The
WINTER
WITCH

A NOVEL

JENNIFER CHEVALIER

Published by Simon & Schuster

New York   Amsterdam/Antwerp   London
Toronto   Sydney/Melbourne   New Delhi

SIMON &
SCHUSTER
CANADA

A Division of Simon & Schuster, LLC
166 King Street East, Suite 300
Toronto, Ontario M5A 1J3

This book is a work of fiction. Any references to historical events, real people, or real places are used fictitiously. Other names, characters, places, and events are products of the author's imagination, and any resemblance to actual events or places or persons, living or dead, is entirely coincidental.

This Simon & Schuster Canada edition January 2026

SIMON & SCHUSTER CANADA and colophon are trademarks of Simon & Schuster, LLC

Simon & Schuster strongly believes in freedom of expression and stands against censorship in all its forms. For more information, visit BooksBelong.com.

For information about special discounts for bulk purchases, please contact Simon & Schuster Special Sales at 1-800-268-3216 or CustomerService@simonandschuster.ca.

Interior design by Ritika Karnik

Manufactured in the United States of America

10 9 8 7 6 5 4 3

Online Computer Library Center number: 1520331549

ISBN 978-1-6682-1642-2
ISBN 978-1-6682-1646-0 (ebook)

For Frederica and Matilda,
witches and philosophers both

SUMMER

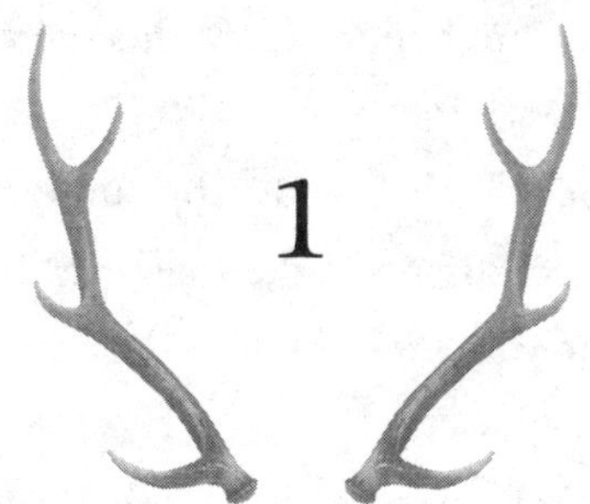

1

They should not have come down to the water's edge. The sea snarled and rushed for their feet with its white teeth, the north wind howling at its back. Élisabeth stumbled backwards, squeezing her rosary in her palm to steady herself.

The captain had said all the brides must stay on the quayside until they were ready to board the ship. But Marthe had insisted she was not going to come all the way to the coast without touching the ocean with her fingertips, and so the two sisters had slipped away from the crowd and down onto the pebble beach. Élisabeth wondered if a sea serpent writhed and coiled within the rough water, while her younger sister bent down to dip her hands into its foam. Marthe touched her wet fingers to her lips.

"It's salty. Like tears."

Élisabeth knelt, slipping the rosary into her pocket. She did not need to taste the sea to know it was made of tears. Every part of this journey was cloaked in sorrow. Still, it is said that a touch of sea-foam on a cloudy day can ease a sea voyage, and so she stretched out her hand.

She felt a thrust in her gut—sharp, urgent—and slowed her reach. *Then again,* she thought, *I would not want to rile a sea serpent, or work a charm I could not control.*

She plunged her hand into her pocket for her wooden beads and stood up. "We should go back."

Marthe gave her a dark look, her usually sunny dimples eclipsed by her scowl. Without waiting for Élisabeth, she marched to the river-stairs that led back towards the harbour. She took them two at a time, forcing Élisabeth to scramble behind her to keep pace.

They passed a row of half-timbered houses that had seen a thousand vessels come and go along the sleeve-shaped channel that separated France from England. The buildings sagged together, windows glinting after the sisters as they rushed towards the quayside.

Ahead of them an old priest in a cassock spoke to a sailor on the main deck of the ship, his finger punctuating the air in short, angry jabs. A blackbird flew past, as sure a sign that the Devil had come to tempt them as if Lucifer himself were setting foot on the ship, with a red apple in his open palm. Élisabeth bowed her head, as if that alone could help her evade Satan's notice, and kept moving towards the ship.

Scattered around the wharf were dozens of small groups of nervous brides.

"Parisians?" Marthe craned to hear the unfamiliar dialects and bumped into a girl with an elaborate coif tied in a bow under her chin.

"Mind yourself." Élisabeth pulled Marthe close, lacing her sister's fingers through her own. She lowered her voice. "At least we can understand them well enough. Father Paul said there could be women from as far as Poitiers on board."

"Poitiers!" Marthe scoffed, shaking her hand free from Élisabeth's grasp. "Why spend the better part of a week in a coach to get here from Poitiers? Surely girls from Poitiers would find passage on the west coast. Honestly, Lili, that priest was as simple as a sock. I'll be glad never to set eyes on him again."

Marthe turned and strode towards a group of young women gathering near the gangplank. Élisabeth bit her lip. Moods came on like summer storms for girls Marthe's age; her sister's ill humour usually passed after a short, violent squall. But this time was different. Marthe had been threatening thunder from the moment they had locked the door to their home in Saint-Philbert and handed over the key.

"Stay close," Élisabeth said as she caught up. Marthe glowered back; the frown did her face no favours. Élisabeth felt the colour rise on her cheeks and looked away.

She studied the women around her, wondering if she could tell which ones came from Poitiers just by their headdresses. On her left was a girl with plump cheeks trying to block a taller one's path. She wore a white linen hood like Élisabeth's own, gathered at the back of her neck.

"Hang back, we don't want to be first," the girl told her friend. Her sharp Parisian accent contrasted with her soft features.

The taller girl put her hand on her companion's shoulder and grimaced, revealing a front tooth so crooked it looked as though it were trying to hide behind its neighbour. "If we're last, we'll get the worst bunk."

"But remember: *First aboard, soon meet the Lord.*"

"We can't put it off anymore," the tall one said, steering her friend by the shoulders towards the *Saint-Jean-Baptiste.*

The women on the wharf started to grow restless. Some, like the first two Parisians, pushed towards the ship, anxious to finally be getting going, done with fretting about where they would sleep and what they might eat and if their meagre belongings would be orphaned on the quayside, just as they themselves were. These girls had no strength left to wonder if they had said the correct prayers to protect against fever, or if it were too much to add a plea to Saint Anne not to be packed into the hold like salted cod in a barrel with the lid nailed shut, but be allowed to see the sky and breathe the sea air. They were done with worries and wishes; like Marthe, they were resigned to their fate.

"Please," Élisabeth begged her sister, who plowed ahead. "I don't want to lose you."

The firm tilt of Marthe's jaw wavered and she stopped. She looked at the throng of girls around them and slowly exhaled. Then she took Élisabeth's hand, and together they bobbed up the gangplank and onto the three-masted ship.

"Keep going down. Then along the lowest deck. Fill the aft bunks first," a gruff voice barked as they were swept down a small staircase into the darkness.

Élisabeth blinked. A stocky sailor stood in the passageway with an oil lamp, the shadows thrown by its light twisted and grotesque. He was arguing with the two Parisians.

"There ain't time for chatter, keep movin'."

"But we want to stay here, close to the hatch."

"Get along, you daft whores!"

There was a rush of movement and the two Parisians scattered. The sailor turned towards Élisabeth and Marthe. "Down the passageway to the stern. Two to a bunk."

"Who will bring our trunks on board?" Élisabeth asked, but Marthe pulled her forward, and if there was a reply, she didn't hear it.

She had to stoop not to hit her head on the low beams spanning the width of the ship. A grating in the ceiling gave the lower deck just enough light for Élisabeth to see the rough wooden bunks lining the walls, providing two layers of sleeping quarters along the sides of the ship. A few coarse blankets were laid in each bunk. The air was already thick with the smell of goats and sheep; nearby Élisabeth could hear the animals' terrified bleating.

She closed her eyes and clutched her rosary. *What in God's name have you done?*

Marthe let go of her hand. "We'll sleep here," she declared, placing her foot on a bottom bunk. She ducked her head and stepped into the coarse wooden box.

Élisabeth had a sudden premonition of her sister climbing into her own grave: wrapped in a death shroud, her feet pointing to the east, a beaded rosary looped around her fingers, the crucifix pressed into her palm. She could not tell how she'd died. Had she bellowed with pain, like Maman? Or had the life slowly drained from her eyes like Papa? Élisabeth shuddered, then crossed herself. Her parents' ghosts melted into the dark corners of the ship.

Marthe pulled her knees to her chest. "Come sit. You're in the way."

"The man said to find bunks at the back." Élisabeth peered towards the end of the deck.

"Don't be a goose," Marthe said.

Élisabeth pressed her lips together. She knew her sister would not budge, so she joined her in the bunk under the light well. She wished she had her holy water vessel with her. The little clay pot would help ease the strange feeling in her stomach, but it was packed deep in her trunk, and so Élisabeth clasped her hands instead, squeezing her palms together as if she were the most contrite sinner on earth. After a moment she released her grasp, letting her fingers glide until they touched in prayer, before her right hand fell into a reverse grip and she squeezed again. She repeated the movement over and over, squeezing tighter and tighter until the friction from her calloused palms worked a spell that allowed her mind to drift.

Take more care, or the Devil will come for you, wayward girl.

She opened her eyes and rubbed her palms back and forth. The floating coffin was stifling. When she tried to draw breath, brambles twisted around her heart. She stopped the squeeze and prayer motion long enough to grab the ribbon in her stays and jerk the knot loose. She closed her eyes as her corset eased its grip, and all of a sudden, she was in the apple orchard where Rémy first touched her hand. When the scent of blossom on the wind—white lilac for innocence, honeysuckle for binding love—foretold a happy marriage.

A clash of voices near the stairwell interrupted her thoughts. Murky light filled the deck as a lady carrying a lamp appeared, a silver cross glinting at her throat; on her heels a pair of sailors followed with more lamps. For the first time since they'd boarded, the full deck was visible. Every bunk, top and bottom on both sides of the cabin, was filled with young women, and in each bed two or three pairs of blinking eyes were fixed on the lady with the lamp. The chaperone they were promised, possibly.

She pressed her lips tightly together for a moment, then her words tumbled out all at once. "We face an obstacle, girls. But there is no reason for fear to overtake us."

"I was not fearful until she spoke," Marthe whispered and nudged herself closer. Élisabeth nodded.

The priest Élisabeth had seen on the main deck strode into the cavern. He was old, and his belly so large it looked as though he were hiding a cauldron under his cassock. By his side was a man with a weather-beaten face and greying hair that curled in waves above his head. The chaperone took a step back as they approached.

"Our very survival depends on it, captain," the priest said slowly, his face pinched, and his head cocked to one side, as if it were painful for him to listen to the other man's concerns.

"Your quest would delay our departure by hours," the captain explained. "The winds can easily shift, and we must take advantage of favourable conditions. If we get stuck in port, we risk eating into provisions that will be needed on the voyage."

A smile crossed the priest's lips, relief perhaps, at this being the sum of the old sailor's argument.

"Captain, your passengers can survive days without food. My concern is for the survival of our *souls*. I must be certain that none of the Norman witches have made their way onto this ship. I must ask every girl to produce her certificate of good conduct."

"Father de Sancy, this is your first journey across the Atlantic. You do not understand how fickle the sea can be. She is not to be trusted. We must leave now, no matter if a stowaway has crept aboard."

"Captain, *you* do not understand." The priest leaned forward, his eyes keen. "The witches I seek were convicted, set to burn. When the king chose to banish them instead, there was outrage across Normandy that they were allowed to scurry away like rats, rather than paying for their crimes."

The captain opened his mouth to speak but the priest held up a finger to indicate he had not finished.

"The Parlement of Rouen took quite a risk in engaging me to track them down, against the wishes of King Louis himself. Does that not indicate to you how dangerous these witches are? You fear the fickle sea. Imagine one of these witches on your ship? The storms she might conjure? Or how she might steal the wind, leaving us drifting for weeks or months on end? There would be no hope of survival."

Élisabeth gripped her hands so tightly that her fingers ached. She wished the men would take their debate elsewhere, but they did not appear to be concerned with frightening the passengers, as if debating within earshot of the brides was like conversing in front of livestock.

The captain rubbed his chin. "What makes you so certain any of these witches are aboard the *Saint-Jean-Baptiste*?"

"According to the courthouse clerk, the most powerful among the Norman witches—their queen, if you will—took a coach to the coast after she was set free. It stands to reason, does it not? Where else would a banished witch hide but on a ship of brides bound for the New World?"

The captain looked around the deck at the girls-for-marrying, huddled and cramped in their cots. Finally, he turned back to the priest. "Very well. Do your search."

The captain retreated and the priest turned to the lady in the shadows. "Madame Étienne, please arrange for your girls to stand before me with their letters of good conduct in hand. And be quick about it."

Madame Étienne fluttered and frowned. "Father de Sancy . . . I can't . . . it's just . . . not all the parishes sent them with certificates . . ."

"Any girl without a letter vouching for her good conduct must rightly be suspected of witchcraft," the priest insisted.

Élisabeth fumbled in the folds of her skirt for her own letter. She pulled it out and stared at the document. It was short: the black scrawl on the paper stretched not longer than the length of her hand. At the very top was an ink spot the size of a coin: the blot that betrayed the lie. The words were a mystery to her; she could not read and did not know what Father Paul had written. Would this inquisitor, this Father de Sancy, be able to see that the words on the page were a deception?

"Father, there are more than a hundred girls on this ship," the chaperone said. "More than a quarter will not have certificates. I can vouch for all of the Parisians . . . I recruited them for the colony myself. They are impeccable . . . irreproachable."

The priest frowned. "Then we shall leave aside your Parisians and interrogate only the Normans. It is among that duchy's women that we will find whom we seek."

"I don't know where they . . ." The chaperone's hands churned helplessly. "The girls from Normandy could be anywhere amongst us . . ."

"Over there!" A voice piped up from the other side of the deck. "I heard a Norman over there, under the light well."

"You girls, there. Come out with your letters ready for inspection."

"Come on, Lili." Marthe swung herself out of the bunk and stood up. "They've heard us speak. They've worked out where we're from."

Slowly, with shoulders hunched, Élisabeth followed Marthe, praying, "Mother of God, Queen of Heaven, pray for us sinners, now and at the hour of our death." She kept one hand on her letter while slipping the other into her pocket to grip her rosary. She could feel the girls around them perk up and watch eagerly for what might happen next. The chaperone swung an oil lamp in their direction.

"Good, good." She sighed, as if all the unpleasantness would come to an end now that she had lined them up in a neat row for the priest to inspect. "I know there are at least a dozen more of you from Normandy. Do stand up so we can proceed."

More girls clutching folded letters rose and shuffled over to where Élisabeth and Marthe stood in the light well. The chaperone moved from bunk to bunk, murmuring to herself, "Paris, Amiens, Paris," ticking off the girls she knew. Occasionally she paused to question a shrinking figure. "Remind me where . . . ?" When the timid reply came back negative—"Reims, Madame Étienne, if you please" or "Orléans, thanks be to Our Lady"—she moved on, leaving the rattled girl to collapse back on her bunk. Others were not so lucky, and despite their protests were gripped by the arm and made to stand up.

Some fifteen girls were eventually herded into the middle of the deck. Carefully, Élisabeth opened Father Paul's letter, ready for inspection, and motioned for Marthe to do the same.

Father de Sancy called for a sailor to hold up a lamp and moved towards Élisabeth. "Your letter, please."

She was instantly struck dumb. She had not expected to be first. Her arms were frozen to her sides, her certificate of good conduct shaking in her hands. She bowed her head to mask her trembling lips.

"Now, I know you cannot be deaf," the priest said. "Because the king has instructed that only good female specimens be sent to the colony."

Élisabeth wasn't certain if he was trying to put her at her ease or get a laugh out of the sailors, some of whom sniggered at her. She glanced at the paper in her hand and almost expected the words to slither across the page, the lies snaking away from the priest's trained eye.

"I-I can hear," she stammered, passing him the letter and ducking into a quick curtsey. The witch hunter peered at the village priest's words. When Father de Sancy looked up at her, she saw his eyes were watery and his nose was mottled red with lumps and veins.

"What is your name?"

"Élisabeth Jossard."

"Have you ever been in attendance at a witches' sabbath, Élisabeth Jossard?" His eyes searched hers.

"No, Father." She shook her head, almost not believing the question. Who would ever admit to such an atrocity?

"Have you been rebaptised in the name of Satan?"

"No, Father," she said more emphatically.

"Has anyone you know died an unnatural death?"

Élisabeth hesitated. Her younger brother had died a fool's death, drinking too much and trying to cross the Orne at night. It was his drowning that had started their string of bad luck. Her older brother had lost a fight with fever and died within the year, and it was the grief over losing both his sons that had caused Papa to fall ill. The whole of Saint-Philbert knew of their exceptional misfortune, but had it been more? Had it been *unnatural*?

"No, Father," Marthe interrupted. "I am her sister, and I can vouch that no one in our family has suffered an unnatural death. Our mother died in childbirth many years ago and our father left us just three months past for the Kingdom of Heaven. We are orphans with no home of our own. We are ready to start a new life in Canada, with the help of God and the king."

Father de Sancy frowned at the interruption and looked from one sister to the other. "I see the resemblance," he murmured, handing Élisabeth back her letter. He turned to Marthe. "Your sister is more comely but appears to be simple. How old are you, child?"

"Almost sixteen," Marthe replied.

"Then you are fifteen. An exaggeration is a lie. Are you a liar?"

"No, Father. I beg your pardon. I am fifteen." If Marthe felt stung by the rebuke, she did not show it. Not for the first time, Élisabeth envied her courage.

"Have *you* ever attended a witches' sabbath?"

"No, Father," said Marthe, her voice calm.

"What do you know of Chamberlen's Secret?" The priest leaned so close to them that Élisabeth could smell the onions on his breath.

Marthe shrugged. "I've never heard of such a thing."

"Yet, we already know that you are a liar. Perhaps you are lying again? How do we know that you have not hidden the Secret about your person? Perhaps deep in the recesses of your skirts?" Father de Sancy's tone had turned severe.

"You can have a look in my pocket, Father. It's got my rosary and nothing else. I have no secrets."

Élisabeth wanted to reach out and pinch Marthe to remind her of her place but instead stood stock-still as the priest studied them. Without another word he moved on to the next bride. Élisabeth's shoulders sagged with relief and her heart thumped so loudly she could not hear their exchange.

She had passed the inquisition. The lie had been believed. Élisabeth raised the letter that had delivered her from suspicion to her lips to kiss it.

Except it was no longer there.

Her hands were empty. Her certificate of good conduct had disappeared.

She looked to her feet, and then all around her. Nothing. The letter had vanished. Then she saw a rustle of movement and caught the eye of a woman jostling back into line a few places down from Marthe. As the light from the oil lamp grew closer to the woman, Élisabeth could see that she did not wear a mended chemise or rough woolen skirt like the Jossard sisters. She had on a rich-coloured dress with a falling collar and long-waisted bodice that sloped into a deep point. Élisabeth peered at the fabric. It was velvet. Velvet for wealth and a promise made to be broken. Velvet for an unbiddable bride. The dress opened at the front to reveal a stain on her petticoats. Maybe mud? Élisabeth was gazing at the frilled sleeves peeking out at the woman's elbow when she froze.

In the woman's hand was Élisabeth's letter of good conduct, instantly recognizable by the inkblot at the top of the page.

She opened her mouth to protest, to alert the old priest to the theft, to clamour for the return of the life-saving letter but halted when she saw the woman's face. It was as dark as the depths of a well, her eyes fixed in a pointed glare. Slowly, the woman raised her finger to her lips.

As if under a spell, Élisabeth fell silent.

Father de Sancy moved towards the woman with the velvet dress. She handed him Élisabeth's certificate of good conduct and waited. The priest squinted at the letter for a second time in as many minutes.

"Recite the Apostles' Creed."

"As you wish," the woman bowed her head and began to say the prayer out loud. Her vowels were crisp and her cadence smooth. Élisabeth ogled to get a better view of her.

"Have you a mole on any part of your body?" the priest continued.

"No." There was a hint of defiance in her voice, but she kept her eyes lowered.

"That's what all the witches say, but when we strip them naked, we can see with our own eyes the mark the Evil One has left upon them."

Élisabeth followed the thief's gaze and saw that her hands were balled into fists.

"Father de Sancy, will removing their clothing be necessary?" The chaperone fluttered at the fringes of the priest's vision.

He waved her away. "Tell me. What purpose does Chamberlen's Secret serve?"

The woman in velvet said nothing.

"Have you ever heard of Chamberlen's Secret?" Marthe asked, elbowing Élisabeth in the ribs.

The priest swivelled around, searching for the interruption. "Hold your tongue! The Devil is about, and I must not be distracted." He turned back to the woman in the velvet dress. "I repeat. For what evil purpose do witches employ Chamberlen's Secret?"

Élisabeth thought the woman with the velvet dress would not answer, so long did she take to speak.

"I cannot fathom any evil purpose this secret might serve."

The priest stood back and squinted, as if trying to read the woman's face. After a moment he handed Élisabeth's letter back to her and moved on down the line.

"What in Heaven's name is Chamberlen's Secret?" Marthe asked when the priest was far enough away not to hear. Élisabeth did not trust her voice to answer. She shook her head, willing her sister to be silent.

Marthe bent down, picking up a sheet of paper. "Honestly, Lili, how can you be so careless? You've dropped your letter."

Élisabeth looked at the certificate of good conduct in Marthe's hand. "How . . . ?" Her mind raced. The woman in velvet was in possession of her letter, was she not? Or had Élisabeth imagined it? She whipped round.

The woman with the stained velvet dress was nowhere to be seen.

She had simply faded into the darkness.

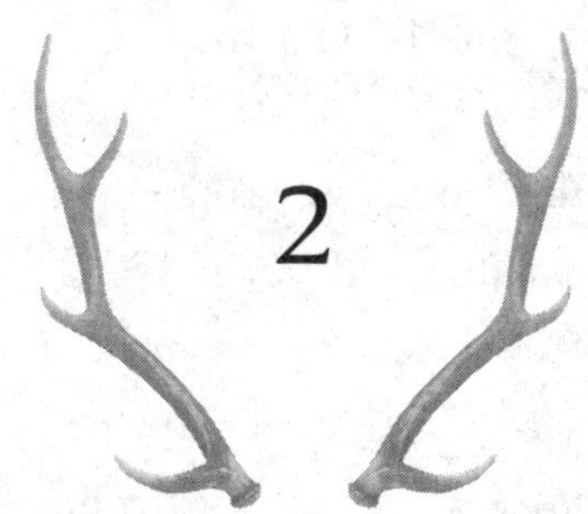

2

Marthe scanned the gloomy corners of the lower deck while the old priest finished his questions. The other girls stared at them from their bunks, whispering among themselves. Marthe smoothed the edges of her cap and fixed her gaze ahead. This was one more trial her sister had forced her to suffer. One more trial she could not forgive.

"Come, Father, dine with me," the captain said, reappearing from the stairwell. He nodded at his lamp-bearing crew as if to move the inquisition along. "My men are anxious to be underway." He bowed slightly at the waist, indicating his deference. "You may continue your enquiries later in our journey, if necessary, once we are safely on course."

Father de Sancy rubbed his bare pate. He seemed dismayed not to have discovered a witch among the Norman girls. The forlorn look lasted a moment, before his mouth hardened. He gave the brides one more frown before allowing himself to be led away.

At once the girls melted. Some fell back into their bunks in a stunned silence, others proclaimed their godliness and piety for all to hear. Élisabeth rubbed her hands together as if she were lathering a cake of soap.

"I don't know how that woman . . . how she . . ."

"Quit your fidgeting," Marthe snapped. She could feel the eyes of the other girls upon them still.

"She did not have a certificate. Did you see? She stole my letter of good conduct, I'm certain of it."

"You hardly merited that letter, Lili. Perhaps it's for the best it landed in the hands of someone whose conduct truly *is* good."

Marthe regretted what she said the moment the barb left her lips. She turned away from her sister's falling face and made herself busy with her own letter, taking it out of her pocket and running her finger along the paper's folds. But who in her position would not be tempted to be sharp, on occasion? It was her sister's fault they were on this ship. Élisabeth's disgrace meant that no one in Saint-Philbert would marry them. And after the barber-surgeon had failed to cure Papa, after their darling father was gone, they were not allowed to stay on their meagre farm. They had been drifting around the cottage like ghosts, haunting their old lives, when foolish Father Paul had come to them with his solution. He said the archbishop was looking for young women who would take up the king's offer of a dowry in exchange for marrying settlers in New France. The village curé then offered to pay for their coach to the coast and sign the required certificates of good conduct if they left by month's end.

Marthe had not wanted to go. She knew from Father Paul's reading of the Jesuit tales the terrors that might befall them: how if captured, Iroquois warriors would chew their fingers to the bone and eat their still-beating hearts. It was madness to agree to such a journey. Marthe had slammed doors and shouted they were not eligible, that Élisabeth's letter was a forgery. She swore that the priest was lying to God, just to be rid of them, the disgraced Jossard sisters. Why else would he swear to Élisabeth's piety and virginity?

Her sister had held up her rosary and said she was as devout as they came.

"Piety is not the part of the letter that interests anyone," Marthe had said, her lip curling. The reddening of Élisabeth's cheeks had confirmed that her sister knew it to be true as well.

Marthe now put her letter back in her pocket. She groped her way back to the bunk in the gloom, Élisabeth trailing behind. They crawled into their wooden casket and sat side by side, each waiting for the other to speak.

"How long do you think we'll be stuck on this ship?" Marthe said finally.

Before her sister could answer, a voice in the darkness replied, "About two months. Maybe less. Maybe more. It will depend on the wind."

Marthe peered out of their wooden cave. She was surprised anyone would speak to them after the priest's scrutiny. The unexpected inquisition could not have helped their standing, yet here was one of the Parisians they had followed on board, hanging upside down from the top bunk, talking to them.

"You from Normandy?" the voice asked. It was the tall girl with crooked teeth they had seen on the quayside. Her cap clung to her head only by the strings at the nape of her neck.

"Yes," Marthe replied. "We are. We're from Saint-Philbert-sur-Orne, half a day's coach ride south of Caen." Until that week, Marthe would not have been able to say how far her village was from the city of Caen. She sat up taller, ready to impart more of her newfound knowledge to these Parisians.

"I could tell from how you talk. It's not as odd as some people say. I can understand you just fine."

Another head suddenly appeared over the side of the bunk. The girl's cheeks were full and her eyes bright. "I'm sorry. Lou doesn't mean to be rude. We like the Norman dialect. It's like . . . it's like drinking cider instead of wine."

"Are you sisters?" Marthe asked, sticking her head into the space between the bunks.

"Near enough," the tall one said.

"Lou was orphaned when she was five, me at seven," her friend explained. "We well-nigh raised each other. We're all from the Salpêtrière—me and Lou, those two on that bunk there, and some others I can't see in this light. I expect you are orphans as well?"

Marthe felt a tug on her heart at the memory of Papa.

"Yes, we are now. Though our mother died when I was four. Lili well-nigh raised me." Marthe clambered out of the bunk and stood so that she was face-to-face with the other girls. "I'm Marthe Jossard. That's my sister, Élisabeth. Lili. What are your names?"

"I'm Marie-Rose and she's Marie-Louise," the plump girl said, smiling. "Though everyone calls us Rose and Lou. When I am a mother, I will insist my own daughters are called by their full names. My eldest shall be Marie-Leonarde-Madeleine and my second shall be—"

"Shut up, Rose," another girl snapped. "Those Normans don't care what you're going to call your pock-nosed children."

The ceiling was so low the one called Lou did not have to stand to hit it with her fist. "If you speak to any of us like that again, God da—"

"Blasphemy, Louise," said a cool voice on the other side of them.

"May the Devil take you too, Apolline," Lou said fiercely, then just as quickly: "What are you eating?"

"A prune," came the reply.

Lou turned towards the voice, her manners instantly gentle. "Can I have one?"

"No."

Lou roared and lunged across the small space between the bunks, trying to grab the fruit. As they fought, Rose slipped into the sisters' wooden box and made herself comfortable.

"Everyone from the Salpêtrière has known each other a very long time," she said, as if that explained the brawl happening above their heads.

"What *is* that place?" Marthe asked, settling next to the Parisian.

"Have you not heard of it? It's a place in Paris for poor women and or-phans. You'll meet everyone soon enough, no doubt. Apolline is the oldest, she's *twenty-six*, so she thinks she's quite a bit cleverer than the rest of us, though she is not." Rose raised her voice so that the older girl could hear the insult.

"And you are the most ill-bred girls I have ever known," Apolline chided. Her voice was drowned out by a chorus of groans.

"She's a bucket of sour milk," Rose whispered. She continued to list the ages and temperaments of all the girls sitting nearby. Marthe noticed Élisabeth frothing her cake of soap again and gave her a kick. Whatever would the Parisians think of her muttering and twisting?

"Is she well?" Rose glanced at Élisabeth with a doubtful expression on her face. Marthe noticed that the Parisian's clothes were tired, even the ribbons lacing her bodice drooped. She shifted to block the girl's view of Élisabeth.

"She'll be fine once we set sail."

"I'm nervous too," Rose admitted. "I've prayed so much these last few weeks my knees are near covered in scabs." Marthe glanced at Élisabeth. In the last month her sister had done more praying than any nun in Christendom. It hadn't helped. "You should not think of the journey," Rose continued, leaning over Marthe to speak directly to Élisabeth. "Think of the reward that awaits us."

"Reward?" Marthe asked. Élisabeth had not mentioned a reward. Her sister had been too distracted to say much other than that they were headed to the most holy place on earth: Ville-Marie, named for Our Lady, a missionary village on an island called Montréal. Marthe had had to bite her tongue to stop blurting out that surely *Jerusalem* was holier than this outpost on the other side of the world, but she did not want to admit that she wasn't certain that Jerusalem was a place that could be found on a map, rather than something that existed only in the pages of the Bible, like camels and palm leaves.

"The choice of husbands we shall have," Rose said, as if it were obvious. "That alone will make the journey worthwhile."

Marthe was startled to see another girl fly into the bunk and perch on its edge.

"Will we really choose for ourselves?" she asked.

"Of course," said Lou, sliding down from the upper bunk to join them. "We're orphans. Who else would choose for us?"

"I was talking to one of the sailors before we boarded." Rose lowered her voice. "He said that in Ville-Marie the men outnumber the women ten to one. I expect we'll have our pick of the best of them."

"When did you slink off and have words with a sailor?" a girl on the opposite bunk said slyly. When Rose ignored her, she climbed down from her perch and crouched nearby. "How will we choose, exactly? Did the sailor say?"

Sour-milk Apolline cleared her throat. "The ship's crew is misinformed. My understanding is that the ratio is not quite as favourable as ten to one—"

"I'm going to line them up, shortest to tallest, and walk up and down the row, squeezing their flesh to see if it's firm," Lou cut in.

"Like choosing a basket of plums at market?" A girl Marthe's age with a snub nose and an overgenerous serving of freckles slipped into the space between the bunks, the better to be able to hear them. Marthe marvelled at how many of them there were. More girls her age than in all of Saint-Philbert, sitting right here, next to her. She shifted so that she was in the centre of the circle.

"No. Not like plums. Like cheese," Rose said.

"How is cheese any different from a plum?" someone asked.

"There are only a few types of plums, but so, *so* many cheeses."

"And cheese doesn't bruise when you pinch it."

There was a burst of laughter before Lou spoke again. "Now that I think on it, it's probably best to line them up based on strength, not height. I intend to get one with arms like tree trunks." She paused, then added, "And a firm backside to match."

All the girls giggled until Apolline broke in. "Don't be vulgar, Louise. I intend to choose my husband solely on his occupation and ability to earn a good living. And I expect you will all do the same."

They groaned, even those who couldn't have known Apolline for more than an hour. Marthe joined in, laughing and shaking her head. Though privately she wondered why the brides protested. How else would one choose a husband, except by judging what he could earn? She sneaked a glance at her sister.

Élisabeth would choose for love, of course.

Marthe sighed.

The girls continued to tell tales of how best to choose a cheese, by pinching or sniffing, then turned to rating various professions. Was a stonemason equal to a blacksmith in the New World, where there was so much to be built? Did a joiner outrank a clog maker? Could girls such as them aim as high as a merchant or a silversmith?

Marthe joined in, pleased to share her thoughts. From their encouraging smiles, these girls seemed to think her as much an authority as an archbishop on such matters. She returned their smiles with her own. She had little experience of friendship in Saint-Philbert—her life had been full enough with her sister and two older brothers—but now, in the near darkness of the lower deck she felt lighthearted.

"We're not likely to be allowed to marry a merchant," a girl with bony wrists and fingers said to the group. She made a gesture like a knife on a cutting board with her hands as she spoke. "I was told we can only choose between craftsmen and farmers."

"I'd prefer a farmer," Lou decided. She made a show of flexing her arm, which made the other girls laugh.

"A hardworking artisan can earn up to six hundred livres a year," Apolline informed them. "A habitant farmer could probably match that. Of course, if you end up saddled with an idle man . . ."

There was less laughter as the group considered her words. An idle man could ruin a girl. And there were worse sins than idleness besides.

"What about you?" Rose turned to Marthe. "Are you in the market for a farmer or an artisan?"

"Well," she hesitated for a moment. She could not remember the last time she had been asked what she wished for. Despite Élisabeth's urgent talk about leaving for Ville-Marie, she had been silent on what they would do when they arrived. "I am a farmer's daughter. So I know what it is to live that life—"

"You shall make a good farmer's wife, then."

"I intend to stay in town," Marthe said firmly. "I have had my fill of reaping grain and shearing sheep. I want to marry a smith or a cooper. Or any crafts-man, really."

Marthe did not want to confess to these Parisians what it had been like to be a farmer's daughter, how despite Papa's never-ending work—the planting, weeding, scything, threshing, and gleaning, year on year until he was near-crippled by the labour—they had always felt the pinch of hunger. After the tithe and the taille had been paid, after the seigneur had taken his due, what was left to the tenant farmer? The yield from the Jossards' plot could barely feed them all when the boys were alive. Marthe wondered if life in Ville-Marie would see her fortunes change. She imagined fine shops in a row, and pointing at everything from copper pots to silk ribbons and telling the shopkeeper to put it on her account. That was the life she wanted. No broken nails and mud-soaked hems. No opening the door to the hapless village barber and watching him fumble and bumble with his tools as Papa coughed blood into his kerchief. Marthe took a breath to stifle her anger. No, she would not be a farmer's wife. There was safety in silver and being able to pay for the kind of physicians who could only be found in town.

"The blacksmith where I'm from does very well for himself," the girl with the bony wrists said. "His family had beef every Sunday."

Apolline came closer to their bunk. "Of course, the real money is in tanning—if you can bear to put up with the smell of the hides and the tools to cure them."

"She means *piss*," Lou sniggered, and then broke into a guffaw at Apolline's curdled expression. "Though this leaky dungeon smells no worse than a tannery."

Rose turned back to the Jossard sisters. "And you, Lili? What sort of man do you want to marry?"

Élisabeth was on her feet in an instant, her movement brittle. "You talk of husbands, as if we will survive the journey. Did you not hear what that priest said? There is a witch aboard this ship."

"Don't pay the curé too much mind," said one of the brides. "Priests are more tormented by witches than those most at risk from their curses."

"And thank the Holy Virgin that the clergy is so vigilant." Élisabeth looked as if she were twisted into a knot and could not breathe. The brides gaped at her. "Do not ask me whom I shall marry. For unless we say our prayers every hour from this day forth, we will very likely never arrive."

Élisabeth crossed herself and walked away into the murk. Marthe sat very still, flushed with embarrassment. Just as she was making friends for the first time in her life, Élisabeth's behaviour would see them mocked or shunned once again. Marthe could not let it happen.

"The truth is, my sister would rather be a nun than a wife," Marthe said loudly enough for all to hear. To her relief, Lou laughed, and the rest joined in. Marthe took a deep breath, willing herself not to stare down the passageway in the direction Élisabeth had fled.

The others might think her sister overly pious, or a fearmonger, or worse. Only Marthe knew the true cause of Élisabeth's protest.

She glanced in the direction her sister had disappeared, then turned back to the other brides, nodding at something she had not heard. She cocked her head sweetly at Rose and was reassured when the Parisian smiled back. Perhaps they would not blame her for Élisabeth's sins.

For there was one thing Marthe understood from all that had befallen them. She would not make the same mistake as her sister.

She would never fall in love.

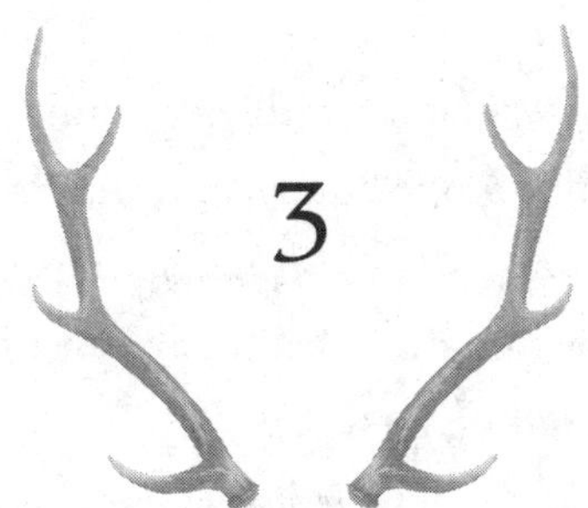

3

Élisabeth could not think straight. Somewhere in the obscurity of the *Saint-Jean-Baptiste*'s lower deck was the woman with the velvet dress. A thief, certainly. And maybe a witch.

For surely Élisabeth had not dropped her certificate like the half-wit Marthe thought she was. Surely it was the same letter, with the inkblot on the top of the page. The priest's words rattled around her mind. Out at sea, who would protect them from a witch's wrath?

She of all people knew what it was to suffer a witch. And she knew she could not survive another.

She must share her suspicions with Father de Sancy.

Élisabeth spotted the deckhand who had greeted them when they boarded, still stationed by the staircase. She slowed her approach.

"Where d'you think you're going?" the sailor asked. He used his chin to point in her direction, his arms firm across his chest.

"I'm looking for the priest."

"Not up here you're not."

Élisabeth stepped back. "Will we never get to go up on deck?"

"Sure y'will. But not until we're out at sea. Captain's orders. Not long back, one of you slatterns jumped ship when it was barely out of harbour. I s'pose the witless creature thought twice about going to Canada to have her scalp sliced clean off her head by savages."

The sailor made a slow gesture with his thumb across his forehead and grinned. Élisabeth's mouth dropped open, and she clasped her hands together. *Squeeze, glide to prayer and past, squeeze again.* She repeated the soothing rhythm to herself twice more while thinking what to say. The man seemed startled when he noticed she was still standing there.

"Get back to yer bunk. You'll be fed soon enough."

The sailor bared his teeth and Élisabeth sank back into the shadows, where she hovered, not wanting to return to Marthe and the other giggling brides. The captain had invited the priest to dine, so if she could find his cabin she might be able to speak to Father de Sancy. She waited in the shadows, watching as the sailor grew bored, picking his teeth with his fingernails. When a shriek of laughter erupted and the deckhand turned away to growl at the unruly girls, Élisabeth did not hesitate. She gripped the railing with both hands and stole away up the ladder to the upper deck.

The wooden beams creaked under her feet as she crept along the corridor, feeling her way with her fingers. After a moment she saw a crack of light out-lining what must be the door to a cabin and crept towards it. She heard a voice as she approached.

". . . I long to be massacred in my bed . . ."

Élisabeth stopped. It was the old priest, speaking loudly enough for her to hear him clearly. She leaned towards the door.

"No, I mean it sincerely! The Jesuits believe they have a stranglehold on martyrdom, but we priests of the Sulpician order are just as anxious to prove our worth to God. I do not mind if I am slain if the Blessed Virgin knows that I died a faithful servant."

She could not decipher the mumbled reply of a male voice. The captain? Then came the high-pitched contribution of the chaperone.

"I agree with Father de Sancy. I too would rather take my chances being captured by the Iroquois than by witches. The troops of the Carignan-Salières regiment have no pistol that can stop a witch, do they?"

The sudden thud of boots coming down the corridor made Élisabeth draw back from the captain's door and rush towards the front of the ship. When she could travel no farther, she waited, crouched in what appeared to be a storeroom full of barrels, her heart beating like a hare's.

The priest *wished* to be martyred. Élisabeth tried to imagine anyone so devout—so confident of their sanctity and contrition—that they would hope for such a thing. To pray, even, for their own slaughter. Papa was as good a man as she had ever known, and even he was frightened near the end. She remembered how he had called her to his bedside on the day she left to work for the Delaunays, his thin, grey hair lying defeated across the crown of his head. He told her to keep her head down and her hand out. He promised it would only be a month or two until he was back on his feet and she could come home. He said the money she'd earn would pay for a barber-surgeon to speed him through his sickness.

Élisabeth pushed away the memory of the squat barber with his large, fumbling fingers. Slowly, she felt her way out of the storeroom back to her position outside the captain's door. Father de Sancy was still talking.

"The king and the court are caught up with their mathematical interests and philosophies and their insufferable Académie," he scoffed. "They are as slavish to the latest thinking as they are to the latest fashion. But they are grossly mistaken to believe that witchcraft can be explained away by natural causes, or that it is the whim of one's imagination. Witches' power is irrefutable. And I believe it is highly probable that within every coven is one with even *more* power than the rest. She who controls the others, like the queen of a hive controls her bees."

"What do you mean, Father? A queen bee of witches?" Madame Étienne sounded puzzled. Élisabeth pressed her ear up against the door. She too longed to understand the priest's meaning.

"Yes. In fact, I am writing a treatise, a compendium of *maleficia*, to detail how it is that some witches have so much power they can possess otherwise ordinary women—women like yourself, Madame Étienne—and bid them to do their will."

"What does the queen witch do to these other women?"

"To other *witches*, you mean. Once she has polluted them with her magic, they are forever tainted. A worker bee's sting is no less than his queen's, after all."

"I see." The chaperone's voice was more muted now. The captain spoke, but again Élisabeth did not catch what he said. The priest boomed back a reply.

"A very good question! Witches are obsessed with the male organ, with making men impotent and women barren. They are addicted to the carnal act and desire nothing more than to fornicate with the Devil as often as they can. But their greatest fiendishness comes in the causing of demonic possession, the scourge afflicting our country of late. I will tell you a tale, if I may. A chilling story. One that I saw with my own eyes at the Hospitalières convent in Louviers, some twenty years ago."

When the priest spoke next his voice was softer. Élisabeth crouched so that her ear was closer to the keyhole, the better to make out his words.

"There once was a young nun who was bewitched and taken to a Black Mass, where she was wed to a demon. As part of the celebrations, the couple feasted upon suckling infants and watched as bystanders were crucified. An orgy ensued, wherein the nun copulated with her demon on the Satanic altar. She performed acts of great obscenity in front of the gathering, kissing his anus for all to see—"

"Father, come now!" For the first time, Élisabeth heard the captain's voice clearly. "There is a lady present."

"No, please," Madame Étienne said. "I want to hear it."

"Well, the horrors had only just begun," the priest continued. "For it was not just young Madeleine Bavent who had been possessed, but as many as eighteen nuns in the convent. They bore all the hallmarks of their curse: blasphemy, fits, staccato movements, animal noises, sudden rigidity then extreme fatigue, the ability to understand Latin and Greek, and their strength! Feats of strength surpassing anything a mortal woman might be capable of."

A bony finger curved up Élisabeth's spine, tripping against each vertebra until it reached the hair at the nape of her neck. A terrible feeling came over her, a notion only just beginning to simmer. She glanced over her shoulder, but she was alone in the unlit corridor. She blinked at the closed door. She knew she should return to her purpose: knock and tell Father de Sancy about the stolen letter. But she yearned to hear more of the priest's tale. She pressed her ear against the door.

"And then the devils spoke to us. I was a younger man then, but by God Almighty, the dialogues I had with those demons when they spoke through the mouths of nuns have marked me my entire life long."

"Father de Sancy, please. Madame Étienne will not sleep tonight with all this talk of witches and demons."

"Very well, captain. As you wish. But forewarned is forearmed."

"I would rest better knowing the outcome for those poor wretches," the chaperone said.

"Be assured, Madame Étienne, we were able to exorcise the demons while building a case against the witches who caused the nuns' suffering. It took us many months and some of the nuns were quite broken after their ordeal. It is no easy thing to cause an unclean spirit to leave a woman's body. We had to shave them and prick them with needles to see if they retained any sensation, or if the Devil had control of their flesh. We then beat them with sticks—"

"Father, I must insist," the captain interrupted. "This conversation cannot continue. I will remain alert to these signs of possession amongst the passengers, in case the worst has come to pass and there is indeed a witch aboard the ship."

There *was* a witch on the ship, wasn't there? Élisabeth's letter had disappeared and magically returned to her, as if the woman in velvet had cast some kind of glamour. After what had happened in Saint-Philbert, surely Élisabeth would recognize the work of another witch. She must tell them what she knew. She must rid the ship of danger.

Maybe she should also confess to the priest the truth about her curse? She lifted her hand to knock.

"Beware, captain. While most of the nuns at Louviers were innocents, demoniacs are not always so. The nun Madeleine, that supposed victim of witchcraft, through careful exorcism and interrogation was discovered to be a witch herself.

"I advise we keep an especially keen eye on the Norman girls during our journey," Father de Sancy said. "I am not satisfied with the answers that I heard today. If any of them should show signs of demonic possession, we shall put them to the Question. So shall I unravel the hive and get to the queen."

Slowly, Élisabeth lowered her hand. A chair scraped across a floorboard, and she realized someone had stood up. She crept away from the door, her legs weak. Candlelight spilled from the cabin into the corridor and Élisabeth cowered against the wall, hoping the darkness would obscure her figure. She could see the captain standing in the doorway.

"I wish you luck with your enquiries, Father." The captain held up his hand, as if to halt an objection. "Though if you are looking for a rack or brodequins to assist with your questions, we do not have such equipment on board."

"It is of no matter, captain. We can make do with a whip or a stick. Just enough pain so that the truth comes out. Remember, I am quite experienced in the art of interrogation."

The door shut and Élisabeth heard the captain's boots striking the ship's boards. When she was certain he had gone, she stole past his cabin, making her way back to the staircase and her bunk. She clasped her hands together to stop them from shaking. *The supposed victim . . . was discovered to be a witch herself.*

What would be worse: allowing the velvet witch to wield her power on the open sea, or confessing her own sins to the priest who might discover her secret and put her to the Question?

Élisabeth slunk down the corridor, bound to hold her tongue, lest the priest put her to the test by cutting it out.

4

During their first few weeks at sea, Marthe could not say what disturbed her most: the feeling of her stomach travelling into her mouth when the ship lurched in rough waters, having to share a bucket with so many other seasick women, or trying to pick a growing army of fleas and lice from her hair. She knew she was in Hell, for the darkness and discomfort could have no other name.

Yet somehow, despite the hardship, she did not suffer. For the kinship she felt on board the *Saint-Jean-Baptiste* was a blessing.

Of all the Parisians, she loved Marie-Rose the best. The girl with the plump cheeks and wide smile prattled all day long, although never over anyone else. She was as happy to listen as to talk. She had questions for everyone she met—Where are you from? How do you fare? Do you miss your mother still?—and when any of the girls could no longer bear the stench of their sleeping quarters or the bickering of their neighbour, they could climb into Rose's bunk and tell all their worries to the girl with the big heart.

By and by Marthe got to know the others as well. Marie-Louise was the one to be admired most, in Marthe's opinion. Not quite eighteen, Lou was among the youngest but twice as bold as anyone aboard. She hung upside down from

35

the bunk she shared with Rose and told rude jokes into the night. She was wiry and strong and liked to leap from bunk to bunk to rally the girls when they felt low. She often fought with snub-nosed Françoise and tiny Thérèse, but as Lou put it, she had known them almost all her life and they were as close as sisters, if not cousins raised next door. Apolline told them that was no excuse for bad behaviour, whereupon everyone jeered and called her an old maid.

"Come now, my little ones," Lou said one afternoon to the fleas caught in the hair on her legs. It was hot and the stench of the sheep and goat manure was so strong Marthe felt almost dizzy. The brides were sitting together in the top bunk, thinking of ways to suspend their boredom as they waited for their turn to go up on deck. Lou had decided to coax her fleas to jump onto Apolline's legs. "Come, Perrette and Nenette, there you go. Good girls. You too, Georgette. Over to that ogre, there."

A flea jumped, startling Apolline, who kicked Lou's arm and caused her to tumble sideways and jostle Rose.

"Stop," Rose begged. "I'm dropping so many stitches that my child's blanket will have a great hole in the middle. Every stitch is already too crooked or too loose."

"Don't fret. You have plenty of time left to fix it." Marthe was combing her honey-coloured hair with her fingers, releasing the braids she had only just made to pass the time.

"Watch your mouth," Françoise said. She was lying on the bottom bunk opposite, her legs in the air, her feet pressed against the top bunk to steady herself against the rolling and tilting of the ship. Her skirts fell to her waist, revealing white thighs. "If I hear another word about how much longer we have on this infernal boat, I'll give you a good thrashing."

Lou jumped heavily down from the top bunk. "I can't stand this closeness a moment more. I'm going up on deck."

"It's not our turn yet," Thérèse told her. "The starboard girls are still up top."

The thought of the starboard girls made them settle. The tragic starboard girls. Each cluster of brides was named for where they slept: the starboard girls, the stern girls, even the goatherd girls for those with the bad luck to be sleeping nearest the livestock. Only a dozen had signed up to travel as far as Ville-Marie, and so they were known as Montréalistes, after the island on which the missionary village had been founded. As the weeks wore on other brides destined for Ville-Marie swapped their bunks so that they could be closer to Marthe's group. There was a plain girl with pockmarked cheeks from Orléans, a blonde from Crécy whose buck teeth made her look like a worried rabbit when she frowned, and young Claire, just thirteen and spoiled by everyone. The Montréalistes knew it was only by God's grace that they were not among the unfortunates sleeping on the starboard side of the ship. A fortnight ago, ship's fever had ripped through those bunks, and several of the girls had died. At the ceremony where they were committed to the sea, every passenger prayed they would not succumb to the same fate.

"God bless the starboard girls," Lou murmured, making the sign of the cross as she sat down next to Françoise. There was a rare moment of silence, then Apolline spoke up.

"It *is* a pity the captain himself is not eligible for marriage." Several of the girls nodded in agreement. The captain had performed the last rites for the dead brides with such sincerity that a small cult had developed around the man, with Apolline its most fervent devotee.

"I cannot believe the priest did not give those poor souls their last rites—"

"Hush, Lou, keep your voice down," Claire whispered. As a fellow Norman, she too had been subject to Father de Sancy's inquisition. She looked over her shoulder into the murky light. "We're better off, now that he's locked himself in his cabin."

The girls from Normandy had been twice as careful to scuttle away when they saw him coming, sometimes forsaking an entire day's fresh air to avoid the old man and his interrogations. The outbreak of ship's fever had been a blessing for them, for the priest had taken to his cabin underneath the quarterdeck and not been seen since.

"Talk of something else," Rose demanded. "What will you do with your bonus from the king, Marthe? Tell me, so that I might think what to do with mine."

"You will not see *me* birthing twelve children for a pension of a few hundred livres," Thérèse said, flitting around the deck like a trapped bird. "You cannot spend it if you're dead. No, thank you. I won't risk childbirth more than seven or eight times."

"Maybe you will desire your husband so greatly you will not be able to stop at eight," Lou said, smirking.

"I agree with Thérèse," Marthe said. "A dozen is too many. There were four in our family. It seems the right size."

"Our mother birthed six of us," Élisabeth corrected her, appearing out of the darkness. Unlike the other Montréalistes, she did not spend her days huddled in the bunks, knitting and sharing stories with the others. She kept to herself, a wraith floating around the edges of the ship.

"I know that," Marthe said in a low voice. "But Rose has bid us to talk of something cheerful. Do not speak of stillborn babes."

Élisabeth leaned against the bunk post, staring into the shadows. She had dark circles under her eyes, no longer the pretty farmer's daughter who had turned every head in Saint-Philbert. Marthe remembered once, walking by the women gathered at the well in the village square, overhearing those child-worn wives complain about Élisabeth's pretty face. She hadn't understood then why *it would only bring her trouble*, and how the wives professed more concern than jealousy, *because the girl doesn't have a mother, after all*. What was so special about her sister's features? It was only later that Marthe began to see what the young men in Saint-Philbert saw, that Élisabeth's violet eyes sparkled in her face like jewels in a coronet, stealing all the attention from her surrounding features: the dark lashes; the long fox's nose with the dusting of freckles; the soft lips.

Marthe tucked a lock of her own churned-honey hair under her cap and looked away. Even now, Élisabeth's sunken eyes would likely attract more attention than Marthe's own pale grey pair.

The ship rocked to one side again and Françoise grabbed the slop bucket to vomit. "When it's our turn on deck, please push me overboard." She flopped onto her back and stared up at the top bunk. "I think I'd rather drown than retch again." There was a spattering of laughter from the others.

"Here, take some mint leaves," said Rose. "I have a few sprigs left."

"What's the use when I'll only be sick again in an hour?"

"That's why I won't change my chemise until we arrive," said Thérèse. "I want to save my clean shirt for when we step off the ship and are swarmed by suitors."

They were murmuring in agreement when Marthe heard the clumping of shoes on the staircase. The starboard girls were returning to their bunks.

"Your turn, Montréalistes," one said.

"It's about time," Lou exclaimed, then stopped and crossed herself. "I mean, thank you," she called after them. She sprang up. "Let's go."

Marthe looked for her sister but Élisabeth had slipped away. Lou put her arm around her waist and Marthe allowed herself to be pulled up the stairs.

There was little space to walk around on the main deck amid the crew pulling on sails and coiling ropes. The girls stuck close to the railings, gazing out at the sea swells, larger today than they had been for some time.

"I feel like dancing," Lou said, kicking her legs in the air. Soon she and Rose were circling around a small corner of the deck, dancing the gavotte or shaking off their fleas; from their jerky movements it was not clear which. Marthe was set to join them when she spotted her sister emerge from below.

"Over here!" Marthe waved. Élisabeth did not respond, instead taking up a position towards the stern of the ship and staring out blankly at the wide ocean.

She clung to the ship's railing with bony white knuckles. Marthe frowned and left the Parisians to join her sister.

"Lili, come and dance with us."

Élisabeth held the railing even tighter as the ship rose and plunged on a swell.

"I danced with Rémy in the churchyard once. Did I ever tell you?"

Marthe frowned. "Yes, you did."

"We could not risk being seen together so we stayed late after Mass. We only spun around the grounds twice, but I will hold the memory in my heart forever."

A tear hovered at the edge of her sister's eye. No sooner had the fat drop started its journey down her cheek than a sailor sprang forward, pushing a dirty handkerchief towards Élisabeth.

"Take this."

It was Michel, the youngest of the sailors, and the only one who did not seem to delight in trying to frighten them. Élisabeth shook her head and wiped her tears on her sleeve.

"Everyone finds it hard to leave home," he said gently, pocketing the grey cloth. "You're not the worst I've seen."

"Who was the worst?" Marthe asked. She cocked her head to one side, hoping to distract Élisabeth from thoughts of Rémy Delaunay.

Michel broke into a wide grin. "Once a girl jumped into the sea as we were setting sail. She thought she could reach the quay somehow. The captain had me fish her out with a net and keep her below deck until she came to her senses. Damn near drowned, beg your pardon for my language. Now the captain likes to get underway while everyone's asleep or eating. Girls are easily spooked, he says, so it's safer for everyone this way."

"Did she live?"

"Oh, aye, she did. I looked out for her after that. I grew quite sweet on her, truth be told. Called her my mermaid, and that made her laugh. Just about the prettiest sound on this earth, my mermaid's laugh." The cabin boy squinted as he gazed out across the waves, as if searching for a tail fin in the deep black waters. "I tell you, if I hadn't been bound to this ship by my term of service . . . I might have signed up for a piece of land near Québec myself so I could marry her."

"Pfff." Marthe could not stop herself from scoffing. Another fool looking to make a love match. She shook her head, then clutched at the railing as a gust of wind caused the ship to list to one side. When she steadied herself again, she asked, "Where is your mermaid now?"

"She married not three weeks after we came ashore." His grin slipped into a melancholic smile. "It was to be expected. She was so lovely, I knew she'd be married straightaway. I'll look for her when we dock at Québec, though. Who knows. I might be lucky and she'll be a widow by now."

As the boy continued to inspect the sea, Élisabeth followed his gaze. The pair looked so mournful that Marthe wondered if she should clack their heads together to knock them out of their misery.

"You girls will get offers right away too," Michel said, suddenly sanguine again. "You won't be in Québec more than a week before you're spoken for, I reckon."

"We're not stopping in Québec," Marthe said, correcting him. "We've signed on for Ville-Marie."

"Why ever for?"

The surprise in his voice unsettled Marthe. She and the other Montréalistes had been asked this by others: Why Ville-Marie? Why not the relative safety of Québec, where the city's walls offered protection from Iroquois warriors bent on breaking the truce and attacking the settlers in their sleep? Élisabeth glanced at him, then turned back to the sea. The sun had slipped behind dark clouds and the wind was growing stronger.

"My sister says it's the holiest place in the New World—maybe on earth," Marthe began, but she could not keep the disdain from her voice.

Élisabeth cut in. "Our whole lives the village priest told us stories about the missionaries' work in Ville-Marie. Some Sundays he read us the Jesuits' accounts of their travels. We heard how the missionaries devote themselves to the glory of God, saving souls in the wilderness all while surviving untold hardship—ice and snow, starvation and torture . . ." Élisabeth shivered as if someone had just walked over her grave. "Imagine surviving simply through holy deeds and divine will? I think . . . I think . . . miracles must happen in such a sacred place."

"We have set sail in search of a holy miracle, you see," Marthe said sarcastically.

The cabin boy looked at them doubtfully. "I imagine the first settlers *were* very pious. Though it has changed quite a bit in thirty years."

"What do you know about Ville-Marie?" Élisabeth said.

"I've seen a lot of New France. And what I know of Ville-Marie is not so heavenly, I'm sorry to say. It's a wild frontier town, filled with fur traders and plenty of wolves."

"Wolves!" Élisabeth exclaimed. The ship rolled again and she struggled to stand upright. Marthe put out a hand to steady her.

"Not actual wolves. At least I don't think so. It's just what they call the men there."

"The men are called . . . wolves?" Marthe asked.

"Oh yes. From the governor on down. There are rumours, so you must take care. I'm glad my mermaid went to Québec after what I've seen of Ville-Marie."

Marthe opened her mouth to press him for more details, but Rose and Lou came dancing over to join them. The wind was whipping Lou's hair so much it seemed as though snakes were writhing on her head.

"Michel! Come dance with us!"

He shook his head, smiling. "Can you girls not see how the sea has changed? The captain will want you all below deck until this storm blows through."

Marthe looped her arm through Lou's. She tried to pull Élisabeth along with them, but her sister was looking out across the ocean, her arms hooked over the railing, her hands clasped together in prayer. For once Marthe could not blame her.

A storm coming. Wolves waiting. She did not know which would be worse.

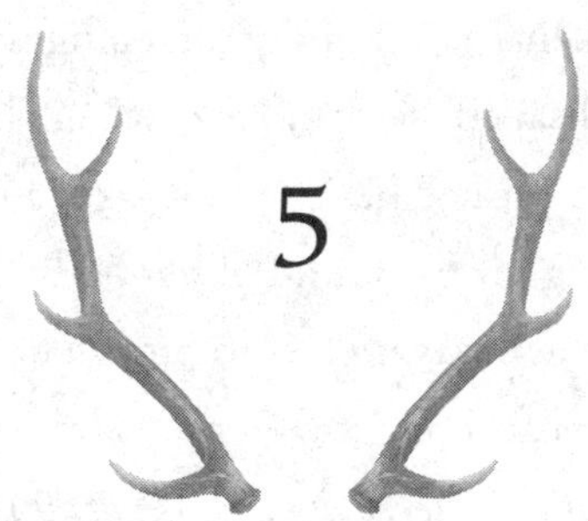

5

That night the sea rose up like the monster Leviathan, determined to toss the ship into Hell, severed from the grace of God. As the *Saint-Jean-Baptiste* heaved and fell, Élisabeth gripped the sides of her bunk until the splinters dug into her palms. The girls screamed and prayed, but the ferocity of the storm seemed even to have shocked the crew, for they could hear the sailors' panicked cries on deck. Élisabeth thought of the priest's warning about witch-conjured storms. *There would be no hope of survival.* Father de Sancy knew this would happen. He had foretold it. Why had she not confessed that the woman in the velvet dress had stolen her letter? The priest could have thrown her overboard and they would have been safe.

The sea convulsed again and Élisabeth clasped her hands together to pray.

Merciful Saint Anne, we cast ourselves at your feet and humbly beg you. Recommend us to your daughter, the Blessed Virgin, that she might serve as our passport and preserve us from peril.

The sound of thunder exploded like a battery of guns above their heads and Marthe shrieked. Élisabeth wrapped her arms around her sister and buried her head against her back. She murmured her prayers as quickly as her tongue would allow.

Holy Virgin, mother of God, serve as our passport and preserve us from peril. Serve as our passport and preserve us from peril.

The ship was a drunken sailor, blindly careening and lurching with no care for those in its midst. Élisabeth remembered when she was six and her older brother, Jean-Jacques, had pushed her backwards off a haystack. Falling, falling, her stomach rising, waiting for the sound of her body hitting the earth. She felt the same now. But here there was no hay to break her fall, only the filthy ship, and the next desperate reel and stagger.

Holy Virgin, mother of God, serve as our passport and preserve us from peril.

Merciful Saint Anne, we cast ourselves at your feet and humbly beg you.

Those girls not praying were retching. The ocean waves rolling over the main deck crashed down the light well and sluiced vomit across the floorboards. The girls were a desperate mixture of prayer and bile, helplessness and panic.

The Devil will come for you, wayward girl.

An echo of her mother's long-ago warning rang in her ears, and she knew, even here, in the middle of the sea, the one with the black feather in his hat had found her. She had tried to run, but the Devil had been following her ever since the day she had succumbed to desire.

Élisabeth put her hands over her ears to block out the sound of the ship's groans. She could not stop the memory of that day in the apple orchard more than a year ago: the blossoms trembling in the breeze, the wind shaking some of the petals loose, covering the ground in a blanket of pink. It was springtime and the sun's heat did not wither them; the days when the fruit would lie rotting on the ground surrounded by wasps were still ahead.

She had run outside to hide from the cook, whose hip hurt, making her more sharp-tongued than usual. Élisabeth had grabbed a trug and said she was going to weed the kitchen garden. Once she was outside though, she had run to the back of the farm, pulling off her cap, loosening her hair, and letting her fingers rub the strain from her scalp. She had thought she wanted to be alone, to fret over Papa's worsening cough, and to give herself a moment to grieve for her brothers, but a figure strolling towards her turned her mind from sorrow to sweeter things.

Rémy approached like a cat with its tail flicking lazily behind him, his eyes catching hers and holding them firm. She'd said good morning and lowered her gaze. But with a cocksure smile, he'd put his hand on her forearm and she'd felt a surge of longing so powerful it felt as if she were an apple tree ripped up by her roots, toppled in a storm.

The ship listed to its side and she screamed.

Take more care, or the Devil will come for you, wayward girl!

She should not have let it go any further than the apple orchard. She should not have agreed to walk with him up to the top of the cliff, where the great rock jutted out over the ravine like a gargoyle guarding a cathedral. She had been warned. She knew what would happen: the Devil comes for wayward girls.

But after months of his tender promises, she had relented. When Rémy whispered his secret plan and tied a stem of yarrow around her ring finger, she'd believed him. He said that they could lay amid the gorse and red sorrel and bell heather as man and wife—and none but the hillside gnomes would be the wiser.

Even then, even after they'd made the climb up to the Roche d'Oëtre—handfasted, secretly pledged to marry—she might have changed her mind. When she gazed out across the valley, past leagues of oaks and ash, to where the river wound past the chapel in neighbouring Bréel, on its way out of Normandy towards places forever out of her reach, there was a moment when it might not have happened. From the top of the cliff, the world had seemed so wide. Élisabeth took a step out onto the ledge and called out her name.

Éli-sa-beth.

Éli-Éli.

Li-li.

That was when Rémy Delaunay had pulled her back from the world below and into his arms.

"I saved you," he had said, though she had not been in danger of falling. "Come. We are as good as married in God's eyes already."

It was enough, this promise, to convince her that their pleasure was no sin. So she'd let him pull her off the rock and into the spiky heather.

Michel the cabin boy ran through the lower deck. "Any maid good with a needle, come help us mend the sails!" he yelled.

Marthe moved as if to answer his call but Élisabeth grabbed her arm to hold her back.

"He needs us!" Marthe shouted above the storm. Lou jumped down from the top bunk and Marthe wriggled free to join her. Élisabeth watched as they staggered towards the trunks and were immediately flung sideways when the ship was caught by a swell. Rose leapt to rescue them. She crawled forward on her knees and guided them back to the bunks.

"What can we do?" Marthe panted, wet hair plastered to her face. Just then an almighty crack rent the air, louder and closer than the last thunderclap. The brides shrieked.

"Devil be damned," Lou swore. "Was that the mast?"

No one knew. Élisabeth grabbed Lou's and Marthe's hands and squeezed them tightly. Only faith or magic could save them, and she did not have any magic.

"Pray with me!" She started to chant the holy words over and over.

Holy Virgin, mother of God, serve as our passport and preserve us from peril. Merciful Saint Anne, we cast ourselves at your feet and humbly beg you.

The words were one long, urgent breath. Her stomach cramped, but she could not spare a moment's worry for the torment inside her. *Serve-as-our-passport-and-preserve-us-from-peril.* Above their heads, sailors hollered for an axe to cut the rigging free. *Serve-as-our-passport-and-preserve-us-from-peril.* Hearing their cries, Élisabeth opened her eyes. Marthe's head was swivelled round, her mouth agape.

"We're going to drown," she cried.

"Pray!" Élisabeth shouted, jerking her attention back to their circle with a tug of her hands. They were lost and the *Saint-Jean-Baptiste* was beaten, no longer a match for the witch's power and the sea's rage. Only the Blessed Virgin could save them.

Michel ran through the cabin again, shouting, "The mizzenmast is down!"

Serve as our passport and preserve us from peril. Élisabeth was exhausted from terror. What would happen if she let go of the others' hands? *Serve as our passport and preserve us from peril.* What would happen if she took a step closer to the edge of the ravine? *Serve as our passport and preserve us from peril.* The words swirled in her head as she turned her face upwards, ready for the end; her eyes lifted to God.

A figure stood next to their bunk.

It was the velvet witch, her dress soaked through, looking more dishevelled than when Élisabeth had seen her last. Which was when? Weeks ago? She caught Élisabeth's eye and leaned towards her.

"Your prayers are no use," she hissed.

"What . . . ?" Élisabeth was struck dumb with terror.

"I said—your prayers are no use!"

Élisabeth grew cold as a terrible realization came over her. The witch had come to mock them as she sent them to their doom.

"What does she want?" Marthe cried, squeezing Élisabeth's hand.

"She said . . . she said our prayers are no use!" Élisabeth wailed, horrified to hear the words that came out of her mouth. Their prayers had to work. It was the only hope they had. She squeezed Marthe's and Rose's hands, as if to jolt the girls back to their purpose.

The witch pushed past Élisabeth, leaning into the bunk so the others could hear her. "No, I said: Have you a needle I can use?"

"I do!" Marthe cried and dropped Élisabeth's hand. "I tried to get to my trunk a moment ago, but I was thrown backwards."

"Show me," the witch commanded.

Marthe clambered out of the bottom bunk and braced herself against the violent motion of the ship. Then, as if by magic, the ship paused in its dance, almost becalmed. The rocking slowed until it became no worse than a mother tending to her nursling in his cradle. Élisabeth's jaw fell open at the demonstration of the witch's power.

"Quickly!" The velvet witch pulled Marthe towards the trunks. "We are in the eye of the storm. It will not last."

They dropped to their knees and Marthe flipped open the lid of her trousseau. Several dozen needles were stuck carefully into a slip of paper, all that she would ever need in her married life. The witch gave Marthe a solemn nod of thanks and grabbed the needles. Then she raced towards the ladder to the main deck and disappeared into the night. Marthe jumped back into the bunk with the others, her eyes wild and fierce with determination.

"She's going to save us," Marthe said.

Élisabeth gripped the frame of the bunk and stared at Marthe in disbelief. *The witch would not save them, she had called the Devil her master to take them all to Hell.* As if in answer, the ship began to heave and pitch. Once again, the girls were tossed in their bunks. Their screams echoed all around.

The velvet witch had to be stopped. She had to be thrown into the sea. Élisabeth had to tell the priest what she knew about the letter, never mind that he might turn his gaze towards her. She had to, if they were to survive the journey. She placed a foot on the floor and gripped the bunk post as she pulled herself up.

"Where are you going?" Marthe shouted.

She turned to answer as the *Saint-Jean-Baptiste* listed on its side and every board groaned, as if the ship were being torn asunder. Élisabeth lost her grip on the post and was thrown forward. Her head cracked on the wooden beam and she crumpled to the floor. Pain exploded across her skull and at once a heavy fatigue fell upon her. She tried to speak, but her words came out in strange tongues. The last thing she saw before she fainted was an apparition of a nun, in a habit of velvet, dark as night, a crown of antlers rising from her head.

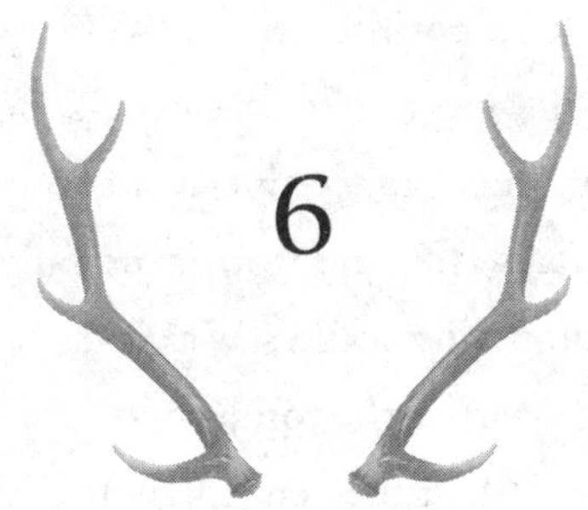

6

Marthe leaned out over the railing, watching the unbroken line of trees. A dark garrison standing against invaders. Below, the river teemed with boats—sloops on business from Québec and barques carrying dry goods, as well as canoes and pinnaces and rowboats—but there was nothing to see onshore but trees.

She shifted uneasily on her feet. "We should be there by now, shouldn't we?"

Lou frowned. "I don't like it."

"We should have stayed in Québec," said Rose.

Marthe looked back at her friends. It was what they were all thinking.

The Montréalistes had left behind the oceangoing *Saint-Jean-Baptiste*—and the bulk of the other brides—in Québec and had transferred to a smaller riverboat five days earlier. There was such a heavy summer rainstorm when they arrived that they had rushed from the king's vessel to the riverboat with barely a chance to bid anyone goodbye, let alone take in the sights of the little town. Now that they were sailing upriver towards Ville-Marie, the wonders of the New World would finally be revealed to them.

Except there was nothing to see at all.

"I'm sure the village will be around the next bend," Marthe said. After all, they had miraculously survived a storm at sea; God would not guide them through such an ordeal only to abandon them in the wilderness weeks later.

Maybe their survival was not due to God's grace. When Father de Sancy had emerged from his cabin, green with seasickness, he claimed the lion's share of the credit for their safe deliverance due to his own intercessions with the Holy Virgin. But in the days after the storm, the sailors had whispered about the woman in the velvet dress who could sew sails faster and more urgently than a galloping mare, leaving Marthe to wonder who she was, and what part she had played in their rescue. When the velvet lady had changed ships with them in Québec and boarded the smaller boat for the island of Montréal, Marthe had felt a frisson of excitement. The mysterious woman was travelling with them to the end of the known world.

But the woman's presence seemed only to add to Élisabeth's despair.

Most of the girls had put the ordeal of the storm quickly behind them, adding it to their trunk of terrible things to consider later, like the weevils in the ship's biscuit and the rats scurrying in gloom-soaked corners. Only Élisabeth seemed truly shaken by their near shipwreck. For weeks after she had smashed her head, she could do nothing but lie in their bunk with her arm flung over her eyes. When awake, she assailed Marthe with questions about tempests and witches and demons while Marthe tried to feed her crumbs of hard tack. Marthe began to think that although the red welt on her forehead had faded, she might have been left demented by the blow.

"Perhaps we won't arrive in Ville-Marie until tomorrow," Rose said. "It *is* late in the day."

"The captain said we would sleep on land tonight," Marthe insisted. "I'm going to get Lili. She shouldn't miss the first sight of the village. We will remember it for the rest of our lives."

Marthe crept below deck, hardly needing any light to find the corner of the boat where they had been stowed like any other exported good, and not even the most precious at that. Élisabeth was sitting near their trunks, scratching the side of the boat with her fingernails.

"We're almost at Ville-Marie," Marthe announced. Élisabeth did not answer. She carried on etching a pattern into the wood, a back-and-forth swirl that grew faster with every loop. "Did you hear me?"

Élisabeth did not look up. "Yes. Yes, I heard. Where is the witch?"

Marthe sighed. "I told you already. Father de Sancy found no witches on board. He went ashore at Québec. You saw him go."

Élisabeth stopped her scratching and rubbed her hand lightly over her brow.

"Does your head hurt still?" Marthe took a step forward to check her sister's injury. Élisabeth pressed her hand to her forehead, blocking Marthe's view. Marthe felt a prickle of irritation and took a step back. "Tonight we will be ashore and the nuns will have a cabbage leaf to lay on your crown. That will soothe your pain."

"I speak of the witch who said our prayers were no use. The one in the velvet dress. Where is she now?"

Marthe bit her lip. She had to get Élisabeth to shore. She was turning in circles, following her mind wherever it led her.

"Come, it's time," she said brightly. "I don't imagine it will be as frantic docking here as it was in Québec, for that was a sight. Girls trying to curl their hair after two months at sea and hitching up their skirts to show off their petticoats. They needn't have bothered. They had neither linen nor lace worth boasting about."

Élisabeth looked up at Marthe. "You believe me, don't you? That woman is a witch."

Marthe sat down by Élisabeth's side. She could not deny there was something intriguing about the woman in the velvet dress. The way she carried herself, tall and proud, and how she stood apart from the others, even now when there were only thirteen of them travelling upriver. After all those weeks at sea, they did not even know her name.

"I admit there is something magical about her, but if there's a hedge witch or a sorceress with us in New France, I shall be glad of it," Marthe reasoned. "We might have need of her magic in the years to come."

Élisabeth stared at Marthe. "How can you speak of witchcraft so lightly? Does it not fill you with revulsion to think of those evil creatures and . . ." She dropped her voice, though there was no one nearby. "The things they do with the Devil?"

"I don't mean evil witches. I mean the cunning folk. Without their help, how else would one cure heartache or remove a wart? Don't forget you too once paid a sol to a soothsayer to hear your fortune. What was she if not a hedge witch? She did you no harm. Except to tell you that Agathe Prévost would marry before you."

Élisabeth bit the corner of her cheek. "Do you think Agathe is married now?"

"Good luck to her if she is. I'll never forget her stumbling into a blackberry bush when Bernard Salé tried to give her a handful of daisies. I've never seen a more awkward couple."

"Perhaps her love for him made her weak at the knees."

"Good grief, Lili!" Marthe exclaimed. "If she were clever she wouldn't fall in love at all. If she must, she certainly shouldn't choose someone who watched slack-jawed as she tumbled into a patch of brambles."

Élisabeth giggled—an uncertain hiccup that Marthe had not heard for months. Her heart lifted at the sound of it. "I should not laugh," Élisabeth whispered, suddenly sober again. "Bramble thorns spell poverty and sorrow. Poor Agathe."

"I am sure she's well enough. You have had greater trials than her. But today your luck shall change."

Élisabeth bowed her head. "I pray you are right. But do not speak of luck. Our fortune is thanks only to God's mercy."

Marthe squeezed her arm and encouraged her sister to stand. Élisabeth wobbled slightly at first, then brushed down her crumpled skirts. Marthe was encouraged by this small act of vanity. If her sister cared enough to smooth her skirts, she was on her way to being herself again. Once they were ashore and settled, Élisabeth would be well.

They emerged onto the deck and were struck by a sky the colour of a dying bonfire. Élisabeth flinched from not having seen the light all day, but Marthe imagined she could only feel better with the warmth of the evening sun on her face. She guided her sister towards the side of the boat and saw that they were no longer moving. They were moored several yards offshore.

"Where are we?" Élisabeth asked, bewildered.

Marthe looked around. There was still no sign of the village. It was not at all like it had been when they docked in Québec. There was no wharf thronging with villagers and soldiers, rushing through the rain to greet them. Here, there was neither sign of any dwelling, nor of any souls at all.

"Where is Ville-Marie?" Marthe asked the others.

"You missed it," Apolline said, her expression cloudy. "And no surprise, for there was little more than a dock and a crowd of native men. That cannot be where we are meant to settle." For once, her voice was uncertain. She turned to face a boatman. "Was that Ville-Marie?"

"Calm yerselves," said a rusty-haired sailor with whiskers to match. "With the fur fair on, it wasn't safe to drop you at the quay in town. The nuns sent word to bring you out here."

"Wasn't safe?" Élisabeth swayed.

"What's a fur fair?" Marthe asked at the same time.

"It's a lovely event where all the great ladies come and show off their furs," the sailor jeered. "It's very grand, you'll see."

Suddenly Lou shouted and pointed at the shore.

"Look!"

A small wooden boat was pushing off from a beach. A woman with a black veil and white coif sat in the bow, a large man in a brown brimmed hat squarely in the middle of the boat. They watched as he rowed steadily closer until the boat was near enough to bump up against the side of their vessel. The nun craned her neck to look up at the crew.

"I've wasted an entire afternoon waiting for you to arrive."

The captain leaned over the side of the riverboat. "We were given instructions not to stop at the quay but to bring the girls-for-marrying here. Are you Mother Bourgeoys?"

"I am not," the nun said crossly, her wrinkled face inspecting the side of the ship. "Well? Get them down. We need them safely ashore before sunset and the hour is late."

The captain beckoned to Élisabeth and pointed at a rope ladder fixed to the side of the ship. "Descend."

"Down the ropes?" Élisabeth's eyes darted to the swiftly flowing river. Upstream the water churned as if there might be rapids.

"Yes. Quickly," the nun shouted from below.

"Do you need help, Lili?"

"No. I am well," Élisabeth said, her eyes fixed on some spot on the shore. "Today my luck shall change. Today the curse shall be lifted."

She gripped the sides of the rope ladder in her fists and swung her leg over the side of the boat. The boatmen whistled at the sight of her pale ankle, but Élisabeth did not turn back; her eyes were locked on the shore. Marthe scrambled after her sister, tumbling into the rowboat.

"It does not look at all as I was expecting," Rose said when she joined them a moment later. The little boat rocked side to side as she boarded and Marthe gripped the gunwales to steady herself.

"We are upriver from Ville-Marie," the nun said, lurching as Lou jumped into the boat with both feet.

"Why did the sailors say it wouldn't be safe to land in the village?" Lou asked.

"Because of the fur fair," the nun said, grunting.

"And will there be great lords and ladies there in their *furs*?" Marthe asked incredulously, for she could not fathom how anyone could wear fur in such heat; even at the end of the day the air around them was almost too thick to breathe. But if the furs were as luxurious as she imagined, who could blame them? Perhaps one day she might do the same.

The nun gave her a look of amazement. "Do you know nothing of where you are?"

"Not really, no."

"The fair is for trading furs, not showing them off. Fur drives all commerce here. The French and English want it, the Iroquois and the Algonquins and the other native tribes have it. That's all you need to understand."

Marthe's heart skipped a beat. So it was true. If there was one thing she had gleaned from their village priest's reading of the Jesuit tales, it was that a fortune could be made in fur. She smiled to herself as she tucked the information away.

Young Claire settled into the rowboat and crossed herself. The nun called back up to the captain. "Send one more down. I only want to make two trips to shore."

The captain nodded at someone on deck and a moment later the woman in the velvet dress appeared. Marthe glanced at Élisabeth who had grown very still.

The velvet lady backed down the rope ladder slowly, her buckled shoe feeling for the safety of the rowboat beneath her. She crouched as she turned and climbed down into the boat, though she was hampered in her movements by trying to clutch an object to her chest. Marthe peered at the bundle but could only make out a thatch of black yarn. The woman moved towards the bench where Élisabeth sat.

Abruptly, Élisabeth jumped to her feet, causing the packed rowboat to lurch from side to side. The woman in velvet lost her footing. She rocked backwards, throwing her hands out for balance. Her bundle of yarn dropped into the bottom of the boat and with a yelp, she tumbled into the river.

In the rowboat, the girls gasped, twisting left and right. The nun shouted at them to sit still while the brides left on the riverboat screamed and pointed. The man in the brown hat jabbed his oar into the river, as if he were trying to spear a fish.

"She's gone!" Marthe cried, peering into the fast-moving water. "Blessed Virgin, the velvet lady is gone." Beside her, Élisabeth was quiet.

The nun trained her eyes on the water. "Pray to God, she will come up again."

Just then, a dark head breached the waves and gasped, not for breath but in rapture. The woman in velvet bobbed up and down for a moment, her arms churning above her head, then disappeared under the water again.

"A sea monster has her!" Lou shouted. "It's dragged her under!"

"Saint Adjutor, protect her!" Rose prayed.

After a long moment the woman reappeared again, closer to shore. She stood and turned back to face the rowboat, the water up to her chest. She waved her hand over her head.

"Go, go," the nun barked at the man in the brown hat, and he drove his oars into the water, pulling them towards land and overtaking the woman in velvet. When the little boat scraped the sandy bottom of the shoreline, the girls leapt from the skiff.

Marthe tottered a little at the feeling of solid ground beneath her feet.

"Thank the Lord you are safe," the nun said, exhaling deeply as she called out to the woman in velvet.

The woman said nothing in return. She had lost her cap in the river and proceeded to squeeze the water from her hair as she waded towards the shore. The river shimmered as she moved through it; the dying sun briefly lit her pale face. When she reached the beach, she put her hands on her hips and looked around her. Then she arched her back and stretched her palms out, as if she were conjuring the rising moon.

At the sight of the pale orb in the darkening sky to the east, a tingling feeling started in Marthe's fingers and toes. Élisabeth was right, the woman in velvet had to be a sorceress. Or perhaps a mermaid. Whatever she was, there was so much magic dripping off her that Marthe longed to reach forward and catch some of it for herself. Three more steps would do it.

"Do not move from where you are," the nun commanded them. "My heart can't take another scare. We won't be a moment; we are going back for the others."

"Wait!" the witch called out. She rushed back towards the rowboat, the other brides scurrying away from her as she approached. When she was alongside the craft she reached inside and fished out the cloth bundle she had dropped when she fell in the river. It was too dark now for Marthe to see it clearly, but she could sense the relief with which the woman clutched it to her chest.

Marthe walked a few paces onto the shore, the sound of sand and pebbles crunching beneath her feet sweeter than angels' song. She crossed herself and looked up to Heaven. Next to her, Élisabeth fell to her knees. Rose and Lou followed and kissed the ground.

The moon had indeed started to rise, bathing the beach in a milky light. The shadows of the trees were growing longer, making it hard to scan the woods for any sign of life. Fireflies flickered for a moment, then vanished, reminding Marthe of summer evenings in Normandy when gleaners combed the fields, the women bent double searching for scraps of grain, the children chasing the tiny fairy bugs. As she gazed up at the lonely majesty of this forest, so far away from home, she heard her sister's feverish prayers—and the splatter of water on stones as the witch wrung the water out of her dress.

"How did you . . . do that?" she asked.

The woman looked up. "What do you mean?"

"I mean, how did you float like that?"

The woman stared back. "I was swimming. I had to, because that fool knocked me overboard." She glared at Élisabeth, who was still on her knees in the sand, clasping her hands.

"I've seen my brothers swim in the river Orne." Élisabeth's voice trembled, her eyes widening. "What you did was not the same. You looked like a—like a sea serpent. Rising and plunging and breathing all at the same time, and with the weight of your wet dress—it is unnatural."

The sorceress raised her chin, the moonlight revealing the haughty arch of her lips. "What do you mean, unnatural?"

Élisabeth said no more and Marthe didn't wonder that she'd lost her nerve. It was risky to challenge a magical creature at any time, let alone under a rising moon.

The woman gave the sisters a fierce look.

"Do you mean to stand and gawk at me?"

Élisabeth stammered, "I-I've just never seen anything like that before."

"That's hardly a surprise. You're a peasant. You've probably seen very little in your life."

A rush of indignation bloomed in Marthe's chest but Élisabeth only pressed her lips tightly together and stared back. Then she turned and walked away. When she had gone ten paces, she kneeled, made the sign of the cross, and lay face down on the sand, stretching her arms wide in supplication.

"I confess to almighty God that have greatly sinned in my thoughts and in my words, in what I have done and in what I have failed to do, through my fault, through my fault, through my most grievous fault."

Marthe rushed to her sister's side. "Lili, you are taking it too much to heart. The boat was overfull. Just apologize and the lady will forgive you."

"I will not apologize to *her*," Élisabeth mumbled into the sand.

"Then get up!" Marthe glanced around to see if the others had noticed Élisabeth lying prostrate on the beach. This was too much piety.

"Leave me be, Marthe."

"If you want to praise the Virgin for our safe arrival, then we shall gather the others and all give thanks together."

"Holy Virgin, with the help of Thy grace, I resolve to sin no more."

Marthe stared, helpless to stop her sister's excessive display. When something in the sand crawled across Élisabeth's chest, she jerked away from the ground and raised herself onto her elbows. The look on her face was utterly forlorn. "I feel the same. No better at all." She nodded at the woman in velvet, now wringing water out of her petticoats. "Perhaps that is why the cure to my suffering has not worked. I am beset by witches."

"You broke your crown during the storm. The captain said it could take months to recover from such a blow."

Élisabeth ignored her and began to work her hands in the peculiar pattern she had developed. "Queen of Heaven, by the help of Thy grace, cleanse my body and my soul. Rid me of evil—"

"Lili! Stop, that woman will hear you."

Though Élisabeth fell silent her hands continued to twist. Marthe knew she should calm her sister and tell her that she believed what she said about the woman in the velvet dress—after all, Marthe could see she was sparkling with magic—but she felt suddenly weary. She let her sister pray and stared back out at the river. The rowboat was gliding back to shore carrying the rest of the women. One of the brides had started singing, her voice clear and high, making it seem as if the craft was drifting forward on an eerie charm rather than the strength of the rower's arms.

"Quand j'étais fille à marier j'étais belle et galante
Quand j'étais fille à marier j'étais belle et galante
Beaucoup d'amants venaient me voir à minuit dans ma chambre . . ."

The skiff scraped up on the rough sand and the remaining girls stepped out of the boat. Their sisters of the sea rushed to join them, chattering and gazing at the New World around them. The dark woods stared back, hiding whatever lay along the forest path: a warm hearth, a good man, healthy children? Or all their deepest fears come true?

One by one the *Saint-Jean-Baptiste* brides fell silent and drew closer to each other, sheep nervous before shearing.

All except one.

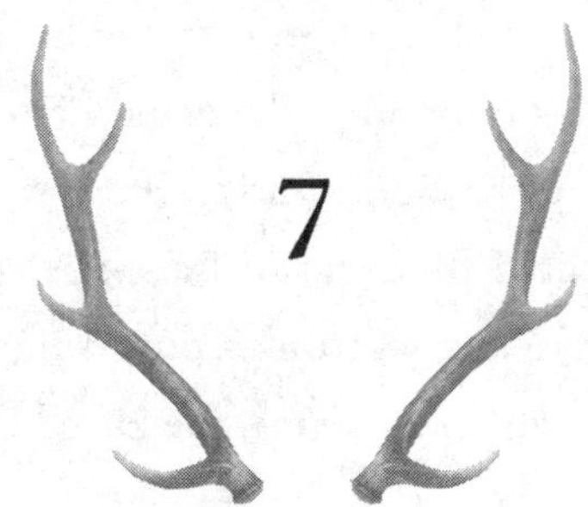

7

A sunbeam danced across Élisabeth's cheek. Her eyelashes fluttered, and for a moment she could not remember where she was. Papa would soon bid her to tend to the chickens before the foxes did, so she should make a start on her chores. She opened her eyes and winced against the bright sun.

The creeping feeling in her belly returned.

She was not on the farm at Saint-Philbert. There were no fires to light, no bread to knead. Her father was not yet a year in his grave and her mother long before him. She blinked away an uninvited image: Papa's blood, spilling onto the cottage kitchen's stone floor. Her linen cloth, insufficient to mop it all up, growing wet and heavy the more she tried. Marthe's anguished wail.

Élisabeth sat bolt upright.

She was in a remote farmhouse on the edge of a vast forest in a strange, new land. All feeling of warmth collapsed as the alarming jabs in her stomach grew more severe.

After two months at sea, she had arrived at the edge of the world, to the holiest place on earth, yet she was still cursed. She knew nothing had changed; could *feel* that nothing had changed. Indeed, it was worse, for like the nuns of Louviers, had she not begun to show signs of demonic possession? What else could explain the feeling of being repeatedly punched in the gut, as if a stag were ramming his mighty antlers against her torso? And on the ship, the priest said the nuns he exorcised had great strength, but also extreme fatigue. Throughout the last weeks on the ship, she could hardly lift her head from her bed! Was it not a sign of possession? During those wretched days and nights, had she not been tormented by devilish dreams? Being stripped naked and pricked with needles from Marthe's trunk, conversing with demons dressed in velvet robes, being laid down on an altar to be kissed below her skirts, the way Rémy had once done.

She pinched her arm to see if she felt pain. It hurt, that was good. But perhaps she should take a needle to prick her body? Would piercing her skin be a truer test of a demon's control? She wished she'd remembered more of what the old priest had said about the symptoms the nuns had experienced. Contortions and convulsions, yes? She circled her knees underneath the blanket to test their grace, and found her limbs still moved with ease.

The churning of her legs woke Marthe.

"Good morning." Marthe sighed, her dimples deepening as she greeted the day. "I had forgotten what it feels like to wake in daylight."

Élisabeth did not reply. They were no longer in the ship's damp dungeon, but she was still mired in darkness. Though, perhaps she should not have expected to feel differently so soon. She had not yet heard Mass or taken communion. Would receiving the sacrament exorcise the curse, here in the holiest village in the world? She tried not to think about what Michel the cabin boy had said, that Ville-Marie was a wild frontier town filled with wolves.

"Lou," Marthe whispered. "Lou. *Marie-Louise!*"

Their friend was fast asleep in the straw mattress next to them, her mouth open, hair mussed across her face. Next to her lay Rose, then Apolline and Claire and all the others asleep on pallets laid out on the dormitory floor. They had collapsed in exhaustion and relief the night before, after the nun had escorted them through the woods and they'd been given fresh bread and meat for the first time in two months.

Marthe prodded Lou's arm with her toe. "Wake up." She tiptoed over to do the same to Rose. When neither moved she tripped over them to wake the other brides, like a fairy tapping them with a wand to release them from their slumbers.

Heavy footsteps sounded on the wooden stairs. The nun from the previous night appeared, accompanied by a younger woman in a similar habit.

"You appear to be lively and ready to work." The nun pressed her lips together and looked around the room. "We're going to start with the laundry and cooking."

"Excuse me," Rose said, raising her hand in the air hesitantly. She received an unforgiving look from the nun in return. "Where is Mother Bourgeoys? When we signed up for Ville-Marie we were told that we would be in her particular care."

A murmur rose across the room. On the ship the Montréalistes had talked about the bargain that they had struck: greater wilderness in exchange for greater tenderness. Marguerite Bourgeoys, they were assured before they left, was as kind as she was devout, and if they agreed to come all the way to the edge of the world she would take care that they were matched to even-tempered husbands who weren't quick to reach for the birch rod.

The nun held up her hands. "She does not live here on the farm. Though you will not find her at her home in town either. She has returned to France on a mission for our congregation." The nun raised her voice above the alarmed whispers. "Mother Bourgeoys has entrusted your care to us. I am Sister Gagnon. This is Sister Brodeur. You needn't worry. Together with Sister Crolo—who is already out in the fields—we will teach you all you need to know before you marry."

"Who will help us find husbands, though?" Marthe asked.

"It is not difficult to find willing bachelors here at any time. And this year they've been given an incentive to marry especially quickly."

Rose's hand started to rise again; Sister Gagnon ignored it and continued.

"The intendant in Québec has decreed that if the bachelors haven't got wives by the first of September they won't be given a licence to hunt and trade." She squared her shoulders. "I've written to tell him that doesn't give us long to get you ready for life on a homestead, but Intendant Talon appears less concerned about you poisoning your husbands with badly cured pork than in making sure you bear sons for the colony as soon as possible, so we'll have to make do with the time that we have."

"Who is Intendant Talon?" Apolline asked. "And why should he want to rush us into marriage?"

The old nun shrugged. "The rules are the rules. And his edict was clear. No wife, no fur trading licence. Seeing as he's the one who runs the fur trade and the courts—the men must do as he pleases."

"But the first of September is three weeks hence!" Lou repeated in shock.

"Precisely. That's why you need to rise and breakfast right away. There's much to learn in a short time."

The room erupted into excited chatter. Rose hopped onto Lou's bed and grabbed her by the shoulders. "Now remember, we shall look for a kind, tall one for you, and whoever is his closest neighbour for me. If all the tall ones are sullen or have excessively bad breath, we shall look for one who is shorter and softly spoken for me, and *his* neighbour for you. Either way, we shall never be parted."

Élisabeth sat on her straw mattress, listening to the other girls. She could not let her own dreams of marriage vanish. She twitched her legs, checking them once again to see if they were free from a demon's grasp. She had to get to the village and receive the holy sacrament as soon as she could.

"Excuse me, Sister Gagnon," Élisabeth called out. "When shall we go to church to attend Mass?"

"There is no church as yet in Ville-Marie," Sister Gagnon informed her, then turned to address the entire group. "Now, your trunks were off-loaded from the ship at dawn and the carter has just arrived with the lot of them, so I've asked our engagés to bring them up—"

"But, Sister!" Élisabeth surprised herself by interrupting. "How is there no church?" Her voice began to falter. "Where . . . where is there a holy place to confess our sins? To take communion?"

"Lord, how you fret." Sister Gagnon frowned and put her hands on her hips. "If you are concerned about where you will be married, I can tell you all weddings will take place in the chapel of the Hôtel Dieu. We do on occasion attend Mass there as well. We are building a church dedicated to Our Lady; the chapel will have to do until that day. Ah, here are the three-year men with your trunks."

Before Élisabeth could enquire when they would visit the chapel, two farmhands in square-toed boots stomped into the dormitory carrying the first of the chests. Françoise and Thérèse elbowed each other from beneath their blankets, goggling at the sight of the men. Élisabeth clasped her hands together. *Squeeze, glide to prayer position and past, squeeze again.* She needed to get to the hospital chapel as quickly as she could. It was her only hope.

"Thank you for bringing me my trunk. It contains everything I own in this world." Thérèse's coy tone caused one of the indentured servants to stop and flash her a smile.

"That's enough of that," Sister Gagnon said, stepping in between them. "He's got two years left on his contract. He's no freer to marry you than the pope."

The workman's grin faded. "And I'm counting the months 'til I can go home," he said, his feet heavier on the stairs as he descended. Françoise smirked at Thérèse, but she seemed to have already forgotten the engagé as she turned to open her trunk.

"I saved this one for my wedding day," she said, pulling out a coarse linen chemise. "Isn't it fine?"

"It seems an ordinary enough shirt for an ordinary girl," Françoise sniped back.

The three-year men soon returned with another of the trunks. Soon all the brides were poring over their few belongings: the headdresses, handkerchiefs, and shoe ribbons they had packed away so many weeks ago. They paid little heed to Sister Gagnon's talk of work in the kitchen and garden. While the other girls mooned over their trunks, Élisabeth left hers untouched.

"Sister Gagnon," she said, rising to her feet. "May we go to the hospital chapel today? I should like to thank the Blessed Virgin for our deliverance. If we do not offer our prayers immediately, we risk the saints' wrath."

"Calm yourself, child. The saints will not forsake you for praying in a corner of this house rather than in Ville-Marie."

The nun turned to direct the farmhands where to put the next delivery of trunks. Élisabeth followed her.

"Would the missionaries in Ville-Marie not be heartened by our example, though, of coming to hear Mass the very day after our arrival? Would we not inspire the villagers with our devotion and piety?"

"Please, Sister Gagnon," Lou chimed in, tripping across the room to plead with the nun. "Élisabeth is right. We must go to the chapel to show everyone how pious we are! Would the bachelors of Ville-Marie not like to see our . . . piety?" Lou wiggled her bottom as the other girls laughed. There was no stopping the brides' pleas now. They crowded around the nun, begging to be allowed to visit the village. Sister Gagnon resisted, pushing past them towards the far corner of the room.

"Where is *your* trunk?"

Élisabeth saw that one mattress in the dormitory was pulled away from all the others. Beside it stood the velvet witch, looking out the window, wearing the thin ratine nightdress she had been given the night before. When she realized the nun was speaking to her, she turned around.

"Are you quite certain that all of the chests have been delivered?" the witch asked. She had the same haughty manner as when she spoke to Élisabeth on the beach. *You're a peasant. You've probably seen very little in your life.* Élisabeth scowled at her, though the witch paid her no mind.

"Yes. All but yours, it seems," the nun said.

"I can't imagine what has happened to it."

The nun sighed. "What is your name? I will send a message back with the carter to check the ship's hold again."

The witch paused and looked down her long nose at the nun. "I am Jeanne. Jeanne Roy. Perhaps you could lend me something until my travelling clothes have been laundered?"

Sister Gagnon frowned. "None of my sisters have clothing that will fit one so . . . slender as you." She looked up to see Élisabeth staring at them. "You. You're thin. Do you have spare skirts for Jeanne Roy?"

Élisabeth froze. She did not want to give this so-called Jeanne Roy—the letter thief, the witch with the velvet dress, the sea serpent—*any* of her possessions. She did not want to be near the dangerous creature.

"I want to go to Ville-Marie," she said meekly.

The nun looked surprised. "Are you trying to barter with me?"

"N-no, Sister," Élisabeth stammered, though from the rush of whispers behind her she knew that's precisely what the other brides thought. "It's only that I want to thank the Blessed Virgin for our survival and not anger the saints. It's been a very long, very frightening journey, and at least a half dozen of us did not survive, and I am desperate—quite desperate—to go to church and take communion. I must tell the Holy Virgin how grateful I am. I do not feel I can eat, or sleep, or rest until I have done so."

Sister Gagnon frowned, then finally the muscle in her jaw relaxed and she cupped Élisabeth under the chin.

"You are a pious girl. Get me a skirt for this one, and if everyone has completed their chores by midday, we can go to the chapel this afternoon."

The brides erupted into applause. Élisabeth heaved a sigh of relief, then remembered what it had cost her. She would have to give the witch a gift. If she did not agree, the trip to the chapel would surely be withdrawn. She glanced at Jeanne Roy, who had turned back to the window, her arms folded across her chest. It would be dangerous to give a witch an item of her clothing, but more so to defy her.

She swallowed and knelt by her trunk. She opened the lid and saw that her linens bore the mark of having been wet and then dried again. A yellow stain crept across two chemises and one of her petticoats. Half of her clothing was ruined.

She reached for the pine-stained petticoat then pulled back. Would it anger Jeanne Roy if the clothes she was offered weren't the very best? The other petticoat was her favourite, one she had spent long evenings stitching by the fire when her brothers and Papa were all still alive, before she left to work in the Delaunay household and everything had changed. She could not bear to part with it. She stared at the linens and felt the turmoil stirring in her belly. She also could not risk vexing the velvet witch. She reached for her best petticoat and her only other skirt. Then she rummaged and found her holy water vessel tucked down the side of the trunk. She clutched the talisman in her hand for protection.

She approached the witch slowly with her eyes averted. She was about to hand the skirts over when she caught sight of a lump on Jeanne Roy's mattress.

A baby's grey corpse.

Élisabeth gasped and dropped the skirts on the floor. She looked to the witch—a snarl spreading across her face—and then back to the dead child.

It was nothing but a homespun cloth doll. Élisabeth exhaled so forcefully she thought she might fall to the ground. She gazed at the witch's familiar more carefully. The shock of tangled soot-coloured yarn on the poppet's head was a rival for its mistress's own black hair. The eyes had been poorly stitched and its arms flopped over its head, while the legs were rigid, ending in heavy stumps, as if Jeanne Roy had not the time nor the inclination to turn the heel and give the poor creature feet. It was so hideous that it was bewitching. Élisabeth could not stop herself from reaching out towards the doll.

"Don't touch it," Jeanne Roy warned.

Élisabeth stumbled backwards as surely as if she had been struck. She turned and started to scamper across the room, squeezing her holy water vessel tightly.

"Wait," the witch called out. Élisabeth felt her legs go rigid, and then experienced an added jolt of fear—for did the priest not say stiffness was an indication of demonic possession? Fixed to the spot, she cringed and turned her shoulders towards Jeanne Roy.

"Thank you," the witch said clutching the skirts in her hand. "For the clothes."

Élisabeth dared to meet her eye. The witch's face was tense, as if she was trying to control her pride—or her fury. Élisabeth did not wait to find out. She dropped her eyes and hurried back to the safety of her own trunk.

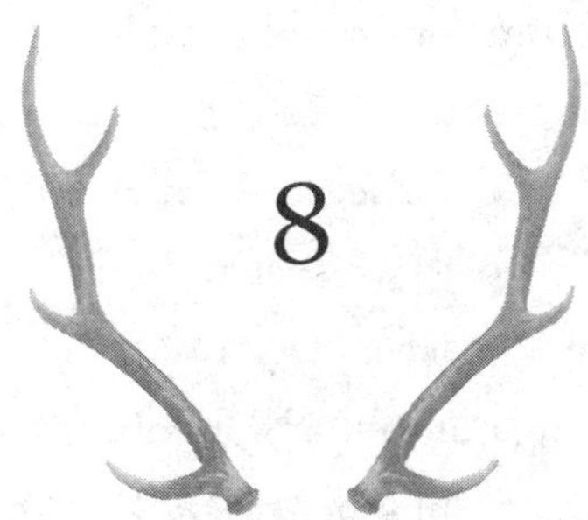

8

The brides' spirits were high as they walked into the village that afternoon. They gaped and pointed at the marvels all around them: bright orange lilies, paler than the hawkweed they knew at home but more brilliant for their size and height; yellow marguerites with furry brown centres that resembled small sunflowers; stalks topped by tiny clusters of white flowers perfect for an elf's bouquet; tall grasses sprouting violets. Bees looped around the flowers in coy circles as some of the brides tried to stop and pick what they could. Sister Gagnon scolded them all for dallying.

Marthe held Rose's and Lou's hands and swung them back and forth as they traipsed through the meadow and across a little creek. She felt oddly seasick from walking on the land, as if she had been so long at sea that she could not stand straight. They skipped ahead and then stopped, waiting for the dizziness to overtake them, then fell to the ground laughing. It was the first day of their new lives and they had everything that they needed: sunshine, friendship, and a generous fifty-livre dowry from the king.

Behind them Élisabeth paused to examine the ground every few steps. She had seemed so anxious to be allowed to visit Ville-Marie, Marthe couldn't understand why she was dawdling now.

"What are you doing?" she asked. Élisabeth looked up at her, her brows furrowed.

"Checking her footprints." Élisabeth nodded in the direction of Jeanne Roy. "To see if toadstools sprout where she treads."

Marthe bent over. She did not see any fungus.

"Do you hear that?" Élisabeth whispered. Marthe tilted her head. There was a piercing hum of what might have been a bird or a cricket, or some kind of otherworldly creature calling out to them. Élisabeth crossed herself and slipped her hands into her pockets, pulling her rosary from one, her holy water vessel from the other. She held them tightly in her fists.

"Can you believe the heat of the day?" Marthe smiled, more as a means to distract Élisabeth than a desire to discuss the weather. "I do believe the sailors' tales of eyelashes turning to icicles and toes freezing black were exaggerations meant to frighten us rather than a true reflection of what this island is like."

"This heat can't last. A storm must surely come," Élisabeth murmured.

"Perhaps. Or perhaps the summers here will be glorious, and the winters mild. Did you see the size of the crops? Everything is so tall."

Her sister did not reply. She squinted into the distance to where Jeanne Roy was leaning over to pick wildflowers. When she moved on, Élisabeth silently followed to inspect the ground. Marthe knew she should keep an eye on her, but enchanted by the delights of the day, she ran to catch up with her friends instead.

They did not meet their first Canadian until they reached a dirt track that Sister Brodeur said bore the grand name of Rue Saint-Paul. A middle-aged man with his chemise open at the neck and a pipe in his mouth lifted his hat and crossed the road to speak to Sister Gagnon. The procession slowed to a halt, which gave Marthe a chance to peer down the road and up a little side street. The roads were earthen, in some places packed hard from use. The few houses in the village had pigs rooting around in the front gardens. Farther down Rue Saint-Paul she could see several figures dressed in black. Jesuit or Récollet priests? Or perhaps like Father de Sancy, from the order of Saint-Sulpice? Marthe had learned the Sulpicians were not just clerics but also the lords of Montréal Island, controlling everything as far as the eye could see.

A pair of nuns in a slightly different habit from Sister Gagnon's also stopped to talk, and Marthe heard Sister Brodeur explain that these were Ursulines, not to be confused with the Hospitalières, who ran the Hôtel Dieu and cared for both the bodies and souls of the needy. She was amazed at the many religious orders and was thinking that Élisabeth could be right about the sanctity of the island, when Lou nudged her.

"Look! A dog pulling a cart."

There was all manner of conveyances on the road: two-wheeled, four-wheeled, some with a place for a carter to sit, others so small they were only fit to move a few goods. All but one was pulled by an ox or a cow; the smallest, filled to the brim with hay, was being led by a mongrel, though the dog was distracted by a feathered lump of carrion he'd discovered in the street, causing his master to strike him with a stick as the cart veered off its path.

"Why does no one have a horse?" Marthe asked Sister Brodeur. The young nun was being pestered with other questions too.

"Is this all there is? There do not seem to be many homes," said Françoise.

"Where are the shops?" Thérèse asked.

"Why is there no proper church?" Apolline frowned.

"There are now as many as fifty houses," Sister Brodeur explained, taking the questions in her stride. "Each artisan has his shingle outside his home so you may know his trade. Few have horses, though I'm sure that will change as our colony grows. Our Lady's church will be built right up that street. Until then, we use the chapel. All things take time."

"How many artisans are there?" Marthe asked.

"Easily two dozen." The young nun smiled, though Marthe was not encouraged by this. Of two dozen men likely only half of that number were in want of a wife, or of a marriageable age. She would not wed an old man unless he was already rich. She needed a husband with strength enough to meet her ambitions.

"Come along," she heard the older nun call to them. Sister Gagnon made sweeping motions with her hands, as if to usher them forward. "I've just been warned there's been plenty of drinking and fighting at the fur fair today. Let's move on."

As if the nun had called him forth with her words, a man with long whiskers started lumbering towards the girls. Sister Gagnon puffed out her chest, creating a barrier between the men and her ducklings, while two more long-beards appeared from one of the side streets. The men staggered towards the brides, staring as if it were more shocking to see a girl in a clean skirt than a black bear on Rue Saint-Paul.

"You there!" the first man called as he loped alongside them. "You're a pretty one." His head turned, taking in the procession. "As are you. Even more so. And you as well."

The smell of brandy and sweat was so overpowering that Marthe was forced to hold her breath. She thought of what her papa might say about the two men lurching towards them. Not fit to breed, better to wring their necks.

"Step back," Sister Gagnon ordered a man in a yellowing hessian shirt. "These girls-for-marrying are intended for demobilized members of the regiment, not coureurs de bois who spend all day in Folleville's tavern."

"Sister, I will have a fortune soon. I'm going upcountry and will come back with enough furs to fill a barque." His beard was so thick and his hair so bushy he looked like a wild animal. Marthe wondered if he were one of the wolves Michel the cabin boy had talked about. Beyond them, down by the river, she could see a crowd larger and more boisterous than a Shrovetide carnival.

Packs of wolves.

"If those girls are going to hear Mass, we will as well," another slurred as he spoke. "Will you stop us from taking communion?"

Sister Gagnon did not reply, only quickened her pace, the men trailing after them into the chapel. She held out a protective arm as she ushered the girls into the empty pews near the front, giving Élisabeth a sharp look as she slid in next to Marthe.

"I should never have agreed to this," she said.

The chapel filled up quickly. More men came to line the walls of the stone room, a half dozen of them panting from having just run to join the service. One clutched a bouquet of hastily plucked wildflowers in his hand, another tucked a bottle of brandy into his waistcoat.

"Get ready," Lou whispered, wiggling her bottom to further provoke the suitors. "They're going to dance around us like a maypole when we're done our prayers." Several of the girls sniggered and Sister Gagnon shot them a fierce look. Beside them, Apolline's stern expression mirrored the nun's disapproval.

While they waited for the service to begin, the brides pestered the nuns for information about the village. Sister Gagnon would not be deterred from her prayers, but Sister Brodeur whispered a few tight-lipped replies to Apolline, and the eldest Parisian relayed what she knew down the pew so that Marthe learned that the fur fair was at its height in August, otherwise the village was very quiet. The Sulpicians had only taken over as the seigneurs of the island a few years ago, and the priests all lived together in a seminary next door. Marthe didn't care about the fur traders and provincial clerics. They were not eligible for marriage and so were of no use to her.

She looked around the chapel, wondering if her future husband could be among the congregation. She craned her neck to the chapel door and saw to her surprise a gentleman walking down the aisle. He swept towards them in a red satin justaucorps stitched with gold brocade. His coat flared at the knees in a way that showed off his calves; Marthe thought he looked like a leopard on the prowl, his stockings were so sleek. A sword hung from the baldric on his shoulder and around his neck was enough lace to trim a dozen good aprons. His right eye was covered by a black patch.

"Congratulations on your beauties, Sister," he said to Sister Gagnon as he stopped by their pew. "They are even more gracious than the girls-for-marrying last year. I hope I may be presented to them later? To welcome them to Ville-Marie properly?"

The nun's body stiffened as she muttered a reply. The gentleman threw back his head and laughed, the curls of his wig shaking. Then he glided down the aisle and took his seat in the front of the chapel.

"What did she say?" Marthe leaned over Élisabeth to tap Rose's arm. "I could not hear Sister Gagnon."

"I don't know. I'm waiting for Françoise to pass it on."

"Who is he?" Marthe wanted to know.

Françoise whispered into Lou's ear, who did not wait to pass it onto Rose, instead blurting out what she'd been told so that the whole row could hear. "Sister Gagnon said, 'Governor, you may meet them only after they are safely married.'"

"He's the governor?" Marthe stretched forward to catch sight of the man. She took in his clothes, his wig, the scent of perfume that filled the air. She had never been so close to someone so wealthy.

"*Acting* governor, Sister Gagnon just said." Rose's ear was still cocked to the murmured conversation beside her.

"Still," Marthe exhaled, as she nudged Élisabeth. "What do you think Papa would say about us being presented to the governor of Montréal?"

"Hush, we're about to start," Élisabeth said.

Marthe dug her elbow into her sister's side. Élisabeth was exceptionally tiresome today: her feet could not stay still, and her knees jiggled like a calf's foot jelly. Marthe glared at her and then pointedly turned away.

Behind her she could see Jeanne Roy rise and walk across the nave to sit next to two women. Marthe leaned back to get a better view. Her eyes widened when she realized they were natives.

"Lili, look," she whispered.

They were dressed in plain tunics, their hair uncovered. But, other than the light cinnamon colour of their skin, they did not look very different from anyone else. Marthe felt almost disappointed. From the stories she'd heard, she had expected something more exhilarating. One even wore a small wooden cross at her neck, not unlike Marthe's own.

"How do you imagine the witch can speak the native tongue?" Élisabeth asked, watching the two women squeeze together to make room for Jeanne Roy. "It must be some kind of spell that allows her to understand them."

"Perhaps they're speaking French."

"French!"

"Don't sound so surprised," Rose said. "Sister Brodeur says that some priests can speak native languages fluently. It stands to reason that those women might speak French."

"Stop staring," Élisabeth said. "The witch will see." She crossed herself and squeezed her hands together. "This chapel is too small." Her knees did not stop bouncing as she spoke.

"Sit still, Lili." Marthe placed her hand on Élisabeth's knee to calm her. Her sister's trembles were turning into convulsions and Marthe was forced to tear her eyes away from the native women. Goodness knows what the congregation would make of Élisabeth, shaking from head to toe and talking of mushrooms and witchcraft. Marthe faced forward and prayed that her sister would settle down before she once again ruined their chances of making a good impression.

No sooner had Marthe fixed her eyes on the back of the governor's head, than he turned around.

She quickly looked away. She studied her hand on Élisabeth's leg. She picked a piece of straw from the cuff of her chemise. She forgot all about Jeanne Roy and the native women. When she dared to look up again, she was shocked to see that the governor was still staring at her.

With his one good eye, he winked.

She dropped her eyes. She could not believe it. The governor of Montréal had just winked at her. What should she do? A wave of determination crashed over Marthe. She would make the most of the chance that had presented itself. She raised her head and looked straight at the governor.

She smiled back.

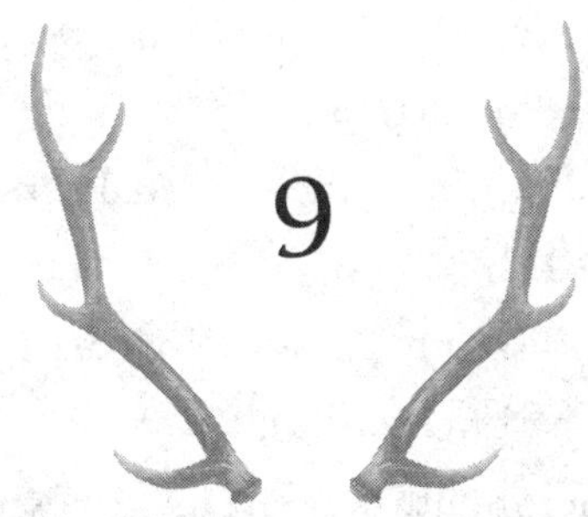

9

A priest with a grey mustache stepped up to the altar for the communal confession. Élisabeth forced herself to look away from Jeanne Roy and the native women. It would not be long now until she would know if the curse was lifted. When the pangs in her belly would cease and she would once again know the sanctified peace that she had lost that night in the tavern, when her life changed with the flick of a witch's finger. Unless—if there were a demon inside her, might she pull a face and recoil as the Eucharist touched her tongue?

She stood to recite the Confiteor in French, then sat when the priest switched into Latin to enumerate their sins. She let the incomprehensible words wash over her and glanced around the nave. This newly built chapel was much smaller than the church in Saint-Philbert. Though still modest, their place of worship back home was infinitely richer than this. Three hundred years old and built from the same uneven stone as the rest of the dwellings in her part of Normandy, the church had the comforting look of an old amber-and-brown patchwork shawl. Inside its walls was the memory of centuries of penitent devotion. Protective, penitent devotion. The contrast with a chapel so new she could smell the sap from the freshly cut pine boards made her worry. Rémy had told her to find the strongest cure she could, even if she had to travel far from Saint-Philbert to discover it. Was this new chapel on the edge of the world sacred enough for the task?

The Sulpician priest rang the altar bells and stepped back to prepare the Eucharist. Élisabeth clasped her hands.

"Stop your twisting about," Marthe muttered beside her but Élisabeth did not care if her sister was ashamed of her.

It was time, finally. Élisabeth prodded Marthe to get up, and when she dallied, Élisabeth pushed past her to the altar.

The body of Christ. Her mouth was already dry when the priest placed the unleavened bread on her tongue. She fell to her knees and nearly wept with relief when she neither grimaced nor brayed from the touch of the Eucharist. Still, her heart beat so forcefully she thought she might die. She remembered a prayer that called on sinners to prostrate themselves before God, so she lowered herself onto her elbows and stretched out face down on the floor. The stone was cool on her forehead.

Have mercy upon me, O Christ, the hope, refuge, and support of sinners.

"Lili has fainted!" A voice behind her cried.

Graciously this day hear my prayer and rid me of this curse. But there was no steam, no contortions, no last howls of the damned.

"It is the heat, there are too many of us in this chapel."

O God my God, I humbly implore and beseech Thee, if there be an unclean spirit within me, cast this demon back to Hell. In the Holy Virgin's name, I pray.

"Stand back, stand back. Let her breathe."

"Get up, Lili," Marthe whispered in her ear. "For pity's sake, get up."

Élisabeth raised her head an inch off the stone floor. Had it worked? Or did she feel the same?

"My sister is very delicate. She needs some air."

I have greatly sinned . . . through my fault, through my fault, through my most grievous fault.

"Let me assist you, child."

"It's the governor, he's helping her!"

"Oh, thank you sir," Marthe exclaimed.

"I need a moment longer," Élisabeth rasped. She could hardly breathe and felt as if she might faint dead away.

"Give me space," the governor said. The crowd stood back. The nobleman crouched over her, hooking her under both arms and pulling her to her feet.

It was too soon. Her head swam and she did not even know if the curse was lifted. She felt the governor's hands travel from under her arms to her waist, where they lingered for a moment, before he set her down on the bench.

"You are quite safe now," he said, his face full of concern. She twisted away. She was not safe in the least. In fact, with his actions, the governor had perhaps snatched her from the safety she had travelled across an ocean to reach.

"Are you well, Lili?" The brides fussed around her.

"She *is* pale."

"Thank you, Governor de Lafredière," Sister Gagnon said gruffly. "We are in your debt."

"I am glad to have been of service." He gave the nun an elegant bow.

Before Élisabeth could rest, Marthe took her by the arm and tried to guide her towards the chapel door. But both brides and suitors surged into the aisle, sending the sisters stumbling into the arm of a pew.

Sister Gagnon struggled to gather her flock. "Everyone out," she ordered the brides.

Most of the men had rushed out of the chapel, lining the pathway to greet the brides as they left, while a few remained inside the nave to pick off any stragglers. Some of the younger girls were swarmed and burst into nervous laughter as Sister Brodeur tried to corral them towards the exit.

No sooner had Marthe and Élisabeth walked through the chapel door than a man with a shy grin stepped forward to address them. He was not old enough to have much of a beard, and his thick brown hair was cut short at the back, making him seem even younger. "May I escort you through the village?" he said to them.

"I need to sit down," Élisabeth said faintly.

"I should stay with my sister."

"It's just . . . I would be honoured to show you my shop," the man persisted. "I took over the business earlier this year. It is the best . . . rather, it is said to be the best bakehouse in the village. I have seen an increase in my income year after year."

"You are a craftsman? With a living in town?" Marthe asked.

"Yes. I am a master baker."

Marthe let Élisabeth's hand drop and stood blinking at the man for a moment. Then she smiled. "Perhaps my sister can wait by this tree until she is well enough to walk." She turned to whisper in Élisabeth's ear. "It will do no harm to get the measure of some of these men before we make our choices, after all."

Before Élisabeth could protest, Marthe walked down the path with the stranger, leaving her outside the Hôtel Dieu. Élisabeth gripped a tree with one hand and tried to steady her breathing. She looked around: Sister Gagnon had been waylaid by the mustached priest at the church door, and the other brides were taking advantage of her distraction to chat eagerly to their suitors. Only Jeanne Roy did not have a man hanging by her side. Instead, she walked through the hospital gates with the two native women, her eyes bright.

Then, Élisabeth spotted a man with a long beard slinking around the chapel door. His eyes were dark and hard, and on his cheek was a scar from a branding iron that marked him as a thief. The skin on the back of Élisabeth's neck prickled. She looked for help but most of the brides had left the Hôtel Dieu grounds and Sister Gagnon was nowhere to be seen.

Élisabeth pushed herself off the tree and started to walk towards the gate. She glanced over her shoulder and saw the man take steps to follow her. She hurried to catch up with Marthe, turning right onto Rue Saint-Paul and breaking into a stride. She did not get more than ten paces along the road before the branded man overtook her. He blocked her path and leered, revealing a gap where his front teeth should have been.

"Hello, my beauty."

Élisabeth stopped in her tracks. She glanced around her. She could see Marthe and her companion in the distance, peering into the window of a house. She tried to move past the roughneck, but he loomed right and forced her to turn on her heel. She started back towards the hospital. Still he followed.

"What's yer name? What's the harm in telling me yer name?"

She felt a jolt in her stomach, as though a horse had reared up and landed a blow. She crossed to the south side of the street. The man followed, weaving and darting around her like a sheepdog herding a ewe. Without thinking, she ducked down the alley to her left.

Several empty market stalls were crushed together along the laneway. Before one of them stood a native man with long hair down his back and nothing on his chest but a silver gorget. Startled by the sight of his bare flesh, Élisabeth quickened her pace past him.

"Don't run, my beauty." The branded man was so close behind her she could smell his breath when he spoke. "If it's a tour of the fur fair you want, I can show you. Bet you've never seen a savage up close before."

"Leave me be," Élisabeth blurted. The end of the alleyway opened onto the common. Élisabeth started to break into a run, then halted. All along the riverbank, as far as the eye could see, were native men and their tents. More men than she had ever seen in her life. Dozens of fires dotted the shore, and the smell of meat cooking rose in the air. French men milled about, drinking straight from bottles of liquor and laughing at two women hiking up their skirts to squat on the ground.

Another drunkard spotted Élisabeth and called out to her pursuer, "Who d'you got there, Claude?" He was tall with greasy hair hanging around his face. Élisabeth froze. She was now trapped between the two men.

"One of them new brides," Claude said proudly. "I'm showin' her the fur fair."

The taller man smiled at her. "He's not worth yer time. Let me show you."

"She's *mine*," the one called Claude growled. The men squared off, as if they might fight.

"Please," Élisabeth begged, breathing in short, quick gulps. "I don't want to see the fur fair."

Her words broke the men's hostility towards each other. They closed ranks and turned to face her.

"That's not very polite," the taller one said. He spat in the dirt and then rubbed his heel in his saliva. "My friend Claude is givin' you a tour. It's not nice to leave a man adrift."

"And if my mate Graton wants to cut in, it's only right to give him a turn."

Élisabeth's heart pounded. "My sister is waiting . . ." Her voice trailed off as both men took another step closer.

"D'you think you're too good for the likes of us just because the governor came to your rescue?" The one with the brand grimaced. "He might get the first swive, but he won't get the last."

"The king only sent you girls over to convince us to stay in this hellhole," the taller one leered. Élisabeth felt a jolt of terror when she saw he was rubbing a knife on his breeches. He laughed at her surprise, raising his knife so that she could see the glint of its blade. Claude leaned in, his mouth open.

"Don't forget your place. You're a whore sent to keep us happy."

He licked her cheek with a warm, slippery tongue.

Overpowered by disgust, Élisabeth erupted.

In a surge of strength, she clamped her teeth down onto Claude's face, pulling back so hard that she ripped his bottom lip. When she opened her eyes, she saw that it hung loose and bleeding from his face.

"Christ, what was that?"

"She bi' me! Tha' whore bi' me!" He struggled to speak through his torn lip.

Before the taller man could grab her, Élisabeth swivelled and gouged at his eyes with her fingernails. He dropped his knife. As he scrambled to pick it up, she kicked him in the head. She heard a crack and he fell to the ground, clutching his face as the blood streamed from his nose and through his fingers.

Staring at the men on the ground, Élisabeth began to shake. It started as a deep pulsing in her thighs that travelled down her calves. Her stomach quivered and roiled, her heart pounded. What had she done?

She ran back towards Rue Saint-Paul, past the empty market stalls, towards the little chapel, now silent as a ghost.

How had she bested two men? Two men at once?

She tasted the branded man's blood as it dripped into her mouth and recalled the priest's words: *Strength surpassing anything a mortal woman might be capable of.*

In that moment she knew. There was no question of how she had managed to savage her attackers.

Like the nuns of Louviers, tormented and broken by unclean spirits, the Devil had control of her flesh.

The witch had not just cursed her.

She had sent a demon to dwell within her.

She was possessed.

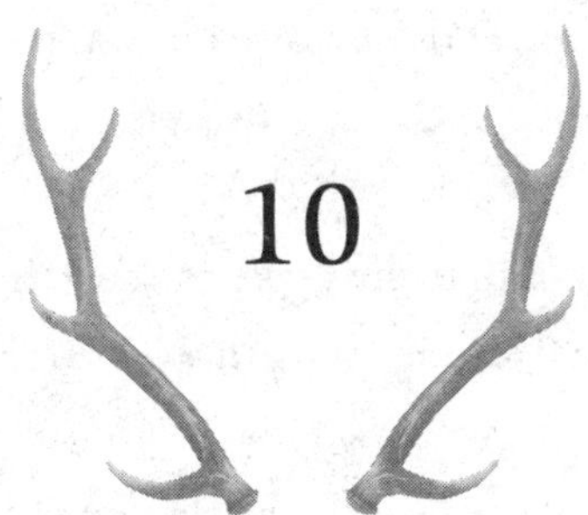

10

The yelps of a wounded animal rang out across the dusty road, distracting Marthe from her companion. The young baker had been detailing his prospects in a nervous and halting manner, and she found herself smiling to encourage him. He was pleasant to look at after all, with a dark forelock he repeatedly pushed off his face. But Marthe steeled herself; she would not be swayed by the baker's good looks and gentle disposition. He said he was without the means to take on an apprentice of his own, and that meant his enterprise could not grow until he had a son. Marthe knew well enough that a child could not be truly productive until he was at least eight or nine years old, and almost a decade seemed a long time to wait until she could prosper. Still, despite his youth, his house was situated in a fine location at the corner of Rue Saint-Paul and a little side street called Saint-Pierre, close to what he said were the largest merchant stores in the village.

She thought about the governor's silk stockings and wondered what they would feel like on her own legs.

The baker pushed his forelock off his brow again and gave her a timid grin. Marthe caught herself smiling back. On the other hand, she knew she could never truly aspire to marry a nobleman like the governor, and she did not want to give up a baker and be stuck with a shoemaker. When times were tough, one could not eat leather.

Another shriek rang out, and she realized it was not the sound of an animal. She turned towards the noise and saw her sister stumble out of an alleyway.

"Lili!"

Marthe began to run. She rushed past the merchants' stores until she was nearly opposite the hospital again. "What happened?"

"Leave me be." Élisabeth collapsed on the ground.

"Are you hurt?" the baker said as he caught up with them.

Élisabeth tried to hide her face in her hands. "For your own sakes, get away from me."

Marthe lay her hands on Élisabeth's back. "Did you faint again? You must have fainted." She turned to the baker. "I'm sure she's only fainted."

The baker shook his head. "She's bleeding."

Élisabeth wiped the blood off her lip, then tentatively probed her teeth with her fingers. "It's . . . their blood. Not mine."

"Whose blood?" Marthe asked.

She pointed back to the alley. "The . . . those men."

"Damned wolves," the baker swore. He darted towards the laneway.

"Maître Verger!" Marthe called after him as he rounded the corner. She blanched at the sight of her broken sister and cursed herself for leaving Élisabeth alone. "What happened?" she asked her. "Were you attacked?"

"Yes! No. At least . . . they were going to hurt me." Élisabeth's eyes were frantic. "But it was not me who bit those men. I am innocent."

"Of course you are innocent if you have been attacked, Lili. What a thing to say!"

The baker trotted back towards them. "No one there," Verger said. "Was it fur traders who did this to you?"

"It was—" Élisabeth blurted out, then took a breath. "No. Never mind. I'm not hurt." She glanced up and down the road, then staggered to her feet.

"Come to the baker's house to rest. It's just down the road. I'm sure Sister Gagnon will understand if we do not return straightaway."

"No." Élisabeth shook her head. "We must go back to the farmhouse. I want to be with the nuns."

"Then I shall accompany you to Pointe-Saint-Charles," the baker offered.

"No," Élisabeth insisted more forcefully. "We will soon catch up with the others. They can't be far ahead." She wobbled as she started to walk west towards the nuns' farm and Marthe knew it was not worth trying to argue. She turned to the baker and tried to smile.

"Thank you for showing me the village, Maître Verger. And your bakehouse."

"Please think about my proposal. I am hardworking and my bread is the best in the entire village. With you as my wife—"

"I must go," Marthe cut him off. "My sister needs me."

"Then let me walk you back. It is not safe—"

"No. Thank you. My sister and I will be quite well on our own. I saw the nuns go by not a moment ago."

She took some satisfaction in the baker's crestfallen look. In all honesty, she wouldn't have minded his company along the walk home, but she worried Élisabeth might do something to further shame her. With a pang of regret, Marthe wondered if she would ever see Maître Verger again.

Élisabeth was walking briskly along the path, her head down with both hands thrust into the pockets of her skirt.

"Lili, wait. Tell me what happened."

"I cannot. I can hardly explain it to myself."

"Try."

Élisabeth picked up her pace and Marthe broke into a trot. "We should tell Sister Gagnon," Marthe panted, the heat so close it made her armpits damp with sweat. "If there are dangerous men afoot, she must alert the governor."

Élisabeth turned on her. "No one must know! If I am . . . if I have become . . . the worst of all things. A creature of nightmare—"

"What are you saying?" Marthe eyed her sister. She was not well; Marthe had been naive to think that she would be better once they landed in Ville-Marie.

Élisabeth strode on, her eyes focused only on her feet. "What are the hallmarks? Think, think. Fits and contortions? Yes. The bark of a dog? The grunt of a pig? Yes. What of pain? Do I feel pain?" She pinched her own cheek and winced. "A little pain, yes. So perhaps it is not true. But this strength! Blessed Virgin, what of this unholy strength?"

"Lili! Stop." They had reached the edge of the little village. The few whitewashed houses had given way to meadow, and the thick forest was within view. Marthe put a hand on her sister's arm.

"You are not yourself. In truth, you have not been yourself since you lost your child."

At these words, Élisabeth's body seemed to cave in on itself, a wheel crumpling on a broken axle. The fever in her eyes dimmed and she was instantly forlorn. Marthe pulled her into a tight embrace. Her sister did not bend; she stood wooden and unaffected until Marthe released her.

"I know how much the loss saddened you, Lili. And for Rémy Delaunay to then refuse to marry you, to abandon you—"

"No." Élisabeth shook her head. "He did not abandon me."

"Of course he did. That is why we are here. He *ruined* you." Marthe put her hand on Élisabeth's wrist. "I know I have been upset about our lot. It is because I believe Father Paul should have insisted on the marriage, rather than signing those letters to be rid of us. I know I should blame Rémy, not you."

"It was not his fault." Élisabeth's hands flew to her ears as if to block out Marthe's words. "It's not his fault. Rémy had no choice but to spurn me." She dropped her voice to a whisper. "The truth is, I am cursed. He had no choice."

Somewhere, a crow cawed. Marthe was suddenly aware that the sun had grown heavy in the sky and thick clouds were gathering overhead. But she could not move. She was stunned, not understanding what she had just heard.

"What do you mean, cursed?"

Fat tears started to spill down Élisabeth's cheeks. "I miscarried because I was cursed." The wind in the trees took up the word and spread it across the forest. *Cursed. Cursed. Cursed.* "Cursed by a witch. And now I am forever barren."

"What are you saying?" Marthe felt the gooseflesh rise on her arms. "Why have you said nothing of this before?"

"I did not want to frighten you."

"But, what do you mean? How can you be certain you are barren? How can you be sure it was witchcraft?"

Élisabeth lowered her hands from her ears. "I saw the witch. I saw as she raised her bony finger and pointed at me—"

"Who?" Marthe's voice was becoming shrill. "Where?"

"At the tavern with Rémy in February. Just before Lent began. It was . . . the Winter Witch."

Marthe struggled to remain upright. She knew the legend about the old witch who lived in the forest on the other side of the Orne. Papa used her name to urge his wayward children to bed, warning them of the hag seen only in the coldest months of the year when she crawled out of the woods seeking a child to devour. The Winter Witch had not taken a human child for years, creeping into the village and stealing away with only the carcasses of stillborn calves left out for the ravens. But everyone in Saint-Philbert knew she was never far away and would one day resume her old ways: causing miscarriages, stealing infants, ruining lives. A chill set into Marthe's bones.

"How can you be certain it was her?"

"Why do you doubt me? I saw her! She pointed her finger at me and I lost my child that night. You cannot deny that is a witch's curse."

Marthe nodded. It was possible, especially if it was indeed the Winter Witch who had crossed Élisabeth's path. The old crone survived by taking the health and fertility that rightfully belonged to youth. If Élisabeth had been cursed by the Winter Witch, that would explain her undoing.

"That is not all." Élisabeth placed her hands over her mouth, pressing her fingers down to stop her lips from trembling. "I brought us here, to the holiest place in Christendom, to rid myself of the curse. But I fear . . . I fear she has done worse than render me barren. I fear she has set a demon to dwell within me."

"W-what?" Marthe's voice broke. She stared at her sister, horror mounting in her heart.

"Not a moment ago I attacked two men in the alleyway and left them broken and bleeding. If a demon has not taken charge of my body, how did I summon such strength?" Tears streamed down Élisabeth's cheeks and caught the blood on her chin, creating a red river that ran onto her chemise. Marthe put her hands on Élisabeth's shoulders.

"No, Lili, that cannot be true." Marthe spoke quietly and urgently, commanding Élisabeth to listen. "Look, look in my eyes. There, I can see my reflection. There I am, right there. That means you are not bewitched. You may have been cursed but there is no *demon* in you."

"Perhaps the demon comes and goes?"

"No! You are nothing like the possessed! Do you not remember the friar that came through Saint-Philbert when the boys were still alive? The one with the demoniac?"

Élisabeth shook her head, wiping her face with her sleeve.

"Nicolas and I went to see them. Were you not with us?" Marthe waited for Élisabeth to nod, to acknowledge the memory, for she could see the day clearly in her mind. The friar had come from the south in late summer, walking with a gnarled cane, calling out for the villagers to gather. When all the wives and children had poured from their homes, he began the exorcism. The possessed woman, a filthy and shambling creature tied by the wrists to a cord around the friar's waist, had rolled on the ground making impossible shapes with her body: her hips raised, her knees behind her ears, her head twisted near off her neck. It was so grotesque that Nicolas had laughed out loud, and the village wives had to tell him to hush.

"Do you not remember? The demoniac had fits for nearly half an hour, barking and moaning and contorting all the time. She crawled around on her hands and knees, licking the cobblestones in the square. Then the friar sprinkled her with holy water and she screamed as if she had been scalded. Lili, you are nothing like that woman—why, you just took communion in the chapel! You cannot think you are afflicted with a *demon*."

For a moment hope blossomed across Élisabeth's face, her blue eyes widening. "That is true, I did not scream in the chapel." Then she faltered and a sob caught in her throat. "Even if there is no demon, I am still barren. I am still cursed. I lost my child, and I can never have another. Not until the curse is broken."

Marthe gently stroked her sister's back while her mind raced. Of course Élisabeth was not possessed—could not be!—but a witch's lesser curse was possible. Everyone in Saint-Philbert sprinkled crushed eggshells outside their door to keep witches away, and traded information about signs of their craft, from mothers' milk drying up to crops shrivelling and animals wasting away. If poor Élisabeth's misfortune became widely known, she would have such a blot against her name. *Their* name. Marthe stiffened at the thought that Élisabeth's shame—once again—might affect her own prospects.

"There must be a way to lift the curse," she said, letting her hand drop to her side.

"There isn't." Élisabeth sniffed. "I've tried everything. I've eaten vervain and dill until I've retched. I've drunk water that had a true relic of Saint Ignatius dipped in it. I've walked backwards around the stone circle at the top of the Roche d'Oëtre in the moonlight. And I came here, to the holiest place on earth and laid on its sacred ground. Nothing has worked. Nothing! I still feel such sharp movements in my gut. I am cursed and I can never, ever have another child."

"There *is* something you could try." Marthe waited until Élisabeth looked up. "The Winter Witch is an old woman, yes? Barren herself." Her sister nodded. "So could a younger, more powerful practitioner . . . break her curse?"

Marthe watched her sister's face as her meaning dawned. Élisabeth shook her head so vehemently the sides of her hood slapped her cheeks. "No. I would not dare—"

"Why ever not? Jeanne Roy is one of us! A sister of the sea. She saved us from the storm. There can be no mightier a sorceress in the whole world than her."

Élisabeth's voice grew shrill. "It is unthinkable to beg a favour from a witch."

Marthe took her hands. "She's not a *witch*. You do not know that she has made a pact with the Devil. She is a mighty sorceress who can heal and mend and cure. There is a difference. And if she is the leader of the banished coven the old priest seeks, she will certainly have the power to break the curse."

Élisabeth pulled away. "If she leads a coven then she is a witch! And there is nothing more evil than a witch—"

"But magic is good!" Marthe insisted. "Magic is holy. Even priests have magic. If one has the power to help and to heal, how can that be evil?"

Élisabeth began to gnaw on her thumbnail, her eyes darting left and right. "I cannot survive another witch."

"You cannot survive as you are, Lili. If Jeanne is as powerful as Father de Sancy says she is, you must make an ally of her."

Élisabeth bit her nail down to the quick, her eyes still scanning the horizon. Marthe felt a surge of frustration. Why could her sister never listen? It was Élisabeth's pigheaded refusal to consider the counsel of anyone but Rémy that had brought them across the sea. The day the village priest had signed the letters of good conduct—the testament to their chastity and piety—Marthe had lashed out and told Élisabeth she would be found out on her wedding night; she would be known for a whore and whipped. Marthe had cursed her sister for her sins and the priest for his lies.

Only a knock on the cottage door had stopped her tirade. It was the Delaunays' wrinkled cook, Old Geneviève, who seemed to know the moment she walked through the door the cause of the sisters' quarrel.

"I told you to stay away from that boy," Old Geneviève said, shifting her weight heavily on her cane. "He's just like his father."

"Rémy loves me—"

Old Geneviève cut Élisabeth off. "Go. Go and forget him. I see you've got them letters. Good. I told the curé that all that gossip was nowt but spite and if it were true, why was there no child to account for? I said you were born unlucky, as sure as you were born with those blue eyes, and if he could talk so much about God's mercy without laying some of it down on you and your poor sister . . . well."

"So *you* are the cause of our misfortune." Marthe glared at the old cook. "You lied to that fool priest so the parish could be rid of us."

Old Geneviève sighed and rubbed her hip. "I am not the cause of your woes. I am sorry for you, Marthe, for you are blameless. But consider, a spirited girl such as yourself might do better in New France than in this tired old village." She turned and spoke more gently to Élisabeth. "And you. Listen to me. Go on that bride ship and start again. Find a better man than Rémy."

"I will go to seek my salvation," Élisabeth said stiffly. "But I won't be anyone else's bride. I love Rémy, I love him and I always—"

The cook had held up her hand. Her eyes were small and dark, smaller still when she narrowed them. "I know it's not easy to listen to folks when you don't like what they have to say. But you must try, Élisabeth Jossard, for your own sake."

On that night, as Old Geneviève had limped out of the cottage and back up the hill, Marthe had wondered why, if Élisabeth and Rémy loved each other so much, they had not fought harder to stay together. Now that she knew the truth about the witch's curse, she wondered why Élisabeth was still so unwilling to heed anyone's advice but his.

She tried again. "Please appeal to Jeanne Roy, Lili. It may be your only hope."

Élisabeth stared at the ground, spitting out a jagged nail. "I suppose she might look on me with favour."

Marthe tried to hide her surprise. She held her breath, waiting.

"It was my letter of good conduct that Jeanne stole to escape Father de Sancy's suspicion. And I gave her my best petticoat this morning because she does not have a trunk."

Marthe exhaled. "Good. All you must do is ask her." She linked her arm with Élisabeth's, urging her forward. "It is a good plan. I know she can help you lift the curse. None of us realized what she truly was until she fell into the river. Then we all saw her magic."

Élisabeth slowed, stubborn against Marthe's enthusiasm. "But she is high-and-mighty. She might refuse me."

Marthe dismissed her sister's doubts. "Then you must choose your time and your words carefully. You will only get one chance to seek her favour."

They walked quickly, Marthe squeezing her arm, wordlessly imploring her to act.

"Yes," Élisabeth said slowly. "Yes, I should choose my time and words wisely."

Marthe felt she might melt with relief. There was a curse, but there was also hope. For every coming dusk, there would also be a dawn. "And you must start with the deepest curtsey and praise her goodness and charity."

"Should I remind her of all that I have done for her?" They walked arm in arm, the wind whipping at the hems of their skirts.

"No. You must be humble in her presence."

"You are right, of course." Élisabeth smiled, a tremulous stretch across her wan face. "I am glad that I told you the truth. And I am sorry that I kept it from you for so long."

"A burden shared is a burden halved." Marthe gave Élisabeth a quick squeeze. She could not help herself from skipping a little as she walked.

"I confess I was overcome with despair when my prayers did not work," Élisabeth continued, her tone becoming lighter. "I imagined that just by setting foot on this island, that would be enough. What a fool I was. This is a better plot. Why, if Jeanne Roy cures me tomorrow, we could even sail back to France with the *Saint-Jean-Baptiste* on its return voyage this week!"

Marthe halted. "Sail back to France?"

Élisabeth looked sheepish. "Yes. Once the curse is lifted, we can go back to Saint-Philbert. I can marry Rémy and . . . and you . . . well, wasn't there that boy from Pont-d'Ouilly who took your fancy? Once I marry Rémy there will be money for a dowry for you."

Marthe dropped Élisabeth's arm. "You want to go back to France to marry *Rémy*?"

"Of course. He only broke with me because of the witch's curse. If I can fall pregnant again, his parents would have to agree to our marriage. That was always our intention, to force his mother's hand. But with the curse upon me I cannot bear a child, Rémy says."

"You *intended* to fall pregnant?" Marthe's voice rose. "It was no accident?"

"Many brides go to the altar already with child. You know what the Delaunays are like. Determined to squeeze the largest dowry out of whoever marries their son, no matter which plain-faced ogre it's attached to. Rémy wanted so much to marry *me*. We knew that if I was with child, they would have to agree to let us wed."

The leaves on the trees were shaking in the wind. There would be a storm soon, but nothing like the squall that brewed in Marthe's breast. "After the way he treated you, you would still go back to France to marry him?"

"It was not *his* choice to break with me. It was because of the Winter Witch."

Marthe's temper flashed. "And what about me, Lili? Why drag me all the way here if you never intended to stay?" She saw the footbridge over the little creek just ahead and started to stride towards it.

"I am sorry, Marthe. Honestly, I don't . . . I don't even know how we would return to France. I doubt the king would pay our passage back, and the cost of the voyage would cripple us. But we must try. I must return for . . . for true love."

"*True love?*" Marthe spat the words over her shoulder. "What about me? What am I returning to? You sold me a story about a king's dowry and a second chance in the New World. And now you want me to risk another deadly sea voyage to return home to . . . to be known as the sister of a girl who spreads her legs to win a husband?"

Élisabeth howled and ran, catching Marthe's arm. "I was a handfasted bride! That means we are as good as married in God's eyes."

"Does it? I've never heard of such a thing. Did Rémy tell you that?"

"I . . . it . . . Rémy loves me!" Élisabeth spluttered, her eyes looking this way and that, before hardening and turning on Marthe. "Listen, I have been looking after you since you were four years old. You will do as I say. And I say we are going home to Saint-Philbert."

"Married in God's eyes? You are such a fool!" Marthe sneered and wriggled free from Élisabeth's grasp. She could not see straight, so blinding was the rage inside her. She grabbed for the first anchor she could think of to stop her drift. "No, I am not going back with you. I am staying here. For I am to be mistress of the best bakery on this island."

"What are you talking about?"

"Verger has asked me to marry him. And I will accept him. *I* will be married—in God's eyes, and in *church*."

"*Who* asked you?"

"Maître Verger! The man who helped you just now."

"Him? You can't have known him for more than a quarter of an hour." Élisabeth crossed her arms over her chest. "It's absurd."

"I've known him for *half* an hour," Marthe retorted. "And he's already a master baker, with his own shop."

"Master baker, what nonsense! He's no older than I am."

"He'll be twenty next month."

Élisabeth threw her hands in the air. "He's lying to you, Marthe, he can't be anything more than a journeyman. He cannot own his own shop. *Best* bakery, what a boast. It is likely the *only* bakery."

"The baker he was apprenticed to has died, and so the business has fallen to him. I like the look of it—and him, I suppose—so if you are going back to Saint-Philbert to marry your devoted Rémy, it will be without me."

Marthe turned and ran towards the nuns' farmhouse. Heavy drops of rain fell on her face as the storm finally shed its tears of frustration. Damn Élisabeth, with her lies and her lovesickness. Her false piety. Marthe would tie herself to this island with a marriage knot so tight that her sister could never undo it.

She ran faster, her skirts flapping, plunging headlong into her fate.

11

Once, when Élisabeth was a girl, a fox made off with three of the Jossards' chickens in a single night. Like every family in Saint-Philbert, they had kept a coop beside their vegetable garden for a ready supply of eggs. Marthe's temper often reminded Élisabeth of the squawks of the birds as they died: outraged fluster followed by a crunch of bones, and then silence. As Marthe's foul mood set in, Élisabeth wondered if she wouldn't be clearing up blood and scattered feathers until long after the wedding.

A fortnight after she had attacked the men in the alley, Élisabeth tried once again to make amends by offering to dress her sister's hair for the ceremony. The girls were in the dormitory, burbling with nerves. Marthe sniffed and declined Élisabeth's offer without a glance, saying that Rose was up to the task and she wouldn't bend her ear with fantasies about returning to France while working her plaits.

"I promise I won't speak of it," Élisabeth said. "But please slow down. Even if we can't go home, you have only just met Verger. Take some time to consider your choices."

"You know what the intendant said." Marthe leaned her head to the right to allow Rose to pin up her braids. "Everyone is to be married by the first of September."

"Yes, but Sister Gagnon says that won't stick. The law can't rule man's heart."

"My marriage has nothing to do with my heart. As such, it hardly matters which stranger I wed. Remember that our purpose in coming to New France was to *marry*. At least mine was, though you appear to have come halfway across the world on a fool's errand."

Marthe cried out and grabbed her head. Rose blushed and removed the pin from Marthe's scalp. "Sorry," Rose said, sending a sympathetic glance in Élisabeth's direction as well.

No matter how much Élisabeth tried to sweep the feathers from the floor, Marthe would not listen to her pleas.

As she made her way along the dirt path from the congregation to the little chapel in Ville-Marie, a familiar sensation churned Élisabeth's stomach. She knew it well by now. It had been with her from the moment she had lost her child all those months ago, the night of the Winter Witch's curse. She clung to Marthe's words—that she was nothing like the touring demoniac, barking mad for all the village to see—but the thought of the woman's public exorcism made her doubt. Marthe's description of the strange twists and thrusts of the woman's limbs mirrored what she felt inside her own body. She had to be possessed like the nuns of Louviers, for what else could it be? With growing dread, she imagined the horror on the *Saint-Jean-Baptiste* girls' faces as a demon hatched from inside her, unfurling sticky, leathery wings like a newborn foal from a mare's womb. She imagined the brides' screams as the demon soared high, high above the farmhouse, sloughing off Élisabeth's snakeskin body and letting it fall back to earth.

She saw Father de Sancy's watery eyes fixed on her, whip in hand, as he demanded to know if she were addicted to the carnal act.

She clasped her hands tightly together and did three rounds of the squeeze and prayer.

When they arrived in the village, the people of Ville-Marie were milling around outside the chapel, waiting for a glimpse of the first of the new brides to be married. There was a handful of women with grey aprons and mended brown skirts, and five times as many men in the same drab colours. Their doublets hung loose and their stockings wilted round their ankles, such was the heat. When the governor swept through in red and blue silk the contrast was so vibrant he looked like a peacock strolling through a flock of sparrows.

"Stay here," he commanded a pair of native children who trailed after him. The younger girl had a missing tooth; she could not have been more than seven or eight years old. She looked bewildered as the older child put out a hand to stop her advance.

"Are those the governor's . . . children?" Marthe looked flushed. Élisabeth wondered if it was the heat, or the beginnings of regret.

"Of course not," Sister Gagnon tutted. "Those are his Panis slaves."

The governor turned and tipped his hat to Marthe, a smile spreading across his face. Marthe faltered. Élisabeth stepped forward to catch her but when Marthe saw her outstretched arms, her face hardened. She turned away, taking Rose and Lou by the hands.

"I must not leave Maître Verger waiting."

Her friends kissed her cheeks, wishing her luck and a dozen sons and reminding her she'd never know a day's hunger by marrying a baker. Élisabeth faded back into the crowd, wincing as if she'd been stung. There was no way to clean up this fit of temper, this mess of feather and bone. Marthe would not bend.

Élisabeth dawdled outside, hanging back by the tree in the Hôtel Dieu yard. The air was muggy, and her chemise stuck to her chest. She watched the native children use a stick to draw a pattern in the dust. She wondered what they were saying to each other, and who the Panis were, and how two of their children had ended up slaves while other natives walked freely down the streets of Ville-Marie. There was so much she did not understand about New France.

Presently a pair of women came up the path, walking slowly and talking as old friends do, not waiting for the other to finish before the next words were spoken. One was a native woman, a woven basket of herbs on her back. Élisabeth gaped when she realized that the other was Jeanne Roy. She stepped behind the tree so as not to be seen.

"I learned all I know from some of the greatest men of our age," Jeanne Roy said, the sin of pride heavy on her tongue. The pair stopped by the slave children. Élisabeth saw Jeanne Roy's companion take an apple out of a beaded bag and offer it to the little girls. The children skipped up and down as they took turns biting into the red fruit.

The native woman looked at Jeanne Roy. "I learned all I know at my grandmother's knee."

The witch paused, considering this. Finally, she nodded her head. "I do not doubt that you had the better education."

The native woman smiled. "Then I will share with you the knowledge of the Haudenosaunee."

Élisabeth peeked her head around the tree. She saw the stranger take a bundle of herbs from her bag and press them into Jeanne Roy's hand. Maybe they were *both* witches? With a start, Élisabeth realized this was the moment to ask Jeanne Roy for help. She would fall to her knees in the hospital courtyard and beg her to lift the curse. Élisabeth stepped out from behind the tree, just as Jeanne Roy spoke again.

"I have nothing so valuable to share in return. Nothing except the story of how I came to be here. I have never told a soul, but it is a lesson I would gladly teach you, should it one day spare you my pain."

"Élisabeth Jossard!" Sister Gagnon's voice rang out from the chapel door. "Hurry, or you will miss your sister's wedding."

The witch turned and saw Élisabeth by the tree, eavesdropping on her confession. Her face turned red with fury.

"I'm coming," Élisabeth called back. She thrust her hand in her pocket and clutched her rosary, slinking past the two women towards the chapel. She wondered what tale Jeanne Roy would tell the native woman about her journey. Would she describe how she had used magic to convince the king to set her coven free? How she had cast a glamour on him from far away? How *did* a convicted witch evade the pyre?

All she knew was that she had ruined her chance to speak to Jeanne Roy and she did not know if she would get another.

Élisabeth felt a shiver up her spine and wondered if the witch were casting the evil eye on her, even now.

12

The first thing that surprised Marthe about being married was that she was expected to share her house with another woman.

The whitewashed wooden building was much like all the others in Ville-Marie. It had a shingle outside announcing the wares within—in the case of her husband's home, bread—a hearth in the middle of the room, and a sloping roof. What was unusual about the baker's house was the thin wall that ran from the back of the house to the front, stopping awkwardly a few paces from the front door. Upon entering the bakehouse customers could see two separate apartments at once. On the left was the room where Maître Verger worked, surrounded by sacks of flour. A hessian sheet pinned to the ceiling obscured a small area at the back of the room where the couple ate, slept, and dressed. But on the right, patrons could see a more comfortable space with a small table and chairs, and two cabinets displaying baskets of bread. A larger sleeping space was carved off from this room, and it was here that the old baker's widow still lived.

"Call me Maman Poulin," she said when Marthe returned from the chapel and walked across the threshold of her new home. "I've lived in this village long enough to have everyone call me mother."

"She's Old Poulin's widow, Barbe," her husband said. "I call her Maman too."

Marthe could hardly remember who Old Poulin was, let alone why his widow was living in her new home, bustling about her shop. Maman Poulin had a portly frame, a sign of many years as a baker's wife, and flecks of silver in her brown hair.

"I told you," Verger said amiably. "Poulin was the baker I was apprenticed to. He died last winter, and Maman has stayed on ever since."

"It was an abscessed tooth that did him in. My poor old bear." Maman Poulin crossed herself and looked up to Heaven. Marthe saw the skin around the widow's neck was loose, though her mouth was set in a firm line.

"By all rights the tooth should have been buried with him, but after the barber pulled it out—in the hopes the infection would not take—he gave it me and I put it in my pocket. It was only after the dirt had hit the lid of his coffin that I remembered the blessed thing. And what was I to do with it then? I could hardly dig up Old Poulin's grave to reunite him with the instrument of his death! So I've kept it in my pocket ever since." The widow rummaged in her apron and pulled out the blood-encrusted molar to show Marthe. "I sometimes pray on it, so that the Blessed Virgin might save me from toothache and the Iroquois and all the other things that bring agony to a settler's life."

"I am p-pleased to meet you," she stammered, aghast at the tooth in the widow's hand. But she was less than pleased when she learned that she and Verger would sleep in the corner of the workroom on the same straw mattress he had used since he was an apprentice, while Barbe Poulin would not budge from the cattail bed where her husband had died.

"You would not like it, ma chère, it may be softer than straw, but it would curse your marriage to sleep where another man has not long breathed his last. You two will rest easier where you are. If I remarry, you can claim my bed and take down the wall between our two halves of the house."

"*If* you remarry?" The words caught in Marthe's throat.

"I cannot be *too* quick about it! How would that look? God would frown upon me, and women would bang pots outside my window and subject me to the full charivari!"

"Of course." Marthe blushed. She didn't want a charivari of villagers screeching and hollering outside of the house at night either. She'd had enough of being tainted by another's sin in Saint-Philbert.

"The best remedy for gossip is to not let the idle tongues begin wagging. Once they start, they rarely stop. I should not want any to take against you, Marthe, so tomorrow we shall put our best foot forward and introduce you to everyone in town."

"Why should anyone take against me?" Marthe asked, but the widow appeared not to have heard.

The next day the widow tucked Marthe's arm under hers and walked her up Rue Saint-Pierre to Rue Saint-Jacques and along the northern edge of the village. Marthe could only absorb half of what Maman Poulin said: Here was the best butcher, though Marthe must take care when ordering, for he frequently scrimped on the fat; here was the clog maker whose shoes were fine, though Marthe should not even think of ordering a pair until they had counted all their sols at the end of the year, for they cost half a livre and the man would not haggle; here were the new merchants' stores, though Maman Poulin insisted they only shop at Le Moyne's, for Madame Le Moyne had been a good friend to Old Poulin and that sort of loyalty always comes back round again. Marthe's head spun from all the widow's instructions.

They passed the inn at the corner of Saint-Lambert where Maman Poulin said many of the soldiers had been billeted before the regiment was disbanded, and was still a cut above Folleville's tavern, although Folleville's was certainly the more popular establishment for soldiers, fur traders, and artisans to drink—and do more besides. She sucked her teeth at that, and while Marthe did not entirely understand her meaning, she did not think it could be such a bad place, for they walked down Rue Saint-Charles and into Folleville's themselves.

"I am friendly with the owner. You too would do well to stay on Anne Lamarque de Folleville's good side," the widow advised her. "Her weekly bread order is enough to keep our bakery in business."

Marthe frowned. *Our* bakery? She had not realized that it was a joint venture between her husband and his old master's widow.

The tavern was already crowded at eleven in the morning. Groups of men sat at mismatched tables, drinking out of pewter cups with carafes of brandy in front of them. A mongrel wandered in between the tables, looking for scraps, and a pair of haggard women in tightly laced bodices sat at the far end of the room, playing a game of shut-the-box. Nearby, lounging close to the fire, was the governor of Montréal. Marthe's eyes widened.

"This is Marthe Jossard. She has married Antoine Verger," Maman Poulin told the tavern owner. Marthe nodded politely while her eyes darted to the far end of the room. She was certain that Lafredière was looking at her, though with his eye patch, it was hard to be sure.

"Have you heard the latest?" The widow's friend leaned forward, her bosom slopping onto the counter in front of her. "The Sulpicians now insist I shut the tavern at nine o'clock every night. Have you ever heard of such a thing? First they threaten to excommunicate us if we sell liquor to the natives, now they think to restrict my hours. Those priests are growing drunk on their own power!"

"They do not make the laws. What would the intendant in Québec say if he knew how bold they've grown?" Maman Poulin tutted sympathetically. "How is anyone to make a living?"

"No other business is so strictly controlled," Anne Lamarque said, straightening up and giving Barbe Poulin a begrudging look. "I don't know if I shall be able to afford your bread anymore. I may have to make my own."

"Oh, ma chère, you can't imagine how much work it would be to make all the loaves you need. This village is fortunate to have our Verger. He is as tireless as my husband once was. The work falls entirely to his shoulders now, since Old Poulin's death. And since he's taken a wife, we have no space in the house for an apprentice."

Marthe looked away, feeling the heat rise to the tips of her ears. She had not considered that her presence in the household might be a burden on the business. She took a step back and studied the array of stone jugs on the shelves behind Anne Lamarque. Would it increase their income if Verger put up shelves in the front room when Maman Poulin remarried and left, so that they could add jam and honey to their list of wares? She was thinking about whether anyone would be lazy enough to buy jam rather than make their own when she felt a hand on her arm.

"A fresh face in this village is as beautiful as the morning sun," a low voice remarked.

Marthe's face responded like the setting sun, a red that deepened the longer the governor's one eye stayed fixed on her. Lafredière wore a different coat today, though his calves were just as sleek in his silk stockings. In his left hand, he gripped a small pewter goblet.

"My lord." She dropped into a curtsey.

The governor's eye looked her up and down and Marthe's cheeks grew even hotter. "I am surprised your new husband has let you out of his sight. May I ask how marriage suits you?"

Marthe raised her chin. "It suits me well, thank you. I have come to New France to make my fortune, just as anyone else. And for a woman, marriage is the necessary first step on that journey."

The governor threw back his head and laughed so loudly that Maman Poulin stopped haggling with the tavern owner and came over.

"Good day, Governor," she greeted him. "I see you've met Maître Verger's bride."

"I have just introduced myself. She tells me she has come here seeking her fortune. What do you say, will she make a success of it?"

"She has made a good start by marrying the best baker in town."

"A necessary step, she tells me." The governor stroked his beard while gazing thoughtfully at Marthe. "Of course there are easier ways to make one's fortune."

"Oh?" Marthe perked up. "Pray, tell. How may my husband and I increase our living?"

"I would be a poor example of how to get rich if I gave away my advice for free," Lafredière chuckled. "What might you offer me in return for my counsel?"

Marthe glanced at Maman Poulin. "We could give you bread, I suppose."

The governor chuckled again, making a show of wiping a tear from his good eye. Then he blinked and fixed it on her. "I would dearly love to try your bread."

"The bakery is always open to you, my lord," Maman Poulin interrupted. "We are on good terms with your servant. I know the fort bakes its own bread, but you may send your woman anytime to collect all the loaves that you like."

"Perhaps I might drop by myself." He did not lift his gaze from Marthe's face.

"Until then, have you no advice that you could share?" she asked. If there were easy riches to be made on the island, she wanted to hear it.

Lafredière leaned forward. Marthe did not know if he was too close by design or if the drink made him unsteady. "Only that you try some way to flee this island. It is worse than purgatory, with hellish flies waging war upon us at night, and savages intent on doing so by day. And should anyone ever try to have a bit of fun . . ." The governor paused and raised the goblet in his hand. He spilled a drop of wine on his coat and he smoothed it down until the damp spot disappeared. "The Sulpicians slam down their pious fists. Remember, they may have been appointed the seigneurs of this island, but I am the closest voice to the king. I say, do not heed everything the Sulpicians say. Make merry when you can."

He winked and sauntered back to his table. The moment he was gone, Maman Poulin turned on Marthe.

"What do you mean, demanding favours from the governor?"

Marthe blinked to deflect the widow's glare. "I thought . . ."

"There is no easy path to comfort for the likes of you and me. Only work and more hard work. Backbreaking, never-ending work." The widow straightened her bodice, then paused. "He's not wrong that there are far too many rules nowadays, though. God would not have given us wine if he did not mean for us to seek solace in it."

"Is it true the Sulpicians have rules about who can drink, and when?"

The widow's head shook. "Oh, Anne Lamarque complains, but it's nothing to the rules bakers must follow. Not only must we vie with the fort to get enough flour, but our prices are fixed. If the harvest is bad, the profit is very mean."

Marthe's heart started to sink. She dropped her eyes to her skirt. It had once been Élisabeth's and had not weathered the sea journey well. "What about fur, Maman Poulin? Would it be better for Verger to trade in furs?"

The widow gave her a sharp look. "Barely married a week and you want your husband to give up his craft?"

"No, I mean, just a little on the side. The three-year men at the nuns' farmhouse all talked of how they might put a hand in the trade, to earn a little extra. And the governor just now said there were easier ways to make a fortune—"

"And what do you think you have to offer the savages in return?" Maman Poulin demanded. "Take care with your big ideas, little mistress, or people will talk. And you'll be the one the charivari mob drags through the streets."

Startled, Marthe bobbed a curtsey and thanked the widow for her advice. But she could not shake the idea that one day soon the governor might come to the bakery. She tucked it into her bodice and kept it close to her heart. She longed for his advice, although she wondered what it might cost her.

13

A few days after Marthe's wedding, Élisabeth stole away from the nuns' farmhouse and down to the river alone. It was creeping towards the end of August and yet the heat on the island had not yet broken. The midday sun left her wilting, so she slipped into the river to cool her feet, as well as her mind.

Her skirts were quickly drenched. She could not be bothered to hold them up and her hem greeted the river as if it were dying of thirst, drinking up the water so rapidly that her skirts became part of the stream, flowing in the current, until she wondered if it might not be easier to let their weight drag her under than to try and fix all that had gone wrong. Marthe was married and would never leave Montréal Island, even if they could afford the passage back to France. Her hope that Rémy would still be waiting for her weakened by the day. And she had failed to make her plea to the powerful witch. All the while, her curse worsened, the spasms in her stomach ever sharper, the feeling of her limbs wanting to coil and lurch stronger, the risk of blasphemy always at the tip of her tongue. Élisabeth was about to fall backwards and let the river take her when she caught sight of a breathless Rose, running through the woods towards the shore.

"What are you doing?" Rose panted, her cheeks red from exertion. "It is not safe!"

"I am perfectly well," Élisabeth lied.

"Do come out of the river, Lili. Sister Gagnon said the men will be here shortly. There will only be a half dozen or so this afternoon so not enough for all of us, but enough to get started. They may only let the older girls meet them, which I think is unfair, given Marthe is already married and she's only just sixteen. I hardly see why I should have to wait for Apolline to sniff around first. Do hurry, or we might miss our chance."

The thoughts of the bachelors descending on the nuns' farmhouse made the demon turn twice in Élisabeth's stomach. She did not want to marry any of these strangers; she wanted Rémy.

"Go ahead. I'll be along in a moment."

Rose looked torn, as if she wanted to haul Élisabeth from the river, but the lure of the impending visitors was too strong. She turned and rushed back through the woods.

Élisabeth slowly waded out of the water, her skirts growing heavier as the river grew shallower. She could not bring herself to wring the water from her clothes; she picked up her shoes and dragged herself back to the farmhouse. She was out of time. It was almost September. The nuns had cloistered the brides for as long as they could to prepare them for their new lives, but today they would start to meet their husbands and leave Pointe-Saint-Charles. She had to summon the courage and the right words to beg Jeanne Roy for help.

As she walked through the kitchen door, she was greeted by a wall of giddy froth. Sister Gagnon was standing by the fire with a wooden spoon in her hand, looking as if she might like to smack someone with it.

"Quiet down now. Remember: no cursing, no belching, no scratching or picking your skin. They've come to choose a wife, not an old sow."

"I thought it was us girls who made the choice," one of the brides said.

Sister Gagnon took out a handkerchief from her sleeve and wiped her brow. "It hardly matters whether you're the pig sent to market or the farmer's wife there to buy it. In the rush to meet and marry I'm not sure who will be choosing whom, or indeed how much thought will go into anyone's decision."

This prompted a frenzied debate. A circle formed around Rose as she explained, bright-eyed, how she would test each of the men in turn with a series of questions that would reveal his true character. Élisabeth took the opportunity to approach the nun.

"Sister Gagnon, must everyone marry before winter? Or . . . or could we stay here with you if we don't find a suitable match?"

The nun pursed her lips. Lou had clearly said something rude because the brides were bent double laughing and Françoise had dropped a spoonful of soup on the floor.

"Get a cloth and clean it up before someone treads in it!" Sister Gagnon looked back at Élisabeth as if she had forgotten she was there. "Heavens no, you can't stay here. My ears will be ringing for months, even if every last one of you is betrothed by the end of the day. Claire, stop throwing salt into the fire. It might ward off evil, but we'll run out before next spring when the ships come back."

The nun marched over to the pack of girls and clapped her hands.

"I'm going to divide you into two groups. If I set the full gaggle on the poor souls coming this afternoon, they'll think twice about marrying at all." She raised her hand and sliced through the herd. "The girls on my left will meet the members of the regiment coming today, the girls on my right will wait for the next batch."

There was a flurry of dancing as brides wove in and out of each other's way to align themselves with their preferred group. Rose edged herself towards those on the left, then beckoned frantically for Lou to join her. Lou forcibly swapped places with tiny Thérèse, who chirped her disapproval and tried to push her way back in.

"Come, Élisabeth, you are with this group," Sister Gagnon ordered, taking

Élisabeth by the arm and escorting her to the centre of the girls who were to be presented that afternoon. "With your younger sister already married we must make a special effort to find a husband for you."

At the mention of marriage Élisabeth felt a squeeze in her gut. She slipped her hand into her pocket to touch her rosary.

"Sister, I wonder if I might be excused to look for Jeanne—"

"Why are you so wet?" Sister Gagnon looked closely at Élisabeth's skirts. "Go upstairs and change. They will be here soon."

"Where is Jeanne Roy?" Élisabeth asked again, but Rose had already grabbed her hand and pulled her up the stairs.

"Let's get you sorted," Rose said. "Maybe today we will both be lucky and find someone as handsome as Marthe's husband." Élisabeth frowned at the thought of the man who had stolen her sister away. "Now, what else do you have to put on?"

"I haven't anything," she said. The witch had not returned her clothing. After laundering Jeanne Roy's velvet dress and satin petticoats, the nuns tutted that they were entirely inappropriate for work on the farm and said she must continue to wear Élisabeth's borrowed skirt.

"It does not matter," Rose reassured her. "With those blue eyes and your fair skin, I shouldn't wonder that you will draw much attention today." Still, she bent down to brush some of the dirt and pine needles from Élisabeth's hem.

"I don't want anyone's attention," she murmured, folding her arms over her chest.

They heard Lou shriek from the kitchen. "They're on the path! They're coming!"

"Wait!" Rose shouted as she flung herself down the stairs. "Wait for me!"

The sound of the front door opening and boots stomping on the floor echoed up to the dormitory. She was out of time. Where was Jeanne Roy? Élisabeth clasped her hands together. *I have greatly sinned.* Squeeze, glide to prayer position and past, squeeze again. *Through my fault, through my fault, my most grievous fault.* She gripped the banister and clenched her teeth as she descended the stairs. She did not care about the bachelors. She had to find the witch.

She stepped into the common room to find the soldiers scattered in small groups, with Sister Gagnon and the brides standing squarely in the middle. Most of the men were dressed in their regimental uniforms: light brown serge coats with grey trim, the buckles shining on their freshly polished boots. The nun stood with her hands on her hips, like a bull facing down a butcher, and it was Rose who clucked around making introductions.

"I am Marie-Rose, this is my dearest friend, Marie-Louise. We grew up in the Salpêtrière in Paris. So did Apolline, though she is much, much older—"

Apolline strode towards a pair at the hearth before Rose could say another word about her age. Rose linked arms with Lou and approached two men who were as mismatched in height as they were themselves. They stared at them as if they were performers at a travelling fair about to start juggling or singing or haggling over the cost of a caramel apple. Élisabeth pushed past them, looking for the witch.

Jeanne Roy was nowhere in sight.

She must be in the garden, Élisabeth reasoned. Perhaps discussing herbs and native wildflowers with Sister Crolo. Élisabeth took a discreet step backwards, hoping Sister Gagnon would not notice her leaving. She put her hands out behind her to feel for the safety of the stone wall.

She took another step backwards and touched wool, not stone.

She whipped round. "I beg your pardon," she gasped when she realized that she had backed into one of the Carignan soldiers—and that she had laid her hands upon his bottom.

His companion guffawed. "I did not imagine the girls-for-marrying would be quite so bold, eh, Francoeur?"

The man she had touched gave his friend an impatient look.

"Please forgive us," he said in a deep voice. "We are in your way. We should not have been hiding in the corner."

"No, it is my fault." She dropped into a curtsey to hide her reddening cheeks. She lifted her head. The soldier was tall and broad-shouldered with a neatly trimmed beard. His hair was neither distinctively brown nor blond, more the muddled colour of wet sand on a beach.

"I apologize," Élisabeth said. "I am not seeking a husband, I should not even be here. Forgive me. I will take my leave of you—"

"You don't intend to marry?" the soldier interrupted. He looked her up and down, his eyes landing on her wet skirts, and the muddy puddle forming at her feet. A flicker of confusion and amusement crossed his face.

"Why should she want to marry?" his friend interrupted. He was shorter and scrawnier, with black hair braided into a tail in the native style. "Marriage is a prison of shrewing wives and mewling children. The forests are pure freedom. I will be happier when I've gone upcountry with the Algonquin, and you would be too."

"Enough, Grandbois." The one called Francoeur gave his friend another sharp look. Then he turned back to Élisabeth. "Let us begin again. How was your journey? I understand your ship came in from Dieppe not three weeks ago."

"It was frightful, actually." Élisabeth's eyes darted around the common room, looking for an escape. A lively group had formed around Rose and Lou; the other brides and bachelors seemed not to be able to resist the pull of the more boisterous party.

"But if you do not intend to marry, why would you make the frightful journey?" the man persisted.

"I mean to return to France. At least, I did . . ." Élisabeth replied, barely looking at him as she judged whether Sister Gagnon would notice if she fled from the room.

"And make another frightful journey back?"

A swish of blue caught Élisabeth's eye. Jeanne Roy swept into the room, like a wicked fairy late for the christening. All eyes turned towards her, the men and women equally dumbstruck. Her velvet dress, now impeccably clean, was the colour of twilight, the fabric swishing smoothly against her petticoats as she moved. The other brides in their drab homespun could never muster such a rich sound. Gold embroidery picked out the boning in the bodice and drew attention to the witch's slender waist. The brides in the room were silent, and the men, who could not have known that Jeanne Roy was a witch, stood straighter, their eyes keener and their ears flattened like hunting dogs obeying a command.

"Please excuse me," the soldier with the braid said, not bothering to look at Élisabeth as he floated towards Jeanne Roy. Élisabeth gaped as he offered the witch his arm. Within a moment they started to take a turn around the room.

"I thought he did not want a wife," Élisabeth said.

"I expect he cannot help himself," Francoeur mused. "She is a great beauty."

"So you say," Élisabeth sniffed, feeling oddly slighted. "Although few are so callous as to rank one woman to another's face."

"Forgive me," he said quickly. "I should have said *you* are a great beauty as well. You are a true flower—"

"Stop." Élisabeth held up her hand. "I do not seek your flattery." This farce had gone on long enough. She had to extricate herself and find a way to speak to Jeanne Roy alone.

The witch and Grandbois had stopped by the farthest window, away from the other brides. They were deep in conversation; Grandbois seemed to hang on Jeanne Roy's every word. *Foolish woodsman.*

"I meant what I said, though," Francoeur persisted. "You are very beautiful."

"It does you no credit to continue like this," she said firmly, taking a step away from him. "I am not moved by overblown compliments. I meant what I said. I am not seeking a husband."

"Is it only the overblown compliments that vex you, or would you accept more middling praise?" The soldier's face was solemn, but his lips quivered with a hint of mischief. "What if I said you were merely passably pretty?"

Unbidden, a smile started at the corners of her mouth. She tried to fight it with a frown but failed, and had to hide her face with her hand. Why did the sandy-haired soldier make her want to laugh? She glanced over to the other side of the room. She was stunned to see that the woodsman had taken the witch by the hand.

"Excuse me," she said to the soldier. She turned to cross the room, desperate to reach Jeanne Roy. Lou instantly blocked her passage.

"Lili! Come meet Jambon," she said. "Bring your beau and come meet mine."

"He's not my beau," Élisabeth said irritably. She glanced at the sandy-haired soldier and then quickly away. He shrugged as Élisabeth untangled herself from Lou, edging towards Jeanne and the woodsman. They were still by the window, though now Sister Gagnon had joined them. Élisabeth inched close enough to hear their argument.

"It seems superfluous to me. Why should it be necessary?" Jeanne Roy challenged the old nun.

"The intendant has his rules," Sister Gagnon explained. "I've given up asking why."

"Then you agree. We can dispense with the paperwork."

The nun put her hands on her hips. "I did not say that. It may not make sense to my old bones, but I do need to see it before you sign the licence."

"But you *know* that my trunk was misplaced. I have been wearing castoffs for goodness' sake! My letter of good conduct was in my trousseau along with everything else."

Élisabeth inched forward again and noticed the soldier Francoeur had followed her across the room.

"That may be so," Sister Gagnon countered. "But the Sulpicians are quite insistent that all procedures are properly followed. I suppose I could appeal to them—although then I'll need an entire afternoon to go into town and come back, and Lord knows that's time that could be better spent on the harvest— but they might agree that a careful reading of the banns would suffice."

Banns? Élisabeth felt a jolt inside her stomach.

Jeanne Roy sighed and turned to Grandbois. "What do you think? If we have to wait for the banns to be read, you'll miss your chance to go on your journey. Why don't you ask someone else to marry you?" She indicated the girls in the centre of the room. "All those others should have their letters."

"Excuse me, Sister Gagnon?" Élisabeth interrupted. "I could not help but overhear that Jeanne Roy does not have her letter of good conduct."

The nun turned and frowned at her. "Yes, that is correct. Every girl must present her certificate before she signs her marriage contract."

"I can vouch for her, Sister Gagnon. Indeed, I know that a Sulpician priest has already seen it." She snuck a sidelong glance at Jeanne, who kept her eyes fixed on the nun. "His name is Father de Sancy. Onésime Gaudin de Sancy, I believe. He was on board our ship but got off at Québec. I watched him examine it with my own eyes."

"Is that so?"

"Yes, Sister, it is. It's God's honest truth. I will swear it, if you need me to."

"That's not necessary," the nun said crossly. "No one needs to swear anything. This isn't a bailiff's court." She thought for a moment more, then threw up her hands. "If a priest has already seen the letter, that's good enough for me. I'll send for a Sulpician, and you can sign the marriage contract later today."

The nun bustled off towards the doorway and Francoeur approached his friend. "Did I hear correctly, Grandbois? You've been crowing like a cockerel for months about the repugnance of marriage, yet you crumple at the first pair of fine eyes?"

"Mademoiselle Roy and I have come to an agreement," he said defensively. "She needs a home, and it will do me no harm to have a hunting licence."

Francoeur turned to Jeanne Roy, his eyes lingering on her velvet dress. "My lady, I am sorry to tell you that you will be disappointed with your part of the arrangement."

The witch gave him a withering look. "Do not be fooled by my appearance. I am quite dogged when I need to be." She turned stiffly to Élisabeth. "Thank you. I appreciate your help."

"It was n-nothing." Élisabeth stammered, then blurted out the next words before she could think. "B-but might you grant me a wish in return?"

"Grant you a wish?"

"Yes, a wish," Élisabeth said, suddenly uncertain whether she should have risked her question. She clasped her hands together. "Only, I have helped with the letter twice now and lent you a skirt."

"I suppose I may grant you a favour," Jeanne Roy said. "What is it you desire?"

Élisabeth took a deep breath. These were the words she had longed to hear. But she would not—could not—speak now. Not in front of the others. She dropped her voice. "I will seek you out when you are alone."

Jeanne nodded curtly. "Very well," she said.

Élisabeth felt her heart lift. It was done. The witch had promised to grant her wish.

And as everyone knew, a witch's pledge can never be broken.

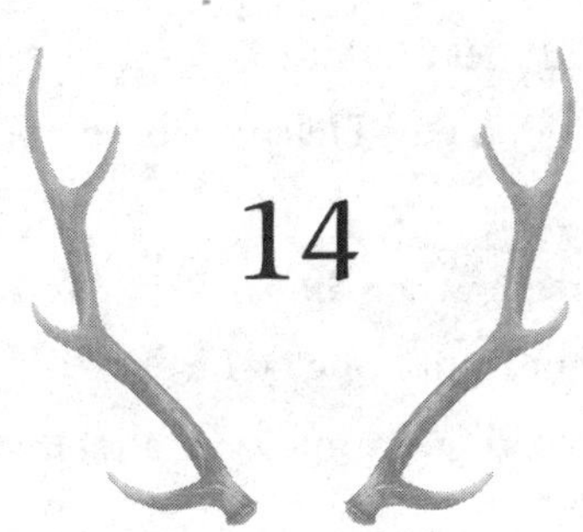

14

The second thing that surprised Marthe about her marriage was that coupling with her husband was not as onerous as she thought it might be. She knew that it would be one of her duties and, at the beginning, had set about it like any other chore. From whispers on board the ship she knew it would hurt, and from how Élisabeth carried on about Rémy she knew it would be tiresome. She had braced herself the first night, lying with her hands by her sides and her eyes fixed on the ceiling. She found, though, that Verger's kisses were tender and his arms strong, and when he pulled her on top of him she found she did not mind what they did together in the dim corner of the workroom. It was certainly more pleasurable than sweeping floors or scrubbing hardened lumps of dough from his clothes. She checked her heart, curious as to how she felt about this turn of events, and decided that she would never experience the crippling exhaustion of *true love*, as Élisabeth put it, but the unexpected comfort she found in Verger's arms at night was not unwelcome.

She knew others suffered a far worse fate.

The bakery was a gathering point for the village and every morning Maman Poulin waited as their customers brought their money and their worries to her door, anxious to relieve them of both. One day, a week or two after Marthe was married, a barrel-chested man with a thick beard and ruddy cheeks barged into the bakery. His wife wafted in behind him, almost colourless by comparison.

Maman Poulin greeted them rigidly.

"Good day, Dufossé, good day, Hélène. I have not seen you in Ville-Marie for many months."

The man bared his teeth when he spoke. "We don't like to be in town when the fur fair's on, but this one"—he jerked his thumb in his wife's direction—"insisted we see about a midwife, as she's so near to dropping her piglet."

"That must have been an arduous journey for you, Hélène," Maman Poulin said, eyeing the woman's round belly. "But you know there's no *licenced* midwife in Ville-Marie. You're best off staying at home and getting a neighbour to help you. Have you any neighbours yet in Côte Saint-François?"

The pale woman stared at the ground as her husband answered.

"Of course we have neighbours," Dufossé said. "There's not as many folk as when we lived in Québec, but soon there won't be a plot of land left on this island that hasn't been claimed. Not that any of these soldiers add to the quality of the habitant stock. Just last week we paid a visit to our neighbour to the east. He was building his house with not a scrap of clothing on his body. Like a savage! Cock dangling free for anyone to see."

"How disappointing," Maman Poulin commiserated. "We are here to make the savages French, not have Frenchmen turn savage. Still, when this heat breaks, we'll having nothing but snow for six months. I expect he'll keep his clothes on then."

As the widow and the farmer exchanged concerns over the weather and the natives, Marthe caught the young wife's eye. "Is it your first child?" she asked.

Hélène nodded but seemed to have nothing more to say.

Marthe stepped back awkwardly and touched the edge of one of the bread baskets on the hutch the way Maman Poulin said she should. Directing the customer's eye to the best loaves, the white ones that cost a few sols more.

"How long have you been in Canada?" Marthe tried again, putting on a pleasant shopkeeper voice.

"A few years," Hélène whispered, reaching a tentative hand towards one of Verger's white loaves. No sooner had she pointed towards a large white miche than her husband reached across the room and cuffed her on the back of the head.

"Who do you think you are, the Queen of Spain?"

The woman stiffened, barely blinking from being struck. Her husband grinned at Marthe as if nothing had happened. His teeth were long and yellow. "We'll take the small one, there."

A faint hue appeared on the woman's cheeks. She did not meet Marthe's eye as she took the loaf, clutching it to her chest as she shuffled out the door. When they had gone, Maman Poulin shook her head and gave Marthe a begrudging look.

"I hope you know how lucky you are, little mistress."

For once, Marthe could not disagree.

15

Hushed voices rose and fell in waves around her. It was not bright enough for Élisabeth to read the angle of the sun, but she would not have been surprised if it were before dawn. She closed her eyes and tried to let the voices fade like a will-o'-the-wisp into a marsh.

It did not work.

"I want you to be happy, Lou."

"I will be. Though, if Jambon's friend does not please you, you need not choose him."

Élisabeth grasped for her dream with her bare hands but it was too late. The moondust started to fade as the voices became clearer. She opened her eyes again.

"But we agreed to marry neighbours so we would never be parted," Rose said. She was lying on the mattress next to Élisabeth, propped up on her elbow, Lou lying flat on her back. When she saw that Élisabeth had woken, her eyes lit up.

"Good morning. You were sleeping so soundly we did not dare wake you."

Élisabeth struggled to sit up, the straw mattress giving way under her elbows.

The empty beds in the dormitory meant most of the other girls must already be up and at their chores.

"What time is it?"

"Midmorning. It's been raining since dawn. Sister Gagnon said she didn't want us churning up mud in the garden and bringing it in on our clogs, so we've been allowed to stay in bed."

"Midmorning!" She glanced at Jeanne Roy's empty pallet. She had not been able to speak to the witch the night before. Jeanne had been surrounded by nuns and giggling girls from the moment the men had left. But today Élisabeth would corner her. She pressed her hands on her stomach to steady the familiar pangs.

"What would you do, Lili? Marry right away, or wait to see if someone better comes along?" Lou fixed Élisabeth with a stare.

"I-I cannot say."

"Well then, what did you think of Jambon? And Lajeunesse? The farmers."

Élisabeth searched her memory. She remembered being introduced to a short man with a big laugh. She could not recall his friend.

"He seemed . . . merry."

Lou turned to Rose and raised her eyebrows. "See?"

"But, Lili, consider Marthe. You wished for her to know the baker a little better before agreeing to his proposal, did you not?"

"True," Élisabeth said quietly.

"Marthe is happy!" Lou insisted. "She knew her own mind and made her choice. So did Jeanne, and now she's on her way to the altar too. Why should I not do the same?"

"You know what is said," Rose frowned. "Marry in haste, repent at leisure."

"What do you mean, on her way to the altar?" Élisabeth said, swivelling to look again at Jeanne Roy's mattress in the corner.

"Oh, you know what she is like," Rose said. "She told Sister Gagnon she had no need for fuss nor festival and saw no reason to read the banns three times. Sister Gagnon was not certain at first, but as it is nearly the first of September and Jeanne is so persuasive I think she came round to the idea. Then Sister asked Agnès if she'd like to hurry up and go too, seeing as she has signed a contract with that habitant from Lachine. Can you believe the man's holdings are only four farms over from her childhood friend from Soissons? She signed as quick as she could—"

"No reason to read the banns?" A fistful of snakes suddenly writhed in her entrails. "What do you mean? Where is Jeanne?"

"She left for the village at first light."

Élisabeth threw her blanket off and leapt to her feet. "How long ago?"

"A few hours, maybe more. She hasn't got a trunk, so they didn't need to send for a carter, and with her soldier being so anxious to make a start for the land of the Odawa, she decided—"

"For *where*?" Élisabeth could not keep the panic from her voice. The witch had left the nuns' farmhouse? Without granting her wish?

"Odawa? Perhaps I did not say it right. The land to the west, somewhere. Her husband wants to be a coureur de bois, trading furs all across the land, which seems terribly daring—"

"Rose, stop talking!" Élisabeth cried. She scrambled to find her skirt and bodice, trying to step into one and pull on the other at the same time. A thought suddenly struck her and she froze. "Is Jeanne Roy going to this . . . Odawa territory too?"

"I don't know."

Élisabeth cursed herself as she tied her bodice laces and pelted down the dormitory stairs. How had she let the witch slip away? In the kitchen some of the younger girls were eating milk curds and maple syrup, their recompense for not being allowed to meet the suitors the day before.

"Where's Sister Gagnon?" Élisabeth blurted.

Claire pointed a finger without looking up from her curds. Élisabeth followed its direction, running into the corridor next to the kitchen. The nun was not there. She opened the door and felt the rain on her cheeks but could not see anyone outside. Then she put her head round the corner of the common room and saw Sister Gagnon standing by the fire next to a visitor.

It was the soldier Francoeur. A small puddle was forming on the floor under his boots.

"Ah, Élisabeth, there you are," the nun said. The soldier smiled at her and wiped a sodden sleeve across his face.

"This young man has come to ask you to marry him."

Behind her, Élisabeth heard a gasp. Rose and Lou had followed her down the stairs, bodices crookedly laced and hoods askew. The soldier's face fell at the nun's blunt delivery. He took off his wide-brimmed hat and rocked back on his heels.

"What are you waiting for?" Sister Gagnon said to her. "Come here."

Élisabeth stared at the soldier in the wet brown coat. He stepped forward to offer her his hand.

"Wait, Sister," Élisabeth turned away from him. The nun was heading for the door. "I don't know this man. I don't know his family or where he's from—"

"Then you have much to discuss," Sister Gagnon said, and closed the door behind her.

The soldier bowed his head. "Our roles are reversed today."

"I beg your pardon?"

"Today my clothes are wet. Yesterday it was your skirts. I'm sure the nuns are looking forward to the winter when all of the matches have been made and they don't have to get out a mop every afternoon."

"I-I had been wading into the river. It is so hot in this country . . ." Élisabeth looked over her shoulder towards the closed door. She had no time for this. She had to find Jeanne Roy or any hope of a cure would be lost. The witch could even now be on her way to Odawa territory. She wondered if she could make it past the nun, who was surely standing on the other side of the door. Élisabeth turned back to her suitor. "Truly, I hope you are not here to propose to me."

He hesitated, then leaned towards her. "In fact, I came because I was curious about something you said."

"Yes?" Élisabeth pressed him, wishing he would hurry his thoughts.

"I can understand one's opposition to marriage in principle—my dearest friend has long argued against it. But why would a girl who came here on a bride ship be so set against it?"

"Look," Élisabeth said, growing more anxious. "Francoeur—?"

"My friends call me Francoeur. Though I was christened Joseph Deschamps—"

"I am not wholly set against marriage. But I cannot marry right now."

He looked puzzled. "What are you waiting for, if I may ask?" The soldier would not be hurried.

"I cannot explain now, I'm very pressed for time."

"You're pressed for time, but waiting for marriage?" The corners of his mouth twitched again. "I'm perplexed."

Élisabeth stared at the man, willing him to get out of her way. He did not seem likely to budge. Indeed, his solid chest and thick arms made him seem as sturdy as an oak. He looked at her and she noticed his eyes were a hodgepodge of hazel, nothing like Rémy's deep brown.

"May I make a suggestion?" he offered.

"If you must." She hoped he did not notice her flushing.

"Do not think of this as a proposal, merely a suggestion." She glanced at the door as he spoke. "When the time comes and you are ready to pick a husband, may I suggest that you choose me?" He stared at her intently, and she felt the heat rise to her cheeks. "I have two hundred arpents of land that stretch down to the river. I've already built a good-size house, though it's not so large that it would take more than twenty cords of wood to heat in the winter. It's large enough for a family of eight . . . ten if we're lucky." He held her gaze until she squirmed and looked away, then he continued in a soft voice. "I have less than some, though more than others, and I am grateful for what God has given me. What I should like more than anything in the world is you—"

"Stop." Élisabeth held up her hand. Her fingers were trembling. Inside her belly it felt as though the demon danced, slamming its cloven hooves into her guts. Francoeur's words were sweeter than anything Rémy had ever said to her. Yet she could not hear him out. His proposal was meant for some other girl—a passably pretty bride who could love a hodgepodge husband. Her task was to find Jeanne Roy and lift the curse. And then find a way to return home to her true love.

"I must go."

"Of course," he said, his smile fading. "It was merely a suggestion."

Élisabeth gave the soldier a brief curtsey and started to leave. She was halfway across the room when Francoeur called after her.

"Wait." He crossed the room and pulled a small bag out of his coat pocket. "I have a gift for you. My favourite fruit. Would you like to try it?"

She took the sack and peered inside at a few handfuls of small dark berries. She looked up at Francoeur. The only gift Rémy had ever given her was a rose, plucked from the vine at the front of the big house. A flower he had snatched back when his mother had rounded the corner and discovered them.

She took one of the tiny berries, no bigger than a currant, and put it in her mouth. The burst of sweetness surprised her. She looked up at the soldier.

"I like it," she said, her voice barely above a whisper.

"They're called blueberries." His smile returned. "Take care not to get them on your clothes. The juice will stain."

"Thank you. I think . . ." She could not explain what she thought. Not even to herself. "I am sorry I must leave you. I must attend my friend's wedding."

"Do you mean Mademoiselle Roy's marriage? I am on my way to the chapel myself."

"You are?"

"I could accompany you."

Élisabeth clapped her hands together. "Yes, please!" She could have thrown her arms around this man, if she had not just refused him.

Sister Gagnon stepped through the doorway. "You appear to have come to an understanding?"

"Yes," Francoeur bowed. "We have agreed that we should attend the wedding of Mademoiselle Roy and my friend Grandbois. May I have your permission to accompany this young woman to the chapel?"

"What about *your* marriage?" the nun persisted. "Are you ready to sign a contract?"

Élisabeth recoiled. "No! I-I don't want to marry him. I only want to go to Jeanne Roy's wedding with him."

"Have you lost your senses?" Sister Gagnon cried. "You cannot go into town alone with this man. Not unless you intend to accept his offer of marriage. Don't be so wayward, girl!"

Élisabeth staggered backwards.

Wayward.

She felt as though a beast had sunk its fangs into her stomach. The demon was rising inside her. It clawed at her with its talons, shredding her heart into ribbons. And why should it not? For surely the Devil never possessed someone he did not find to be in mortal sin.

The nun crossed her arms. "So, what do you say? Will you marry him?"

"I cannot." She looked at the soldier's hodgepodge hazel eyes, now downcast, and steadied herself against the rush of emotion sweeping over her. Sister Gagnon threw her hands in the air.

"Then you shall go to your bed and think about your situation. A bride who refuses to marry! Good Lord, what a thing. Francoeur, I am sorry for your wasted journey."

The nun pointed at the door, ordering Élisabeth back to the dormitory. Élisabeth stared at Francoeur, who gave her a sad smile. Then she looked at the nun and saw the hard set of her mouth. She could not believe what was happening. Jeanne Roy was on the cusp of disappearing, and with her Élisabeth's last chance to be rid of the curse. Without the witch's remedy, who would want a barren bride? Barren, and possessed by a demon.

"Go!" the nun barked and Élisabeth fled up the stairs. She ran into the brides' room and flung herself onto her mattress, her breath coming in short gasps.

Only then did she remember the small bag of blueberries in her hand. She sat up. The bag had been crushed underneath her when she fell. There was now a mottled blue stain on her chemise, right above her heart.

AUTUMN

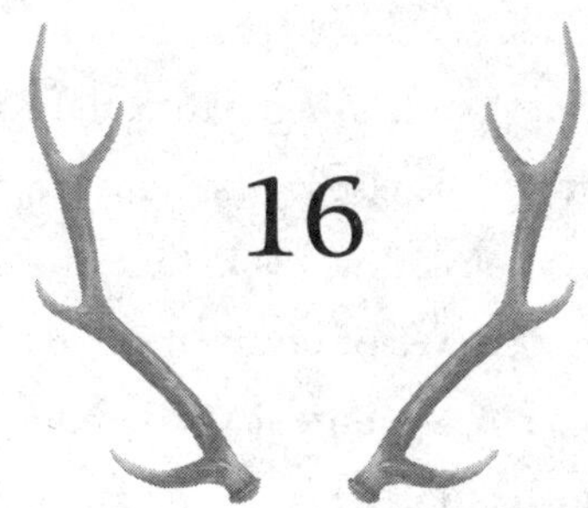

16

It was the time of year when the fairies came out at night to paint the leaves in copper and gold, yet crabgrass still sprouted between the fat pumpkins. The October weeds were stubborn. The odd creeper had kept its hold throughout the summer and Élisabeth had to dig with some determination to root them out. She plunged her fork into the earth and gave one a twist, using her other hand to pull the fringed willow herb loose.

Her thoughts were not so easy to purge.

She had lost the witch. Jeanne Roy had disappeared into the forest and Élisabeth had missed her chance. She was cursed with no hope of a cure, possessed by an unholy spirit, as sure as she could tell. One by one the other brides were marrying and leaving the farmhouse, and soon she would be left with no choice but to do so too. She would have to marry a stranger. But would it last? She was a barren bride. She could not give a farmer his sons, a cabinetmaker his apprentice. How long before her husband sent her back to the nuns' farm, shunned for not being able to do the only task God put her on earth to perform?

She would be sent into service again. It would be like it was at the Delaunay household: the hours long and uninteresting, the mistress demanding, the cook cranky. She had thought she would die of loneliness.

Until she'd met Rémy.

It was true that the cook had warned her to keep to her work and stay away from him. *He's a chip off the old block, that boy is.* Élisabeth had not wanted to understand Old Geneviève's meaning. From the start Rémy Delaunay had shown her a kindness that no one else in the household had.

"I knew your brother, you know," he'd said one afternoon when she was washing up. He'd rolled the sleeves of his chemise to his elbow, revealing thick, dark hair on his forearms. For a moment she'd thought he meant to help her with the cooking pots, but he took a seat at the table instead. "I liked him very much. It's a shame that God had to take him so young."

She'd nodded and kept her eyes fixed on scraping burnt parsnips out of the bottom of a cast-iron pot. Everyone from Falaise to Flers had known Jean-Jacques; he had been Saint-Philbert's favourite son. She told herself it was not remarkable that a well-to-do man such as Rémy had liked her brother, everyone had liked him. She'd put the kindness out of her mind and continued to scour the pot.

Still, that spark of sympathy had kindled something in her, and she began to look forward to the moments in the day when their paths would cross. At their first meeting after the burnt pot, Rémy had given her a cheery wave as she lugged water from the well. Another day he had winked when his mother had corrected Élisabeth on how to set the table. A whispered slight against the cook had made her laugh out loud, and for the first time since her brothers had died, Élisabeth thought it might not be impossible to be happy again. She related all of her encounters to Marthe in exacting detail when they saw each other at Mass on Sundays.

"He said Old Geneviève's underarms shake like blancmange when she whips cream. Isn't that funny? Now that he has said it, it is all I can think of when I watch her whisk."

"Why would he say such a thing?" Marthe had frowned. "She's been with his family since she was our age."

Élisabeth had kept her eyes fixed on the altar and ignored Marthe. Her sister was too young to understand that it did not matter what Rémy said about the old cook, only that he had sought her out and shared his confidences with her. It was what had kept her alive in that cold farmhouse on the hill.

She shuddered, as if the cold were still upon her, and a clump of crabgrass broke off in her hand before she could loosen the root. She threw the stalk to one side. Perhaps it had been cruel to mock the old cook's wobbly flesh, but that had not been her greatest sin.

Don't be so wayward, girl.

She turned the nun's words over, this way and that, examining what Sister Gagnon had meant, guessing at what she knew. She thought about the day she had walked with Rémy up to the clifftop to lay amid the heather. *We are as good as married in God's eyes already.* She remembered the stem of yarrow on her ring finger, and how it had not lasted, how it had disintegrated with the washing of the cooking pots.

Wayward girl.

The nun's words burned just as much as they had the day her own mother had seared her with that brand.

Élisabeth had been chasing after her younger brother and the game was getting rough, their faces streaked with dirt and tears from laughing and fighting. Her mother said good girls didn't play in the dirt. Good girls sat by the hearth and helped their mothers with the mending. But Nicolas had thrown a stick and hit her shoulder, and that had started it. She'd sprinted after him. She was two years older and twice as strong and could easily catch him. When she did, she had a mind to pinch his cheek until he squealed.

She did not close the gate, as she knew she must, and the chickens ran free, scattering across the field.

At first she'd laughed to see them run, a poultry army in disarray. It did not matter if they ran loose. Even at the age of ten, her older brother, Jean-Jacques, could be relied upon to catch them one by one and put them back in their hutch. *My angel*, Maman called him. Maman had no such words for Élisabeth now. The new baby she was carrying made her more disagreeable by the day, and she no longer stroked Élisabeth's hair when she went to bed at night or whispered soft prayers in her ear. Nowadays Maman did nothing but complain that her back ached and her feet hurt, and she could never catch enough sleep.

Mind your sister.

Mind how you behave.

I am losing my mind with you, girl!

When Maman flung open the cottage door and screamed about the hens, Élisabeth knew she should hang her head and apologize. She knew she should have been minding Marthe, not chasing Nicolas. But why should the fault be hers, when it was Nicolas who had thrown the stick?

She screwed up her fists into tight balls. She shouted that her younger brother deserved to have his ears boxed, and her sister was a pest that no one wanted clutching at their skirts. Of course Marthe then wailed and stretched her arms out to be picked up, her usual ploy. Élisabeth was surprised to see Maman push Marthe away. Her mother slumped down on the doorstep, overcome. She looked at Élisabeth then, her words as heavy as stones.

Take more care, or the Devil will come for you, wayward girl.

The very next day the babies came—two of them, as it turned out—and took Maman with them to the grave. Élisabeth sat small in the corner when the neighbour's wife said that it was over, and at least now Maman was in Heaven where she belonged. Marthe had wept like the baby she was, but Élisabeth had not looked up. She had kept her red-rimmed eyes on the mending in her lap.

"Lili?"

Élisabeth raised her head and peered through the withering pea stalks at Lou. She could not say what time of day it was; she had a suspicion she had not yet eaten. The demon took up too much space in her belly for her to feel hunger. She grimaced and sat back on her heels.

"Is it time?"

"Yes."

She looked down at her hands caked with soil. The dirt under her fingernails would never come out. She rubbed her hands together to remove the worst of it and quickly ran through the squeeze and prayer. She stopped when she saw Lou giving her an odd look.

"Dirt on my hands," she muttered.

As she opened the back door to the farmhouse the noise of high-spirited girls billowed towards them. They walked into the kitchen and saw half a dozen of the brides crowded around a deck of cards, some seated on the long benches, the younger ones sitting directly on the table. She made her way to the stone sink and poured well water over her hands. As she had predicted, the brides could not be rushed into marriage by the first of September. They were enjoying their season of courtship altogether too much.

"I had a stack of five at one point," Thérèse bragged as she shuffled the deck.

"So? I had at least six. You can't walk out the door without tripping over another one," Françoise replied, steadily sharpening a pencil with a paring knife.

"That engagé doesn't count."

"I'm *not* counting him, more's the pity. With that firm backside he'll be snapped up when his term of service is done." Françoise clicked her fingers to make her point and there were giggles all round.

"Shall I deal you in?" Thérèse asked, looking up at Élisabeth.

"No," Élisabeth shook her head. "We are going into the village to see Marthe before Apolline's wedding starts."

"Shame. The winner gets your Francoeur."

"What?" Élisabeth forgot to protest that he wasn't *her* Francoeur. "Has he proposed to someone else?"

One of the younger brides rolled her eyes. "Not yet, but he will. This game will decide who gets him."

"What do you mean?"

"Do you expect him to pine for you?" Françoise smirked. "It's been a month since he proposed. I'm minded to add him to my own pile to consider."

"Ignore them," Rose told her. She was standing by the door with Lou, her cloak around her shoulders. "It's just a game." Élisabeth crossed the kitchen to collect her shawl.

"It's ten men for every girl, remember, and we hold all the cards," Thérèse called out.

Rose patted her shoulder. "If you have an interest in Francoeur, just tell us and we'll make sure he's not one of the men they are playing for."

"I do not," Élisabeth said coldly. She rammed her fist into her pocket and felt for her beads. She would recite her rosary on the walk into town. She had not been wayward to reject the soldier, no matter what the nun had said. And she had done no wrong in walking to the clifftop with Rémy.

She had been a handfasted bride.

Hadn't she?

17

The autumn wind was brisk enough to send the shingle on the outside wall clacking back and forth, and all day Marthe was not certain if customers were opening the door and coming into the shop or if the wind was merely toying with her. She swept her broomstick across the bakery floor, leaving a small pile of flour in the corner. She did not like the wind. A gale had been howling the night her brother Nicolas had disappeared. It had been the same time of year, when the night comes early and the harvest is in. Their elder brother, Jean-Jacques, had paced across the cottage's stone floor, saying out loud what none of them knew to be true, that Nicolas was a sensible lad and he would return home from the tavern with nothing but a sore head and a tall tale. Élisabeth, then sixteen, had bent over the fire, adding so many sprigs of thyme to the tripe stew that she ruined the only meat they would have all week. Finally, Papa had sent for the soothsayer. The old woman arrived with a grimace, shaking her head about having been called out into the night's fury. She led them into their vegetable garden and plunged a pair of silver scissors into the earth, balancing a sieve on top of the handle. The instrument careened in the wind, but she persisted with the charm, calling out to Saint Pierre and Saint Paul, asking them if Nicolas still lived. *Turn, if yes! If no, stay still.*

The sieve had spun round on the scissors, giving them all false hope.

A fresh clatter caused Marthe to drop her broomstick. Was it the wind, or was there someone at the door? She was still hoping the governor would come by the bakery. The longer he stayed away, the more consequential she imagined his visit would be. She hoped she had made a good impression, enough that he might offer them some small patronage—using his power to require that the fort purchase its bread from Verger, for instance. But more than that, Marthe dreamed that the governor would stride into the humble bakehouse and reward her with the secret of how to trade furs with the natives. The secret of how to grow rich.

She tucked her broomstick behind the door to ward off evil and took a seat on Verger's workbench. Her husband was asleep, having shuffled off after the night's bake, placing a kiss on the nape of her neck as he went through to their quarters. Maman Poulin was in her salon, preoccupied with some scheme that she had not shared and that Marthe dared not enquire about lest she be told off for prying. The widow could be testy at times.

Marthe looked around the empty room and felt uncertain of what she should do next. She wondered what Rose and Lou were doing on their farms, and if they had moments of loneliness too. Her thoughts were drawn back to Nicolas, his unkempt hair, his easy laugh. In the end they had found his body by throwing a communion wafer into the river Orne, the magic of the Eucharist revealing where her brother had drowned. If he had not died, would any of their subsequent troubles have come to pass? Marthe wished she could have paid for a Mass for his soul. When she grew rich, she would buy for prayers for them all.

A gust of wind blew the bakehouse door open. Marthe leapt to her feet and tucked a strand of hair under her cap.

"Good day?" she called out.

"Hello, Marthe."

It was Élisabeth. Marthe had not seen her sister since her wedding day six weeks earlier. With the memory of Nicolas stirring in her heart, part of Marthe yearned to run to Élisabeth and tell her all the thousands of little things that had happened to her since she'd left to be married—how her husband hummed while he worked and she could not decide if it was endearing or annoying, how difficult it was to live under the widow's critical gaze, how she had not bled this month and had been sick every morning for a fortnight.

Élisabeth stood in the hallway, dark circles under her eyes, her hands twisting together. Something about the gesture triggered Marthe's impatience. She would not forgive her sister's deception too readily.

"Good day, Élisabeth."

"You will not call me Lili?" Élisabeth smiled, a ghostly twitch that did not light her face.

Marthe held her head high. "Not at the moment, no." They stood in silence until Marthe could no longer bear the void between them. "What are you doing here?"

"The nuns said I could attend Apolline's wedding. They have not granted me permission to leave the farmhouse since the day Jeanne Roy married; I've been kept back so that I might show my contrition and contemplate the Seven Joys of the Virgin . . ." Her voice trailed off, her head hung in misery. She took a breath and tried again. "I came to town early, with Rose and Lou, to see you. I've asked them to give us a moment alone . . ." Élisabeth's hands were frothing furiously now. Marthe wanted to reach out and calm them, to halt her sister's distress. "Because I know . . . I know the nuns are not the only ones I have angered."

"No, they are not." Marthe remained resolute, placing her hands on her hips.

Élisabeth fell silent again, staring at the floorboards as the wind wailed outside. Marthe frowned and tapped her foot, wondering how long she could hold out. Her anger had melted away long ago, it always did. But her sister ought to suffer a little longer for the lies she had told.

"Do you think me wayward, Marthe?" Élisabeth said, her voice barely above a whisper.

Marthe hesitated. "You were certainly led astray."

Élisabeth looked up, suddenly urgent. "The Devil comes for wayward girls, does he not?"

"Our Lady in Heaven! How am I to know what the Evil One does?"

Élisabeth nodded, her hands still twisting. "I am sorry for what I did. I should have told you the truth about the curse. And about my wish to go home."

"It is an impossible wish," Marthe said gently. "You must know that."

"I do. I do know it. Yet I cannot help wishing it."

The sisters stood for a moment, the silence around them growing again. The skin around Élisabeth's eyes was blotchy and her lashes damp. She hesitated for a moment, and then the words tumbled from her mouth.

"Marthe, I am suffering. My anguish is so great, I fear I must be possessed. A wicked spirit has surely made its home inside me, I can feel that it has. Some days the beast leaps and dances so much I feel that I might faint."

Marthe glanced over her shoulder towards Maman Poulin's half of the house, pulling Élisabeth into the workroom. "You seem thinner, but nothing worse than that. Put these wild thoughts of possession out of your mind."

"My bones have grown sharp, it is true. No matter how much bread and lard I eat, the demon inside me consumes it all."

Marthe settled her sister onto a stool by the edge of the hearth while she searched carefully for her words.

"I am fortunate in some ways," she said. There was an easy answer to Élisabeth's riddle, and she needed her sister to see it. "We have all the bread we could ever want to eat. We also have meat or fowl several times a week. And there's a pig in the yard that will see us through the winter."

"You have all the luck of the stars." Élisabeth looked mournful and Marthe felt a twitch of frustration.

"You could be as lucky! When Rose and Lou last came to town they told me there's a good man, a habitant, who wanted to marry you. Why did you refuse him?"

Élisabeth squeezed her hands together. "You know I cannot marry."

"Because of Rémy?" Marthe's voice was sharp.

"Because of *me*. I think . . . I *know* now that I will never marry Rémy." Élisabeth's voice wavered. "But even if I resign myself to living on this island for the rest of my days, how could I wed Francoeur, knowing that I am cursed?"

Marthe furrowed her brow. "I told you. Ask Jeanne Roy for a simple or a charm to help you."

"I missed my chance. She was never alone. And now she has vanished."

"Vanished?"

"She married a woodsman and disappeared."

"Well, then. She is likely living on one of the more distant seigneuries if she has married a woodsman. They will come to town now and again, to sell their firewood."

"No. I believe they have travelled upcountry to trade furs. Never to be seen again."

"Oh Lili." Marthe sighed. Her sister was seeing only darkness when there were shards of light everywhere. She need only turn towards the sun. "You don't know that. Who is to say that she might not return home in the summer, when the fur fair starts up again?"

"She could be anywhere in a thousand forests. I am forever cursed."

Marthe gave in and put her hands on top of Élisabeth's. "You will see her again. In the meantime, do not succumb to these bleak thoughts of possession—"

Élisabeth leapt up, pushing back the stool so hard that it let out a screech as it scraped across the floor. "How can I not? You do not understand how much I suffer!"

Marthe was on her feet quickly, looking over her shoulder to see if the widow had heard them. She put a hand on Élisabeth's back, hoping to soothe her into silence. "Tell me, then. Tell me about your suffering. Quietly, though."

"There must be a demon inside me. I know what you believe, Marthe, that I am not like the demoniac you and Nicolas saw. But what else can explain all of these sensations inside of me?" Élisabeth's voice was rising again.

"Do be quiet," Marthe pleaded.

"On the ship I heard the old priest tell the captain what to watch for. He said fatigue was a sure sign of possession. You saw me, Marthe—I could not rise from my bunk for weeks!"

"You broke your crown, Lili."

"But the strength! The unholy strength that allowed me to attack those men! I know I have not had a fit as yet, but what if that is still to come? What if it is only a matter of time before I'm grunting like a pig, or—or howling and gnashing teeth like a wolf, and sticking out a long, slithering snake's tongue—"

"Oh, ma chère! What horrors you describe."

Maman Poulin peered around the corner, her black eyes glittering. Marthe froze as the widow stepped into the room. "Tell me, what manner of creature do you speak of? Is it a goblin? Or a demon?"

Marthe stiffened. How much had the widow heard?

"Y-yes," Élisabeth blanched. "A demon."

Marthe stood up. "Lili," she said cautiously. "This is Barbe, the widow Poulin, whose husband was once the baker here. She lives in our house still. Barbe, this is my sister, Élisabeth."

"Lili? What a pretty name. You must call me Maman Poulin. I've lived in this village long enough to have everyone call me mother." The widow curtseyed and Élisabeth followed suit. "Now tell me, what sort of demon grunts and barks and has the tongue of a serpent?"

"I don't know," Élisabeth said nervously.

"Where did you see it?"

"She has *not* seen it," Marthe interrupted before Élisabeth had a chance to confess to anything. "My sister heard the story from a woman who passed through our village in Normandy. The woman angered a witch, so the hag sent a demon to plague her. Lili was just telling me how she still worries about the poor cursed soul. My sister has a very sentimental nature." Marthe kept her voice so steady she wondered at her own ability to spin a tale from the air. Maman Poulin's eyes narrowed for a moment, then her face crumpled into a picture of concern.

"It is a most cruel thing to be cursed by a witch," she sympathized, shaking her head. "Why, there was a girl here in New France who was cursed, several years ago now. By a male witch, if you can imagine! A filthy Huguenot. He sent demons to harass her when she refused to marry him. Then he poisoned the air so that the children could not breathe. They died in droves, gasping for breath, poor lambs. I will never forget the sound."

"What happened to the girl?" Élisabeth rose from her stool anxiously.

"She recovered once they caught and killed the witch, thank God. She went on to marry and have a dozen children. But it was not the only time it has happened here. There was also once a nun who was plagued with a demon. Satan himself came to her at night, as cold to the touch as the dead."

"Satan was here in Ville-Marie?" Élisabeth whispered, crossing herself. Marthe watched uneasily as she took a step closer to the widow. She did not need Maman Poulin filling her sister's head with dark tales. In the distance, church bells started to ring.

"Lili, the bells!" Marthe leapt on the distraction. "We must go or we'll be late for Apolline's wedding."

"It's only a few strides to the Hôtel Dieu from here, and the first bells are but a warning that it is time to gather," Maman Poulin said without looking at Marthe. She patted Élisabeth's arm. "How fortunate to be wed on a Monday, don't you think? The charm from yesterday's holy sacrament will still be upon them. Now, tell me more about this dreadful demon."

Maman Poulin pulled Élisabeth into a snug hold and led her out of the bakery. Marthe could do nothing but follow behind, her sister's shadow.

"The woman . . . she came through our village several years ago. She spoke of feeling . . . much turmoil inside her," Élisabeth started as they walked down Rue Saint-Paul. "I-I wish I could tell you more. The woman, she found it hard to describe."

"You mentioned a howling like a wolf."

Élisabeth hesitated. "I suppose."

"And having a tongue like a serpent."

Élisabeth's face was becoming pinched with worry. Marthe frowned.

"The girl would have rested easier knowing which of the demons it is," the widow said.

"Which of the demons?" Élisabeth stared at Maman Poulin.

"Yes. There are so many of them, and each has its own weakness. It is important to know which one ails her so that the priests may know how to defeat it."

"I believe the woman should not have thought about it all!" Marthe chirped from behind. "It only distressed her further. It only added to her worries."

The widow stared at Marthe with an open mouth, then turned to Élisabeth. "Your sister is surely the most callow little mistress I know. Of course the woman was right to worry. It must be her only concern."

The wind blew so forcefully that Marthe's hood was almost lifted off her head. She grabbed it with both hands, her knuckles white.

"She was nervous to tell any priest . . ." Élisabeth said. "Lest the exorcism be the death of her. For she heard that it is a procedure of . . . of great violence."

The widow shrugged. "I do not know if that is true. You could ask the Sulpician priest who lately arrived in Ville-Marie how it is performed. He is a great expert on witches and demons. I'm sure he would also know which one has afflicted this woman. He could write to your curé and explain what must be done, should she return to your village again."

"An expert on witches?" Marthe tried to insert herself between the two women.

"Yes, a witch hunter from France. His name is Father de Sancy." The widow gave her a backwards glance. "He's the cleverest man who has ever set foot on this island, or so I heard him say."

"We know him." Élisabeth began to lather soap between her hands once again.

"He was on our ship on the journey over," Marthe explained. "Though he mostly kept to his quarters. He would have no reason to remember us."

"You must speak to him." The widow ignored Marthe and turned to Élisabeth. "Tell him what you know of this woman."

"I shouldn't like to disturb him with such a tale."

Marthe could see the widow clinging ever more tightly to Élisabeth's arm, forcing her hands apart.

"Lili is right," Marthe agreed. "No good will come of telling this priest about a woman back in Saint-Philbert. It's a French story that must stay in France."

"Nonsense. It is best that we understand as much about the workings of the Devil as possible. Lest he tries to strike here again."

Before Marthe could counter the widow or pull Élisabeth aside to plead with her not to draw the inquisitor's attention for nothing, another gust of wind lifted her hood right off her head, tossing it in the air and down the street. She scurried to capture what she had lost, while Maman Poulin drew Élisabeth into a tight embrace. Marthe wondered why the widow was so taken with her sister when she had had nothing but strict words for Marthe about how to cook and clean and take care of her husband. Was it Élisabeth's frailty or the frisson of magic that drew Maman Poulin in?

"I will accompany you, chère Lili, if you like," Marthe heard the widow say when she had recovered her headdress. "Shall we go together to see the priest?"

Marthe's heart sank as she heard her sister's answer.

"Yes, Maman Poulin. I'll seek out the priest and ask him about this demon."

18

It was a full fortnight before Élisabeth came back to Ville-Marie to visit the priest, shortly after Lou's and Rose's wedding ceremonies had taken place. The Parisian girls married at the same time, to men whose plots of land lay next to each other, just as they had promised. Lou stumbled over her vows—for she only knew Jambon by his regimental nickname and balked when she was asked to take someone called Jean Dupuis as her husband. Her laughter upon realizing her mistake rang out like morning church bells. Rose spoke little before—or after—her marriage to his friend Laurent Lajeunesse.

Élisabeth waited outside the chapel for Maman Poulin. She had barely taken note of the weddings. She was still agonizing over her decision to seek out Father de Sancy—she alone knew how he extracted his knowledge, and she could not loosen the fear that he might discover her secret and call for her to be stripped naked and pricked with a needle—but she could no longer live with the uncertainty of the feelings inside her. Besides, Maman Poulin seemed so sure of the righteousness of the enquiry and Élisabeth liked the plain-spoken widow. With Maman Poulin by her side, Élisabeth felt she no longer had to carry her burdens alone.

As they walked from the Hôtel Dieu to the Sulpicians' seminary though, the spirit inside her seemed to snake into her legs, trying to hide in her knees. She set her mind to putting one foot in front of the other, surprised at how difficult the task was. When they reached the front door of the stone seminary, a servant answered, and the widow took charge. They were soon shown along an unlit corridor into a room with large windows. Élisabeth had never seen so many books—the church in Saint-Philbert counted itself lucky enough to have a single missal—and yet here in Ville-Marie there was an entire case of prayer books. Father de Sancy sat behind a small table in the corner, a quill in his hand.

Maman Poulin cleared her throat. "Father?"

"Do not speak," the priest said, not looking up as the feather scratched across the paper.

Élisabeth felt a rush of heat race up her spine and wondered if the demon were blowing smoke from its nostrils inside her. She swayed from foot to foot to try to lull the creature to sleep. The priest paused and placed his quill down on the table.

"Men may read the words I am writing today for centuries to come. But I cannot think when a female is dancing around the room before me."

Élisabeth flushed and crossed her arms over her chest protectively.

"Father, we are sorry to disturb you," Maman Poulin tried again. "We asked to speak with you today because my young friend has an important question that we know only you can answer, for you are a great man with much knowledge."

"Yes, yes," the priest dismissed her flattery crossly. "I remember our appointment."

"This is Élisabeth Jossard, newly arrived from Normandy," Maman Poulin said. From his blank stare Élisabeth realized that the priest did not recognize her from the inquisition on the ship. "She is the guardian of a frightful secret, for she met a woman in France who is possessed of a demon. And the matter is so terrifying to her—indeed the description of the turmoil the poor soul faces fills us all with such horror—that we wanted to ask you about it so that you may soothe our nightmares."

The priest leaned forward, his eyes glinting. "Normandy, you say?" Élisabeth could only nod. "Were the authorities in your village aware of this demonic possession?"

The widow looked at her expectantly. Élisabeth dropped her eyes to the ground, evading the priest's gaze. "I . . . I do not know, Father."

The priest sat back in his chair, wheezing. "It would hardly matter if they were. The courts in Rouen are struggling to prosecute even the most heinous crimes, now that the king has turned soft. It is left to witch hunters like myself to deal with all the heretics, witches, and demons—no matter how many cases there are. The amount of work to be done is almost insurmountable."

"You are a champion," the widow said quickly. "Your reputation is widely known. It's all the talk of Ville-Marie, how well-versed you are in the fight against witches and demons and the like. We are lucky to have you amongst us."

Father de Sancy waved his hand to dispel Maman Poulin's words. "What is it you want to know?"

All the questions Élisabeth had wrestled with since the day she was cursed started to churn inside her. Did the sharp jabs in her womb mean that she was still barren? Or did a demon account for all the strangeness inside her? And if so, could the magic of one witch defeat the curse of another? Might she drink a potion or beg Jeanne Roy for an enchantment, rather than suffer being beaten, pricked, or God knows what other violence in search of a cure?

"She describes a creature so strange and fearful that it does not sound like anything I have heard of in all my life," Maman Poulin started.

"She feels jabs in her belly," Élisabeth said.

"It is far worse than that," the widow interrupted. "She describes a mangled beast from Hell."

Élisabeth listened as Maman Poulin began to weave a tale of a wolf with horns, talons, wings, and a serpent's forked tongue—a nightmare so colourful and intricate they would wear it for the rest of their lives, a garment to be handed down for generations. The longer she spoke, the more Élisabeth could feel such a creature moving inside her.

"What do you think, Father de Sancy? Have you ever heard of such a demon?"

Father de Sancy leaned back in his chair and rubbed his considerable stomach. "Of course I have."

Élisabeth's hand flew to her mouth. The priest knew which devil dwelled inside of her! She put her thumb in her mouth and began to chew on her nail as the priest spoke.

"We've made great progress in our understanding of Hell's creatures. I myself assisted with the Greek translation of the works of the inquisitor Michaëlis."

"And what does this Michael say about getting rid of demons?" Élisabeth asked. She found it hard to look the priest in the eye, only glancing at him when his gaze was not fixed upon her.

"Michael-*isss*," the priest hissed. "And while his work was significant, my own treatise is not without acclaim. Though of course I have built upon the work of giants."

"Giants!"

The priest gave Élisabeth a severe look. "Great thinkers. Men you would never have heard of."

She put a knuckle into her mouth and continued to gnaw, finding some respite from her fear in the pain. "Are you famous because you helped those nuns?"

"Ah, my reputation *does* precede me. You are referring to my work on the demonic possessions at Louviers?"

Maman Poulin, astonished, turned to Élisabeth, who managed a meek shrug. "Yes, I mean those nuns. Though I cannot understand why the most pious of women could be possessed," Élisabeth said.

"Perhaps they were not as pious as they pretended," the priest replied. "It is well known that the female is a slave to her filthy lusts."

Élisabeth looked up at the priest and flinched when she saw that his eyes were bearing down on her.

Father de Sancy inhaled sharply and continued. "We exorcised more than a dozen demons from those nuns and burned the witches who cursed them."

"What sorts of demons were they?" Maman Poulin was almost breathless.

"Terrifying legions from Hell," the priest said, though he did not seem frightened. He extended his legs and placed his hands behind his head, his elbows pointing out to the sides of the room. "Did you know, I spoke to the demon Leviathan himself at Louviers?" Father de Sancy's eyes grew misty and his voice softened. "He was right there in the room, communicating with me through that poor Sister. The audacity of his words . . . it was remarkable. If I live another seventy years, I will never see such wonders again."

"How did you know it was Leviathan?" Maman Poulin asked.

The question pierced his thoughts. He remembered their presence and sat up straight in his chair. "We learned through time and experience to recognize the different demons through the behaviour of their victims."

"What sort of behaviour? What do you mean?"

"Sinful behaviour, of course. For instance, if your village girl is lustful, it could be the demon Rosier who inhabits her. Should she whisper during Mass, it is very likely Belias, a fallen prince of virtues. I do not think a demon as great as Leviathan or Beelzebub would bother with a peasant girl, but they have scores of lesser demons under their command. In one of the most celebrated cases, a demoniac had as many as thirty devils inside of her! Including Beelzebub the lion, Cerberus the dog, and Astaroth the pig. Without meeting your girl to examine her, I cannot tell you which demon afflicts her."

Élisabeth swayed. Should she own up to her tyranny of symptoms and let the priest examine her? Should she risk being shaved and beaten until her skin turned blue? No, no. She could not survive the shame of it. It would be better to do as Marthe suggested and entreat Jeanne Roy to help her with a potion. If Jeanne Roy could be found.

"Father, could it be something simpler than a demon?" Maman Poulin asked. "What about a werewolf?"

The priest snorted. "Nothing but folklore. Creatures of fantasy."

"Could a demon be a wolf and a serpent at the same time?" the widow persisted. "The girl Lili met had snakes *and* a wolf inside her."

The priest reached for a book and opened it. Élisabeth dared to take a step closer. On each page were loops of black writing, as well as sketches of stars and crosses and circles—all manner of magical shapes.

"Many spirits can have muddled limbs and borrowed features. *The Lesser Key of Solomon* details the characteristics of seventy-two demons. Here is a prince of Hell with the head of a lion and the feet of a goose. Oh, and here you see the fifty-first spirit, Balam. He has three different heads from three different creatures, and the tail of a serpent. Ah, interesting. It says he rides a bear and can make men invisible."

Father de Sancy flipped the pages of the book, lost in his research again. "Why look, here is another. Marchosias, a great and mighty marquis of Hell. He appears in the shape of a cruel she-wolf with a gryphon's wings and a serpent's tail, vomiting fire. It says, 'He is a strong fighter and giveth true answers to all questions.'"

"Mar-co-see-us?" Élisabeth shivered as the syllables tripped off her tongue. If this particular spirit was a fighter, could that account for how she attacked the men in the alley? She peered at the scratches of ink on the parchment, wondering at the connection between the black lines and the rising turmoil in her stomach. "Is he a wolf with wings and a serpent's tail?"

"Yes, that is how he appears. Oh, I would dearly love to exorcise this devil from whomsoever he inhabits. If Marchosias is bound to tell the truth, I would learn a great deal." The priest shut the book and laboured to stand up. "Now, I haven't time for any more questions."

"Please." Élisabeth stopped him. "How . . . how can this demon be defeated?"

The priest grunted with disapproval, as if her question were too simple to warrant a proper reply. "Exorcism. Thorough, precise exorcism. Sometimes it takes weeks. Sometimes years."

"So long," she murmured.

"Yes. To be frank, it's sometimes hardly worth saving these demoniacs, there's so little of their souls left by the time the demon departs. Don't look so alarmed, child! Many of them are secretly witches anyway. Only fit to burn."

The priest gave them both a slight nod as he departed, leaving them alone in the library. Élisabeth tried to take a step towards the door but her legs failed. Maman Poulin caught her as she stumbled.

"Thank the Holy Virgin you left Normandy," the widow whispered as she pulled Élisabeth close. "You are safer here in New France."

Élisabeth clung to the widow. Her teeth chattered and she could feel a fluttering in her stomach as the demon—did the priest say Marcosi was its name?—attempted to unfurl its wings.

Was she not worth saving? Was she as good as damned?

"Come, we will go back to the chapel to absolve ourselves from such dark thoughts."

They took the path between the seminary and the hospital until they reached the chapel. Élisabeth followed Maman Poulin into a pew, barely noticing as a handful of other villagers slid into the seats nearby. At least she understood how she had savaged the men who tried to attack her in the alleyway. Marcosi was a wolf. His fangs were what must have torn the lip of the branded man. And if the demon had gryphon wings as well? Well, that would explain the feeling she had of being ready to take flight whenever he was at his most unsettled. Even the existence of a serpent's tail made sense, for he often slithered around her body and into her bowels. Everything she had been feeling for the past months could be explained, now that she knew there was a great marquis of Hell inside her. She gripped her rosary between her palms and rubbed the beads against her knuckle bones while the Latin droned on around her.

Mea culpa, mea culpa, mea maxima culpa.

She could not tell the priest—she could not face the shame of undressing before him, or the pain he would inflict. But if she could not tell the priest, she could not confess her sins. If she could not confess, she could not take communion, putting her soul ever more in peril.

My fault, my fault, my most grievous fault.

She was so lost in her thoughts that she did not see the soldier Francoeur until she left the chapel.

He was talking to another man on the churchyard path, his sandy curls unmistakable. Élisabeth felt the demon unfurl his wings in her stomach and flap them mightily. She pressed herself against the chapel door to prevent Marcosi lifting her off the ground. She hoped Francoeur had not seen her.

"Whatever's the matter?" Maman Poulin had not missed her cowering by the entrance.

"Maman Poulin, I . . . I am quite shaken by all we have heard today. I need to sit a moment longer."

The widow followed her gaze. "Isn't that the habitant who made you an offer?" She had a shrewd look on her face. Élisabeth swallowed. Of course Maman Poulin would know of Francoeur's proposal.

"I cannot speak to him. Not now."

"Goodness, child." The widow sighed loudly. "Then leave him to me." She pattered down the path after Francoeur. Élisabeth stood in the shade of the Hôtel Dieu walls, rubbing her rosary between her hands, feeling the beads against her bones. Surely one witch could undo the magic of another. Surely she would not need to submit to torture to be cured. She felt the demon turn twice in her stomach. *Stay down, Marcosi,* she prayed, though she knew he did not obey her. She waited until she saw the widow curtsey and the soldier walk away before creeping forward to rejoin her.

"I think he was lingering in the hopes he might speak with you," Maman Poulin said. "I said you were unwell, and he was disappointed, for he cannot stay in town."

Élisabeth looked away in the hopes she might deter the widow from saying any more. She did not want to discuss Francoeur. She wanted to figure out how to dispel the evil spirit that dwelled within her.

Maman Poulin prattled on, oblivious.

"He was here to fetch flour for his neighbour's wife. Can you believe his neighbour has turned coureur de bois and gone west to Odawa territory, leaving his new wife alone all winter?"

The demon Marcosi thrust his horns into her gut. The blow was so fierce she almost fell forward.

"Some men." The widow shook her head. "You shouldn't let that one get away, Lili, for he would not do that to you."

"What did you say?" Her voice caught in her throat.

"Francoeur is a good one. He's thoughtful and speaks as he should."

"No. About his neighbour."

"Oh. He's left his wife to go off and trade furs."

"Did . . . did he mention . . . did he mention the wife's name?" Élisabeth's whole body began to tremble.

"Ma chère, look at you, you have been bitten by the cold. We'd best get home. A brisk walk will chase the shivers away—"

"Please! Did he tell you his neighbour's name?"

"Good grief, girl, there's no need to shout. He said her name is Jeanne. Jeanne Roy."

Élisabeth did not hesitate. She searched the horizon and saw Francoeur heading down towards the river path. She hiked up her skirts and ran pell-mell after him. She could hear Maman Poulin cry out but she did not stop. She did not even feel the ground beneath her feet. Her hair came loose at the back of her hood, her stockings fell down around her ankles.

"Francoeur!" Élisabeth called out. He turned and stopped, putting his hand up to block the sun from his eyes.

"Élisabeth?"

She stopped in front of him, breathing heavily. He grinned at her dishevelled state. "You are unwell, I understand?"

She blushed. "I did not see you in the chapel. I ran after you because . . . because I feared you would think me very rude for not wishing you a good afternoon."

"I could never think badly of you." Francoeur's expression clouded over. "I was thinking badly of myself. After our last meeting."

"You have nothing to feel badly for, it is I who . . ." Her voice trailed off, then she looked up. "I liked the blueberries very much."

He nodded thoughtfully. She squinted into the afternoon sun, wondering how to proceed. "I understand you live very near my friend Jeanne Roy. I did not realize you were neighbours. Tell me, how does she fare?"

"The duchess?" Francoeur scratched his beard. "She has remarkable fortitude. She seems to manage very well all on her own."

"Élisabeth Jossard!"

The tenor of the widow's voice made Élisabeth fear she was about to catch a slap. She looked up and saw the widow trundle towards them, her bosom jiggling as she ran. When she caught up she pulled Élisabeth away by the elbow.

"What are you doing? Throwing yourself after that man like a wolf on a rabbit! When I said you shouldn't let him get away, I did not mean for you to chase him through the streets."

"I wasn't—"

"I do understand." The widow took in the figure of Francoeur standing just out of earshot, his hands clasped behind his back. "You can't leave clean laundry on the line for too long, lest the wind carry it off. But, Lili, let the man come to you, for pity's sake."

"No, Maman, you misunderstand. I do not want to marry him—"

"There's no need to play coy now. Half the village has seen you run after him. The other half will know about it by tomorrow. I would say you've made your decision."

Maman Poulin pushed Élisabeth towards Francoeur and took an exaggerated step backwards, though Élisabeth had no doubt she could still hear perfectly well.

"Lili has something to say to you," she encouraged.

The wind ruffled the pine trees, and a raven cawed, once, twice. A sign a change was coming, or an ill omen. If it were the latter, then there was nothing she could do but pray. If it were the former, well. Everyone else seemed to understand what she must do. It was only Élisabeth—poor, lovelorn Lili—who was too stupid to understand. A spinster could not travel around the island, looking for months on end for the strip of land where Jeanne Roy had settled. A spinster could not charge into the tavern, lay a shiny écu on the table and call for the best rider in the land to bring the witch to her. A spinster would sit in the congregation's farmhouse, outstaying her welcome, bearing reproachful looks from the nuns and their hired hands as the cabbage and turnips ran low in the winter months. She would waste her best years waiting for the chance to happen upon the missing sorceress in the market at Ville-Marie. She needed to marry Francoeur to get to Jeanne Roy, but she would need Jeanne Roy's magic to make a marriage to Francoeur work.

She looked at the sandy-haired soldier. She judged him to be five to seven years older than she was. Old enough to marry, young enough not to be set in his ways. He was not small and lithe like Rémy. He had arms like tree trunks, as Lou would say. Élisabeth looked at the tight fit of his doublet against his chest. She could not deny he was strong. Francoeur would make a good husband.

But she would make a terrible wife. A wolf with gryphon wings lived inside her. She was barren. By marrying Francoeur, she would ruin his life.

Unless the witch could cure her.

The raven cawed again, mocking her dilemma. *What will you do? What will you do?* For all the brides' talk of choices, she had none. She clasped her hands together and began the squeeze and prayer.

"Élisabeth?" His hodgepodge hazel eyes filled with concern, and something inside her relented, just a little. She took a deep breath and spoke softly, so that Maman Poulin could not hear.

"The truth is . . . I am afraid."

He reached forward and took her hands in his, squeezing gently so that she could not rub them together anymore.

"There are many things in this world to fear," he said softly. "I promise you that I am not one of them."

She looked up at him. "So. We shall be married?"

Francoeur nodded, a flicker of amusement on his lips. "If that is your desire, then yes. I accept your proposal."

Élisabeth's heart lifted and sank at the same time, a tipsy dance. It was decided. She would never marry Rémy. She would never return to France. She would wed this habitant and hope the witch could cure her so that she did not make both of their lives a misery.

In the pine trees, the raven cawed.

And in her belly the demon waited, an ember that would set the whole forest on fire.

19

On the day of Élisabeth's wedding, the *Saint-Jean-Baptiste* girls came down to the river to tie garlands onto Francoeur's canoe. There were few flowers so late in the season, and the ruby and gold leaves that had garlanded the autumn weddings in an aura of riches lay rotting on the ground. The brides made do with late sneezeweed and goldenrod and tickseed, tucking the sunny buds into the gunwales of the canoe.

"Oh my lover, come to see me, in my chambers, ho!
Oh my lover, came to see me, Papa beat him so."

"Françoise!" Apolline snapped. "Keep your smutty verses to yourself. If anyone hears we shall be mistaken for whores."

"Who would care if I sing a sea shanty?" Françoise threw a stalk of yellow tickseed into the boat. "We're all married women now. We can do as we please."

"I'm not married yet," young Claire piped up.

"Being married means we must set an example in the village," Apolline continued. "For younger girls like Claire."

Claire rolled her eyes.

"You are acting like Old Poulin's widow," Marthe told Apolline as she wiped her hands on her apron. "She's been talking of organizing a charivari to put Anne Lamarque de Folleville in her place."

"She wouldn't dare!" Thérèse said. "Would she?"

"No, she would not," Marthe agreed. "Folleville's tavern is our greatest customer." Still, Marthe was not entirely confident in what she said. The way the widow's eyes lit up when she described the slights she was dealt at the hands of others and how her enemies should suffer made Marthe worry she was the kind of woman who would set fire to her home—Marthe's home—just to watch it burn.

"I think the canoe is pretty enough. Let us go and see if Lili is ready," Marthe said. She led them off the village pier and back towards the bakehouse. She was glad of the company of the other girls, though in her heart she wished it were Rose and Lou who had stayed in town to marry a nail smith or a cobbler, rather than heading out for the farthest côte on the island with their farmers and leaving her with only prudish Apolline and the others.

They arrived at the bakery and went straight into Maman Poulin's salon. Élisabeth wore a clean chemise and cap and an uneasy expression. The widow sat opposite her. Marthe beamed at her encouragingly while Maman Poulin, seemingly not to be outdone, placed her hands on Élisabeth's knees.

"Ville-Marie has never seen a more beautiful bride," she said, her chest puffed out, as if Élisabeth were her own daughter. Marthe wondered if the widow's words were meant kindly, or if she had found a way to slight the rest of the recently married women.

"Your shop is divine, Marthe," Claire said, gazing at the hutch with its baskets of bread and the warm fire in the hearth. "Just what you always wanted."

"Wait until you see the improvements I intend to make," Marthe said. "I want to put a shelf up over there." She motioned to the far wall, over Maman Poulin's head. "And I wonder if we might stock a little jam and honey for the convenience of our customers. Maybe even some small beer."

"Jam and honey?" Maman Poulin recoiled. "Are you mad? This is a bakehouse, not a farmer's gate. And *beer*? People will not buy such a thing, little mistress, they make it themselves!"

"What's all the ruckus?" Verger had woken. He shuffled across the room to place a kiss on Marthe's cheek, his face creased with sleep.

"Your wife has ridiculous ideas that you must put a stop to, Verger. Selling jam and small beer. Of all things!"

"Jam?" Verger chortled. "Who would want to buy jam from a bakery?"

"I was thinking of ways to increase our profit," Marthe mumbled, embarrassed to be told off in front of her friends.

"Maman Poulin," Élisabeth interrupted. "Surely in a bakehouse the notion of brewing one's own bouillon is not such a terrible idea, for do you not already have the knack of fermentation?"

"Silly Lili." Maman Poulin turned and placed a kiss on her forehead. "What a thing to be thinking of on your wedding day. Ignore your sister, for she is full of nonsense. Her husband will need to take a firm hand with her. Or else who knows where her wild ideas will end." The widow glared pointedly at Verger, who scratched his stomach.

"Marthe, may I see you in the workroom?" he said. Marthe could feel both shame and the heat of her temper rising in her chest. She flashed Maman Poulin a glare and stomped across the hallway to the other side of the house. Her husband shuffled after her.

"Have patience," he whispered when they were alone. "New France is desperate for wives. A widow is as good as a maid here. Maman Poulin will marry soon enough and leave you to direct all manner of improvements in the bakery."

"When?" Marthe demanded, ignoring his gentle tone and arranging her features in what she hoped was a look of disapproval, the same face she had seen Apolline make many times. "She is already forty. And she was not capable of providing Old Poulin with any children. Who would want her?"

Verger gave her a reproachful look. "Be generous. I do not want to force her from the home and enterprise she has spent her life building."

"But it is *my* home now. I am your wife. And yet she picks at me every day, like a sore that will not heal. What about me?"

"Enough, Marthe," Verger said, his voice uncharacteristically stern. "Stay your plans until Maman Poulin leaves. Let's have no more talk of jam."

"And what if she does not leave? What if she does not marry, *ever*? What then?" Marthe's cheeks were red with frustration.

Verger dismissed her concerns with a swish of his hand by his ear, like a dog rooting for a flea with its hind leg. He shuffled towards the back door, off to seek solitude by his bread oven in the yard.

Marthe tried to compose herself. Her humiliation thrummed all the way down to her curled toes. She could not bear to walk back into the widow's salon, so clearly chastised and defeated. She patted her cheeks to test their temperature, willing herself to calm down.

It was no use.

She realized she had married for neither love, nor money, and in the widow Poulin, she had a demon of her own she must defeat.

20

Then they were alone, yoked together with as little notion of how they came to be bound to each other as a pair of dumb oxen.

Élisabeth had been anxious to get to the chapel the moment they had signed the marriage contract—her marking an *x* on the parchment with two short, determined strokes, him writing his full name—Joseph Deschamps, known as Francoeur—but he had pushed back the wedding until he could finish the house. He told her she would not be pleased if he brought her to a home without shutters. The oiled paper he used for windowpanes would let the winter air in, chilling their bones and getting their married life off to a cold start. When the moment was finally upon her, she pushed away all thoughts of Rémy and Marcosi, the two creatures that tormented her, and walked down the aisle. Maman Poulin wept, Marthe pleaded with her not to leave it too long before she visited, and the other brides cheered as she left the chapel on her husband's arm.

Now, trotting down to the river with her trunk balanced on his shoulders, she tried to steal a glance at her husband. The trousseau was large and blocked her view of his face.

"I thought the farm was to the east?" she asked. He shifted the trunk higher on his shoulders.

"It is. We are going down to the river to make the journey by canoe."

"By canoe?"

"Why do you not walk on my other side so that I may see you?"

She hesitated, then dropped behind him to appear on his right. He was half a foot taller than she was, and with her white cloth cap pulled tightly around her face she had to turn her body fully to see his eyes. He gave her a smile.

"I am not such an ox that I can carry this trunk all the way to Côte Saint-François. We will travel in the dugout so that I am not spent by the time we arrive."

"How far away is your farm?" she said after a moment.

"*Our* farm is a half hour downriver. Double that time on foot." He paused for a moment, then continued. "Mother Bourgeoys told me you girls-for-marrying judge a man by his holdings, not his heart. Yet you have asked very little about our situation."

Élisabeth stared at the river before them. She could not think of anything else to ask about her new home. The demon inside her was yowling like a barn cat birthing kittens. He made so much noise that Élisabeth was surprised her husband could not hear it.

"We do have a cow," he continued when she did not speak. "In the winter when she gives no milk, I harness her to a sled to speed my travel, although she doesn't like it."

"Where do you travel to?"

"Here and there, up and down the côte. Until the snow comes the river path is only passable on foot. The road is too uneven and rocky for a cart to make the journey."

They reached the village dock. The dugout canoe was already loaded with a sack of flour, a gallon of lamp oil, and a new sickle and flail for next year's harvest, all purchased on credit with her dowry. There was only space left for her trunk and the two of them. Élisabeth blinked at all the wilted flowers tucked into the gunwales as Francoeur put her chest down.

"Next year I hope to purchase a bull, and one day before we are old, I hope we'll own a horse and sleigh. I imagine our winters will then be full of visits not just with our neighbours, but old friends beyond our côte too."

"About our neighbours," she began, seeing her chance. "How long does it take to get from your house to Jeanne Roy's?"

"The wind has whipped your cheeks red raw. Do you have something warm to put on?"

For a moment she could not fathom what he was talking about, she was so anxious to plot her path to Jeanne Roy's home. Then she remembered herself and knelt to open her trunk. She took out a woollen cloak and draped it around her shoulders.

"Does it button up, so that your hands are free to paddle?"

"Paddle?"

He gestured to the loaded craft. "It will be faster if we paddle together."

She buttoned her mantle at the neck, then stood blinking at the canoe. "It looks like a . . . pea pod. Is it safe?"

He laughed. "It's safe. The dugout is not as fine as a birchbark canoe, but I cannot afford one of those. Still, it's a good deal more useful than a pea pod." He knelt down and handed her one of the paddles. "You hold it here, and here. It's not difficult, you'll see."

He reached for her arm to help her step into the hull. She was startled by his touch, and the wooden craft lurched back and forth. He gripped the gunwales to steady it.

"I see the wedding fairies have been decorating." He smiled at the yellow flowers strewn around the boat as he leapt in after her. He pushed off from the quay. "Like this," he said, plunging the paddle into the river. She turned to look over her shoulder, then clenched her jaw as the canoe swayed with her movement. She gripped her paddle more tightly and dipped it into the water. "That's it."

It took several minutes for her to grow accustomed to paddling and she did not speak while she put her mind to the task. She did not want to appear incapable. He would come to realize how useless she was soon enough.

Once she had made peace with paddling, she turned to look back at him and tried again. "How far is Jeanne Roy's house from yours?"

"Mere minutes through the woods. You'll have plenty of days in her company this winter, I am sure. Though I don't doubt at first we will find the duchess more often at our hearth than her own."

"Why is that?" She did not need to ask why Francoeur called Jeanne Roy a duchess. The witch had clearly arrived in the côte with the same haughty airs she had put on at the nun's farmhouse and on the *Saint-Jean-Baptiste*.

"Grandbois is an adventurer, not a farmer. I convinced him to take a plot of land next to mine when we were decommissioned from the regiment. We built cabins, but they are only truly fit for animals. The floors are earthen, and the roofs are made of thatch. Last winter there were nights I thought I would freeze to death it was so cold. In the spring I set about as fast as I could to build myself a proper house. Grandbois did not. Jeanne is living in that old cabin."

The air coming off the river was damp, and Élisabeth's hands were white with cold. She wished they had bought some wool in the village before setting out, for she would need to knit a pair of mittens almost immediately. She wondered what spells Jeanne Roy intended to employ to keep herself warm until springtime.

"I would like to see her as soon as possible," Élisabeth said finally. "First light tomorrow, if I may."

"That's a fine idea. I will come too and see if there is any service I might perform for her."

"No," Élisabeth said, glancing over her shoulder at him. "I should go on my own. She will speak more freely to me, as a woman, and I shall determine whether she bears any resentment against Grandbois for leaving her in such harsh circumstances."

"That's an even better idea." She heard nothing but the sound of the paddles in the water for several minutes, then Francoeur spoke again. "We are a good match, Lili. We work well together."

She felt a stab of guilt. If Jeanne Roy could not cure her, Francoeur's contentment would quickly desert him. She dipped her paddle into the river, thinking of how to respond.

"I was not accustomed to anyone but Marthe calling me Lili until we came here. It was her childhood name for me. She could not say Élisabeth." She lifted her arm to take another stroke and a splash of cold water soaked her sleeve. "How did you come by your regimental name?"

"I am told I have a sincere heart."

She turned back to glance at him, to see if he was teasing. His face was solemn. "I expect you will now want me to call you by your Christian name."

"No. Call me Francoeur." There was a note of bitterness to his voice. "I do not even remember who the boy called Joseph Deschamps was."

"Truly? You cannot tell me anything of your life before you joined the regiment?"

"We're nearing our côte." He ignored her question and pointed to a house just visible from the water. Smoke curled from the chimney and a dull glow came from behind the shutters. "That house belongs to a man called Dufossé. He's a curmudgeon, though I grant him allowances. His wife had a child that died soon after it was born. I'm sure a healthy son will soothe his ill temper."

"Did his wife survive her ordeal?"

"Yes, she is quite well. Though a quiet mouse. You will meet her soon enough. One day you will have children the same age, I don't doubt." At the mention of the duty she owed her husband, the demon Marcosi slithered through her bowels, curling in a ball in the pit of her stomach. "Our house will be the next we see, then a short ways after is Jeanne's cabin."

They passed another stretch of unbroken forest. Dusk had descended on them; whatever sunshine had filtered through the clouds in the afternoon was long gone and they continued the last part of the journey in near darkness.

When they reached the shore of their own ribbon of land, Francoeur beached the canoe. Once she had stepped out, he walked through to the bow and hauled the craft out of the water behind him.

"I had hoped to show you in daylight," he said as he emptied the canoe of its goods. "There's the house. Do you see? Next to it is the old cabin. I use it as a barn now for the cow and the chickens. The pig has already been slaughtered, though. I ran out of feed at the first frost."

She squinted to see the house in the pale starlight. It was built of square pine logs that dovetailed together, with a high sloping roof and neatly white-washed walls. It was solid and handsome, the type of home where a farmer's wife might plant an apple tree out front and gather the windfalls every autumn to sweeten pork and watch her children climb its branches. But no farmer's wife would let her children sleep under its leaves, Élisabeth reminded herself, for any child that slumbers beneath an apple tree is likely to be stolen away by fairies.

Élisabeth shivered and made the sign of the cross.

"They look like giant's fingers."

"What?"

"The trees. They're so bony and bare. They look like giant's fingers reaching towards us."

He studied her for a moment. "They're just trees. You will see in the morning how many I've already cleared to plant our wheat."

She wrapped her arms around herself. "I don't believe . . ." She paused, then shook her head and started again. "I don't believe I have ever been so far from other folk in all my life."

He stared at her again, then beckoned. "Come, I will show you inside. You will see how comfortable it is."

He heaved Élisabeth's trunk onto his shoulders and led her up the path. When they reached the house, he opened the door, and she noted the scent of freshly cut pine. Inside, he set her trunk down and reached for a flint to light a crow's beak lamp. The wick sputtered to life illuminating the whole room.

"I built that table, and those two chairs. You'll see the hearth opens on both sides, so that it heats the whole room. We can add another chimney on the far wall as our family grows. Over there is where we will sleep."

There was a straw pallet on the floor, a cherrywood cradle by its side. Élisabeth blanched.

Her purpose in Francoeur's home could not be plainer.

She felt a twist inside her and rubbed her chest so that Marcosi might loosen his grip on her heart.

This is not how she imagined she would pass her wedding night. Once, she thought she would spend it in the Delaunays' house on the hill. She remembered how she'd met Rémy in the orchard to press him on the details of their wedding, long after they had walked up the hillside together—after the apple blossom had gone and the wasps had come. Rémy had not answered. He'd pulled her towards him and pretended to examine her face for flaws. *Too many freckles,* he'd teased and then elaborately shrugged, as if freckles were the sort of thing one couldn't be too particular about if one were looking for a good wife. She'd swatted his arm as if he were one of the insects trying to suck all the sweetness out of the windfalls. *You love me,* she had insisted, and he had laughed and nuzzled her ear, the sound of his voice blending in with the drone of the wasps all around them.

Élisabeth shook her head. It was not freckles that mattered if one was choosing a wife. It only mattered that she be able to produce a child to lay in a cherrywood cradle.

"This winter I'll build a cabinet bed in the corner," Francoeur continued, nodding in the direction of the far wall. "In the winter we can pull the doors shut to keep warm. What do you say to walnut?"

She took a step backwards to touch the wall, tracing the knots in the logs with her fingers, letting them fall into the grooves. She did not know what to say to walnut. What did it matter to her whether he built them a box of walnut, or cherry, or enchanted applewood? She glanced at her husband, her eyes lingering on his broad chest. She thought about how they had met, when she'd mistakenly laid her hand on his buttocks. She remembered the firmness of the muscle beneath the soft serge and imagined the moment when he would pull the doors to the cabinet bed shut on a winter's night, locking them into their marriage bed.

Nothing for them to do all night but burn with infernal fire.

She felt a rash of heat spread across her chest and thrust her hand into her pocket. She pulled out her holy water vessel and stretched to place the talisman on top of the lintel. When she turned back, Francoeur was standing in front of her.

"Élisabeth, I am very glad that I married you," he said, holding her gaze.

She dropped her eyes. "And I you."

He took her hand and laced his fingers through hers, then pulled her close to his chest. The smell of woodsmoke and sweat was dizzying. She felt Marcosi's tail coil between her legs. To her horror, she felt the beast begin to growl with pleasure.

Francoeur bent forward. She stood as rigid as a possessed nun, waiting for her husband's touch. But he surprised her by brushing past her lips and landing his kiss on the curve of her neck.

Her flesh responded in a thousand tiny bumps. His rough beard caused her to shiver all the way to her toes and the demon to flap his wings. Her lips parted, about to moan, when she caught herself. She shuddered instead, full of shame. It was as the priest said. *The female is a slave to her filthy lusts.*

"No!" She pushed Francoeur away, though she did not know if she was telling her husband or her own self to stop.

"Very well." Francoeur brought her hand to his lips and kissed it before releasing her. He smiled but Élisabeth looked at the floor. She felt sick.

"Élisabeth, look at me," he said softly. She bit her lip to brace herself; his hazel eyes were full of concern. "Are you frightened of what is to happen next?"

Marcosi laughed so loudly Élisabeth knew that if she opened her mouth to answer Francoeur, the wolf's howling would echo through the house. No, she was not frightened of carnal relations. She was afraid of what the demon was making her feel. *Where is the sin? He is your husband now.* But she had also been Rémy's handfasted bride, hadn't she? And that union had been cursed. The Devil would not have come for her if she had not been in mortal sin. If she gave in to lust again, would she ever be rid of the demon?

"We don't have to rush to bed just because it's our wedding night," Francoeur continued. "We have months—years—to get to know each other. We do not need to start our family tonight."

"And what if . . . children do not come?" Her voice caught and came out as a rasp. She placed her fingers on her throat.

"Of course we shall have children," he said. "God will bless us. One day this house will be so full of noise and disarray that you will laugh when you think back on this night, and your worries about being alone in the woods."

She pulled her hand away and stood up.

"I am tired," she mumbled.

"Will you eat some bread before you sleep?"

"I am not hungry."

She made the sign of the cross and knelt by the mattress, murmuring the Pater, the Ave, and the Credo. She was aware of Francoeur kneeling to join her in prayer. When they were finished, she rose and waited for him to turn his back. She slipped off her skirts and bodice until she was wearing nothing but her shift and slid under the blanket.

She heard Francoeur's suspenders hit the wooden floor. The straw rustled as he joined her in bed. Though when he rolled onto his side, he took care to keep his distance so that she could not feel his back against hers.

She closed her eyes. Good. As the village priest had instructed her, she would go to sleep thinking of death, eternal repose, and the sepulchre where Jesus' body lay.

Touch him, the demon Marcosi whispered to her in the dark. *Lay your hand on his thigh*. She made a fist with her hand.

No. If she could not bear children, if she took pleasure in the marriage bed, it would break the holy sacrament of marriage. She would not bend to Marcosi's will. She would not slip into sin. Not until the witch cured her curse and made her fruitful again. She opened her eyes again.

"Francoeur? Are you awake?"

"Yes."

"I think tomorrow I will be hungry. After I visit with Jeanne Roy, I . . . I am certain my appetite will return."

"I'm sure it will."

The straw rustled again.

"Lili?"

"Yes?"

"We do have all the time in the world."

She nodded in the darkness.

Press against him. Lay your hand on his back.

She clutched her hand to her side, squeezing her eyes shut and saying her prayers over and over again.

One more day and she would see the witch.

One more day and the demon would be turned to dust.

21

The soldier wiped his runny nose on his sleeve, then gestured towards a wooden house across from the old barracks. Marthe gripped her basket in her hand as she stepped through the fort's main gate. With the Iroquois truce bringing security to the village and the troops of the Carignan-Salières now decommissioned, the fort was falling into disrepair. The handful of men left behind seemed the sort to have been forgotten in the refuse pit, without enough sense to find their way out. Marthe brushed past the sickly soldier and made her way across the compound to Governor de Lafredière's door.

She had given up waiting for him to visit the bakery. She could not stand the idle torment of wondering when he might come and what advice he might give her. She had decided to take matters into her own hands. It had not taken her long to realize that her husband's stores of flour were fixed and meagre, and with just a little more of the precious grain Verger could increase their living by baking more bread. She hoped that with so few soldiers left, she might appeal to Hannibal Flotte de Lafredière to give them a few sacks of the fort's flour.

She rapped on the front door and then pinched her cheeks to redden them. She had put on a clean skirt and laced her stays as tightly as she could, forcing her breasts up and over the top of her bodice. It was the best she could do with her waist already starting to thicken. Ever since she had felt the tiny butterfly wings start to flap inside her womb, her shape had started to change. She was overjoyed to see evidence of the child growing inside her—though perhaps too fast? When she had confessed her news to Barbe Poulin, the widow had not seemed pleased. Within a week she had started tapping the side of her nose, muttering that Marthe was putting on weight far too quickly.

Marthe wished she'd kept her condition to herself. Perhaps that was why she did not tell the widow or her husband where she was going when she left for the fort.

The iron hinges groaned, as a mean-faced servant, her thick eyebrows knit into a scowl, pulled back the door. "What do you want?"

Marthe smiled brightly.

"Good day, I am the baker's wife, Marthe Jossard. I have come to offer the governor a basket of our finest loaves and some buttered taffy, as it will soon be the Feast of Saint Catherine." Marthe flashed the servant her dimples. She had sweated over the taffy the night before, telling Verger she was delirious with cravings for the sweet treat. In truth, for a measure of molasses, she was betting she could advance her family's standing.

"Saint Catherine's Day is not for weeks." The servant reached her hand out. "But I'll take it."

"May I come in? I should like to give it to the governor myself."

The woman stood solidly in the doorway, gazing at Marthe. "I wouldn't, if I were you."

"Please. I'll only stay a moment."

The servant's mouth drooped, weighted down with whatever regrets her thirty-some years had brought her. Marthe was embarrassed, suddenly, to be standing before her, bright-eyed and well-groomed.

"Suit yourself," the servant muttered.

She stood back to let Marthe pass. "My lord," she called out sarcastically. "You have a visitor."

She took Marthe's cloak and led her into a large room where the governor lounged on a settee. Two men sat opposite him. The salon was filled with more items of furniture than Marthe had ever seen in her life. Paintings and mirrors hung from the walls, as well as a gilded crucifix. There were several stuffed chairs, elaborately embroidered, as well as the upholstered settee where Lafredière reclined. Marthe marvelled that he had brought such luxuries with him from France, and imagined the chairs were so comfortable she would be content to sit in one all day long.

"It is definitely a weapon," one of the men said. "The way the old priest described it."

"Well of course it's a weapon, you dunce. But what does it *do*?" The governor looked up and noticed Marthe standing by the door.

"You have a visitor," the servant repeated more loudly.

"So I see." The governor's voice flashed with irritation and Marthe thought he might snap at them both. Instead he rose and flicked his fingers at the men. The gesture was enough to make them stand. "Find out who Chamberlen is. Someone will have heard of him."

As the men filed past, one of them leered at Marthe. She was astonished when the servant cuffed him on the arm and muttered for him to mind himself. Marthe clutched her basket of bread tighter as Lafredière approached.

"Good day, pretty wife. What a pleasure to see you again."

Marthe stared at the governor of Montréal. He was not wearing his wig, and his eye patch was askew. As he got closer she could see a cluster of puckered flesh where his eye had once been. She hesitated. Without his wig and gold-brocade coat he seemed just like any other man. She checked herself and curtseyed, remembering her purpose. He was a nobleman and she had come to advance herself.

"I have come to offer you a basket to celebrate Saint Catherine's Day," she said.

"How delicious." Without looking at the bread and taffy, he handed the basket to the servant. "Bring us some brandy." He took Marthe by the arm and escorted her towards the chairs. The door shut with a conspicuous click.

Marthe sat in one of the stuffed chairs and noticed it was not quite as comfortable as she had imagined. She was gazing around the room when she heard the crash of pewter on the other side of the door.

"My servant is clumsy," Lafredière said. "Lazy too." He leaned towards her. "What do you think? Should I get rid of her?" He winked mischievously.

Marthe was taken aback. The governor of Montréal was asking *her* advice? She paused, choosing her words carefully.

"Perhaps the work is too much for one person. Could you not hire someone else to help her?"

"You are clever," he purred, although she could not think how her comment could be deemed especially intelligent. "I grant that she may have more work now, with the Panis having run away."

"Your slaves . . . ran away?"

"You had not heard?" He sounded surprised.

"No, my lord. I am not one to trade in gossip like a fort's trumpet." She thought about Barbe Poulin—she was not inclined to call her *Maman* ever again—blaring everyone's business all over the Place Royale.

The governor leaned sideways on the settee, looping his long legs over one arm. His manner was so informal that Marthe felt uncomfortably prim, sitting upright in the chair opposite him.

"But you are the baker's wife. The women of Ville-Marie like to gather in your home, I'm told. If *you* had not heard of their disappearance, then perhaps my subjects are not discussing me behind my back."

"I . . . I had not heard anything."

He eyed her again, then swung his legs off the arm of the settee and leaned towards her.

"Let's talk no more of it. The slaves were only children and not good for much. Easily replaceable for a few hundred livres. Though I will have to wait until summer when fresh ones come in with the furs. And that is tedious." His voice dropped, forcing her to lean closer to hear what he said next.

"This country is an icy Hell from November to April. Once the rivers freeze, we are locked in, without supplies. No spices, no slaves. None of the comforts of life."

Marthe hesitated. She could not think what to say to this man, so rich he could buy another of God's creatures to wait on him. She realized he was no longer looking at her eyes, but at her swelling bosom. She began to doubt the wisdom of trying to tighten her stays. She leaned back in her chair and his attention shifted to her face.

"Perhaps if your woman is overwhelmed by her work, you might consider our bakehouse providing you with your daily bread?"

The governor laughed out loud. "Well played, pretty wife. I had forgotten that you are on this earth to earn your fortune. For a moment I thought you were paying me the compliments of the coming feast day." He pouted at her, and she squirmed.

"My lord, forgive me. I do want to earn my fortune, I do. But our stores of flour are running low. I . . . I was thinking perhaps if the fort has any surplus grain, you might have it milled for our use."

She eyed him warily, waiting for his reaction. He smiled and patted the settee.

"How interesting. Why don't you come over here, so that we may negotiate the terms of your request."

Marthe looked over her shoulder. The servant had not returned with the brandy. She wasn't sure if it was proper for her to sit so close to the governor. In fact, even though she was married, she was not certain she should be sitting alone in a room with him at all. When she had imagined her visit, she pictured more members of the household being present. Lafredière seemed to sense her indecision. "I won't bite," he said.

She thought of the little bag of coins she knew her husband kept hidden behind the hearth and thought how it might fatten if he could only bake more bread. She rose and moved closer to the governor. Lafredière left his hand on the seat between them.

"So you want more flour so that your husband may work harder. Yet you do not realize how easy it is for you, as a woman, to earn a fortune yourself." His lips were only inches from Marthe's ear. She put her hand to her cap and started to smooth the rough cloth as she spoke.

"My lord, I should have thought that it is only right that my husband, being so young and strong, would be the one to earn—"

Lafredière shook his head, and she fell silent. She was close enough to see a blue vein throb in his temple and fine red lines showing from underneath the powder on his cheeks. She had not imagined a gentleman would powder his face the way that ladies did. She leaned as far back from him as she could without appearing to be rude.

"There are a thousand men in this colony with brawn. They all want to run into the woods and come back clutching five hundred beaver pelts. None is distinguishable from the next. It is the women here—the very, very few women— who are desirable. And do you know what that means?" Marthe shook her head. "You are in a position to take advantage of that scarcity. You may trade on it."

"What do I have to trade?" she asked.

Lafredière smiled. Then he reached out and picked a hair from her bodice, a stray she had not noticed when she had combed and plaited and prepared herself for her visit. He held it between his fingers for a moment, then let it drop to the floor.

"What about a kiss?"

Marthe felt a wave of sickness come over her, worse than she had felt since she had fallen pregnant. She tried to stand up. The governor grabbed her arm and pulled her down.

"Don't run away. You came here for my counsel," he reminded her.

"Forgive me, but—"

"Listen to me," he cut her off. "Ask yourself what a kiss is worth. You give it freely to your husband at night, don't you?" She did not answer. She felt the skin under his grip start to burn and glanced at the door, measuring her escape. "I would shower you in silver and gold, for a kiss."

"No." Marthe tried to pull away. His hand tightened on her arm, and she could not stop herself from whimpering from the sharp pain of the cinch. He leaned in towards her, his lips parted. She could smell brandy on his breath. She flinched and turned away, bracing for the feeling of his mouth on hers. Then at the last moment, he bowed his head and kissed the top of her breast.

"Silver and gold," he murmured, tracing his lips along the top of her bodice. His hand pinned her in place so that she could not move. The sour smell of his breath was so overpowering she wanted to gag. She knew she should scream for the servant, but if she came now Marthe would be humiliated. Maybe even ruined, like her sister. Poor Élisabeth, forever wringing her hands and muttering her prayers. Marthe could feel the governor's spittle on her breasts and the bile rose in her throat. No, she would not be ruined. She gathered all her strength and jerked herself away.

She ran for the door but Lafredière was too quick. He blocked her path and slammed her against the wall. In an instant his hands were around her neck, his one eye bulging as he glared at her, beady as a falcon's.

He began to squeeze.

Marthe could not draw breath. She felt the child inside her flutter. She tried to scream but her voice came out as a squawk.

"You won't earn a sol that way," he snarled, lifting one hand from her neck to slap her into silence. The reprieve from the chokehold was enough to allow her to gasp. She drew in one long, ragged breath. But before she could call for help, his hands were wrapped around her throat again.

Suddenly the servant walked in, holding a decanter of brandy. Her face was blank.

"Your drink, my lord."

Lafredière released Marthe and she stumbled towards the door, her hands hovering like a halo around her throat. She could hear Lafredière shouting but she didn't look back. She reached the door and yanked it open. The hinges screeched. She tumbled outside and was struck by a blast of cold air. She ran across the fort's crumbling compound. When she was safely through the gate, she collapsed against the palisade, trying to catch her breath. She'd started to pray, when a hand on her back made her jump.

It was the servant, with her cloak in her hand.

"You forgot this," she said.

Marthe grabbed it. She could barely speak. "What . . . what in Our Lady's name . . . ?"

"I tried to warn you," she said.

"You did not," Marthe rasped.

"You knew well enough what sort of man he is. Everyone does." Marthe clutched the cloak to her chest and reached up to touch her swollen neck. "You got off lightly," the servant muttered. "He's done far worse to others."

"Worse?"

The servant nodded, her lips pursed. Marthe noticed the lines around her eyes.

"Why do you stay in his household?"

"I'm married to one of his men."

Marthe looked at the servant. Had she come on a bride ship just like her? For all their talk of choices, she realized how easy it was to make a bad one. And once made, how difficult it was to undo. She put her cloak around her shoulders and tied it so that the crimson thumbprints on her neck could not be seen.

"I am sorry for you. Maybe you can run away, like the Panis did?"

The servant snorted. "You may believe they ran away, if it makes you feel better."

"What do you mean?"

A wave of anger crossed the woman's face. "You're one of the stupidest girls I've ever seen, with your basket of taffy, preening around in front of that man. Get away from here!"

"I didn't preen—"

"Take my advice. Say nothing about this and go on with your business. No one has to know you were here."

"I will do no such thing. I will tell the Sulpicians what he's done."

The servant shook her head. "Then you are a greater fool than I thought. He'll ruin you for speaking out. Do you want to see his men sent round your bakery every other day, checking your prices and peering into every sack of flour for mites and mice? And that would be the least of his revenge. Last year a habitant objected to some of the governor's soldiers stomping through his fields, ruining the crops as they hunted on his land. Lafredière saw the poor man hung from a wooden horse with sixty-pound weights on his limbs, just for complaining."

Marthe gaped at the servant, wordless and horrified. What had she done? She had wanted to help make her family's fortune, not take away the little they had. Hannibal Flotte de Lafredière was the governor of Montréal. A nobleman with an estate to return to in France. She was an orphan barred from ever returning to her village in Normandy.

As Marthe ran away from the fort, tears streamed down her cheeks. She was an idiot for believing she could make something of her life. How had she been so stupid? Her hands trembled as she crossed the bridge over the Little River.

But how could she blame herself? It was her sister's fault for lying with Rémy. If Élisabeth had not been so naive, she would not have had cause to drag them both to a place utterly forsaken by God. Élisabeth was a fool, and Marthe would never forgive her.

Except—had Marthe not just made the very same mistake? She had turned to a wealthy man to secure her future. And if she said nothing, then she would be no better than Élisabeth, wringing her hands and wishing for a cure for her misery.

No. Marthe would not fall fearful, like her sister had done. She would tell someone. She would see the governor punished.

Now, more than wanting to get rich, she wanted to get even.

22

At first light Élisabeth got up and dressed. By the grace of the newly built, solid wooden floors, she padded silently across the room and slipped outside before her husband awoke. The air was crisp and the woods silent, but for birdsong and the river lapping against the shore. She could see where Francoeur had cleared some trees, but still felt surrounded by menacing giants, as if a maple or oak might bend down and grab her with a rough limb.

She pushed the lower branches away from her face as she stole through the woods. She had listened carefully to Francoeur's description of the côte and knew Jeanne Roy's home would be along the forest path to the east. Though the settlers talked of bears and the Iroquois with equal dread, she told herself that Marcosi the wolf could rip the flesh off anything that tried to attack her, be it man, bear, or tree. Before long, the cabin appeared. It was made entirely of birch with a tangle of thatched branches and moss for its roof. Clay and sod had been stuffed into the gaps between the logs; smoke rose from a makeshift chimney. Élisabeth stopped. It was a fairy-tale witch's hut, something her mother might have warned her about. She approached with caution and knocked on the door.

After a moment Jeanne Roy appeared. She raised her eyebrows when she saw Élisabeth.

"You."

The witch's hair fell loose down her back; it did not look as if she had combed it in the two months since they had last met. Her velvet dress was covered in dirt and twigs and herbs, as if she had been rolling in the autumn leaves. Despite this, the arch of her eyebrow and the set of her jaw told Élisabeth that Jeanne Roy had lost none of her pride.

"I have come to pay my respects to you." Élisabeth bowed her head and sunk into a deep curtsey.

"All the way from Ville-Marie?"

"No, from next door. I married your neighbour, Francoeur."

The witch looked at her with such curiosity that Élisabeth felt as if she were a frog trapped in a wishing well, while an inquisitive child poked her with sticks.

"He said he was going off to be married. He did not say to whom. Come in."

The cabin was small and warm, like an animal's den. On the walls were more furs than Élisabeth had ever seen in her life; beaver, certainly, but also other creatures she recognized as marten, mink, and perhaps weasel. Two stools squatted in front of a stone fireplace held loosely together with wattle and daub. A black cauldron hung from a hook over the flame. There was no other furniture save a long table placed against the back wall. Upon it was a mess of branches and dried herbs and a very thick book. On top sat Jeanne Roy's strange doll, staring at them with dead eyes. Élisabeth avoided looking at it and stared instead at the feeble hearth.

"How will you keep warm, if it's as cold as they say it will be in the winter?"

"I have been invited to stay with a friend." Jeanne Roy sat down on one of the stools, gesturing for her to do the same. "Though I expect I will be able to manage for some weeks yet. I do love the cold."

"Which friend?" Élisabeth knew Jeanne Roy had barely spoken to any of the other brides.

"My friend Wari. She's Agnier, but she lives in the Jesuit mission village across the river at La Prairie. When the ice and snow set in, she will come to fetch me."

"She's what?" Élisabeth balked.

"Agnier is the French name for her people. I believe others call them the Mohawk."

Élisabeth stared blankly.

"One of the Haudenosaunee Confederacy." Jeanne gave her a defiant look, then let out a deep sigh. "She's Iroquois, Élisabeth."

"Iroquois! You . . . you will spend the winter with . . . the Iroquois?"

Jeanne Roy tipped her head back to laugh. "Why should I not?"

"Because they are our enemies! Sister Gagnon says they—"

"I'm not in the least bit interested in what that nun says."

"But are you not frightened of them?"

"No. I am intrigued by them. Wari says in her village grandmothers have the final say in all matters. They decide what crops shall be planted, what punishment the guilty deserve, who shall marry whom. Just think what we could learn from the Haudenosaunee! Had we French half their sense, I might not have been saddled with either of my husbands." Jeanne Roy folded her hands and looked suddenly chagrined, as if she regretted speaking so freely.

"You've been married before?"

"Yes, Élisabeth. I am not the first widow to take a ship to the New World in search of a better life."

"Forgive me," Élisabeth said quickly. She knew she must not pry; Marthe said she must flatter and encourage the witch to look well upon her so that she would grant the wish she'd promised. "What a burden to have been widowed so young."

"I am not in need of your pity."

Élisabeth could not put a foot right. She shut her mouth and thought of how to put the witch in a generous mood. Jeanne Roy stood to reach for a pitcher of water, pouring it into the cauldron hanging above the fire. As it hit the hot iron, the water hissed and the steam rose, drawing out the dank animal smell of the cabin. Jeanne Roy pinched leaves off bundles of herbs lying on the stone hearth and added them to the cauldron.

"I have not talked about my life in France for many months. Francoeur warned me I would want for company alone here in the woods. Perhaps he was right."

"You may confide in me," Élisabeth offered, seeing her chance. "I too have a past I do not speak of. And a very grave problem. Though I believe you can help me."

The witch looked up from stirring the cauldron. "What makes you think *I* can help you?"

"I . . . I . . . it was my sister's idea. Marthe suggested it. Without your help a fate worse than anything you can imagine awaits me."

"I can imagine a great many terrible things," Jeanne Roy said softly. "I doubt your fate is worse than any of them." She gave Élisabeth a long look. "It is true that I have helped many women in my time, though I am curious how your sister came to know it." She paused and spoke in a low voice. "Are you worried about bearing a child?"

"Yes. I am. Can you see it just by looking at me? Can you tell that I am barren?"

"Barren?"

"I cannot bear children."

"I . . . I thought you were concerned about being *with* child."

"No!" Élisabeth recoiled, realizing the witch's meaning. "Quite the opposite. I am barren. Cursed to be childless forevermore."

Jeanne Roy narrowed her eyes. "How do you know that you cannot bear children?"

"I will tell you my entire story willingly, if you promise to help me."

"Of course I will help you," Jeanne Roy said, placing her hand on Élisabeth's shoulder. The witch's touch made the demon Marcosi twist in a circle and whine, knowing his end was near. "It is what I have trained to do."

Élisabeth realized then the breadth of Jeanne Roy's power: not just a witch of forest and fable, but a sorceress with *training*, with knowledge that could surely defeat the rustic spells of the Winter Witch, a hag of no standing compared to her. Élisabeth felt a wave of relief wash over her. She laid her hands in her lap and cleared her throat.

"Shortly after my two brothers died, my father grew ill. To pay for his treatment I went into service. The eldest son in the family favoured me with his affection and soon we were in love."

Jeanne Roy made an indistinct sound. Élisabeth studied the witch but she continued to stir her potion without comment.

"My family was poor, and I had no dowry. Rémy's parents thought more of themselves than they ought to have done and would have never consented to our marriage. So Rémy came up with a scheme that would force his mother's hand."

Élisabeth grew warmer as she spoke. She parsed her words when describing their passion on the clifftop, leaving out their continued meetings in the orchard and cellar, or wherever Rémy found to press himself upon her. She explained his plot to conceive a child and then announce it to his parents so that they could not refuse the match. She made sure the witch understood how alone they were, how they had not a single ally in the household, how even Old Geneviève, the cook, muttered dour warnings. Jeanne Roy listened intently while pouring the brew she'd made into a tin cup and handing it to Élisabeth. She took a tentative sip. The potion slid down her throat, scalding Marcosi and causing the demon to dance on his hind legs and whimper with pain. Élisabeth glowed at this proof of the witch's powers. She leaned in closer.

"So you see, on Saint Agnes's Eve I was not obliged to eat dumb cake and walk backwards up the stairs to know whom I would marry. My dreams were already assured. Then, they turned into a nightmare."

A slight frown formed across the witch's face. "Go on."

"Nine months ago, in February, I was with Rémy in the tavern by the mill." Élisabeth found her words slowly, remembering the night that the household had gone out to celebrate Shrove Tuesday. While the others dallied behind, Rémy had accompanied her down the hill, walking beside her, so it had felt like they were walking out together, just the two of them, though he'd been careful not to touch her elbow.

"We were about to tell his parents, knowing that my condition was certain. We were perfectly content, united in our joy. But no sooner had we settled at a table than a powerful witch stormed into the tavern, ablaze with fury. She pointed her finger—"

"Stop." Jeanne Roy's face turned dark. "What do you mean?"

"A witch came into the tavern. She pointed her finger and laid a curse upon me. I lost the child that very night."

A sharp sadness came over Élisabeth as visions of that night flashed like lightning in a summer storm. Rémy laughing as he returned to the table with a stone jug. The bitter taste of the wine. Élisabeth leaning closer to her lover, whispering to him what it felt like now that the child had quickened. And once that word—*quickened*—had escaped her mouth, the door blowing open in one wintery breath. She had turned, expecting to see Old Geneviève, whose hip troubled her more at night, limping in to join them. Instead, an unsettling sight: a haggard crone with long grey hair, dressed in rags. Cloudy eyes casting around the room, seeking something she could not find. Then, the raised hand, the long bony finger pointed at Élisabeth.

'Twas for you.

At first, Élisabeth had covered her mouth to hide her titter, but Rémy leapt up and rushed towards the hag. She saw a flash of silver and an ashen face.

Rémy came back to the table, his voice shaking as he told her what the Winter Witch had done. She shook her head—*that cannot be, I have eaten no fruit nor been touched by her hands, how can I be cursed?*—but the turmoil in his eyes told her the truth. Her brow grew slick with sweat and her breathing shallow as the spell began its terrible work. She stumbled back to her father's house, whispering prayers to ward off the cramping. But the holy words—*grace, blessed,* and the one she could barely utter without choking, *sinners*—rang with such sibilance that it sounded like she was hissing through a forked tongue.

That was when the child slipped from between her legs in a slick of dark blood, and the demon took its place in her belly.

"I cannot believe it." Jeanne Roy sounded dismayed.

"It's true," Élisabeth murmured through tears. "I cannot have another child until the Winter Witch is killed or the curse is lifted by a more powerful sorceress."

The sound that broke from Jeanne Roy's lips was as ragged as an animal being slaughtered. She placed her hands over her eyes and her knuckles grew white as she pressed her fingertips against her forehead.

"You are not barren . . . because an old woman . . . pointed her finger at you." She spoke haltingly, struggling to form the words.

Élisabeth did not understand. "But I saw what she did. Rémy explained it to me. I lost the baby that very night."

Jeanne Roy rubbed her forehead, as if trying to smooth out the creases on her brow. She began to mutter in a way that made Élisabeth uneasy.

"You stupid . . . ignorant . . . *peasant.*"

Élisabeth flinched. Inside, the demon Marcosi began to growl.

Jeanne Roy's voice rose. "Do you really believe that? You believe that a woman can simply point her finger at you and by her will alone do you harm?"

"Yes, of course." Élisabeth blinked. Jeanne Roy's anger was startling. "Such curses are near impossible to break. Rémy spent weeks searching the woods to find the hag and kill her. When he did not succeed, I came to this holy land at the edge of the world to lay myself down on its sacred soil. Yet that too has not worked."

Jeanne Roy's face twisted and her voice shook. "You sent your lover to *kill* her?"

Élisabeth grew wary. She lowered her voice to prevent Marcosi from hearing what she said next, lest it stir the demon further. "The Winter Witch still lives. If she were dead, my demon would have disappeared."

"Your demon?"

"He is called Marcosi. When the Winter Witch pointed her finger and cursed me, she must have caused him to grow inside my womb. It is why I am barren."

Jeanne Roy groaned. She wrapped her hands around her own neck and kneaded the base of her skull. She took a deep breath and gazed at Élisabeth, shaking her head. "It is the stupidity more than anything else that I cannot abide. Malice is comprehensible. One need only read the Bible to understand that men are greedy and hateful. It's the ignorance—the *wilful*, lazy ignorance!— that is so . . . so reprehensible."

Élisabeth flinched. She had known that approaching a witch would be dangerous, that Jeanne Roy was bound to exact a heavy price. But she did not know she would have to bear insult as well.

"I am not stupid," she said quietly.

"Are you certain?" Jeanne Roy taunted her. "Let us look at your story again. In the study of natural philosophy we are taught to include only what we know to be true—what we have proven—in our observations. Shall we try that and see what truth your story reveals?"

"I don't know what you mean."

"Of course not, because you have no education. I presume you cannot read or even write your name. No? Of course not. So let us go over your tale of 'witchcraft' again. Let us see if there is another hypothesis we might consider."

"I don't know . . ." Élisabeth saw the bottled fury in Jeanne Roy's eyes and stopped. If the witch wanted her to start from the beginning, then so be it. She would have to explain herself more clearly.

"We lay together for many months. I told Rémy I was with child after I felt the quickening. He said he would tell his parents—"

"Stop. A question. Was he pleased to hear you were carrying his child?"

"Yes, of course he was." Élisabeth thought back to the moment she had felt the baby flutter inside of her and had run to tell Rémy that what they had suspected was for certain. He was not in the house, and the old cook grumbled he was more likely than not in the tavern. Élisabeth had found him in his usual place by the window, a tankard of cider before him. He was laughing with the innkeeper's daughter. The girl was wiping the table in such a way that made her breasts jiggle. But nothing the pock-faced barmaid could flash at Rémy mattered now that Élisabeth was with child—she had won. She had whispered her news into his ear, letting her lips graze his lobe, and had pulled back, ablaze with triumph. He had smiled, slowly.

"It was his idea that we should lay together. He said, 'I will tell my parents' and then 'we will be married before you start to show.' So yes, he was very pleased."

"And *did* he tell his parents?"

Élisabeth faltered. "He did not have time to speak to them before . . . before the witch cursed me. I . . . I was not at that moment staying at the Rémy household because my father had taken a turn for the worse. I was at home, helping Marthe care for him. Before too long Rémy knocked at our door and said he wanted to step out with me to celebrate."

"How long after you had told him did this occur?"

"I don't know . . . It was February. A fortnight? Not more."

"Thus he had known for two weeks about your condition and had not told his parents. Continue."

Élisabeth swallowed, the demon twisting furiously in her gut. "We sat down, we called for our drinks, the witch came in. It was as I said."

"What did you eat before your miscarriage?"

"Nothing. Food had not been sitting easily in my stomach, as is normal before the quickening. We drank wine, too sour for my liking, but Rémy said it would do me good. The witch came in soon after."

"I see."

"You may think me a fool to drink to my own success before it was assured, but at that moment I believed myself to be the winner of a prize beyond all imagination, to be marrying my true love. Then I saw a movement at the window. A telltale sign of a witch. A shadow, something you see out of the corner of your eye, then when you look there's nothing but a creeping feeling up your spine."

"That is why you believe the woman was a witch? That you didn't turn your head in time to see her through a window?"

Élisabeth forced herself not to scowl. She had not said it right. Jeanne Roy made it sound ridiculous, but Rémy had been definite. "Rémy told me she was a witch."

"And did you believe everything your lover told you? Or did you gather any proof of this woman's ability to perform magic?" Jeanne Roy's tone was so biting that Élisabeth wanted to scream, but she knew if she did, that would be the end of her chance of a cure. Still, she raised her chin as she continued.

"I had a feeling when I saw her. The tavern door opened and a gust of cold wind rushed into the room. There was the Winter Witch, the one Papa had always warned us about. The one who feasts on infants and has long sought to do our village harm. She noticed me and fixed her eyes on me with a . . . with a fiendish expression. I remember she had a witch's mark on her cheek, under her eye. She lifted her finger, and it was gnarled and bony with a long, black nail."

"You could see her fingernails from where you were sitting?"

Élisabeth ignored the question. "''Twas for you,' the Winter Witch called out, pointing at me, and Rémy jumped into the air with fright. He understood right away what was happening. He rushed at the old witch and pushed her out the door. I could hear the hag screech as he did so, like glass shattering on a flagstone, loud and sharp. Then I saw Rémy fling a silver coin at her, as you are supposed to do to keep the curse from sticking. He came back to me and told me not to mind a thing, he would take care of me, and he wrapped my cloak around my shoulders, and told me to finish my drink. He was very tender, very caring, and he said he would take me out the back so that the witch could not lay her eyes on me again. I was terrified to see Rémy so affected, so I made him tell me who the woman was. He said he didn't want to frighten me further, but I insisted. He started to weep as he told me the truth. That she was the Winter Witch."

Jeanne Roy formed a steeple with her index fingers and tapped it against her frowning mouth. The slow, deliberate movement looked like she was casting a spell.

"And did Rémy explain how she came to pick on you of all people?"

"She lays curses on beautiful girls because she is jealous of their youth and wants it for herself. Rémy said that she wanted me because I am quite pretty . . ." Élisabeth paused, aware of sounding boastful. "But do not think me so vain as to believe that. I have since wondered if it wasn't Madame Delaunay who caused the witch to come for me. She was always suspicious of her son's affection for me. I believe it was she who encouraged the cook to keep us apart. Old Geneviève was forever telling me to stay away from Rémy."

"And what happened to the woman after she was pushed out the door?" Jeanne Roy's voice was tight, as if she could not breathe. "You said your lover could not find her?"

"No. She was gone with the frost in the morning. It's what she's done for a hundred years, and she could go on like that for a hundred more. Until she is killed, I can never, ever bear children. I had thought I could lift the curse by coming to Ville-Marie, but I was wrong. I can never bear children, unless you, Jeanne, can break the curse."

"Me? What part do I play in this fantasy?"

A spark escaped from a crackling log, falling at their feet. The witch snuffed the cinder out with her heel. Élisabeth took a deep breath to force the keening demon down. She sank to her knees, her hands clasped together.

"I know you are a far more powerful and accomplished sorceress than the Winter Witch of Saint-Philbert. I saw what you did when the ship was in danger of sinking. And you magicked my letter of good conduct out of my hand! I've seen you swim like a mermaid in the sea. Please, for pity's sake, you must have a spell that can counter the curse that afflicts me."

For a moment there was only silence and the crackling of Jeanne Roy's meagre fire. Then came a noise so startling it nearly knocked Élisabeth backwards. It was a cackle as dry as the bark on the outside of Jeanne Roy's hut and just as brittle. The witch was laughing.

Jeanne Roy shook her head. "I cannot begin to think what to say to you."

"Say anything. Please. I spoke to Father de Sancy. He said the demon is a great marquis of Hell. Marcosi is a wolf with a serpent's tail and gryphon's wings. He will fester inside of me until I no longer know myself. Perhaps . . . perhaps the demon shall turn me into a wolf with wings myself!"

Suddenly the witch looked weary. She stopped laughing.

"You will not become a wolf with wings, Élisabeth."

"I might. Maman Poulin says werewolves—"

"No. You won't. You are a harebrained fool who has listened to too many stories and who has chosen to believe them without a shred of reason or common sense. There is nothing I can do to help you."

Élisabeth could hardly understand what she was saying.

"I am cursed. This is not a *story*. A demon lives inside of me. How else can you explain everything that has happened to me?" She stood up; Marcosi was agitated by the witch's disdain and roiled her guts.

"Very simply." The witch stared at her evenly. "Consider for a moment that witches and demons are *not* real."

"They are real. As real as the trees outside. As real as God."

"So you say—"

"It's not me who says so. It's Father de Sancy. It's the church! Do you deny God's truth?"

"Consider, just consider, that witchcraft does not exist. Magic is not real. Let us think of what other reason there might be for everything that has happened to you—"

"Nothing can explain why I lost a child that had already quickened! Nothing can explain why my guts churn like there's a monster inside me, or why I can't ever catch a full breath of air. There is a demon in my body, put there by a witch," Élisabeth said, her voice cracking, unable to hold back her tears.

"Many women miscarry, even after the quickening. It is not an act of witchcraft to lose a child. You are more than likely perfectly able to have another."

Élisabeth spluttered. "The Winter Witch pointed her finger at me! An old crone never seen in the village except in the darkest time of year, stumbles into the tavern and screams at me, a girl she does not know? Why would she point at me?"

"Perhaps she is afflicted with madness. Perhaps she only comes into your village in February because the wood she has carefully gathered all year has run out and it is cold and she is starving and begging for help to survive until the spring."

Élisabeth flushed. "She did not beg for help. She pointed and screamed *'twas for you.*"

"Maybe she was trying to warn you."

"Warn me about what?"

"Let us consider a new notion. Firstly, let us consider that witches are not real. They do not exist. I suggest the woman is a mad beggar, deserving of our pity. You say that doesn't explain her behaviour entirely. Fine. Let us gather the evidence. You are an unmarried servant engaged in fornication with your mistress's son. No, wait, don't be angry. Is this not a fair and true assessment of your situation?"

Élisabeth glared at Jeanne Roy. The demon flicked his tail, his annoyance mounting. The witch stared down her long nose at her and continued.

"The boy led you to believe that by conceiving a child you would force his parents' hand into allowing you to marry. The cook in the household suspects as much and warns you against the boy. You take no heed of that warning. Eventually you do conceive, and you let him know of it. He promises to tell his parents, yet he does not hurry to do so."

"That's not fair—"

Jeanne Roy waved away Élisabeth's protest. "Next, he asks you to meet, not at his parents' home, but at the tavern. He encourages you to partake of wine so sour that it is unpleasant to drink. Then a woman enters the tavern in a state of distress. Something has alarmed her. The boy is also fearful, almost terrified of her presence. He rushes forward and pays her a princely sum of money, a whole silver écu, and pushes her out the door. Then he arranges for you to slip out the back, making sure you do not meet the old woman again, lest perhaps she explain herself. After that your lover announces that you will never have another child because of a curse and he's done with you."

The cold-blooded manner in which Jeanne Roy spoke felt like a box to the ears. Élisabeth stood, staring at the velvet witch, full of hatred. Still Jeanne continued her tirade.

"Those are the facts. But we still have questions. For instance, why *was* your wine so strangely bitter? Had the barrel gone off and made you sick to the point of losing the child? Or is it possible—and I am only suggesting this as an idea to be considered—that Rémy poisoned your drink to make you miscarry? Had he grown tired of you? Had he come up with a way to be rid of that which bound him to you?

"And that night in the tavern, did the old woman see you and realize that the boy never intended to use the poison draught he bought from her on rats or cats or whatever he had told her? Did she see him slip it into your drink from the window? Was she dismayed and tried to warn you—*'twas for you!*—only to be attacked and pushed out the door by the man who said he would protect you?"

The demon was screeching in Élisabeth's ears. Jeanne Roy was pitiless, she would not stop. Élisabeth wanted to kick her right into the fire.

"That's . . . not . . . true."

"Perhaps not. It's possible that you miscarried because the baby was not meant to live. It's possible that you feel possessed by a demon because you have been hysterical with grief since you lost your child or gripped with shame for your acts of fornication. It is possible that you suffer from melancholy due to an imbalance of the biles in your body. Any of these are better theories than that of a witch bearing a grudge against your beauty coming into a tavern to lay a curse on you. That's the dull-witted thinking of a peasant. And that, I am afraid, is the only *real* curse you bear."

Élisabeth clenched her fists to stop her body from trembling, striking them against her own hips. She seethed. Jeanne Roy was not only a witch, but a thief and a liar. A lying witch who refused to help her. Tears blurred her eyes, and instead of Jeanne Roy in front of her she saw the Winter Witch, cursing and taunting and thwarting her. She could no longer keep the demon down. When she spoke next it was with Marcosi's forked tongue.

"I have a few notions about you, Jeanne Roy, or whatever your name is. Would you like to hear them?"

The witch crossed her arms. "I am certain to be amused."

"You were not meant to be on that ship. You had no trunk. No letter of good conduct. You snuck on board as a stowaway because *you* are one of the Norman witches that Father de Sancy hunts."

"Can you prove it?"

"No, not until I discover your real name and see if it is the same as that of the witch queen that Father de Sancy seeks. For your name is not Jeanne, that is for certain. And Roy? *King?* It's so obvious now. The king saved you from the stake and so you took his name."

Jeanne Roy's eyes glittered like ice. "And what if I am one of those falsely accused women from Rouen? Those women of learning, or desperation, or both. I have served my sentence. I have left France—banished as the king decreed—to live my life in exile. Father de Sancy has no cause to arrest me."

"Unless you are accused of witchcraft again," the demon said quietly.

"Do not threaten me, Élisabeth," Jeanne Roy snapped. "I am not the only one who owns a scandalous past."

"Then help me be rid of this curse," Élisabeth cried, sinking to her knees again. "Why won't you help me? I will keep your secret, and once I am cured you will never hear from me again."

"The only thing you need curing of is stupidity, and I have no herbs or tinctures for that," Jeanne spat.

A strangled cry burst from Élisabeth's lips. "You have potions. I can see them, there! And there's a book of spells on your table. You *are* a witch! Why won't you use your power to help me?"

"I am not a witch! That is no grimoire! That is my journal. I am a student of science. I have trained with the greatest accoucheurs in Europe. I have studied midwifery and medicine in Paris—I have done what no other woman has done. I will not be thwarted by a fool with a grudge. Not again."

Jeanne Roy laid her hands on Élisabeth's shoulders and pushed her out of her hut. She stumbled outside, wide-eyed and gasping as the witch slammed the door shut.

"Jeanne! Let me in," she cried, banging on the door. There was no sound from within. Élisabeth took a step back and looked wildly around. The demon Marcosi, spared execution, began to chuckle. She stumbled away from the cabin, started to make her way through the woods, but the branches of the bare trees grasped for her. She ran, jagged as a hare, too overcome with despair to relinquish any speed, too distraught to shield her face from scratching twigs.

It could not be true. It could not be.

For if witchcraft did not exist, then every choice she had ever made since the night in the tavern was without purpose, or reason.

WINTER

23

A dropped spoon is a sure sign of visitors coming, and if it falls face down, they'll be bringing bad tidings. Élisabeth looked at the back of the wooden spoon on the floor and the pork dripping spattered across the pine boards. She braced herself for the worst.

The sky was the same colour as the snow on the ground, a bruised white that made it difficult to tell where the horizon began and ended. The visitors' red woollen hats made them visible on the river path long before their ox-drawn sled pulled up to the house. One very tall, one short and barrel-chested, she recognized the grim faces of the two Carignan-Salières soldiers who had married Rose and Lou. Élisabeth wondered how bad the news would be. In her womb, the demon Marcosi sat up on his hind legs, ears flat against his head, and waited.

They had had visitors enough in the two months since she had been wed, but the untamed demon inside her had made it impossible for her to exchange anything more than greetings with the well-intentioned neighbours who had come to call. In the first weeks of her marriage, she had curtseyed and said good day to a dozen of them, but with Marcosi strutting around unfettered as a cockerel after Jeanne Roy's rejection, Élisabeth was tongue-tied and awkward.

Jeanne's voice tormented her still, as sure as if her words were shards of glass stuck in her palm.

Consider, just consider, that witchcraft does not exist.

Is it possible that Rémy poisoned your drink to make you miscarry?

Had he come up with a way to be rid of that which bound him to you?

She could neither join in the neighbours' admiration of the crucifix Francoeur had newly hung above their hearth, nor weigh their advice about storing straw in the rafters and putting aside salted fish and peas in the cellar. She could not unstick herself from her own thoughts, and soon enough the visitors stopped coming, amid whispers that Élisabeth was odd, or at the very least dull, and quite likely simple.

Her husband was undeterred. He had insisted she would find companionship among the wives living in Côte Saint-François. At first, he had suggested Jeanne Roy come to dine, but when Élisabeth blanched and begged Francoeur not to invite her into their home, he retreated. Then on Saint Martin's Day he brought her with him to pay the rents. The Sulpicians did not have a manor house in the seigneurie, so the habitants met their landlords at one of the neighbour's houses. Élisabeth thought the man called Dufossé boorish, and his wife, Hélène, an unfortunate creature ducking and cringing at her husband's every glance. The only moment of kinship Élisabeth felt with the woman was when they realized that they had travelled to New France on the same ship, a few years apart.

Finding her tongue, Élisabeth mumbled, "I suffered the entire journey."

"When we set sail, I was convinced we would all die," Hélène replied. "I jumped overboard, thinking it was better to drown close to Dieppe than out in the ocean, for at least near shore they might recover my body rather than leave me to be taken by sea monsters. One of the sailors rescued me."

"You're the mermaid!" Élisabeth exclaimed, drawing the attention of the other neighbours. She was forced to explain that she had heard the story of a girl who jumped into the sea from the sailor who rescued her, and how he thought of her as his mermaid still. Dufossé stepped in to jeer at his wife and told everyone assembled that she was a mooncalf, not a mermaid. Hélène hunched her shoulders, closing in upon herself, and the men continued their talk of how to convince the seigneurs of the need to build a grist mill. Once their backs were turned, she took a step closer to Élisabeth.

"You met Michel?"

"Yes," Élisabeth nodded. "And I believe he must be in love with you, for he left the ship in Québec to search for you. He has a notion you might be a widow and free to marry him."

"He loves me still?" Hélène's eyes had widened.

Élisabeth had looked at her pale face, thinking what it would be like to have a friend in the lonely stretch of near-unbroken forest she now called home. She and this woman might meet again at her table and share stories of the lovers they left behind. Then Élisabeth thought of Rémy. Had he tired of her, as Jeanne Roy said? Thrown her away, like an apple core for the pigs? If so, *why?* He said she had too many freckles, was that the reason? She should have scrubbed her face with apple cider and honey. She agonized over what she had done wrong and fell headlong into silence.

After that, Hélène had retreated, shrinking further into herself until she became so invisible that no one seemed to notice her sitting alone by the hearth, staring into the fire.

Francoeur soon gave up trying to foist companionship upon her, and she and Marcosi were left alone. Until the spoon slipped through her hand on the morning of Epiphany, and she knew something was about to change.

The two old soldiers stomped their feet at the door, letting thick chunks of snow fall from their boots.

"Élisabeth, what can we offer our guests?" Francoeur said. He had no foreboding; he seemed delighted by their unexpected company, eagerly taking his comrades' coats to hang them on pegs by the door.

"There's spruce beer. Or the blueberry wine."

"Good Lord, no!" Short, stocky Jambon smacked his palm to his forehead. "Mistress, has he tried to make you drink the blue vinegar?"

The one with the baby face who had married Rose chuckled. "He bought it from a pretty maid at market," Lajeunesse said. "He never manages to finish a bottle, yet he always goes back for more."

"Now lads, you'll land me in trouble with my wife," Francoeur said hastily. "*She* is the most beautiful woman on this island. Although she pretends she's only passably pretty."

He tried to catch her eye so that she might share in their private joke, but Élisabeth looked at the floor. Why could she not smile back? Laugh at his little joke, touch his shoulder when he passed by, draw him close to her at night, as Marcosi urged her to do?

No, no, no. If the witch would not help her, she would fight the demon by not giving into sin. She must be as pious as the Holy Virgin. It was the only way to keep the demon down.

Consider, just consider, that witchcraft does not exist.

Impossible. If witches did *not* exist and magic was nothing more than wishes, then she was neither cursed nor barren. If the Winter Witch were merely an old woman looking for firewood, then Élisabeth could have stayed in Saint-Philbert and accused Rémy of seduction. The courts might have forced him to marry her. If witchcraft did not exist and Rémy was a liar, then he was not her true love. She had thrown her life away for nothing.

If witchcraft did not exist, she could lay with her husband without sin.

Stupid, ignorant peasant. Harebrained fool.

Jeanne Roy's words were as poisonous as an adder's bite. Who was she to call Élisabeth stupid? She might not be able to read or write her name, but which of them was living in a warm house with an able husband, and which of them was living alone in a hut made from little more than brambles? She felt Marcosi stretch and dig his sharpened claws deep into her belly. She grimaced.

The ache inside of her was all the proof she needed. What else could explain her gut-wrenching spasms if demons did not exist?

No, she was not stupid or harebrained. Witches were real. Demons walked among them.

She knew it for certain, for she lived with one every day.

"Give us the blue vinegar, then. We shall drink a toast to our wives." Jambon clapped his hand on Francoeur's shoulder, bringing Élisabeth out of her thoughts. She stepped away to fetch the wine.

"My friend, we have come to you for your counsel," Jambon said. "I am sorry to say we have bad news about Lafredière."

Élisabeth poured the blueberry wine into tin mugs and placed one in front of each of the men. Francoeur placed his forearms on the table, staring straight at Jambon.

"What's he done now?"

Jambon looked at Élisabeth uneasily. "He attacked one of the village wives."

"Tell me." The words shot out of Francoeur's mouth.

"Lafredière fell upon her and choked her until she nearly lost breath. It happened a few months back. We only learned of it when we went into town to sell firewood a few days ago."

"Who?" Élisabeth asked warily. "Who did he attack?"

Jambon swallowed and glanced at Élisabeth again. "I was told to keep the woman's name to myself. She does not want to bring shame upon her household."

Francoeur kept his eyes fixed on Jambon and nodded. "Was she badly hurt?"

"Her neck was bruised, but he did not break any bones."

Élisabeth felt the demon rake along her spine, its tail knocking against every bone. She took a step back from the men to hide her shudder.

"That's not all," Jambon added, leaning across the table towards Francoeur.

"Lafred's slaves have gone missing. The two Panis girls. He claims they've run away. Only, after what happened in New York, we did wonder . . ."

Francoeur sat quietly, digesting what Jambon said. His fingertips traced the grain in the wooden table; the skin around his eyes was tight, as if he were wincing.

"What happened in New York?" Élisabeth asked. Her husband ran his hands over the edge of the table, measuring something in his mind. He did not look at her.

"So we came to you, of course," Jambon continued. "We have to stop him. Once and for all."

The muscle in Francoeur's jaw twitched. "You don't need me. You could have alerted the authorities yourselves."

"Lafredière *is* the authority in Ville-Marie."

"The church, then."

"What can the priests do?" Jambon said. "They don't have pistols or muskets. They can't stop him. They might not even care about missing slaves and throttled wives."

"They might if he's killed those girls."

"Killed them?" Élisabeth steadied herself against the table.

"Who in Ville-Marie would care about a pair of Panis slaves?" Lajeunesse shook his head. Everyone at the table understood his meaning. In a land of reluctant brides, indentured labourers, and new farmers trying to outwit winter to survive, who indeed would look beyond their own hardship to care about the fate of two Panis girls?

"I do not know much about their alliances," Francoeur said slowly. "But if we French are allied to the Algonquins and the Huron, perhaps the Iroquois count the Panis as their allies. The children's deaths could be the spark that causes the truce to be abandoned. The church would certainly care if the Iroquois took up arms again."

"Why do you believe he's killed them?" Élisabeth demanded. "What happened in New York?"

The taller man let out a sound halfway between a snort and a guffaw. "New York was the finest mutiny in the history of the French army. It was when your husband took a stand against Lafredière," Lajeunesse said.

"I'll tell her," Jambon interrupted. "I'm better at telling stories." He leaned back and cleared his throat. "It was a wintery day in January. Almost five years ago now to the day, in 1666. We had marched south to burn the Iroquois villages—"

"That's enough," Francoeur said, shaking himself from his stupor. Élisabeth could see his jaw clench. "You need to decide what to do about Lafredière, not dwell on old tales."

"*You* need to decide," his friend whined. "You're the captain of the côte."

Francoeur frowned, chewing the inside of his cheek. The room was silent, all eyes on him. Then Jambon piped up.

"You could shoot him again. Only this time, don't miss."

The demon shot upright so quickly that Élisabeth almost fell over. She gripped the table again.

"You tried to kill the governor of Montréal?"

"To be fair, he wasn't the acting governor then," Jambon said. "Only our captain."

"And he had it coming," Lajeunesse added.

"There will be no shots fired." Francoeur stood up. "We have to appeal to the intendant in Québec. Get the civil authorities involved if the military can't tame him. We can tell Intendant Talon what Lafredière has done and demand that he be recalled to France."

"Why would the intendant listen?" Jambon stayed seated, scowling at his friend's suggestion. "Lafred is the Marquis de Salières's own nephew."

"We will make him see the risk of ignoring Lafredière's crimes. If we petition the intendant in person, with the signatures of anyone who knows about his behaviour, the authorities will have to see sense. Between the villagers he's harassed and the men who were with us in New York . . . there will be a hundred signatures, maybe more. If we bring them to the intendant and explain what's at stake, he cannot ignore it."

"If *we* bring the evidence? So . . . you'll do it?" Lajeunesse stood up.

Francoeur's hands tightened on the back of his chair. He stole a glance at Élisabeth. "If he's attacked one of the village wives . . ."

"Hell's teeth," Jambon grimaced. "Another long winter's march for us then."

"We're going to freeze our balls off. Again." Lajeunesse cupped his hands over his groin.

"I will pack our bags," Élisabeth offered, stepping towards her husband.

"Élisabeth, you cannot come with us," Francoeur said gently. "It will be a difficult journey and may take more than a month to reach Québec. A woman cannot travel for so long in such cold."

"You would leave me here?"

She had grown used to how her husband lumbered around the house with his hammer and nails, making a racket as she plucked a bird or skinned a rabbit for their dinner. She wondered what it would be like to sit by the fire, peering at her darning in the dim light, and not hear him hum, or smell the sweet tobacco he stuffed in his pipe. She wondered why he did not roll over at night and insist she perform her duty as his wife.

"I would die without you," she stated.

He stroked his beard and smiled. "You would *die* without me?"

Their guests tried to smother their smirks. Élisabeth walked away from the table, beckoning for Francoeur to join her by the hearth.

"It is no lovelorn declaration," she said. "It is a fact, I cannot survive here alone."

"Forgive my teasing," he said, at once serious. "Of course you cannot stay here alone. But you cannot travel with us either."

"What would you have me do then?"

"I'll bring you to stay with your sister in town."

"Is it not more dangerous to be in Ville-Marie with the governor stalking the streets for women to choke?" She slipped her hand into her pocket, seeking the smoothness of the rosary beads against her fingertips.

"You could stay here, if we ask Jeanne Roy to come and live with you."

"No!"

Jambon and Lajeunesse peered at them from the other side of the hearth. She lowered her voice. "No. I won't have her in this house."

"Then I will take you to your sister's. A month or two with Marthe and Verger. Does that not sound fine?"

She tried to imagine it. She thought of Marthe and Maman Poulin sitting at the table in the warm bakery, sharing stories. The other brides from the ship—Thérèse and Françoise, even Apolline—visiting every day. The bustle would be more cheerful than her own hearth. But it was at her own hearth that she longed to stay, with Francoeur.

"Will it really be as long as a month or two?"

He reached his hand out to stroke her cheek. "By the time I am home, winter's back will be broken and we will start afresh in the spring." She wanted to turn her face towards his calloused palm. Start afresh. She wished he would kiss her. What harm could come from one kiss? She almost wished she had abandoned her piety, listened to Marcosi's sly whispers and touched him that first night, and every night afterwards.

Start afresh? If only she could.

"Élisabeth, I know life here is not easy."

"I do not mind the work," she said quickly.

"I mean to say, it is a lonely life. You will be happier with your sister. And when I return, we will begin again." He leaned down and spoke softly. "We can start our family then."

She blinked several times to hold back the tears stinging her eyes. Never mind a long winter's march. The one thing her husband required of her she could not do.

She was barren. Useless.

And now he wanted to be rid of her.

A wilful tear slipped down her cheek. Francoeur took her face in his hands and stared into her eyes. "Élisabeth, what frightens you so? Is it me?"

"What do you mean?"

"I see you jump when there is a knock on the door or praying as if the Devil himself is near. Do you fear that I am some kind of brute, like . . . like Dufossé?"

"No, of course not." She stopped and looked at her hands. She wished she could tell him the truth about the Winter Witch and the curse and how the old priest said the spirit had the jaw of a wolf and the tail of a serpent and black gryphon's wings as well. She could not. The friendly crinkles around her husband's eyes would melt into a gaping mask of horror. He would turn her over to Father de Sancy to be stripped and whipped. Or never come back to collect her from her sister's house. She would be shunned, again.

"It's not you that I'm frightened of," she whispered.

"Then what?"

She faltered. She could see Jambon stretch his arms above his head, impatient to be going. They had to start their journey now or risk travelling at night.

"You are right. It is the loneliness I fear."

"Then we shall take you to the bakehouse and surround you with people all winter long."

He took her hand, his mind made up. He seemed so satisfied with his plan, the mending of his broken wife. Élisabeth felt her heart ache as he pulled her to her feet. She smiled as best she could.

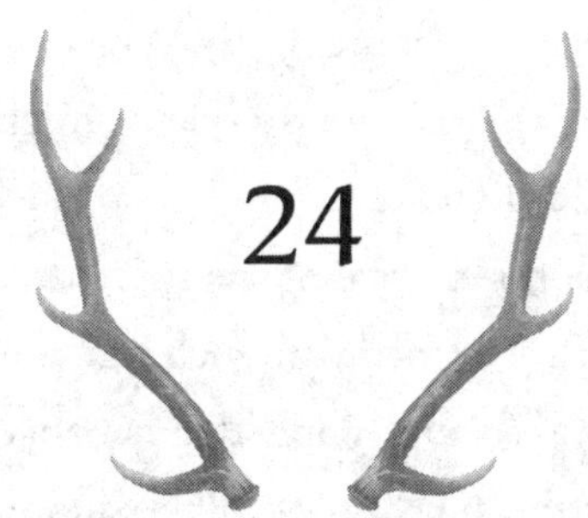

24

"They've been baked too long, they're burnt on the bottom," Marthe said dully, examining each loaf of bread as she laid it into the shop baskets. "We won't be able to charge full price."

Verger shrugged in a way that set her teeth on edge: an insouciant gesture of both submission and idleness. "Just adds flavour, Old Poulin used to say."

Marthe kept her eyes on the bread, stifling her rage. "Well, they're also flatter than usual, so you're doing something wrong."

Verger did not answer, which was somehow worse than a shrug.

"Did you hear me? The loaves are over-risen. I do not know how you can claim to be a master baker when your bread is so irregular."

"If you will not let me be master of the one thing that I should, then what do you expect?"

The sound of her husband's fist on the table brought a smile to her lips. For weeks, she had been angry. All she wanted was to scream, slam doors, and beat her fists against the wall. She hoped her amiable husband would give her cause to do so.

Turning towards him, Marthe glowered and touched her neck. After the attack, her bruises had turned the colour of rotting dandelions, a chain of decaying flowers stretched from her nape to her throat. In the presence of customers and Barbe Poulin, she'd hidden them with a scarf and complained loudly of the cold to cover her shame. Only Verger had seen the extent of her injuries. Verger, who had a childish notion that he might challenge the governor of Montréal over what he'd done.

"You, master of my honour? Please," she sneered. In her heart she knew she was being unfair. But her fury burned with such heat it made her reckless. She did not understand why she was so angry, only that her anger made her cruel. "If you so much as tread near the fort our bakery will be shut down within a sennight."

"And yet you appeal to your brother-in-law, with no fear of the repercussions for his livelihood?" Verger shot back.

"That was not my doing—Jambon and Lajeunesse said Francoeur would know what to do. They said he has dealt a blow to Lafredière in the past." She paused, wanting her next words to bite. "And I trust them to solve this matter more than you."

She watched as her husband's slim frame caved in defeat. His fist was still on the table, though now it grew slack, lying impotently against the wood. He gave her a long look and pointedly raised his shoulders to his ears and down again. She wanted to grab a loaf of bread and hammer him over the head. Instead, she turned back to her baskets and listened for the slam of the door as Verger left for the tavern.

She tried to steady her breathing. She could not blame her husband; what had happened was not his fault. But her temper—always her greatest sin, her sister said—was like nothing she had ever known before. She could not sleep for the fury that crackled inside of her, burning all day and all night. It was so blinding she wondered if the demon that inhabited Élisabeth dwelt in her heart as well.

She heard the door and felt herself soften. When she was not enraged, she was close to tears. She turned, ready to run into Verger's arms. She would forgive him, though of course there was nothing to forgive.

"Good day, Marthe."

Marthe halted, taking in the sight before her. It was Jeanne Roy, her cheeks ruddy and her eyes bright. She wore a native-style woollen blanket coat, belted at the waist, underneath which Marthe could see a pair of tall moose-hide boots. The snowflakes caught in her hair glittered like starlight. Marthe was so astonished she sank into a deep curtsey.

"Whatever are you doing? I am not your better." Jeanne Roy laughed, stepping into the room. "At least not in this country. May I present my friend Wari?"

Marthe noticed a native woman standing behind the witch. Again, she fell into a curtsey, not knowing how else to greet the stranger. The woman was dressed the same as Jeanne Roy, but with an intricately beaded bag over her shoulder and long black braids hanging below her cap. She leaned two pairs of snowshoes against the wall as she came in.

"Wh-what are you doing here?" Marthe stammered, then checked her rudeness. It would not do to anger Jeanne Roy, who held Élisabeth's fate in her hands. "May I offer you a drink?"

"We have come to buy bread," Jeanne Roy smiled. "This is a bakehouse, is it not?" There was a faint trace of imperiousness in her voice that Marthe did not like, but she did not show it. She bobbed her head.

"Of course, of course, you must have come from some distance." Marthe glanced at the snowshoes. "Please sit and take some small beer with me."

The women arranged themselves around Barbe Poulin's table; Marthe was relieved that the widow had gone out on some errand she would not reveal. She poured spruce beer into pewter mugs and sat down.

"What brings you to town to buy your bread?" Marthe asked. She wasn't sure if she could enquire after Élisabeth's health in front of the native woman. She did not know how much the stranger knew about Jeanne's magic.

"I am on my way to spend the winter with Wari at the mission village across the river at La Prairie," Jeanne said, her eyes shining. "I will live in a longhouse with her and other Oneida and Agniers until the spring comes."

Marthe blinked at the pair sitting opposite her. She could not imagine living among the natives in a longhouse—whatever a longhouse was—though a year ago she could not have imagined a native and a noblewoman sharing her table. Her heart lifted for the first time in weeks. This experience was a richness of a sort.

"Will your family mind Jeanne staying with you for so long?" Marthe asked Wari, thinking of the widow crusted onto the hull of her own home.

The Agnier woman did not move. "The small pox killed my family."

"Oh." Marthe's face fell.

"My home is now with the other Haudenosaunee at the Jesuit mission. Others who have converted to your faith." Wari folded her hands in her lap. She spoke French well, with a lilting accent. Marthe could not help staring at her.

"And why . . . why did you become a Christian?" She knew from Jeanne Roy's sharp look that her question was impolite, but she could not contain her curiosity.

"Five years ago, French soldiers burned our villages and our crops." Wari fixed her eyes on Marthe. "When peace came, so did the black robes. They spoke of safety in a place along the river. They said we could worship God freely there. I wanted a place where I could sell my herbs and be free to trade medicine with your people." The Agnier woman nodded at Jeanne. "That's why I became a Christian. For safety."

An image of the governor's bulging eye flashed into Marthe's head. She put her fingertips on her throat and gently rubbed the skin where he had grabbed her. Wari was wrong to seek safety on this island.

"This is a town full of wolves," Marthe said bitterly. "None of us is safe amongst these men."

"You speak too rashly," Wari replied. "There are good men and bad men, just as there are good and bad women. In all things, there is balance."

Marthe paused, trying to find fault with the woman's words. But in her heart she knew her husband was a good man, nothing like Lafredière or the customer who had struck his wife in the bakery for daring to want a finer loaf. Her father had been a good man too. Marthe pictured Papa, sitting down at the table with his children all around him, laughing as they spoke over each other to be the first to tell him all that had happened during the day. Her fingers slowly pinched the flesh on her neck as she thought about Papa slumped in the same chair where he ate his cheese and bread, his blood spilling over the rim of the small clay cup and onto the floor. A good man, gone too soon.

"Then I will pray for safety," she whispered. "For my family as well as yours."

The native woman nodded. "I will pray for you too, and for Angélique."

"Your child must be kicking by now." Jeanne Roy turned abruptly to Marthe, her tone brusque.

"Why, yes," Marthe said, bewildered by the shift in the conversation. She did not know who Angélique was, and there was more she wanted to ask Wari. But she longed for the sorceress's advice, and so she turned to Jeanne and shared her deepest fears. "I sometimes worry I will not survive my time in childbed."

Jeanne nodded. "Every woman worries. I have helped girls in worse circumstances than you give birth to healthy children."

Marthe's ears perked up.

"You're a midwife?" It made sense; most midwives had a bit of magic in them. Though they were almost always mothers or grandmothers themselves. "Do you have children of your own?" she asked.

"No." Jeanne Roy's tone was sharp. "I studied in Paris with one of the greatest accoucheurs in Europe."

"Accoucheurs?" Marthe's nose wrinkled.

"Man-midwives you might call them. It's quite common now for well-born ladies to have one attend to them in their labours."

Marthe rolled her eyes. "A *man*-midwife? I expect they'd be just like Verger, talking about sows and piglets, nary a clue what it is to carry a pumpkin around inside for months."

Jeanne Roy smiled. "It's true. Most men don't know a baby's head from a melon. But the man-midwives are different; they are highly skilled. One of the best in France taught me all he knows."

"Why would any woman want a man to assist her while she is labouring?" Marthe asked. "Is it not shameful for a man to see a woman in her confinement?"

"It is not shameful in the least," Jeanne said. "Women want Mauriceau near them in part because fashionable ladies want what other fashionable ladies have. But also because some mothers would die in childbirth without him. Mauriceau has a brilliant mind and methods for every difficulty, the very latest advances for turning a breech, stopping certain types of blood loss, extracting a stuck child. He was—he *is*, he still is—frustratingly remarkable." She was lost in thought, biting her lip so hard Marthe thought she might draw blood. Marthe thought of her own mother's end. She wondered if this Mauriceau could have prevented her mother from dying in childbirth.

"Was Mauriceau the one who taught you how to be a man-midwife?" Marthe asked quietly.

"Yes, François Mauriceau is the best of all the accoucheurs in Europe. I learned a tremendous amount, though there were parts of his learning he sought to keep hidden from me."

"You are a skilled medicine woman now," Wari broke in. "And because you are here, your skill will grow."

"Yes," Jeanne said, her face brightening. "Marthe, did you know the Iroquois can cure a wound in eight days that would take French doctors thirty?" She turned back to Wari. "I meant to tell you. I've been thinking about a new remedy for chest ailments. I think we should start our studies with the leaves of maidenhair."

"I thought we might start with a root, as it is wintertime. Were you not interested in the ginseng I brought you?"

Marthe watched, agog, as the two women debated how they would spend their time over the long winter months, which plants they would test, which tinctures they would brew: a pair of cunning folk plotting their potions at her table. She was so caught up in the conversation that she did not notice Barbe Poulin come in.

"What is this?" the widow demanded. Marthe leapt up. Barbe Poulin took her by the elbow and pulled her into the workroom. "Why is there an Indian sitting at my table?"

"You always have customers sit with you to while away the time."

"Not *savages*." Barbe Poulin's voice was cold. "Get rid of the pair of them."

"No," Marthe said. She put her hands on her hips and faced down the widow. "I won't. They are my guests. They will stay in my house as long as they like."

The widow glared at Marthe, her eyes narrowing. Marthe did not flinch. She had been desperate for a fight to ease the rage in her heart, and if her husband would not go to war with her, the widow could take his place.

"Marthe, we will take our leave of you," Jeanne Roy called out from the hallway.

"Wait!" Marthe turned on her heel, running to catch them. The Agnier woman had taken the snowshoes and was already outside. "Let me give you some bread." She took three loaves from the shop baskets and pressed them upon the midwife. "They are my gift. In turn I hope you might help me, if you can, when I am in childbed?"

"Of course, I am at your service."

"And Élisabeth? Might you be able help her too?" Marthe whispered, careful that the widow not hear her plea. "With her curse?"

Jeanne Roy's eyes turned to stone. "Your sister is deluded about what ails her."

Marthe hesitated. "Do you mean to say . . . that is, has she spoken to you about the curse? And the . . . the demon?"

"Yes."

"Jeanne, I cannot believe she is possessed, she shows none of the signs. What do you think? I accept she might be cursed with barrenness but not *possessed*. Yet when Father de Sancy told her about a wolf with wings, a marquis of Hell, she became convinced that this demon haunts her. He planted a bad seed in her mind that has grown into bindweed."

The witch wrapped a scarf around her head. "Her imagination has interfered with her reason."

"So that is all it is? Her imagination?"

"No. That is not all." The sorceress paused with her hand on the doorknob. "I have thought a great deal about Élisabeth's condition since she came to see me in November. And I do believe there is an explanation for it."

Marthe looked over her shoulder to ensure the widow did not approach. "Tell me."

"I believe your sister suffers from melancholy, an ailment caused by an excess of black bile."

"Black bile?" Marthe was confused. "Is that a type of dark magic?"

"No." Jeanne gave her an incredulous look. "It is one of the four humours in the human body. To be in good health the humours—the blood, phlegm, and the black and yellow biles—must all be in balance. If a person has too much of one and not enough of another, they become ill."

"I don't understand. I've never heard of humours."

"No, I don't imagine you have." The witch's voice lilted with superiority. "Galen's philosophy of medicine is not something I would expect most people to understand."

Marthe was suddenly impatient. "Well then, how do you cure this black bile? *Can* it be cured?"

"Yes, it can. Élisabeth's black bile has overwhelmed her spleen and polluted her blood. A small cut with a lancet will let the bad blood run out so that she might be cleansed. I would happily bleed your sister. And then I believe she will be well again."

Marthe felt a wave of desperation wash over her as Jeanne Roy nodded and thanked her politely for the bread. She stood staring at the back of the door when the midwife had gone. It was too cruel. There *was* hope for Élisabeth, a cure that would ease her suffering. But she would never submit to it.

Not after what happened to their father.

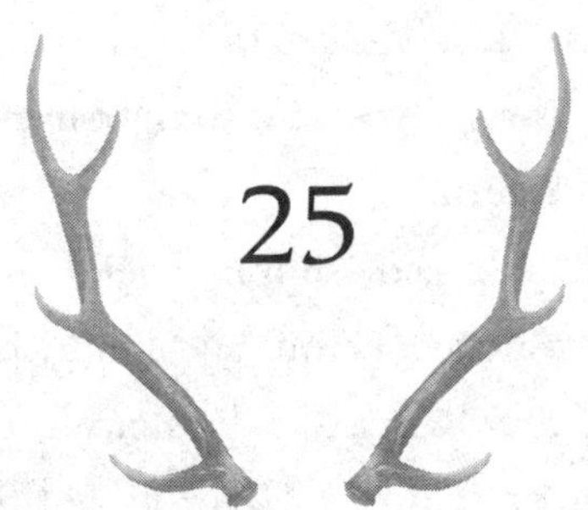

25

When the sleigh pulled up outside the bakery, Francoeur gave Élisabeth a tender kiss, helped her disembark, and drove away, leaving her feeling as if her heart were being torn from her chest. Maman Poulin pulled her close, staunching the bleeding. She embraced Élisabeth as if she were her own child—pinching her cheeks and exclaiming that she was skin and bones and needed to be fed until she was as plump as a chicken and fit to roast.

"What sort of scandal is it that makes your husband rush off and leave his bride so soon after he is married?" Maman Poulin prattled as she pulled Élisabeth into the salon where customers gathered. Marthe stood in the corridor. Élisabeth could see she was vying for her attention, but she was exhausted from having been jostled and lurched in Jambon's ox-drawn sleigh for the better part of an hour. She paid no attention to Marthe and sank into a chair.

"The governor has attacked one of the village wives," Élisabeth said, untying her cap and scratching her head. "Francoeur is going to see about having him recalled to France."

"What a to-do!" Maman Poulin's eyes gleamed as she leaned forward. "Though I've been in this colony almost since its founding and have known scandals much worse than that." She poured Élisabeth a cup of beer and continued her tale. "One of the worst was the girl-for-marrying from La Rochelle who landed in Québec already fat with child. She tried to pass herself off as a virgin fit to be married! The recruiting agent paid a hefty fine for the deception, I can tell you. The girl was sent straight back to France, and I expect she got fifty lashes on her return."

"How terrible," Élisabeth said, slipping her hand into her pocket. She vowed then that no matter how generous and kind Maman Poulin was to her, she would never tell her about Rémy. She did not want fifty lashes on her back.

"Lili, you must want to lie down," Marthe said from her position at the door. Her sister was behaving as if she did not dare step foot into the widow's room. "It is long after nightfall."

"I am tired," Élisabeth said. *And heartsick*, she thought.

"We haven't any ticking or fresh straw to make you a mattress of your own, so you shall make your bed with me," Maman Poulin insisted.

"Why should she sleep with you?" Marthe asked crossly.

"Because, little mistress, in case you have forgotten, you share your bed with your husband. Whereas I have plenty of room for your sister. You will like my pallet, Lili, it is made of cattail. Though I confess I never sleep entirely easy. I would prefer a house with a second story so that I could pull a ladder up behind us at night and thwart the Iroquois from scalping us in our sleep."

"Have you ever known anyone who was scalped, Maman?" Élisabeth asked. Marcosi stirred and she felt the demon's hot breath in her throat.

"Oh yes. Yes, indeed," the widow said, providing no further information.

"But the Iroquois do not come into the village anymore. Not now there is a truce," Élisabeth said.

"On the contrary. I saw one today."

All of a sudden Maman Poulin leaned forward and sliced her thumbnail across Élisabeth's forehead. Élisabeth shrieked, startled at the mock scalping. The widow started to laugh, the sound of a donkey's honk filling the room. Élisabeth laid her hand on her chest to see if the demon was sharpening his claws, readying himself to attack. Would Marcosi try to sink his fangs into Maman Poulin's flesh, here in her own home? But Élisabeth found that the demon did not mind the jest. Perhaps Marcosi was placated by the fact that Maman Poulin was as fearful of him—and all of his demonic kin—as Élisabeth herself was. As the sound of braying echoed around them, the spirit inside her curled himself into a ball and settled his horned head down upon his paws for a rest.

Élisabeth took a deep breath. Perhaps it would not be such a bad thing to spend the winter in Ville-Marie with Maman Poulin. While she would do well to make sure Maman Poulin did not glean anything about Rémy, the widow's influence might be just what she needed. She was certainly righteous, keeping track of slatterns and fallen women, and pious, for her regard for the church higher than none. Maman Poulin would take care that their winter was free of both witches and sin. And besides, Marcosi seemed soothed by her presence. Élisabeth felt her shoulders loosen for the first time in many weeks.

Yes, a winter with Maman Poulin would do her good.

She did not notice that Marthe had left the room.

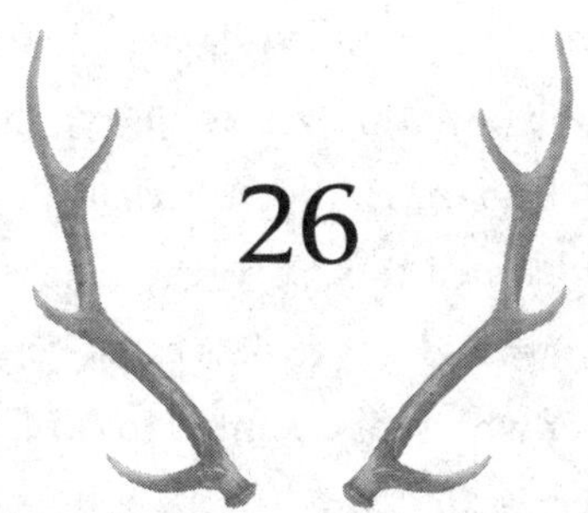

26

Marthe strode along Rue Saint-Paul, her breath billowing out of her mouth as if she were on fire. It was the coldest she had ever been in her life, yet she knew that with one long scream the bonfire within her could warm the village to the heat of a summer's day.

"My eyelashes are stuck together," Élisabeth complained.

Marthe pulled her shawl more tightly over her ears. She could not bring herself to agree with her sister, even though she could feel her own lashes sticking with every blink.

"Did you hear me? My eyelashes have frozen together. And I think my toes might turn black."

"It's really not that far to the merchant's stores."

In the month since Élisabeth had come to stay, Marthe had grown accustomed to stepping out into the cold air to cool her rage. She liked how winter gripped her by the shoulders and shook her, taking both her breath and her thoughts away. Marthe could not understand why her anger and tears were still so close to the surface, but it was only by storming down the freezing road in a quick march that she felt soothed.

She had not told Élisabeth about the governor's attack. She'd thought she might, but her sister had quickly fallen under the widow's spell, and Barbe Poulin was too set on stoking her fears about the daily dangers of New France: rough labourers, fast-flowing rivers, open flames, freezing fingers and toes, natives (especially the Iroquois), werewolves, the Devil, witches of course, Protestants determined to sneak into the colony, as well as all other manner of heretics and sinners. Marthe had learned to sort wheat from chaff, and she knew that almost everything the widow said was useless husk; very rarely was there a grain that could be trusted in her words. She wanted to confide in her sister about the very real thing that Governor de Lafredière had done but knew Élisabeth was preoccupied with other worries.

"Maman Poulin says she knows of a miller whose apprentice turned into a loup garou. Can you believe it, Marthe? The miller met the werewolf one night and slashed its ear with his knife. The next morning his apprentice came to work with a bloody ear. That was how he knew it was one and the same man."

Marthe tucked her mittened hands into her armpits. She had heard the story, and many more, often enough. She did not answer.

"Do you think . . . do you think I should be concerned about that happening to me? I don't mean about being attacked with a knife. Marcosi would kill anyone who tried to touch me. I mean about becoming a werewolf. Because Maman Poulin said—"

"I can't bear that you call her Maman. She is not our mother. She's not even Verger's mother. She's the former baker's wife who refuses to leave my house."

Élisabeth paused for a moment, letting a puff of frozen breath escape her mouth. "Don't be so hard on Maman Poulin. Think what it would be like if Verger died. Wouldn't you want to stay in your home rather than hand it over to a stranger?"

Her defence of the widow acted as dry kindling on a flame. "We have the largest oven in Ville-Marie behind our house," Marthe snapped. "It's the *only* home where a baker could live. It is *not* the only home where a baker's widow could live. Especially when she could remarry at any time."

She pushed the door to Le Moyne's shop open and stormed inside, Élisabeth right on her heel. Madame Le Moyne nodded from the far side of the room.

"Perhaps Maman Poulin hopes to fall in love before she marries again," Élisabeth murmured.

Marthe snorted. "You are a goose, Lili. If Verger should die, I would carefully consider my choices and marry whichever man does not have his mother— or any other woman—already living in his house."

She paused by the iron stove Le Moyne kept burning ostentatiously in the centre of the shop, a symbol of luxury Marthe could never afford. She gritted her teeth and strode over to the shopkeeper.

"Do you have any wool? I am in need of warmer socks," Marthe asked, scanning the shelves of linen and bedding.

"It's not cheap to come by," Madame Le Moyne warned her. Marthe shot a glance at her sister, who was warming her hands by the iron stove.

"I know. We *were* warned about these terrible winters, but some of us were determined to come, regardless of what it cost us in comfort."

The shopkeeper offered her commiserations and a small bag of unwashed fleece for as good a price as she could manage, given the time of year and the fact there would be no more of it until the springtime when the few sheep on the island were sheared. Marthe talked her down a dernier or two but could not get her to budge further. Madame Le Moyne seemed content with the sale and showed her appreciation by adding a tidbit of gossip in for the price.

"Did you hear about the woman who keeps house for Governor de Lafredière?" she asked. The shopkeeper's expression was a mixture of sorrow and a smirk.

"No." Marthe lifted her chin, bracing herself.

"She has left the fort and is staying at Folleville's. I don't know what she's thinking, running away like that. It's not as if her husband doesn't know where she is. He could go claim her at any time." Madame Le Moyne lowered her voice. "And as bad as it is at the fort, you know Anne Lamarque de Folleville won't let her stay without earning her keep. Soon enough she'll be forced to earn her living on her back."

Marthe tried to smile and managed only a grimace. She could not remember the grip of Lafredière's hands around her neck. It was his bulging eye, the sound of the brandy decanter smashing on the floor, and the servant's haggard face she could not forget.

"Apparently the Sulpicians have caught wind of it and are furious," Madame Le Moyne continued. "It's all anyone can talk about."

"Pray, forgive me," Marthe mumbled, grabbing her wool and rushing for the door. The servant often came to Marthe in her nightmares; she did not want to think about what must have happened to convince her to finally flee. Élisabeth followed several paces behind as they scurried back to the bakery.

"Blessed Virgin, shut the door!" Barbe Poulin cried as they came in. Marthe hovered by the entrance, wondering if it would be best to take another turn around the village before facing the widow. Élisabeth rushed straight towards her, placing a kiss on each of her cheeks. "Do you want a nip of brandy to warm you up, Lili?"

There was a firkin on the table, fat-bellied and full of trouble, as well as several smaller bottles. In the widow's hand was a funnel. She looked up at them expectantly.

"What are you doing?" Élisabeth asked, then quickly added, "Why are you only filling the bottles halfway?"

"I'm leaving room for water."

"Whatever for?" Marthe scowled. The room was filled with the sharp smell of eau-de-vie. Barbe Poulin looked like she was set to challenge Folleville's tavern business with the amount of liquor before her.

"I am going into the fur trade." The widow smiled like a satisfied cat.

"What?" Marthe gasped.

Maman Poulin placed the funnel into one of the bottles and filled it halfway up with brandy. "You heard me. I am going to trade brandy for furs."

"But that was . . . I wanted to trade furs!" Marthe was finding it hard to breathe. "Only, I did not know what to trade . . . or who to trade with . . ."

"Is that allowed, Maman?" Élisabeth asked doubtfully. "The Sulpicians have threatened to excommunicate anyone who sells liquor to the natives."

"The governor of Montréal himself has given me licence to do it." The widow bustled to the other side of the table and reached for a pitcher of water.

"He—what?" Marthe thought she might faint. The child inside her kicked and she staggered towards the doorframe. "When? When did you speak with him?"

"You heard him yourself," Barbe said, her tongue jutting out of her mouth as she set about her task. "At the tavern some months back. He quite clearly stated that we should not mind everything the church says. And he *is* the king's representative here."

"Well, if the governor has given you permission, I suppose it cannot be sin—" Élisabeth began.

"He said no such thing!" Marthe braced herself against the wall and rubbed her belly to soothe the kicks. "He gave you no licence."

Barbe Poulin pretended she had not heard Marthe. "At any rate, I can't afford more than the one firkin just now. I'll have to make it last if I'm going to get enough furs to turn a nice profit. The savages won't know any better if it's half river water." She put down the pitcher. "Tell me, how was Le Moyne's?"

"Marthe paid a hefty price for the wool and I doubt she'll get more than one pair of socks out of it," Élisabeth said, shaking her head.

"You should have waited until spring. I did warn you," the widow told Marthe.

"What would you have me do about my feet?" Marthe glowered. "They're always cold." She wanted to ask whom the widow intended to trade with, and where she had purchased so much brandy. She also wanted to tell the Sulpicians what the widow was planning.

"Cold feet means you're having a girl," Barbe Poulin announced. "Verger will be so disappointed."

"Cold feet means that it's winter!" Marthe boiled with frustration. The widow's gaze fell upon her again, pointedly lingering over her large bump. Marthe stopped rubbing her sides and crossed her arms over her belly.

"Maman Poulin, did you hear about the governor's servant?" Élisabeth sat down in a chair at the table. "She has left his service and is staying at Folleville's."

"I did not hear that. How did I not hear that?" Maman Poulin raised her eyebrows.

"Madame Le Moyne said that Anne Lamarque will demand that she earn her keep through whoring," Élisabeth said. "The Sulpicians are said to be ready to step in."

The widow crossed herself. "There is no greater sin for a woman. None at all." She pursed her lips in concentration then she reached for a loaf of bread.

"What are you doing?" Marthe asked. She dreaded the prospect of Barbe Poulin interfering—and doubted the governor's servant cared about falling into sin, given the type of men she had fled.

"I'm going to Folleville's, of course." The widow made a pious little click with her tongue against her teeth. "We do not get to Heaven on prayers alone. Our actions count equally, and saving another's soul is worth a hundred indulgences." The widow tied a scarf around her neck. "And if I can't persuade that poor wretch to return to her husband, I might at least be able to tell Father de Sancy what I know of Anne Lamarque's vile business. Oh! I can't wait to see the look on her face! Come with me, Lili, we do God's work today."

"Don't go," Marthe said plaintively to her sister. "I have the wool to card and spin. We could do it together, in front of the fire, like we did in Saint-Philbert . . ."

Her voice trailed off. She did not want Élisabeth to cross paths with the priest again, lest he fix another devilish notion in her head, another weed that would sprout and spread, impossible to root out. And maybe, if they had more time alone just the two of them, she might confide in her about the governor's attack. Maybe if the widow were not nearby, Élisabeth would listen. Marthe might win her sister back.

"Stay in by the fire when there's a woman on the edge of ruination and priests set to rain God's judgement down upon her?" Barbe Poulin clicked her tongue again, indicating what she thought of Marthe's ideas.

Élisabeth looked from Marthe to the widow. She clasped her hands in front of her and began to twist them. "I won't be gone an hour," she said finally, pulling her mittens back on. "It is the right thing to do. I can help you with the wool when I return."

The bonfire inside Marthe roared back to life, sending sparks into the air. Once again, Élisabeth had chosen to drink poison rather than nectar. Once again, Marthe had lost.

"Suit yourself," she said coldly and stormed across the hallway to her side of the house, her heavy belly slowing her gait. She would not share her secret with her sister. She would see the servant's face in her nightmares again. The anger inside her would grow, filling every inch of her small frame.

She wished with all her heart that there was a door to her room rather than just a burlap curtain. She wanted to hear the satisfying slam of wood, rather than the muted swish of fabric, as she flopped down into her bed.

<h1 style="text-align:center">27</h1>

There wasn't another soul on Rue Saint-Paul. Élisabeth and Maman Poulin bowed their heads against the cold, linking arms to move as one down the street. Élisabeth clutched the lapels of her coat tighter as they hurried past the Sulpicians' seminary, the grey stone dwelling that bore down upon the little village. She was starting to regret having followed the widow outside. She preferred joining her by the fire, listening to her talk as she knit. No one knit faster than Maman Poulin. She could produce a whole stocking in a single evening, the click-click of her needles keeping pace with her opinions. Élisabeth was soothed by the constant activity. The demon Marcosi did not trouble her excessively in Maman Poulin's presence. He slumbered, wings wrapped around his fur-covered body, only one ear cocked and alert. He no longer leapt against her rib cage, trying to break her bones in his bid for release. And for that reason alone, for the calm she felt when Maman Poulin was nearby, Élisabeth would accompany the widow to Folleville's, or out into the frosty night, or wherever she wanted to go.

She pulled the tavern door open, and they were struck by a wave of warmth and pipe smoke. Even in the middle of the day, in a town of only a thousand settlers, Folleville's was busy. It was newly built, but the scent of fresh timber could not mask the smell of sweat that hung in the air. Élisabeth had been to the tavern a handful of times since she had come to stay at the bakery, and on each outing it did not fail to both captivate and alarm her: the noise of pewter mugs slamming down on the wooden tables, the sweet strains of a fiddle matched by the beat of a pair of spoons, the laughter of fallen women in dark corners.

Someone shouted, "Shut the door!" and Élisabeth did as she was bid. Maman Poulin barrelled towards the bar, licking her lips.

"Good day," Anne Lamarque greeted them from behind her counter. Maman Poulin laid the loaf of bread upside down on the counter: a sign of bad luck meant to put the innkeeper on notice.

"The crumb on this new loaf is as fine as any Verger has ever baked. I could not let you miss out," Maman Poulin said pushing the bread towards Anne Lamarque.

"My husband came by this morning to collect our order," she said, eyeing the widow but taking the bread. "I am surprised that you did not know. Though I will not say no to another. Verger is a credit to Old Poulin's skill."

"I am as proud of him as if he were my own son. Though I will confess to you that I sometimes wish he had married this one here, rather than her sister. Lili is as dear to me as any daughter could be."

The innkeeper gazed at Élisabeth, her expression blank. Then she picked up a cloth and began to wipe the counter. "Verger and Marthe have been joined together by God, so put that thought out of your mind, Barbe Poulin."

"Oh, I'm not saying that Verger isn't lucky to have Marthe. She's as sharp a girl as you'll ever meet. It's only that sharp girls are like sharp knives. You need skill to handle them."

The widow followed Anne Lamarque as she moved down the bar with her cloth. Élisabeth rocked back on her feet and felt the pinch of her boots on her heels.

"I hear that you have a new guest staying with you," Maman Poulin continued. "And that she may be forced to take the path of the Magdalene."

The innkeeper stopped wiping the counter and stared at the widow. "Who told you that?"

"It is known across the village."

"It's not true."

"Not true that a certain servant is staying here, or not true that she may be forced into sin?"

Just then the door opened and a parade of men in black cassocks marched into the tavern. Folleville's customers grew still at the sight of the Sulpicians. The fiddle player dropped his bow. Men standing by the fire slid into seats or turned their attention to their drink. The fallen women melted away until the room was full of nothing but artisans, fur traders, and three-year men.

At the head of the procession of priests was Father de Sancy. With a start, Élisabeth noticed one of the men that Marcosi had attacked in the alleyway months ago. She remembered the stench of his breath when he licked her cheek. The demon uncoiled himself from his sleep and sat upright as Élisabeth shrank back towards the bar.

Anne Lamarque glared at Maman Poulin. "What have you done?"

"Nothing!" the widow exclaimed. "I have only just heard of it myself. I did warn you that it has already spread around the village."

"May I help you?" the innkeeper called to the priests.

"Anne Lamarque de Folleville?" Father de Sancy stepped forward, gazing around the room, taking in the men with their red eyes and unbuttoned shirts, a dog in the corner licking its groin. The priest observed it all before turning back to the innkeeper. "There wouldn't be any natives among your customers today?"

"Of course not."

"You understand the punishment for serving liquor to the Indians?"

"My tavern only serves Frenchmen," she replied.

"And what about French women? It is a woman whom I seek today."

Élisabeth took a step closer to Maman Poulin, hoping the priest and the man Marcosi had attacked would not notice her.

"There is no law against a woman having a drink." Anne Lamarque's voice was even.

"I believe a good deal more than drinking happens in this place." The priest wheezed and pressed his hands to his chest before continuing. "I suspect you are up to your neck in debauchery." He pointed to the man Marcosi had attacked in the alley, the one with the brand on his face, hiding among the priests. "I am looking for this man's wife. I believe she is staying here?"

Anne Lamarque crossed her hands over her chest. "That man is a disgrace, as is his master."

"Very well." The priest paused, his tone reasonable. But something about his manner made Marcosi jab his talons into Élisabeth's gut as he angled for a better view. "If you cannot produce his wife, perhaps I might spend the afternoon in conversation with you, Madame de Folleville."

"Me?"

"I am curious why, of all the taverns and inns in Ville-Marie, yours is always the most frequented. Why are you so popular?"

"I serve the best wine and the best food. That is my secret," she replied steadily.

"There is no magic involved? There is no book of spells to draw the most powerful men in New France to your door? What of the tales of you owning a grimoire written in Latin and Greek?"

Anne Lamarque made a show of shrugging her shoulders, though Élisabeth could see her click her fingers behind her back. A man in the corner rose to his feet and slid up the stairs.

"There is no witchcraft here. I don't doubt there are some who are jealous of my success and try to spread lies." The innkeeper glanced at Maman Poulin.

"Then shall I put you to the Question?" The priest's voice grew as soft as a cooing pigeon. "Just to make sure?"

The tavern held its breath. Marcosi gripped Élisabeth's throat so tightly she struggled to swallow. She ached to clasp her hands together in prayer but dared not move lest she draw the priest's attention. Then, out of the corner of her eye, she saw someone on the stairs. The man Anne Lamarque had sent upstairs returned with the scowling servant in tow. The innkeeper nodded in her direction.

"There is no need for any questions, Father. Here is the woman you seek."

Anne Lamarque slowly turned her back on the phalanx of priests, picking up her cloth and rubbing the already clean countertop. She did not watch as the servant was given a shove and landed in the grip of her husband.

But Élisabeth did.

"Let this be the end of wives straying from their husbands in this village," Father de Sancy called out. The effort made him cough into his fist. When he recovered he continued, "I have been dismayed by the behaviour of the women in this colony. I have seen bare collarbones, powdered hair, rouge." He rolled his tongue over the last word as if he regretted it leaving his mouth and wanted to hold it in his embrace a moment longer.

"The women here have turned themselves into instruments of Satan, seeking to please men's eyes. Do not forget, it was Eve who introduced sin into the world. And for that sin, women must be forever penitent. Shame and submission must be their watchwords. They must walk with their heads bowed." He struggled for breath. "I decree that from this day hence, women who wear powder and jewellery will be refused communion."

Across the room a whore stifled a snigger. Father de Sancy rounded on her.

"You find my warnings amusing?"

The woman dropped her gaze. Élisabeth noticed her hair was powdered and her cheeks unnaturally red. She suspected it had been some time since her last confession.

"I would not laugh if I were you. For there is a witch in Ville-Marie."

Folleville's customers shifted in their seats. The haranguing of their wives and whores was one thing; one of the Devil's concubines in their midst was another.

"Ah, I see, this does concern you. As it should. For the queen witch of the Normandy coven is surely here. And she is more than usually dangerous, for she is in possession of Chamberlen's Secret."

A hush fell over the customers. Marcosi's forked tongue flicked up the back of Élisabeth's neck, standing the fine hairs on end.

"What is Chamberlen's Secret?" Maman Poulin asked, loudly enough for the priest to hear. Élisabeth cringed as he turned his gaze on them.

"It is a tool that witches use to perform acts of great evil."

"May the Virgin in Heaven protect us!" Maman Poulin crossed herself, and Élisabeth quickly copied her.

"You are right to pray to the mother of God, for this tool allows witches to rip a child straight from its mother's womb into their greedy, gaping mouths. Witches are insatiable for babies' blood. None of your children are safe as long as she is among you."

The demon fed on Élisabeth's fear, growing bolder and wilder with every scrap of worry he was thrown. Élisabeth started the prayer-and-squeeze ritual, wringing her hands together.

"Are you any closer to finding the witch, Father?" someone called out.

"Not yet," the priest admitted, folding his hands on top of his large belly. "I searched for her in vain in Québec. But then I learned of the devilry in this frontier town and understood that I'd find her in Ville-Marie."

Father de Sancy surveyed the men in the tavern. "Do not worry. Witches cannot stop themselves from committing their evil deeds. I need only wait and watch, and she will act. A child will die. It is only a matter of time."

Élisabeth felt perspiration prickle under her arms. She knew where the priest could find his witch. She should tell him about Jeanne Roy. She owed her no allegiance; Jeanne had done nothing to help her. And if she did have Chamberlen's Secret, as the priest said, she was more dangerous than Élisabeth could have imagined.

But when the priest put Jeanne Roy to the Question, might he ask her about the other brides? Would she tell him about Marcosi? Would Father de Sancy exorcise Élisabeth's demon with needles and whipping, only to then decide she too was a witch, and burn her at the stake?

As she wrestled with her thoughts, she watched the man with the branded face grab his wife by the back of the neck and laugh as he pushed her towards the tavern door. The servant hit and kicked him as he dragged her, with every blow cursing God's name for making her a woman.

28

Word had travelled around Ville-Marie that Father de Sancy hunted a witch in their midst, and the villagers had grown watchful and wary. Now when Marthe fled the bakery in search of a moment's peace from Barbe Poulin, she no longer met smiling housewives, newsmongers strolling the streets to engage in a little gossip. She saw only the stern gazes of men who questioned why she was afoot alone.

Marthe reached the corner of Rue Saint-Paul and Rue Saint-Joseph. Her feet were swollen and her back hurt. She was not even seven months along, yet she felt like the whale that swallowed Jonah. Marthe stopped, eyeing a nun outside the hospital door. She could continue walking past the Hôtel Dieu or she could cross the icy street and loop down to the river. No, the Saint-Laurent was too far and she might run into the governor.

She seethed with frustration to be tethered such a short distance from her own hearth.

A ribbon of birds rose and twisted in the sky, the tail of the flock rippling into the afternoon sun. Marthe watched them fly, thinking of the fat pigeons they should have for their dinner—if only she could pluck and truss the birds without Barbe Poulin commenting on the feathers she'd left on the breast. The ribbon arced and disappeared into the distance and Marthe felt a stab of despair. She wished she could fly away too.

A familiar figure crossed in front of the Place Royale and Marthe leapt at the diversion.

"Apolline!"

The older girl looked around and squinted into the sun. Marthe hiked up her skirts, and placing her foot in a patch of ice that had begun to melt, crossed the road.

"Look at the state of your shoes!" Apolline tutted. Marthe looked at her feet. How like Apolline to worry about mud on wooden clogs, as if a damp cloth wouldn't make them right again in a moment.

"Don't mind about my—"

"I wanted to catch you," Apolline interrupted. "But we must speak privately. Come with me to Françoise's home." Without waiting for an answer, Apolline turned back in the direction she came from, towards Rue Saint-Gabriel. Marthe followed, intrigued.

"It's been many weeks since you've been by the bakehouse," Marthe said as Apolline turned off the main road. "I do hope you are still enjoying our bread." She chided herself for sounding so desperate. Her husband had four hundred livres a year. If she hadn't spent months dreaming of fur-lined riches, perhaps she would not feel their circumstances were wanting. But the widow had stolen her dreams, and now Marthe was set against both the widow and the fur trade.

"Yes, of course," Apolline replied. "It's nothing like what we had in Paris, but certainly better than I would have expected." She pushed open the door to the sabotier's shop; it had been some time since Marthe had been to Françoise's home. She liked the bald cobbler her friend had married. Though he was older than most of the husbands, he had crinkles around his eyes from too much smiling.

"Françoise!" Apolline called out, and after a moment, the girl emerged from the back, tiny Thérèse right behind her.

"Ooh, Marthe. You must not have long to go before you deliver your child," Françoise said.

"I'll thank you to know I have more than two months left," Marthe said through gritted teeth. Françoise gave her a curious look and Marthe regretted letting her temper loose.

"I'm sorry. I know I am rather large. I wish . . . I wish there was someone I could ask to be certain when I will deliver. If I count nine months from my wedding night, it should be the middle of May . . ." Marthe's voice trailed off. She also wished Barbe Poulin would stop mentioning the size of her belly. A thought occurred to her. "Apolline, perhaps I could ask your husband?"

"Blessed Virgin, don't even think of it! Le Picard only attends a labouring mother when she's near dead and the father wants the babe cut out of her belly. Though in most cases the child follows her straight to Heaven."

"Oh," Marthe said weakly, sparing a thought for what it must be like to be married to a surgeon. Apolline's husband's wages must exceed that of a baker's fivefold, but she didn't envy her friend the screams from her husband's patients when he pulled a tooth or cut off a limb. "I wish . . . I wish I could ask Jeanne Roy."

"That is what I need to discuss with you all," Apolline said, craning past Françoise and Thérèse. "Is your husband home?" Françoise shook her head and Apolline continued. "There is to be a search party organized. One of Jeanne Roy's neighbours has gone missing."

"Do you mean Lili's husband?" Marthe said. "He is away on business."

"Of course not," Apolline said. "The entire village whispers about the nature of Francoeur's mission. This is someone else. I do not know the man."

"What concern is it of ours?" Thérèse asked. "If a man has fallen into the river or been buried under a carpet of snow, spring will soon enough reveal what winter has done with him."

"I worry . . ." Apolline started. "I worry that a man's disappearance might be seen as strange, given the times."

She did not need to say more. The village was on edge, seeking signs of sorcery everywhere. Did Benoît's cow sicken and die because it was old and had not enough feed over winter, or was it the work of witchcraft? Was Folleville's oldest customer unable to lie with his wife because of drink, or had a spell been cast over his male member? A missing man could not now simply be dismissed as winter taking its wage. Not when he lived so near to Jeanne Roy.

"But Jeanne is not at home," Marthe said suddenly. "She left in January to stay at the mission village at La Prairie. I spoke with her the day that she left with her Iroquois friend. She is likely across the river even now. She could have had nothing to do with her neighbour's disappearance."

Thérèse and Françoise exchanged a glance. "An Iroquois friend?"

Marthe nodded, thinking of how strange that seemed. The priests tried to convert the natives, and the nuns tried to educate them. But only Jeanne Roy tried to befriend them.

"My sister says that Jeanne Roy has a book of spells in her cabin. And all manner of devilish herbs. Not to mention that frightful doll. If the priest finds them—"

"She will burn," Thérèse said, finishing Marthe's thought.

Apolline drew a deep breath, and her face took on the look of prim self-assertion Marthe imagined she must have been born with. "We cannot know if she brought her magical instruments with her when she left for the mission village. I propose that we travel to her côte and rid the cabin of its effects. Bury them under the snow. Or cast them into the river."

"What if someone should see us?" Françoise asked doubtfully.

"We shan't be seen," Apolline scolded her.

"I worry . . . I worry we will put ourselves at risk," Thérèse said. "For some-one who has not always looked so kindly upon us."

Marthe looked closely at the other girls. Françoise's cheeks were plump; Thérèse had the wan look of someone who had been sick all morning; and Apolline's waistline had developed a small paunch.

"We must!" Marthe urged. "We have no choice. We shall all be in childbed before the summer is out and she is the only midwife on the island. And not just a midwife. A trained accoucheur."

"A *what?*" Thérèse asked.

"I don't really understand what that is," Marthe admitted. "All I know is that we shall all be in need of her magic soon enough."

"How long does it take to get to her côte?" Apolline asked.

"My sister says it's little more than an hour's walk."

"The days are getting longer," she said. "If we leave now, we can be back before nightfall."

"I shall run back to the bakery," Marthe said. "We shall be in need of food on our journey, even if we are only gone a few hours."

"Will it be safe to walk so far out of the village?" Thérèse asked, meaning: Might the Iroquois capture them? There was always a risk that a hunting party might breach the peace. But between a rogue attack and facing childbirth alone, Marthe knew which she feared the most.

"Recite your rosary and beg for Saint Anne to protect us," she said, wishing there were more they could do.

Marthe hurried back to the bakehouse. If the man was missing, Jeanne might be blamed. She shuddered, and not from the cold. As much as she was drawn to magic, the idea of searching through the hedge witch's hut for enchanted tools frightened her a little bit.

She threw open the door to the bakery and made straight for the front room to collect some bread. For once she was thankful her husband slept all morning. She would be gone before he woke. She crammed two loaves into her bag and was turning to leave when she was startled by the sight of her sister standing silently in the doorway. Marthe let out a gasp.

"You startled me!"

"Where are you going?" Élisabeth asked.

"To deliver some bread."

"I thought all the orders had gone out. Maman Poulin took the regulars not half an hour ago."

"Well, she left one order behind."

Élisabeth frowned. "Marthe, I know how you like to walk about but it's not safe with a witch on the prowl."

"You know as well as I do that the witch they seek is Jeanne Roy. And we have nothing to fear from her." Marthe spoke with more confidence than she felt.

Élisabeth glowered. "She's never done anything to help me."

Marthe hesitated. She did not know whom to believe. Élisabeth, who was desperate for Jeanne to rid her of her demon, or Jeanne, who wanted to prick her sister's arm with a lancet to drain her black bile. Marthe felt if only she could sit them down and make them talk to each other they might come to some kind of understanding. She decided to confess.

"Lili, truth be told, I am going to Jeanne Roy's cabin with Apolline and the other girls. One of your neighbours has gone missing. It won't be long before a search party goes to your côte. And who knows what magical objects and charms Jeanne has hidden in her cabin. If anyone finds them . . ." Marthe's voice trailed off.

"Which neighbour?" Élisabeth asked.

"I don't know. Apolline did not say."

Élisabeth twisted her hands in front of her, lost in contemplation. Suddenly she looked up. "I will join you," she said. "If Father de Sancy is right and Jeanne Roy is in possession of Chamberlen's Secret, we must look for it in her cabin. After all, it might . . . it might be the tool I need to banish the demon."

Marthe hesitated. The village was abuzz with gossip about the magic wand that was said to give the witch her power. She knew from her visit to the fort that Governor de Lafredière also wanted to find it. Perhaps someone other than a witch *could* figure out how to use it. But after what Jeanne Roy had said about Élisabeth's condition, Marthe wasn't certain that a magic wand was the cure her sister needed after all.

"I can't imagine Jeanne would have left Chamberlen's Secret behind, if it is so powerful," Marthe said. "Still, I would be grateful if you joined us."

She gave her sister a shy smile. Élisabeth smiled back, and Marthe's heart lifted. Perhaps a long walk would do them both good. She reached for her blanket coat from the peg by the door and belted it around her waist. She handed Élisabeth her own coat, just as the door flew open. Barbe Poulin stepped inside.

"Where are you two going?" the widow asked. The look on her face indicated she was not pleased. "Marthe, have you plucked the birds for our supper yet?"

Marthe glanced back at the pair of pigeons on the table. They lay limp, trussed by the legs. She thought of the ribbon of birds she had seen earlier, rippling and waving as they disappeared over the horizon. Her frustration was so great she wanted to break into a sob.

"Maman Poulin, we are obliged to journey to my home this morning," Élisabeth said suddenly. "I've had word from a person who walked by the house that a shutter has come loose."

"Oh no," Barbe Poulin said, her concern knit across her forehead. "You mustn't let a loose shutter flap in the wind. It could damage the frame."

"Precisely," Élisabeth said. "So we have decided to make a day of it, Marthe and I, along with some of our sisters from the ship. We will be back before nightfall."

Marthe marvelled at Élisabeth's smooth lie. Though what Barbe Poulin said next made her heart sink.

"What an idea! I shall join you."

29

They collected the other *Saint-Jean-Baptiste* girls from the clog maker's shop and walked along the river path on the edge of the forest. The day before, a dreary sleet had fallen unlike any Élisabeth had ever known in Normandy, a cold rain that had frozen when it hit the ground, lacquering the house and trees with a glaze of hard ice. The landscape looked like it had been coated in whipped egg whites. Élisabeth wished she had brought the snowshoes her husband had purchased from the Algonquins; they would have helped her balance on the icy path.

Still, Maman Poulin was merry company, telling the girls everything she knew about those who dwelled in the houses they passed. The long, thin ribbon farms ran down to the river, each with its own stretch of waterfront, so they had occasion to cross dozens of homesteads. Several times along the way the widow stopped to talk to the habitants as they rushed out of their homes and down to the river to greet them. On the first occasion, Marthe whispered her plan to the others: that she, Thérèse, and Françoise would forge on towards Jeanne's cabin, while Élisabeth and Apolline tarried behind to keep the widow distracted. Élisabeth muttered that Marthe would not know her house, let alone the witch's hut, but Marthe said from all she had been told she would not mistake it.

Before Élisabeth could protest further, the widow had drawn her over to greet a habitant and his wife.

Marthe and the two others stole away, growing smaller and smaller in the distance; when the widow called out for them to cool their heels, it was too late. They were gone.

"Now this is a sorry home," Maman Poulin told Apolline when they finally reached the western edge of Élisabeth's côte. "Dufossé and his wife rarely come into the village. Hélène lost a child soon after she delivered it, and I don't think he has ever forgiven her. I say we stop and pay her a visit."

"Oh Maman, I worry that we won't get back before nightfall," Élisabeth said, glancing at Apolline. "We have stopped so often already."

"We must. A baker's wife keeps a village's secrets at her breast, and I know enough about this pair to insist that we look in on them."

"Pray, let me travel on ahead," Élisabeth begged. She had no desire to see her mouse of a neighbour Hélène in her misery. "I will tie up the broken shutter, and when you reach my door, I will have the fire started and we may eat our bread and cheese at my table. I am sure that Marthe and the others are already there."

The widow was like a general: she did not like her troops to move without her command, and she had already lost half her company. Her face rumpled at the mutiny she faced.

"Do not fear, Maman Poulin," Apolline broke in. "I will see Élisabeth safely to her door. You look in on the poor, childless mother and we shall see you within the hour."

They took their leave of the widow and walked eastwards as quickly as they could.

"I will forge on to Jeanne's cabin to help the others," Apolline said as they neared Élisabeth's house. She stifled a shriek as her boots slipped on the ice. "Can you make a show of having mended a broken shutter?"

"Don't worry about me. You go on and find the others. And Apolline? Keep your eye out for Chamberlen's Secret. If you see it, whatever it is, do everything in your power to keep it safe."

Élisabeth showed Apolline the path through the woods where she would find the witch's hut and then turned to open the door to her home.

Inside, it was so cold she thought no amount of firewood could ever warm its wooden bones. She looked around the room. She had forgotten how perfect her home was. How the door fitted smoothly in its jamb. How the backs of the newly built chairs curved gracefully. Francoeur had sanded them over the course of the month of December, and he had promised to build more when their children came and claimed a place at the table. Élisabeth's gaze fell on the straw mattress, lying plumped and waiting on the floor.

The mattress where she had let him believe that her piety and fear stopped her from lying with him, when all the while she had longed to feel his calloused hands on her body. Like a wolf on a rabbit, as Maman Poulin said.

Yet the grace of the sacrament of marriage came from its fertility, and she knew from the feeling of the demon sharpening its claws on her womb that she was still barren. Without children, their marriage bed would have been a pit of sin.

Consider, consider. Witchcraft does not exist.

Élisabeth crossed the room, sweeping her hands across the hearth to try to locate the tinder in the dim light. What if Jeanne Roy was right? What if witches were not real? But if that were so, *why* had she lost her baby?

Rémy wanted to be rid of you, that's why.

She tried to ignore the demon's taunts, but she could not help but think of her lover: Rémy with his wiry frame and feline appetite, pouncing on her day after day, pawing at her stays as if she were a doll for him to undress. She found the tinder and clutched it in her fist.

She must have been mad to think herself in love with him. She must have been a fool to believe they would marry.

She dropped to her knees to build the fire and saw there was barely enough kindling to catch, and not a log left inside to burn. She would have to bring some in from the woodpile. The woodpile Francoeur had carefully cut and stacked before the onset of winter.

All around her it was plain what she needed.

Francoeur, who had built a home for her with his bare hands.

Francoeur, with shoulders so broad and arms so strong she ached when he changed his shirt, giving her a glimpse of his bare chest.

Francoeur, who had left her.

Élisabeth did not have time for tears; the widow would be upon her soon. She rose and made for the door, stepping outside and slipping on the slick ground as she made her way to the woodpile. It too was covered in a layer of ice. She ran her hands over the wood but could not pry a single log free from the pile.

"Hell's teeth," she muttered, kicking a frozen log and immediately feeling a stab of pain in her toes. She clamped her mouth shut so that Marcosi could not slip out on a string of curses. She turned towards the cowshed. Her husband had stored enough wood for the entire winter in the shed, cords and cords of it cut down from the back of their farm. Her boots skidded on the ice as she shuffled over to the meagre cabin, the same as all the settlers had erected when they first arrived: thin trees bound together with wattle and daub. She reached the door and saw to her dismay that it was barricaded by a drift of snow.

"Blessed Virgin, give me strength." She kicked at it and found that once the crust of ice had been broken, the snow underneath was soft enough to be pushed aside with her foot. She cleared enough to open the door a few inches and squeezed inside the shed.

She blinked, adjusting to the dim light, aware of shapes in the darkness around her. She squeezed her eyes shut and opened them wide again.

There, on top of the woodpile: a man, sitting.

Élisabeth screamed. She stumbled back to the door. She grabbed it and pushed frantically against the snow to be let out. The door caught on the drift on the other side. She looked back.

His skin was blue, his eyes frozen open.

A ghost carved from ice, waiting for a gathering of his fellow damned before awakening to walk the earth.

The fellow damned . . . like her?

Horrified, Élisabeth banged on the door with her palm. She shouted the names of all the saints in Heaven. With a surge of Marcosi's strength she lunged, breaking through the door, tumbling into the daylight, tearing her sleeve and the pale skin underneath. She fell to the ground and scrabbled on all fours back towards the house, howling. She looked up and saw her sister running through the woods towards her.

"Lili! Are you hurt?" Marthe cried.

"Her arm is bleeding!" said Thérèse, close behind.

Élisabeth's lips formed a hoarse rasp. She struggled to her knees as her cap slipped off and her hair fell loose against her face. Marthe squeezed her arm tightly and said something she could not hear. Panting, Élisabeth bent over and tried to get the air back into her lungs, but the demon had grown so large inside her there was no room for her to inhale.

Marthe moaned. "Good grief, here comes the widow Poulin."

"What's happened?" the widow called out from a distance. "I heard screaming."

The voices swirled around Élisabeth, making her dizzy. She was hot and cold at once. She was certain she would faint.

"Tell me what happened," Marthe urged.

"Dead," she croaked, pointing at the cowshed. "Man." She was aware of Marthe squeezing her arm again, and Françoise or Thérèse crying out for God's help.

The widow reached her side and latched on to her other arm. "What has happened?"

"Lili saw something . . . someone . . . dead in the shed."

Maman Poulin threw her body around Élisabeth's, squeezing her as tightly as a bear. "Mary, Mother of God, it must be him. Is it the neighbour, Dufossé? He went missing three weeks ago. His wife, Hélène, has just told me so herself. Oh, the poor wretch, to have died without confessing his sins."

The horror of the man's perfectly composed, perfectly frozen body came back to Élisabeth and she began to stammer. "It *is* Dufossé. He is sitting . . . sitting in the cowshed."

"Sitting?" Maman Poulin was incredulous.

"On the woodpile."

"Then he is alive?" asked Françoise.

"He's fr-fr-frozen," Élisabeth stuttered. "On the woodpile."

Maman Poulin shook her by the shoulders. "That can't be right. What do you mean, he's sitting on the woodpile? Sitting down, frozen solid?"

Élisabeth swallowed. The widow's lips were drawn in a firm line. There *was* something strange about Dufossé sitting with his hands folded in his lap. He seemed almost comfortable. Élisabeth's fingers began to tingle.

"I must see him for myself," Maman Poulin said, standing up and straightening her skirts. She walked towards the shed, grim-faced and silent, Françoise and Thérèse at her heels, Élisabeth and Marthe close behind. They filed through the open door.

Élisabeth blinked.

Dufossé's eyes were fixed somewhere on the cabin's far wall. His beard was full of ice, his lashes trimmed with frost.

"Witchcraft." The widow gave an almost contented sigh.

"Why so?" Marthe challenged her.

Maman Poulin shot her a peevish glance. "It is the strangest thing I ever saw."

"I cannot bear to look," Thérèse said, her voice catching on her words.

Apolline leaned closer to the dead man. "He must have frozen to death."

The widow shook her head, disbelieving. "Look at him, sitting there with his hands in his lap. Why would anyone just sit down and wait to freeze to death?"

"Maybe he could not get back into the house?" Françoise suggested. "There was a good deal of snow outside the door."

"Nonsense. Lili broke through the door and look at her. She's the size of a sparrow."

"Perhaps he was drunk," Marthe said. "And could not find his way home. Perhaps he fell asleep."

"With his eyes open? Sitting up? Who sleeps sitting up in the cold?" Maman Poulin sneered. "No. There is only one explanation for what happened here."

"My husband is a surgeon," Apolline announced, though everyone knew Le Picard's profession, "and he sees a good many corpses. If witches were behind every frozen body in this land, they'd be responsible for half the deaths each winter."

"Precisely," the widow said. "Witches *are* responsible for half our troubles. The Iroquois are responsible for the rest."

"What . . . what are we to do about him?" Élisabeth finally found her voice. She averted her eyes from the dead man's gaze, but she knew the half-moon slits in his blue face continued to stare straight at her.

"We must tell Father de Sancy, of course," Maman Poulin said. "And I suppose we should let Hélène know that she is a widow now."

"Do we just leave him here?" Élisabeth asked.

"He's doing no harm where he is. He won't be buried until the ground thaws in May."

Élisabeth hid her face in her hands so as not to look at the dead man again. One by one the others made the sign of the cross and left the cowshed. Maman Poulin strode purposefully ahead, determined to be the first to bring the grim news to the man's widow. Françoise stopped Élisabeth before she could follow.

"Why would Jeanne do such a thing?" Françoise whispered, kicking the snow pile with her boot.

"I thought she was a sorceress, a magical healer. Not an evil witch," Thérèse said nervously.

Élisabeth was about to reply that Jeanne Roy had never done one good thing for her, when Marthe pinched her arm.

"That's enough," she snapped. "Do not speak Jeanne's name aloud again. Especially not in front of the widow."

"Why not—"

"Because we cannot have her accused. This is the spark that starts the fire. We cannot, must not, let her burn."

"But what if she killed that man?" Élisabeth demanded. "What if a child is next?" She blinked and no longer saw Dufossé's blue face. She saw the Winter Witch, her finger pointed, lips trembling.

'Twas for you.

Marthe pinched her again, harder.

"Ow," Élisabeth cried.

"Mind what I said. Do not speak Jeanne's name aloud," Marthe's voice was low and urgent. "Especially not in front of the widow."

30

The village simmered with anticipation. Marthe watched with growing unease as her neighbours cast about, looking for the queen witch of the Normandy coven at every turn. A man had been bewitched to death. Such wickedness would not go unpunished. They put their faith in the magnificent witch hunter, Onésime Gaudin de Sancy, and the widow Poulin, who spared no details in her telling of the story to her customers. They lingered in the bakery, getting in Marthe's way as she tried to sweep up flour and mop down bread baskets, hanging on the widow's words: *There he was! Hands raised, mouth agape, a tableau of horror, pointing at the space where the witch had stood as she cast her evil spell.*

Some said they would make the trek all the way to Élisabeth's house to see the frozen corpse in the cowshed, though if they did, they never came back to counter the accuracy of the tale the widow wove.

Marthe hung her cloak on the peg as she stepped inside the bakery. Her walks were no longer as soothing as they once had been. Now when she pounded the dirt paths of Ville-Marie, forcing the earth to absorb her fury, she met simpletons in wide-eyed agreement with the widow—that a witch was to blame for a man's death—all while the brutal governor of Montréal attacked women and girls without censure.

The sharp clatter of Barbe Poulin's voice rang out from the front room, admonishing Élisabeth what to do and what to think. Marthe stood apart, watching them from the doorway, unwilling to sit at the table no matter how much the weight she carried made her groin ache. Élisabeth's feet were up on a trunk, her head in her hand. Barbe Poulin had stuffed a morsel of bread into her mouth and was chewing with her mouth open, her tongue forcing the sop of bread forward and back until it was the consistency of porridge. Marthe did not like to bother God with much, but she could not help saying a small prayer for the widow to swallow her food.

God paid no heed.

"Well then, little mistress, bring us the news," Barbe Poulin trilled. The mashed sop was visible for a moment, then disappeared again behind her tongue. "We all know how you like to get about."

"Did you cross anyone's path?" Élisabeth loosened her hood and pulled it off her head.

"There was no one out but me," Marthe mumbled, eyeing the brandy between them on the table. The widow had first opened one of her diluted bottles after they had returned from their grim discovery. A little something to calm their nerves. Now it was becoming habit. But the drink did not seem to have steadied them much, for the alarm Marthe saw on the streets of Ville-Marie was fourfold in her own home.

"What drives you out to walk the streets," Barbe Poulin said snidely, "I can't imagine. There is a witch afoot, for goodness' sake. Use your head."

"Chérie, won't you stay inside?" Élisabeth pleaded, a crease in her brow.

Marthe beckoned for her sister to join her in the hallway. She would not step foot inside the widow's web.

"I won't forget what I saw for the rest of my days," Barbe Poulin said as Élisabeth rose. "Eh? Lili? Do you recall? The poor soul's hands raised, like so, trying to shield himself from the spell that took him?"

"Yes, Maman," Élisabeth said as she crossed the room. "What is it?" she said to Marthe.

"Must you sit and drink with her all day while she embellishes her tale?"

"I have done nothing of the sort," Élisabeth said, though her face was flushed. "Perhaps only a little sip or two. You know how the demon torments me, even more so now. Brandy helps Marcosi sleep."

"Eh? What's that? Who is Marcosi?" the widow called from her salon.

Marthe threw a glance to Élisabeth. Barbe Poulin lurked at every corner, sniffing out her words like a bitch after another dog's urine.

"No one, Maman," Élisabeth said, blushing. "I said the brandy makes my toes sleep."

"Ah, mine too, child, mine too." The widow put her feet up on the trunk.

Marthe lowered her voice. "Take care, Lili. If you are drinking to tame your worries, you are headed for ruin."

Élisabeth steepled her hands in prayer. "You do not understand my suffering."

Marthe could not bite her tongue any longer. "Oh, but Maman Poulin does?"

"Marthe, I have been thinking. Given Dufossé's death, I do not believe I should deceive Maman Poulin any longer. I must tell her about Rémy, the demon, Jeanne, all of it—"

"No! You mustn't. Jeanne had nothing to do with that man's death, as you well know. And if you tell Barbe Poulin about the demon, how long do you think it would take for the widow to betray you to the priest? She will see you accused of both fornication and witchcraft before the day is out."

Élisabeth frowned at the reminder of her past sins. "Marthe, listen to me. I know what I risk, but I am *possessed*. I must conquer my fear and tell Maman Poulin. She cares for me; I know she does. She will help give me the strength to go to the priest to be exorcised, now before matters worsen—"

"Lili, do you not see that all the blame that widow has whipped up will land on *you*? You could be accused of causing Dufossé's death!"

"But what can I do? What in Heaven's name can I do? The demon writhes in my entrails and squeezes my heart. It is so angry. One day soon, this unholy spirit will surely command me to howl like a wolf in public or force me into contorted leaps across the Place Royale—"

The bakery door opened and a gust of cold air swept the floor. Marthe watched the colour drain from Élisabeth's face, then turned to the figure filling the doorway.

Francoeur.

His beard was bushy and his clothes filthy. Nights of poor sleep were written in the lines on his face. Behind him grinned her two best friends in the whole world, Rose and Lou.

Marthe ran towards them and threw herself into their arms.

"Thank God. Thank God in Heaven and the Blessed Virgin and all the saints. You are here. Thank God, you are here." She did not dare ask how or why they were here, or if Francoeur had been successful in his petition against the governor.

Rose kissed her cheeks once, then twice, then all over again for luck, while Lou's laughter filled the hallway.

"Our husbands collected us from our farms on their way back from seeing the intendant in Québec," Rose explained, gesturing behind her at Jambon and Lajeunesse. "It was on the way." The men crowded through the door so that the small space filled with the smell of tobacco and tired travellers. "They have the petition, and a decision. They said they were exhausted and wanted nothing more but to collapse into bed, but we said, 'No chance, take us to Ville-Marie!' And so we happened upon the idea of all coming together."

"Francoeur?" Élisabeth wobbled towards the door. She stumbled, reaching for him through the crowd. Francoeur caught her by the arm and a tentative smile spread across his face.

"I've got you."

He bent down to kiss her on the cheek as Élisabeth turned her face towards him. Their lips met. She put her arms around his neck and closed her eyes, pulling him closer. They didn't break away until the widow pushed herself into the hallway and declared, "Oh, there will be a rumpus in bed tonight if I'm not very much mistaken!"

Élisabeth pulled back and blushed. Francoeur's ears were as pink as her cheeks. "Forgive me. I am not . . . myself," she told him.

Marthe rolled her eyes at her sister. "You are *fine*, Lili."

But Francoeur gave Élisabeth such a tender look that Marthe felt instantly rebuked. In the small, crowded hallway, he saw no one but his wife.

"Come in, come in," Barbe Poulin said, ushering the group into her salon. "You were gone ever such a long time, Francoeur." Barbe Poulin turned to the travellers to take their cloaks and hats. "I am not complaining. It has been a delight to have my chère Lili here. But what on earth kept you so long?"

"I'll keep my hat," Francoeur said, shaking his head at the widow. His eyes took in the bottle of brandy on the table. "Before I collect Élisabeth, I must speak with my sister-in-law. Marthe, may we talk alone?"

"Francoeur?" Élisabeth's voice shook. "What is it?"

Marthe felt another stab of frustration with her sister. If Élisabeth had stopped wringing her hands about her own woes to listen to Marthe's, she'd have known the truth of Francoeur's mission. That she, Marthe, had suffered a *true* demon, rather than Élisabeth's imagined one.

"Follow me," she said to Francoeur, aware of Élisabeth's eyes on her back as she crossed the hallway to Verger's workroom and shut the door.

Marthe braced herself. "How was the petition received?"

Francoeur's expression softened.

"We accomplished what we set out to do," he said, but when her face lit up, he held up his hand. "It is not entirely a success. Lafredière *will* be recalled to France. He'll be sent to Québec immediately to await the spring ships. He'll be dispatched on the first to return to France and the colony will be rid of him. But there will be no investigation into the missing slaves. And no record of what he did to you. He will only be written up for debauchery and selling liquor to the natives."

Marthe put a hand to her neck. No one would ever know what he had done. He would be gone, but he would never be guilty. The weight of disappointment was so heavy she thought she might slump to the floor.

"Marthe, I'm sorry. It was the best we could do. Lafred's uncle is the Marquis de Salières. He argued for him, and it is hard to counter the commander of the regiment. Take heart that although Lafredière will not have to account for what he did to you and the Panis girls, he will be gone from the island of Montréal before the roads melt."

"How long will that be?"

"The intendant sent his soldiers and his sleigh with us. They'll collect Lafredière and leave as soon as the horses have rested."

"What if he doesn't agree to go?"

"The intendant's men have the authority to take him by force. He can leave as a bandit in chains or as a nobleman with footmen to wait on him. It will be his choice."

"I expect he'll leave as a lord, which is more than he deserves," Marthe said bitterly.

"I should say so. Now, I will speak with your husband. I will pay him for any costs he's incurred for boarding Élisabeth, and take her with us to the inn—"

"Francoeur, wait. I must speak with you about Lili."

Marthe hesitated, struggling to put into words what she could not understand. "Jeanne Roy came by the bakery some while back. She said that . . . rather, I believe how she explained it is . . . Élisabeth has too much black bile. She is off-balance." When Francoeur gave her a puzzled look, Marthe blurted out the rest. "Élisabeth suffers from melancholy."

Marthe could tell he was not wholly surprised. "Melancholy," he said, and stroked his bushy beard. "I knew that she found our life on the farm difficult. She was often . . . distressed, I think, by being so far away from you. I had hoped this time with you would have soothed her nerves."

"I'm afraid that dreadful widow has upset her nerves even more. Barbe Poulin has thrown Ville-Marie into the grip of a witch hunt." Marthe's temper flared momentarily, thinking of the poison that had been poured into all their ears. "Jeanne says the only cure is to open Lili's vein with a lancet or a fleam." She shook her head mournfully. "Bloodletting."

Francoeur nodded, a tight military movement. "Good. Bloodletting is not such a burden to bear. If it cures her of the sadness in her soul, then we shall try it immediately."

"Oh, Francoeur. You do not know. Our father . . . we tried to bleed him to cure his fever." How could she explain to Francoeur how appalling their father's end had been? She looked at the floor. "I cannot imagine Lili would ever let a lancet near her."

The hessian curtain separating the rooms moved and Verger appeared, his face crumpled with sleep. He looked shocked to see Francoeur in his workroom.

"Welcome back, brother." His face was neutral as he put his arm around Marthe's shoulder. "I hope you have made a safe journey."

"It was a success," Francoeur said.

Marthe shook Verger off, stepping out of his reach.

"Why then, you are my wife's saviour," Verger said, his voice both flat and forlorn, his arm left hanging by his side. "The saviour of Ville-Marie."

"I'm no saviour," Francoeur said sharply. Then he took a breath. "It is not very late in the day. I will ask Jambon or Lajeunesse to take a skiff across the Saint-Laurent to fetch Jeanne Roy. We will see her before we return home to our côte."

"No!" Marthe cried. "You mustn't bring Jeanne to Ville-Marie!"

"Whyever not?" Francoeur looked puzzled. Marthe glanced back and forth at each of them. What could she say? They had found no book of spells, no magic wand in Jeanne's cabin. But every one of the brides on the *Saint-Jean-Baptiste* knew what she was: a cunning woman, an enchantress, a sea serpent in female form. With confession on the tip of Élisabeth's tongue, if Jeanne returned to the village now, the flint would surely strike the steel and she would be named as the witch they were hungry to set aflame.

"Lili will not want to be bled" was all Marthe could think to say.

Francoeur gave her a patient smile. "If Élisabeth is unwell, as you say she is, then we must look for a cure. I will send for Jeanne straightaway."

Marthe could not return his smile.

31

Her husband's face was drawn and serious when he emerged from his conversation with Marthe. Élisabeth wished she knew what her sister had told him. Marthe would not have spilled her secrets; she was too quick to deny Élisabeth's suffering to tell Francoeur she was possessed. But what had they discussed? Élisabeth watched as her husband pulled his men to one side and spoke to them quietly. Within moments Lajeunesse had taken his coat from the peg and slipped out of the bakery. Francoeur refused the drink Maman Poulin offered him, and stood up stiffly, almost rudely, to announce that they must be on their way or they would be without rooms for the night.

Élisabeth and Francoeur walked side by side down Rue Saint-Paul. Jambon turned left to take Lou and Rose to the inn a few streets away from the river; Francoeur explained that there was nowhere left for them to stay for the night but Folleville's. As he spoke, she noticed that his shirt was worn at the neck and determined she would make him a new one. She would use what was left of her dowry to get some serge from Le Moyne's and stitch him as fine a shirt as he had ever worn. She would not settle for buttons made of bone; she would show him how she felt with buttons wrapped in silk.

She imagined him unbuttoning his new shirt to reveal his bare chest and felt the stirring of lust. She shook herself to loosen the demon's grip on her mind.

"Francoeur," she said abruptly. "What did you discuss with Marthe?"

"I explained that our petition was only a modest success."

"But why tell her—"

He pulled open the door to the tavern. The room was full, voices were high and bright, and faces pleated with laughter. In the corner, a boy with wispy hairs on his chin smacked a pair of spoons between his hand and his knee as an older man cranked a bow across a fiddle.

"I too would like to hear about your petition." She was aware she sounded petulant, even jealous, as he steered her towards a table.

"I will tell you all," he said, looking over his shoulder towards the bar. "Though I felt I should take a moment to reassure Marthe privately that she is safe. The governor has been recalled. He cannot hurt her again."

"Why would—? Hurt her?" At once Élisabeth realized what she should have known for months. All the parts of the riddle were now clear: the governor had attacked one of the wives, Francoeur had leapt to the woman's defence, Marthe had been sullen and angry all winter.

How had she not known? Why had Marthe not confided in her?

She felt a spasm of despair. Marcosi had prevented her from seeing what should have been plain. The unholy spirit had blinded her to her sister's pain. She thought for a moment of all the hours she'd spent in the widow's company, and how hard Maman Poulin was on Marthe.

Through my fault, through my fault, my most grievous fault.

"There's Anne Lamarque," Francoeur said, rising to his feet. "Stay here while I see about a room." He strode towards the bar, spent a moment in conversation with the innkeeper, then followed her upstairs.

The fiddler started on a sombre tune, weaving his way among the tables, his head shaking in time to the music. Élisabeth knew the song. It was about a shepherd who went to gather wildflowers for his true love, but he took so long that his milkmaid died while waiting for him. For some reason the lament filled Élisabeth's heart with an unbearable sadness. She closed her eyes and listened to the grey-bearded fiddler sing, wondering if it was too late to beg for her sister's forgiveness.

The fiddler and the boy on spoons stopped playing abruptly. Élisabeth opened her eyes. At first, she did not recognize the man they gawped at in the doorway, for he was not wearing his wig.

"Good afternoon, good citizens of Ville-Marie," Governor de Lafredière bellowed. He swept into a mock bow. "So pious. So devout. So *treasonous.*"

The patrons clutched their drinks. No one spoke. The demon hammered his fists against Élisabeth's heart. This man had choked her sister. He had tried to kill Marthe.

"Yes, treasonous. Do you think you can be rid of me? That I will not have my revenge against those who wronged me?" The governor unsheathed his sword and pointed it at every person in the tavern, turning in a circle. When his gaze landed on Élisabeth he stopped.

"Where is she?"

Élisabeth trembled and said nothing, though she longed to tell this monster what she thought of him.

"Are you a mute? Or just stupid? Where is your sister?" Lafredière's lace cravat was loose, his justaucorps unbuttoned, the gold brocade unravelling on one side. "Where is the baker's wife?"

As she gaped at the dishevelled nobleman, she could feel the pressure in her gullet as the great marquis of Hell shook his horned head. She remembered what Father de Sancy had said: that the demon Leviathan had spoken to him through the weak flesh of a possessed nun. *Possessed.* She clamped her hand over her mouth lest Marcosi take command of her tongue.

"I will not be sent home in disgrace on the word of some little tart," Lafredière sneered. "Where is the lying whelp? Where is the baker's bitch?"

It was too late. With a sickening feeling, Élisabeth felt Marcosi rise from the chair. With complete power over her trembling body, the demon turned to face the governor.

"You pathetic cur," Marcosi boomed, his voice clear and bold. "You have the mind and the morals of a rabid dog."

Not one person in the room breathed. They stared at the girl and the governor. Lafredière gaped at her, licking the spittle from the corners of his mouth.

"Do you believe that it is on the girl's word *alone* that you are banished?" Marcosi continued. "Fool. Your own men turned against you—every soldier on the march to New York. Every one of them still laughs at your weakness, your impotence, the worm-filled hole where your eye used to be—"

Lafredière roared and lunged for her neck. Marcosi vanished. Élisabeth ducked and put her hands over her head, bracing for a blow that never came. Instead, through her fingers, she saw the governor crumple, tackled from the side. Francoeur had Lafredière pinned to the floor. He grabbed for the governor's hands, but Lafredière twisted away. Francoeur drew his fist back and punched his head. Blood erupted from Lafred's nose and his eye patch slid off, revealing puckered skin stitched closed in a dreadful, permanent wink.

"You whore! I will see you hanged!" the governor shouted at her.

Francoeur sprang, this time grabbing Lafredière by the waist. The governor slapped at his hands but Francoeur flipped him over onto his face and placed his knee on his back. Lafredière twisted, trying to lift his head.

"You are supposed to be locked in the fort," Francoeur panted. "How did you escape?"

"Oh look, it's Francoeur." He spat out his name like a wad of tobacco. "The worst of the slapsauce ruffians on this miserable island." The governor squirmed, trying to free himself. "Do you think for a bag of coins my jailors wouldn't let me say goodbye to my people?" he shouted at the room. "My people who have turned on me!"

"The people have never been with you." Francoeur's voice was as low as a growl.

"They love me!" the governor roared.

"And yet not one of them ever came forward to reveal who shot you. It's as if they wanted you dead."

Lafredière tried to turn over, but Francoeur pressed his knee in deeper. "Was it you?" the governor said. "Are you the coward who shot me? Once my uncle hears of it, you *will* be hanged."

"Your uncle has forsaken you. In the morning you will be off the island and on your way back to France. Hundreds signed our petition, willingly. The Montréalists want nothing more to do with you."

Someone threw Francoeur a whip to tie Lafredière's hands.

Lafredière laughed and gnashed his teeth as he tried to wriggle free. "You pig. You think you have won? Soon I will be back home in France. And you will all be here in Hell."

Francoeur snapped his fingers at a boy by the bar. "Run for the bailiff. We'll put him in the pillory until morning."

He stepped off Lafredière's back and two men came forward to haul the governor to his feet. They whisked him out the door and towards the Place Royale, their prisoner writhing and cursing as they went.

Élisabeth gaped after him, stumbling backwards into a chair. Francoeur sat down next to her.

"What were you thinking?" Her husband's eyes searched hers. She turned away. How could she explain what had just happened? "Élisabeth? Tell me what you were thinking, speaking to him like that. He could have killed you."

A sense of great weariness came over her. Finally, it was time to confess.

"No, husband. He could not hurt me. Marcosi would savage anyone who tries to touch me."

"Marcosi?" Francoeur froze. "Who is Marcosi?"

She blinked, trying to find the words.

"I see." Francoeur swallowed. He laid his hands on the table, pressing his fingertips into the wood. "Do you love him?"

She shook her head, drawing her hands into her lap. "No," she whispered, shaking her head. "I hate him."

"Élisabeth, listen to me," he said, leaning forward. "I would not begrudge you if you once hoped to marry another. I have a past too."

She looked down at her hands. The skin between her thumb and forefinger was cracked and red from the number of times she had wrung her hands.

"I want to know about your past," she said.

"Then I will tell you, if it means you might tell me about your Marcosi." He laid his hand on top of hers. When she did not speak, he began.

"I will start, then. My father was a cruel and violent man. My mother was forced to take refuge with the Poor Clares for her own safety. I was not yet grown when she left, only fourteen, and I was lonely. To avoid my father's fists, I spent time down by the docks. I met a girl—"

"I don't want to hear about your other women." Élisabeth pulled her hand away, then immediately wished she had not. "I want to hear how you became a hero. How you shot Lafredière."

"I am no hero."

"Your friends talk as if you are."

Francoeur looked away, as if what she had said was painful. She followed his gaze. Some of the customers stroked their beards as they glanced at her husband. One nodded respectfully, another tipped his hat.

"It is a misunderstanding." He put his hands on the table. "But if I confess all, you must tell me what possessed you to take him on."

"Yes. I will tell you what possessed me," she whispered.

He drew in a deep breath and sighed. "Very well. You know half of it. We were sent to burn the Iroquois villages and crops. Lafredière was not acting as the military governor then, he was our captain. A worse officer you could not imagine. He knew nothing of fighting, or marching, or anything except that as the nephew of the regiment's commander, he was to be obeyed. We were not dressed for the journey and when a winter storm rolled in, we could not see two paces ahead. Yet still he ordered us onward. We were snow-blind and lost within a day. By the end of the month sixty men had died."

"Frozen?" Élisabeth murmured, thinking of Dufossé in the woodshed.

He nodded. "We were so lost we didn't know where we were. We crossed into English territory—what used to be Dutch land not so long ago. There was no grand, glorious battle with the Iroquois. We shot at a few trees and were forced to beg or buy food from settlers. One Dutchman called me a shitten rogue and spat on the bread before handing it over. I didn't care. I stuffed the food in my mouth and begged him for more."

"Why did you shoot the governor?"

He tugged on his beard as if he wanted to feel the sharp edge of pain. "Our allies, the Algonquins, were meant to guide us to the Agnier villages. But on the morning we were due to leave they did not appear. Of course they had stayed behind to wait out the storm, as they thought we would. They were dumbfounded that Lafredière would march us into a blizzard. When the snow settled and they saw that we had left, they tracked us down.

"We did not meet them until we were on the journey home. Our men were broken: frozen, starving, and mutinous. Lafredière saw a chance to deflect their anger away from his disastrous decision to lead us into a winter war. He started shouting, blaming our soldiers' deaths on the Algonquins. He accused them of working with the Iroquois. He grabbed one of them by the throat and raised his pistol to his head. And before I knew what I was doing, I aimed my musket."

"That was when you shot him?"

"Yes," Francoeur's voice was soft now. "But I missed. I only grazed his skull, though I took his eye."

"But you intended to kill him. You wanted him dead."

"I do not know what I wanted. I saw the Algonquin man—a boy, really—about to be murdered in cold blood and I shot my commander to make him stop. Everyone thinks me some kind of hero, but it was no more than rage. My rabid actions proved I am no better a man than my father." Francoeur shook his head. "Besides, within the year we returned and burned the Iroquois villages and food, along with two old women they'd left behind when they fled. So, no, Élisabeth, I am not a hero."

She looked at his face, his lip curled in distaste at his own actions. She reached her hand across the table.

"It is not your fault if you gave in to rage when you shot Lafredière," she said softly. "A demon took possession of you."

He snorted and looked down at his hands. "You could say that."

"I understand."

Francoeur took her hand, a tentative smile spreading across his face. "Élisabeth, let us forget our past sins. Let us imagine we have only just been married, that tonight is our wedding night. Whatever sort of man Marcosi is, I know I can make you forget him. Do not blush! I know I can. I can make you happy. Let us forgive and make each other forget."

A gnawing began in Élisabeth's chest. Heartache. An axe blow that bled and bled until there was no life left, only the stiffness of a corpse that could no longer feel. It was time to tell the truth.

"Marcosi is not a man." She bit her lip and looked across the room. Francoeur's smile faded.

"I do not understand."

"Marcosi is a demon," she whispered.

"What?"

"A wolf with gryphon's wings. A great marquis of Hell. I was cursed by a hag known as the Winter Witch. She caused me to be barren, and sent a demon to torment me. I am possessed."

"Possessed?"

"I should never have married you. I'm sorry that I did. I know I have ruined your chance of happiness—"

"Wait, Élisabeth, listen to me. None of this is true. It is as Jeanne Roy said.

You are suffering from melancholy. This is only an excess of black bile. There is no demon." He grasped for answers like a drowning man after a ship's rope. "It can be cured. It can be cured by bloodletting."

She recoiled. Closing her eyes, she saw the lancet being dug into her father's arm. The startling red against the fresh white linen laid out to catch the blood. Then she thought of Jeanne Roy—arrogant, self-satisfied Jeanne Roy—sneering at her, *a peasant*, and lecturing her about natural philosophy. How could she possibly know what ailed Élisabeth?

"It is not black bile. It is not melancholy. It is a demon, I know it."

Francoeur let go of her hand. Élisabeth saw his eyes travel across the room as though searching for an escape. "Very well," he said, pressing his mouth firmly shut. "We shall see."

Élisabeth blinked back her tears. He did not believe her.

If she could cut open her chest so that he could see the beast sitting there, quietly gnawing on her heart and her bones, she would.

32

Marthe lay on her side on her straw mattress unable to sleep. The ticking was rough to the touch but she did not lift her cheek from the burlap. She could feel the child inside her struggle. She placed her arm around her belly.

"Hush, baby."

The more the child pressed against her, the more she felt the walls closing in around her. But where could she go? Fifteen paces outside of the village there was nothing but forest all the way to the end of the world, and the cost of a return passage to France was a lifetime of labour, too dear by half. She was trapped. Under the thumb of a shrew who marked her every step and a man too weak to stand up to her.

Her child kicked again. A foot was at once in her groin and in her throat. He must be the most active of all the babies on the island. She felt a surge of pride.

"You shall go far," she whispered. "I may have travelled across an ocean, but I can go no farther. You, though, will run as far and as fast as you like. You will touch the stars."

"Marthe?" Her husband's voice sleepy. "Why are you still abed?"

She thought about not responding, feigning that she had spoken in her sleep. Was this the only place she could hide from her husband and the widow now, in her dreams? But if sleep was her only escape, what was the point of living?

"I'm tired," she said finally.

"Is the child moving again?" Verger loved to hear about the exploits of his son, as if the child were already grown and sending them letters boasting about his accomplishments from afar. For a moment Marthe thought about relenting, about curling her back into his warm body and murmuring her fears to him. But it had been too long since they had sought comfort in each other's arms. She would not reward him with tales of his child now.

"I'm getting up. I can hear customers next door."

"Rest here with me. Maman Poulin can see to them."

"Don't call her Maman," Marthe said through gritted teeth. "She is not your mother."

She hauled herself out of bed and pulled on her bodice, lacing the ribbons loosely. She did not care how she looked. Modest or slattern, comely or unkempt, she truly did not care what anyone in Ville-Marie thought of her. How ridiculous she had been to primp for the governor of Montréal. How stupid to have thought she could throw herself into the path of wealth and good fortune. Lafredière was right. He would be led from the village in a sleigh and horses, waving like a king to his people, while they were all left behind in Hell.

She made her way across the hallway and saw her sister and Francoeur in the widow's salon.

"Good day." Francoeur was formal, standing by the door, fidgeting. "We've come for my wife's trunk."

Marthe knew he must be waiting for Lajeunesse to return with Jeanne Roy. Élisabeth sat at the table, wan and morose.

"Where's Barbe?" Marthe muttered.

"Asleep," Élisabeth said. "When she saw we were not customers she went back to bed."

Good, Marthe thought. She deserves her sore head. But there was no doubt the widow could hear them well enough on the other side of her curtain.

At that moment, Rose and Lou rushed in with Jambon at their side.

"Is it true?" Rose began, taking off her coat and hanging it on a peg. "Our innkeeper said there was a fight at Folleville's last night. He meant it as a boast that his inn is a better sort of establishment, but I am certain it must have bedbugs for I could not stop scratching all night long. And then he told us that the fight was between the governor and *you*, Francoeur! Imagine how shocked we were to hear that man was loose in the village. Jambon made us go straight to the tavern to hear what had happened, but we found you had already left! We have been chasing you all over town."

"Lafredière?" Marthe's hands froze on her stomach. She turned to Francoeur. "I thought you said it was safe."

"Don't worry. The governor spent the night in the pillory and the intendant's guards will take him to Québec this morning."

Élisabeth gave Marthe a rueful look. "I'm sorry I did not know what he did to you," she mumbled.

Marthe looked away. It was far too late for her sister's comfort now. She had sat by the widow's side for almost three months, listening as Barbe Poulin cackled and dreamed up ever more frightening creatures to terrify them both: drooling goblins, giant Iroquois werewolves, yellow-toothed witches. Not once had her sister been curious about the real danger the women of Ville-Marie faced.

Rose prattled so long about the night's events that no one heard the door open. All of a sudden Lajeunesse peered around the corner with a toothy grin. Then he stepped back to reveal the prize he had delivered.

Jeanne Roy's cheeks were bright and rosy from the cold. Her twilight-coloured velvet dress could be seen beneath the native shawl on her shoulders. As she walked into the widow's salon, the rich fabric rustled and the room was filled with the scent of pine needles and woodsmoke, and the crispness of a winter's day.

"Madame, you are a sight for sore eyes," Francoeur said. He exhaled like he might crumple with relief. Rose and Lou swept into reverent curtseys and Marthe rose to take the native shawl that was wrapped around Jeanne's shoulders. Only Élisabeth remained seated.

"I am sorry to have interrupted your visit to La Prairie," Francoeur continued.

Jeanne Roy nodded graciously. "It is no matter. I am happy to assist." She looked at Élisabeth. Before Jeanne could speak, Barbe Poulin came bustling into the room. Marthe knew that she had not been able to resist the temptation of greeting their guest. The widow looked Jeanne up and down with an appraising eye.

"Good day. I'm the old baker's widow," she said. "You may call me Maman Poulin. I've lived in this village long enough to have everyone call me mother."

"I never knew my mother," Jeanne Roy remarked. "I am not in need of one now."

The widow opened her mouth and then closed it, as if she could not think of what to say.

"You do not know the excitement we have had, Jeanne," Lou cut in. "The governor of Montréal has been banished. He was choking girls and doing other stuff besides. And Lili found a man frozen on top of her woodpile. He was dead, of course." Lou shivered and danced on the tips of her toes, unaware of the danger she was stirring.

"It was a terrible accident," Marthe said hurriedly.

"It was witchcraft," Barbe Poulin said at the same time. "I will not forget it for the rest of my days. Blue and stiff as a board. The man's eyes locked on the place where the witch who killed him stood to cast her spell."

Jeanne Roy's nostrils flared. She looked at Francoeur and then back at the women. "Excuse me, I have business with my neighbour," she said coldly. "Is there somewhere we might speak alone?"

"Come with me," Marthe said, beckoning Jeanne and Francoeur across the hallway. When she realized Élisabeth had not followed them into Verger's workroom, she dashed back and motioned to her. "Lili, you must come too."

Francoeur and Jeanne Roy had their heads together when she returned with her sister.

"You are certain there is no other option?" Francoeur said.

"None that I, nor any other student of medicine, knows of." Jeanne Roy's eyes were flat and steady. "I have my tools. If you are ready, we can do it now."

"Tools?" Élisabeth asked.

"Élisabeth, I have sent for Jeanne Roy so that she might help you with your melancholy. I fear you are in need of help. She has brought her lancet. She is going to bleed you."

Élisabeth looked stunned, the expression on her face a mixture of fury and fear. "Y-you brought her here? For this purpose?"

Francoeur stepped towards her. "Yes," he said. "Yes, I did. Élisabeth, I am worried about you. Let Jeanne help you."

"I already asked Jeanne for help and she refused me."

"We are discussing medicine now, not folklore," Jeanne Roy replied, her voice dripping disdain.

"Medicine? Do you mean gibberish about *black bile*?"

"It is curious to me how humoral theory, understood since the time of the ancient Greeks, can be called gibberish by one who believes in *witches*," Jeanne snapped. "That is *true* gibberish."

Élisabeth began to wring her hands, looking from Jeanne to her husband. Marthe could not let her twist any longer.

"Lili, listen. I know you fear what happened to Papa. But Jeanne says that if we let out a little bit of your blood, it will release the . . . demon. Isn't that right, Jeanne?"

"No, that is not correct," Jeanne said. "There are no such creatures as de-mons. Or witches. But letting a vein breathe will let out the bad humours that are making your sister ill."

"Let my vein breathe?" Élisabeth was veering into panic. She turned to Francoeur. "*Breathe*? She will butcher me. And then God help us all. Marcosi will not stand for it! Marcosi will attack—"

"Stop." Francoeur held up his hand. "It is because of this . . . this *thing* that we must listen to Jeanne. A little bloodletting will not kill you."

"But it *did* kill my father," Élisabeth cried, her eyes darting between them. "Every time the barber came with his nasty little knives, Papa only weakened. So the barber said he must take more, more, *more*. He gouged Papa's vein with his fat fingers and then, too late, he tried to stop the flow. The cut was too deep. The blood would not stop. The fool stammered and squeezed our father's arm, as he lay bleeding at the kitchen table. He was such a strong man. But he faded away, as meek as a lamb. And I could do nothing—nothing!—but take my cloth and wipe his blood from the floor."

"A country barber with no training might kill a patient," Jeanne Roy said softly. "But I won't make that error. You will be safe."

"But you *know* the cure I need. I asked you to use your magic and you laughed at me. You called me a peasant! You said I was ignorant."

"I did not mean it as an insult. It is a fact. You *are* ignorant. You talk of magic and have no education, no learning—"

"I *do* have learning. I know my sums. I can run a household and a farm, which I wager is more than you can do." Élisabeth was speaking quickly, like a rat in a trap, scrambling for any escape.

"Listen. You need to be bled to get well. The more you argue against it, the more you demonstrate your ignorance."

"I do listen! I listen and learn all the time. I listen in church, and at market. And here in the bakery." Élisabeth's tongue slowed. "And I certainly listened when Father de Sancy told us about Chamberlen's Secret."

Jeanne Roy took a step backwards and nearly bumped into Francoeur. "What do you know about Chamberlen's Secret?"

"I know how powerful it is," Élisabeth said, her voice steady. "And I know it must be *you* who has it."

Jeanne Roy paused, and looked at Élisabeth as if she was assessing her for the first time. Finally, she shifted her weight and spoke.

"It is true. I do have Chamberlen's Secret. But whatever that priest has told you is wrong. It is certainly not what you imagine. It can be no use to you. What you need, Élisabeth, is to be bled."

"Chérie, listen to Jeanne," Francoeur reasoned. "Don't be so wayward."

Élisabeth's hands flew to her ears. Her eyes were wild, and a red flush crept up her neck to her cheeks. Marthe took a step forward to calm her sister but stopped when Élisabeth began to scream.

"*Maman Poulin!*" Élisabeth rushed out of the workroom. Marthe gasped and bolted after her, Francoeur and Jeanne Roy close behind. "Maman Poulin!" Élisabeth cried again. "Jeanne Roy has confessed! *She* has Chamberlen's Secret!"

Marthe's heart raced. The child inside her began to kick furiously as Élisabeth lifted her hand and pointed her finger at Jeanne Roy.

"She . . . she killed the man on the woodpile. She is the witch that Father de Sancy seeks. Jeanne Roy is the queen of the Normandy coven!"

33

"Ridiculous," Jeanne Roy snorted, but there was a look of fear in her eyes that gave Élisabeth a strange feeling of power. "I did not kill anyone. Why would I do such a thing?"

"Because . . . because . . . you are the Winter Witch!" Élisabeth said, her mind racing. It made sense. Jeanne was no different from the hag that cursed her. She loved the cold; snowflakes glittered in her hair. They were one and the same. Winter witches both.

"What are you saying?" Maman Poulin reached her hand out, whether to steady herself or ward off Jeanne Roy, Élisabeth could not tell. "Who is the Winter Witch?"

"She comes out in the darkest months to steal what is not hers. She took Dufossé's life. She cast a spell on him to make him sit down and die. Now she wants my blood. Next she might . . . she might take Marthe's baby! Or any of your children." Élisabeth pointed at Rose and Lou, then at their husbands. Marthe covered her mouth with her hands. Élisabeth's ears rang and she could feel sweat under her arms. A feverish heat spread across her chest and back. This was the cost of finally finding her tongue. The toll of righteousness, now that she was no longer afraid to tell the truth.

"Blessed Virgin, stop!" Marthe grabbed her belly.

Élisabeth spun round to address the group. "She was banished from France. She made up a new name. She stole my papers to be allowed passage to Ville-Marie."

"It's not true," Rose quivered, but there was doubt in her voice.

"It is," Élisabeth said, raising her chin. "Ask the witch herself. Do you deny it, Jeanne Roy, or whatever your name is?"

Every pair of eyes in the room turned to Jeanne Roy. Marthe looked nervously at her, shaking her head, as if willing her not to speak. The men shifted on their feet, unsure whether this was women's business, or something more serious. Slowly, evenly, Jeanne Roy crossed her arms.

"I am not a witch, and I am not a queen," she said.

Rose and Lou exhaled as one. The men rubbed their beards and Francoeur started to unclench his fists. But then Jeanne Roy's lips twitched. She pressed one hand to her mouth as if she were stifling a scream. She released her fingers and held her hand up, instantly stopping all activity in the room, as if she could control the movement of every man and woman before her with a flick of her fingers.

"But it is true that Jeanne Roy is not my name. And that I was among those poor souls banished by the king."

Maman Poulin gasped. "She *is* the witch queen!"

"Jeanne, stop," Marthe cried. "Don't say any more."

"No. I am tired of all the stupidity. The days of magic-riddled nonsense must be behind us." She lowered her hand, and they were suddenly able to move again. Jambon put his arm around his wife. Francoeur took a step towards Élisabeth, but she evaded his grasp. Jeanne turned to meet their gaze.

"I was the victim of a false accusation, made out of jealousy and spite. I would have been put to death for that lie, but the king granted me clemency. He knows, as all but the most ignorant do, that witchcraft is not real. It is a salve for silly minds. For those who do not have the fortitude to approach their problems with the patience and hard work they require. The king knows it, anyone with learning knows it. And it is only by shedding the true light of reason on this superstition that it will wither and die."

"So you do not deny it?" Maman Poulin asked, gleeful.

"There is nothing to deny," Jeanne Roy retorted. "Witchcraft is not real. I was convicted of nothing and banished for nothing."

"And what of the dead man in the barn?" Maman Poulin said. "He was bewitched into sitting down to freeze to death!"

"Enough," Francoeur thundered. "Élisabeth. Recant your lies now."

"But she admits it herself!" Élisabeth said.

"She admits no such thing. That man's death was an accident. Jeanne has done no wrong." He turned to his neighbour. "I am sorry. My wife is not well, as you know. We will see you safely home. Jambon, Lajeunesse, make room in your sleigh for Jeanne."

The two men looked nervous until Rose prodded her husband's shoulder. "You will come to no harm," she whispered to Lajeunesse. "She is a white witch."

"And you," he turned to Élisabeth, "come with me." She could feel him fume as he laid her cloak on her shoulders and pulled her outside.

"Don't be angry." The wind whipped across her cheeks. "I was only doing what I should have done from the start: my duty. I had to let you know what she really is."

"What is your duty, Élisabeth? All I know is that you want to avoid the treatment that you need. Now your fear of a lancet may have condemned a soul to death."

"But that witch is a danger to us! She is the one Father de Sancy seeks."

"Élisabeth, your melancholy has made you wild. You must come home and rest." He moved to grab her by the arm.

She cringed, ducking away from him. "Don't!"

Francoeur closed his eyes and placed his hands over his face. Then he ran them through his beard, tugging at the ends until he winced. He opened his eyes, giving her a long look. Finally, he turned to grab the snowshoes he had propped up against the house.

"Francoeur? What are you doing?" He slipped his boots into the wooden rackets and started lacing them up. "You heard her yourself. She admitted she has Chamberlen's Secret." Her husband stood up, his feet laced in, and started to walk away. "Francoeur! Wait!"

He stopped and turned back towards her. "We are a lost cause. We cannot be saved."

"What do you mean?"

"We cannot chafe alongside each other any longer. It seems I cannot help you. What's more, you cringe and cower as if you fear that I will hurt you. We must let each other go."

"But we are married."

"We have not lain together." The accusation fell to the ground, weighted with lead. "The church cannot object to an annulment."

"An annulment?" All at once the demon unfurled his leathery wings. Francoeur wanted to end their marriage? Marcosi grabbed for her heart and clung on, squeezing until she could hardly breathe. "The church will never agree to dissolve—"

"Oh, it will. Only last year a man complained that he was bewitched and could not perform the duties of a husband. His marriage was annulled and he wed someone else within the year."

She grabbed both of his arms. "No! Francoeur . . . wait. I love you."

For a moment, his silence made her hopeful. She stared into his hazel eyes, willing him to feel as she did, willing him to kiss her. But he stood still and soon the cold settled on them, weighing them down. His beard and mustache grew white with frost. She wanted to reach out and put her fingers over his lips and feel the ice melt under their warmth, but she did not dare.

"Goodbye, Élisabeth."

He shook himself free of her hands and turned away. She stared at his back as he strode down the street. She stood frozen, feeling the life drain from her. The demon let go of her heart and slumped against her rib cage, wings drooping. She could feel the bruise forming where Marcosi had gripped her, purple and tender. When Francoeur was so far away that she could no longer see him, Élisabeth sat down in the road.

Not dutiful, or good.

Barren. Useless.

And forever wayward.

She could not make sense of it all. She curled up into a ball and lay her cheek on the snow, hoping that like the man in the shed, the cold might take her too.

SPRING

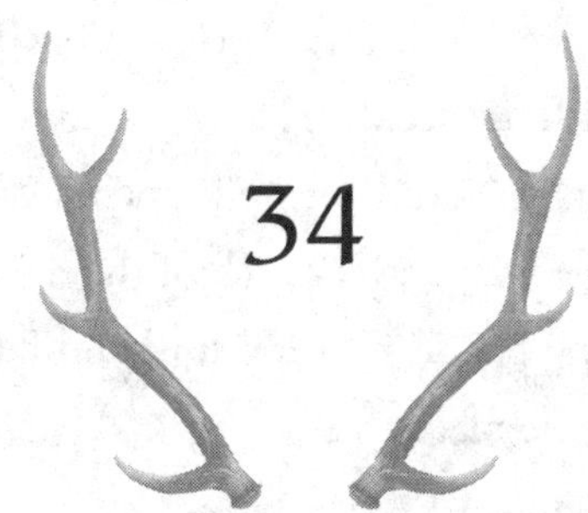

34

Not long after Francoeur had left, his snowshoes leaving heart-shaped marks in the path behind him, Élisabeth followed him out of town. When she could no longer see his tracks, she trudged the path she imagined her husband had travelled, and when she reached their house in Côte Saint-François, she let herself in.

He was not at home.

She took the holy water vessel down from the lintel and dropped to her knees in front of the crucifix. She prayed for the Blessed Virgin to take pity on her and send her husband back to her. She recited her rosary and begged God to forgive her sins. She pleaded and bartered and beseeched until her knees ached and her head spun. Only the demon Marcosi answered her prayers.

You heard what Francoeur said. You are a lost cause.

"His anger is misplaced," she told the demon. "I did my duty by letting the village know about the witch."

Your duty was to curb your tongue and to lay with your husband. Why did you never do your duty, wayward girl?

"And when he discovered I was barren, Marcosi? What then?"

The church cannot object to an annulment.

They argued like this for days, the demon and the wayward girl. Élisabeth threw herself into her chores to distract herself from the voice in her head, to prove that she was not without use. She baked bread with what was left of their flour. She swept the floors until the wispy branches of the broomstick threatened to score the pine. She wiped every inch of the house free of cobwebs, running her cloth over the log beams that her husband had stripped of bark with his own hands, caressing the places his fingers had been.

Still, Marcosi was relentless.

Your fear of a lancet may have condemned a soul to death.

It was true. Not an hour after she had accused Jeanne Roy, Maman Poulin had scurried to the seminary to tattle to Father de Sancy. Soon the bailiff and the executioner were sent to retrieve the witch. She was found on the river path, heading east with Rose and Lou and their husbands. The bailiff tied her by a rope to the back of a sleigh, like an animal brought to slaughter, making her march back to Ville-Marie on foot. She was blue-lipped and shivering by the time they reached the village. A mob gathered to gawk and jeer. When Father de Sancy declared that the most powerful sorceress in all of Europe stood before them, someone called out that though the witch's hands were bound, she might yet have the means to summon her master, the Devil. Another in the crowd cried out—beware!—he could smell brimstone. Élisabeth had looked at Jeanne Roy's face, drawn white with terror, and took no satisfaction in her neighbour's fate. She had gazed blankly at Maman Poulin, gleeful in the centre of the mob, and turned to leave the village.

Alone at the farmhouse, Élisabeth now stared across the length of their land, down to the river. The snow that had once blanketed the landscape had started to shrink, and the land to thaw, turning to mud. She wondered how long she had been locked in debate with her demon. How many days? She did not mark the passage of time. She wondered what was happening in town.

She wondered if the witch still lived.

What if Dufossé's death was an accident, wayward girl? The cold in this country has its grip on all our throats.

She could stand no more of the demon's poison tongue. She would chop wood until it brought her some peace. She strode outside and grabbed Francoeur's axe. The hem of her skirt dragged in the mud, but she did not move into the shade where the ground was cold and dry. She raised the blade above her head and brought it crashing down upon the log in front of her. The pine cried out as it split, two halves tumbling to the ground. It felt good to punish the logs. She picked up one of the split halves and laid it on the oak stump, raised her axe above her head again, and tried to silence Marcosi's voice.

Perhaps what the witch said is true. Perhaps I am merely black bile.

She slammed the axe down onto the stump and picked up another log. She tried to focus her attention on the wood before her, but her mind was not her servant.

"How can you say that you are naught but black bile, Marcosi?" She leaned on her axe as she addressed the beast. "I can feel your claws when you sharpen them against my insides. I can feel your tail knocking against my spine. Do you deny what I can feel? I can feel, therefore witchcraft is real."

Two thoughts twisted together, the first not able to take root before the other weeded it out.

Witchcraft is real.

Witchcraft does not exist.

Élisabeth made a sound as if she were trying to blow out a candle. "Melancholy." She raised the axe again. She did not want to admit to Marcosi that she did not know what Jeanne had meant by *melancholy*. She understood that it was a kind of sorrow, and the Blessed Virgin knew that she had many of those: the loss of her mother, then her brothers, her beloved child and the hope for a good marriage, and then finally Papa, the final fraying of the rope before it snapped. But why then did she feel no sadness? Only the angry demon curling and unfurling in her body, leaving fear in its wake?

"Witchcraft is real, Marcosi, and Jeanne is its most powerful practitioner. I have seen her grimoire with my own eyes. I have seen her familiar! What other purpose does that terrible doll serve? Do you not remember what Maman Poulin said, about the power of familiar spirits—gargoyles that breathe through their mouths, and cats that speak Latin as clearly as I speak French?"

She raised her axe, bracing for the demon's retort.

Cats that speak Latin? That is absurd.

Élisabeth froze, axe above her head. Marcosi was right. That *was* absurd.

Then she imagined Jeanne Roy's sneering face. *How ignorant you are to believe that cats can speak at all.*

She grunted and brought the blade down hard on the stump. She misjudged and the axe glanced off the wood, striking her knee. She dropped the axe to the ground and swore.

Once the curse left her lips, she could not stop. Élisabeth flung her head back and let loose a savage moan. It filled the woods and echoed through the trees. It caused the crows to stop and stare at her wretchedness.

Francoeur was gone. She had been wayward, and the Devil had come for her. Everything her mother had once warned of had come to pass.

She howled until the birds grew frightened and took flight. She howled until her throat hurt. She howled until she felt Marcosi stretch and grow until he thrust his wings into her arms, his horns into her skull. The demon put her on as if she were a suit of fine cloth, and found it fit him very well.

You will never be rid of me. For now I am you. A she-wolf with wings. A warrior. A great marquis of Hell.

Élisabeth sat down on the oak stump, her howls turning to sobs. She buried her face in her hands. She could not go on. She was cursed. Her husband had left her. Her sister had turned against her. She had condemned a woman to death. What was she if not one of Hell's wolfhounds, living alone in the woods?

Alone in the woods, like the Winter Witch.

How long she stayed on that stump she did not know. She could hear the dripping of the melting icicles on the roof of the house. Her tears dried and left salt streaks on her face. It was only when she heard a twig snap that she looked up.

Her neighbour Hélène was at the edge of the woods, her eyes wary. Élisabeth gave Dufossé's widow a cold stare.

"I thought I heard . . . an animal. Are you well, neighbour?"

Élisabeth considered the question. Was she *well*? She was a demon. But if she were a she-wolf with wings, she could fly wherever she pleased. She could dance at midnight by the light of the moon. As a demon, she could walk into the forest, swishing her silken tail, her yellow eyes alert. She did not have to be frightened of living alone. She could leave her chicken-hearted dread behind.

"Yes, I am well."

Hélène hesitated. "May I join you?"

Élisabeth did not reply and Hélène approached cautiously, perching on a stump nearby. "Have you had any word from the village?" the neighbour asked.

Élisabeth shook her head.

"I saw it all, you know. Jeanne had already reached my house when they caught up to her." Hélène looked at her hands. "I ran down to the river path. I tried to tell them it was not witchcraft that killed my husband, but liquor. They did not want to hear it. The executioner said that if I defended her, they would assume that I too . . . that I . . ." She could not finish her thought. She rose suddenly and crossed her arms, glaring at Élisabeth. "Why did you do it?"

Élisabeth folded her hands in her lap. She wished her neighbour would leave. She did not want to hear any more. She turned and stared out at the river, trying to ignore Hélène's glare. A handful of skiffs were already out on the open waters, hurrying firewood and other supplies across the river. Élisabeth saw a native woman in a canoe, paddling close to shore. She squinted at her, watching her progress.

"You seem able to keep your counsel now," Hélène said. Still Élisabeth gazed at the river, wondering where the woman in the canoe was going. Hélène stepped in front of her to block her view of the Saint-Laurent.

"You did not have to cause us all such grief! It was a simple enough thing, and you ruined it."

Élisabeth stared at her neighbour's pinched face, then glanced back to the water. The native woman was disappearing out of view, now hidden by a thicket of trees on the riverbank.

"At least tell me again what he said to you. So that I may know if it was worth it."

"What would you have me tell you that you don't already know?" Élisabeth's voice was hoarse from howling.

"I want to hear all of it," Hélène demanded. "From the start."

Élisabeth tore her eyes away from the river. She was weary but she knew her neighbour would not leave until she was satisfied. She took a breath. "Father de Sancy told us that the witch queen—"

"I don't care about the damned priest!" Hélène cried. She took a step closer. "I want to know about *Michel*. Tell me again what he said about coming to look for me. How he hoped to find me widowed."

Élisabeth blinked. Hélène meant the sailor on the *Saint-Jean-Baptiste*. The one who had saved her when she jumped overboard.

"Tell me about Michel, and how he calls me his mermaid still." Hélène let out a deep sigh and collapsed onto the stump, putting her head in her hands.

Élisabeth recognized that sigh. It was the sound of exquisite longing. She thought of what she had once done to be reunited with Rémy. The lunacy that came of longing.

A wave of understanding came crashing over her.

"Hélène, did you lock your husband in our cowshed?"

The neighbour lifted her head from her hands. Her shoulders were hunched, her meekness returning at the mention of Dufossé. "I will never own it," she whispered.

"You shut him in, to freeze to death?"

Hélène said nothing.

"How?" Élisabeth persisted. "How did you do it?"

"It was a simple enough thing," Hélène said in a small voice. "He'd been stealing your wood all winter, ever since Francoeur left for Québec. Dufossé was in and out of your shed every few days. I only needed to fill him up with brandy and follow him. Then I shut the door and barred it. At first he was angry to be trapped, but I convinced him the door was accidentally stuck. I counselled him not to break it down lest you realize he'd been thieving. I bid him to sit quietly on the woodpile while I dug him out. Then I sang him a song. The same lullaby I sang to our child, before my husband shook him to death for crying for his mother in the night." Hélène's voice was bitter as she rose from the stump and brushed down her skirts.

"With the brandy's help it did not take long for Dufossé to fall asleep. He felt no pain as he died. More's the pity."

Élisabeth felt sick, as bilious as she had ever been on the sea-tossed ship. She stared at Hélène. Jeanne Roy had not caused her husband to die. The witch had not bewitched the neighbour into awaiting his own death. It was the work of a mermaid caught flailing in a cruel man's net, luring him with her siren song.

Consider, consider. Witchcraft does not exist.

What had she done? Suddenly Élisabeth felt the urge to run, to flee the monstrous mistake she had made. She stood and turned towards the forest.

"Where are you going?" Hélène called after her. "You will not tell anyone, will you? I will not own it! I will never confess!"

Élisabeth felt her heart pound as she ran past the house Francoeur had built with his bare hands. She reached the path at the edge of the woods. It had not been trodden for weeks and there was still snow in the shadows where the sun did not penetrate. Still she pressed on, not stopping when she slipped and branches tore at her face.

She reached the witch's hut and pushed open the door.

A native woman was inside.

Élisabeth blinked to adjust to the gloomy light. The woman wore a blanket coat pulled snug around her waist with a bright scarf. Élisabeth had seen her before, at the Hôtel Dieu chapel, talking to Jeanne Roy.

"It's—it's you," Élisabeth said, her breath coming in sharp pants.

The woman gave her a disinterested look. "I'm Angélique's friend, Wari."

"Angélique is her real name?"

"You must be the neighbour."

Élisabeth realized the entire village must know that she had been the one to accuse Jeanne Roy of witchcraft. "I am, yes."

"The one with the demon spirit."

Élisabeth was stunned to hear the truth from this stranger's lips. She looked away, her eyes sweeping across the hut. Jeanne Roy had clearly spread her story, even as she refused to help. Élisabeth could not bear the stranger's gaze. She stared at the cabin walls, still hung with furs and bunches of dried herbs, then shifted her eyes to the wooden table, where a goose feather lay next to a pile of stones and a pot of ink. Small glass bottles half filled with liquid were clustered nearby. The cabin was so thick with magic the air nearly shimmered with spells. It was absurd to deny it. Élisabeth turned back to the witch's friend.

"What did she tell you about my demon, then? She who claims that demons and witches do not exist."

Wari sat down on a stool by Jeanne Roy's small fire pit. She pulled off one of her boots and wiggled her toes, then felt inside and pulled out a pine needle. Only when she put her boot back on did she turn to face Élisabeth.

"It is true that Angélique does not believe in demons. But I am curious about how you manage to live with one inside you. What is that like? Does it cause you to suffer greatly?"

Élisabeth gawped at the woman. "No one has ever asked me that before." It was true. Marthe was embarrassed by her. Jeanne Roy had ridiculed her. Francoeur tried to fix her. But no one had ever asked her to merely describe her affliction. She sat down next to Wari.

"I do suffer," Élisabeth confessed. "More than anyone could imagine." Élisabeth gazed at the goose feather on the table at the back of the hut. "Although . . . although I expect it is what I deserve."

"You deserve to suffer?"

"Yes. I was wayward, in France. I led a wayward life. I did not do as my mother taught me."

"I'm sorry, my French is not perfect . . ." Wari wrinkled her nose. "What does it mean, *wayward*?"

Élisabeth considered this for a moment. "I suppose it means that I turned away from the right path. And so the Devil sent the Winter Witch to curse me."

"You chose your own path? I would call that freedom."

Élisabeth was so shocked she laughed out loud. "No, no, this is not freedom. This suffering—snakes in my knees and wings in my belly—this is not freedom, this is . . . this is fear."

Wari nodded. "I suppose it *is* frightening to travel an unknown road."

Élisabeth was struck dumb by the woman's words. Once again two ideas twisted together: She was wayward, she deserved the demon's torment. Or she was wayward, travelling an exhilarating new path.

Wari stood up, appearing tired of their conversation. "Perhaps your demon has given you new strength. I wish you luck."

Élisabeth mirrored her, leaping to her feet. "What do you mean by strength? Can I be rid of this demon? Can I . . . can I bear children? For I fear that the feeling of the spirit lunging and growling inside me means that I am still barren. That I am still cursed."

The stranger pulled her shawl tightly around her shoulders. She looked past Élisabeth to the door. "Why did you not accept the cure that Angélique offered you?"

"She was going to bleed me! Opening my vein cannot cure a demon. Magic is what is needed. Jeanne could have broken the spell, but she kept her magic to herself."

The woman looked at her. "If you believe Angélique has magic, then why would the cure she offered you not also be magical?"

Élisabeth faltered again. She had not considered this. She knew there was always a price to pay when seeking a witch's help. That blood sometimes had to be spilled. Perhaps Jeanne Roy's talk of bloodletting was merely the price of the magic she meant to perform. If only the witch had explained that, rather than making Élisabeth feel so stupid and small.

"I . . . I thought she would give me a potion. Something to drink."

The woman adjusted the strap of the bag against her shoulder. She made for the door.

"Wait," Élisabeth said. "Do you think witchcraft is real? Is Jeanne Roy truly a witch who could cure me of my demon?"

Wari relaxed her grip on the strap of the beaded bag. "These words—*witch*, *witchcraft*—are French words. I would call Angélique a medicine woman. Is that the same as *witch*?"

"I-I don't know," Élisabeth said. "I think one is born with magic, but medicine must be learned."

"Angélique learned her medicine." Wari stopped and studied Élisabeth's face. Then she sighed. "I want to tell you something about Angélique. Something that I hope will bring balance to how you see her. Will you listen?"

"Yes," Élisabeth said in a small voice.

"Angélique had a teacher who showed her many wondrous things. But when her skill surpassed his own, he accused her of stealing his knowledge—as if knowledge is something that can be owned by one man alone. He sought to stop her rise. He told the church that she was a dangerous witch. The innocent women she cared for were also accused."

"The Normandy coven," Élisabeth said, barely above a whisper.

"Their torment lasted weeks. Terrible things were done to them, in the name of God. All those women, suffering for nothing more than having a little learning. So when you ask me if she is a witch, this is all I can tell you."

Consider, consider. Witchcraft does not exist.

Élisabeth felt a tug on her heart as she thought of the child she had lost. And all that she had lost since: Rémy, her home in Saint-Philbert, and now Francoeur. What if Jeanne was right? What if Rémy had wanted to be rid of her, and witchcraft was *not* the root of her misfortune?

"If witchcraft does not exist, then I have been sorely deceived," Élisabeth sniffed. But who had deceived her but her own self? She had taken Rémy's hand and walked up to the clifftop. She could have listened to the old cook's warning and kept her distance. She might never have fallen for his eel-tongued promises. But she had not listened. She had *wanted* to lie with him at the top of the world. She was wayward, after all. She had chosen her own path. "What I mean is, I have been a fool. A wretched goosecap fool." Élisabeth took a deep breath. "It is as Jeanne Roy said. I have been . . . ignorant."

For the first time since she had entered the witch's hut, the stranger's face softened a little. She reached out and put her hand on Élisabeth's arm.

"You are young. Perhaps you are not ignorant, only innocent." The woman's words caused tears to prick at the corners of Élisabeth's eyes. She blinked them back as Wari continued. "The question is, what will you do to grow wise?"

Élisabeth wished she could unravel the last six months. She might try the cure Jeanne Roy offered. She would consider Marthe's happiness as much as her own. She would give herself the chance to fall in love with her husband.

Too late, too late.

As if Wari could read her thoughts, she rose. "It is late," she said. "And I have far to travel."

"Wait," Élisabeth said, blinking up at her. "You asked what I would do to grow wise. I don't know. I don't know what to do."

Wari paused and then opened her beaded bag. She reached her hand into its depths, and then pulled out Jeanne Roy's ragged doll.

Élisabeth started to recoil from the dreadful poppet. Then she stopped.

She had once been afraid of the familiar spirit. In truth, she had been afraid of everything: the doll, the Winter Witch, the native people she saw in the village, the demon inside her. She had been frightened out of her wits. Yet here she was, in a witch's hut with an Iroquois woman, reconciled with her demon. And she was safe. Perhaps she had no cause to fear any of the things that frightened her.

She reached for the ragdoll. She was surprised at the weight of it. It was heavy, like a sack of plums. She held it in her lap.

"Thank you for your kindness in calling my ignorance by a gentler name," she said. "But you are right. If I have been innocent, then I must grow wise. I must undo what I have done. This doll . . . Jeanne prizes it above all other things. Do you think it has the power to save her?"

Wari gave Élisabeth a mournful look. "I do not know."

"We can take it to her. Perhaps she can use it . . ." Élisabeth looked doubtfully at the cloth creature, its yarn eyes unravelling, its feet dirty and frayed. If Jeanne Roy wasn't a witch, what good would a child's plaything do? The impossibility of the task sat heavily on her.

"I need to convince the old priest that she is not a witch, while hoping that she truly is, so that she might have the power to escape. I don't know how to undo this knot."

Wari held her gaze. "Angélique is being held in a prison within the grounds of the old fort."

Élisabeth bit her lip. She had accused Jeanne Roy of causing Dufossé's death by witchcraft. What could she do to make Father de Sancy doubt her word? How could she protect Hélène, who did not deserve to die for defending herself against a brutal man? And how could she convince Francoeur to love her once more?

She sat with the witch's familiar on her knees, feeling the weight of the doll pressing down on her. Jeanne Roy said she was an ignorant peasant. Élisabeth knew that was not true. Now she had to prove it. She had to think. She had to figure out a way to save the witch and win her husband back.

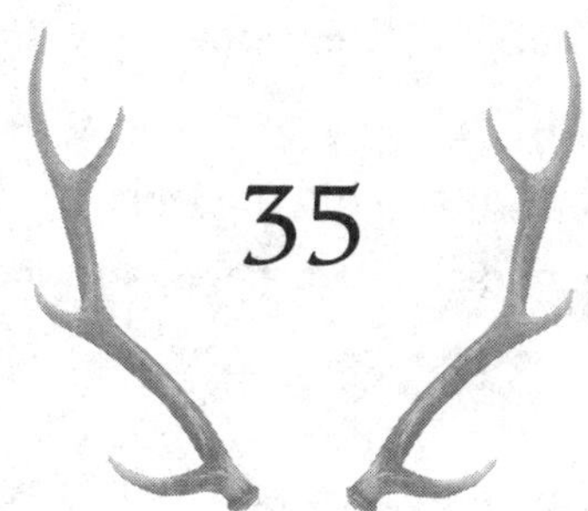

35

The sickening sound of the chapel bells rang out across the village, each clang reverberating deep into Marthe's bones.

She wished she were braver. If she had more daring, she would stand outside the fort—now twice consecrated to make sure the Devil could not come to the aid of Ville-Marie's most prized prisoner—and chant her prayers out loud so that Jeanne might hear them through the walls and know that she had supporters still. But if Marthe did that, the village might point their fingers at her next. And worse, she might hear the grunt of the executioner as he did the priest's bidding, and the low moans of their victim, the witch.

Marthe had brought fresh bread and water to Jeanne that morning, and her stomach had turned at what she had seen: ankles bruised and twisted from being shut in the brodequins, and fresh lash marks on her back and arms. She remembered the pain and terror of the governor's hands around her neck and could not fathom how Jeanne had withstood the Question for more than two weeks. Perhaps it was because Father de Sancy was going about his task languorously, standing over his prisoner hour after hour, day after day, watching as the executioner hammered the brodequin boots while he asked her precisely when—and how—she fornicated with the Devil.

"How much longer, do you think?" Thérèse asked in a forlorn voice. Marthe shrugged, a timid movement that the others barely registered.

"The other Sulpicians have left the chapel," Apolline told them. She had all the answers as usual. "So Nones has finished. It can't be much longer." She made the sign of the cross, and the others did the same.

"I pray for Jeanne every night," Françoise murmured.

"Look, Marthe," Thérèse nudged her with an elbow. "Maman Poulin is already at the wall."

"Don't call her Maman," Marthe said.

In the distance the widow peered through a gap in the palisades. She took a step back to speak to a woman standing next to her. The woman laughed and tried to look through the crack herself, but Barbe Poulin pushed her away. Marthe knew the widow rose early to claim the peephole for herself. Marthe's stomach churned at the thought of what she saw.

"I need to sit," she said and took a step away from the other girls. She lumbered over to a fallen tree on the edge of the commons and eased herself down, feeling her heavy stomach settle between her legs. She grunted as she moved. The burning in her chest had not stopped and she felt as though her heart were on fire. The others were not as fat with child and pestered her with questions about what to expect in the months to come. Marthe wished she knew.

She needed Jeanne Roy. She needed her so badly it fueled the burning in her heart and kept her awake at night. Jeanne would know what to do to ease the fire in her chest. She would have a simple or a potion that would take the ache away. And when she gave it to her, she would tell Marthe not to worry, the child would arrive safely from Heaven and all would be well—words Marthe was desperate to hear.

"I don't believe my eyes." Thérèse let out a whistle and then rushed over to the tree where Marthe sat. "Your sister is on the path."

Marthe grabbed Thérèse's hand but even then struggled to pull herself to her feet. Her back hurt and there was a dull ache in her groin. It felt as though the child could come that very day. But she had not even been married eight months—the child could not be born so soon. She felt a stab of panic. Since Jeanne's arrest, Barbe Poulin had repeated her muttered warnings about girls who were whipped and sent back to France for being spoiled before marriage. The widow knew her own power; now she had the priest's ear. Marthe shuddered, thinking of Jeanne's battered ankles and bloodied back. She put a hand to her own throat. No, the baby could not be born so soon. She would be whipped raw if he was.

"You are bold to show your face here." Françoise glared at Élisabeth when she reached them. "Go and stand with those gleeful hags who wish our sister of the sea harm."

"I mean Jeanne no harm," Élisabeth said meekly, holding up her hands. Her face was flushed and she was breathing as if she had run from afar. "I have come to save her."

Apolline snorted. "It is you who have condemned her! And us all. For there is not one among us who will not be in need of a midwife soon."

"I promise, I am here to make amends—"

"It's too late!" Thérèse cried. "She is in his grip. He tortures her at least twice a day. It's been going on for more than a fortnight. She cannot hold out much longer."

"Marthe, please." Élisabeth turned away from the others. "I was not myself. The demon, it . . ." Her voice trailed off for a moment, then she drew breath. "No, it was not the demon, it was me. I made a grave error. I will set it right."

"How can you fix this, Lili?" Marthe demanded. "Father de Sancy has found his witch queen. The only reason she is still alive is that she has not confessed to the crimes she is accused of. But she will surely die by his hands if her ordeal goes on much longer."

"I know what to do." Élisabeth beckoned the girls closer. "We will petition the king, just as my husband did to rid us of the governor. The king saved her once before, when he banished the Normandy coven. We will write a letter—"

"Write a *letter*?" Marthe exclaimed. "A girl who cannot even write her name will write to the king?"

Élisabeth only hesitated for a moment. "Apolline can write it," she said, nodding in her direction. "Or Rose, or Lou. They will be here by nightfall. Jeanne's Agnier friend has gone to fetch them in her canoe. If every one of us young wives—everyone who was on the *Saint-Jean-Baptiste* this year, and on bride ships in years past, or indeed any woman who is expecting a child or one day hopes to—if we all sign and tell the king that without a midwife to safely deliver our babies the whole colony will founder, then she will be freed! We do not need to send it to France, we need only do as Francoeur did and take the letter to Intendant Talon in Québec."

There was a wildness about her sister that Marthe did not recognize. Her knotted hair was long and loose, like a mane she had not brushed for weeks. Her eyes shone with a fierceness that was unsettling.

"Lili, listen. Listen to the bells. They ring to keep Satan at bay while Father de Sancy and the executioner are with Jeanne, torturing her. They believe it is how they keep themselves safe, so that the Devil does not come to her aid. Those bells ring for hours on end, every day."

"Then we must not delay! Thérèse, you and Françoise go round the village. Apolline, your husband has a horse, does he not? Send him west to fetch the others—"

"Lili, listen to me!" Marthe stopped her. "How long do you think it will take to get your petition to Québec? Francoeur was gone two months. Go up to the fort and look. You will see that Jeanne does not have time for your plot to succeed."

The determination in Élisabeth's eyes waned. She shifted on her feet and looked across the commons towards the fort. "Very well. Show me."

Marthe led the way to the bridge across the Little River, towards the run-down wooden fort, leaving the other *Saint-Jean-Baptiste* girls on the commons.

As they approached, the widow Poulin saw Élisabeth. Her eyes widened and her mouth formed a round hole the shape of a cherry stone.

"Oh, ma chère, you are here!"

Marthe bristled as Élisabeth kissed the widow on both cheeks. "Good day, Maman Poulin."

"I do not like to be the bearer of bad tidings." The widow licked her lips and leaned forward. "But the witch still has not confessed. It can't be long now, though. The priest is doing good work. He's very precise in his questions. Just now, he asked her if she has lain with Satan. Isn't that frightful?"

"None of it is true," Élisabeth started, her voice soft and her eyes lowered. "I was wrong to accuse Jeanne. I am here to recant what I said."

"Don't be a ninny-hammer!" the widow exclaimed. "She's a witch as sure as I'm a widow. The truth will come out. I have also heard him ask about Chamberlen's Secret." Barbe Poulin whispered the name of the magical tool with awe.

Marthe had an urge to kick her in the shins.

"Dufossé froze because he was drunk," Élisabeth explained. "Jeanne Roy has done no ill to anyone."

The widow gave both sisters a withering look. "That's not even her name. She's Lady Angélique de La-Dee-Da. She cast that spell on your neighbour, and if she's not stopped, she'll go after our children."

"Please, Maman," Marthe grabbed the widow's arm. "I beg you. We need Jeanne's skill. She trained in Paris with the man-midwives. We need her."

"For goodness' sake!" The widow shrugged Marthe's arm away. "Look for yourself. You will soon hear her admit all manner of horrors." The widow pulled Élisabeth towards the crack in the palisades and Marthe could not help but follow. Tentatively, they took it in turns to press their eyes to the peephole.

"Can you see her?" the widow asked.

"Not well." Still Élisabeth did not pull away. Marthe leaned her head against the wall, feeling sick. She wished she could sit down. The thought of what was happening in the middle of the fort's compound was too much to bear. The ache in her back had grown much worse and had spread to her belly. She heard the sound of a whip and a strangled gasp of pain that was so close she could feel it on her own flesh. She grabbed her stomach with both hands.

"What did the witch say?" Barbe Poulin glinted.

"The priest is still asking about Satan," Élisabeth replied. "Jeanne has not spoken."

There was another crack and Marthe felt the whip bite into her belly again. She doubled over. She could not prevent a moan from escaping her lips. She had to get away from the sounds of the whip on flesh. She stumbled away from the fort, clutching her belly in her hands. She staggered back across the Little River to the commons and saw that the other brides had disappeared. They could not bear the sounds of Jeanne's torture either. They would have gone home to pray. She did not blame them.

Marthe reached the safety of the bakery and shut the door, breathing steadily through her nose. The pain eased. She straightened her shoulders and turned to see Verger rounding the corner from the workroom, flour dusted on his face and his beard.

"How now, *wife*?" he asked. She cut him with a look. He had been sulking more of late, asking pointed questions, now even seeming to query their marriage vows. Barbe Poulin's malice had made it to his ears.

"I am well," she grimaced. Suddenly, the pain was upon her again. She gripped her belly and cried out. Verger was instantly by her side, all trace of anger melted.

"Marthe? Are you well? Is the child coming?"

"No," she grunted, looking at the floor. "It is a bit of bad fish that turns my stomach, is all."

"I shall run and fetch Maman Poulin, she will know what to do."

"Do not . . . call her . . . mother." Marthe's words were strangled and raw.

"Come and lie down, chérie, and I will fetch Barbe—"

The pain eased and Marthe stood up straight again. "Do not instruct me! You're barely more than a boy the way you carry on, following after her apron strings as if she had *any* claim to good sense or judgement."

Verger dropped his outstretched hand and his back stiffened. He shouted back, "If I am barely more than a boy, it is because you forbade me to act as a man! How do you think I feel, not being able to challenge Lafredière for fear of ruining us? Then you ask your brother-in-law to be your champion? How am I to feel?"

Verger wiped his hand across his forehead, leaving a streak of flour on his brow. Marthe glowered. He was no more use than a cart with one wheel. She could feel her temper rising.

"Why do you think you could take on the governor of Montréal when you could not take on the widow Poulin? You have done nothing to ensure she marries and leaves our house. You are ignorant of how she spreads rumours about me around town. You are ignorant of her scheme to sell liquor to the natives. You are an ignorant boy who does nothing and says nothing and I wish . . . I wish I had never married you!"

Something shifted inside her and suddenly water rushed from between Marthe's legs. She grabbed her belly as Verger sprung forward.

"Marthe, chérie—"

"Oh, leave me in peace," Marthe sobbed, pushed him away. "I have just wet myself, for pity's sake!"

The door flew open and Barbe Poulin barrelled in. The widow took in the sight of the water on the floor and a triumphant smile spread across her face.

"I knew it," Barbe Poulin jeered. "Your child comes and you are not yet eight months married. You sly whore."

"Maman Poulin, please. Marthe missed the chamber pot," Verger started, then recoiled when she rounded on him.

"You fool! The waters mean the child is coming. Just look at the size of her belly! She's well past her term. Count on your fingers, boy. That bastard is not yours."

Verger's jaw dropped. His hands dangling by his side, uncertain what to do. While he hesitated, the widow turned to Marthe, a vicious glint in her eye.

"You came into this house, pretending to be a maid, and married this blameless man. I will tell Father de Sancy! I will see you whipped in the pillory for this!"

Marthe laid her head down on her knees. If it was true, and the child was coming, she did not need to fear the whip, for she was as good as dead. The child was too early; he would die and take her with him to Heaven. She wished, as she had a thousand times before, that she was rich enough to send for the best man-midwives in all of Europe, as the fashionable ladies did.

"Whipping is too good for a common hedge-whore like you." The widow's voice pierced her thoughts. "I'll see you and your bastard cast out of Ville-Marie for good! I'll see you sent back to France—"

And then came the sound of Marthe's salvation.

"Shut your mouth, you old toad! How dare you say such a thing to my sister?"

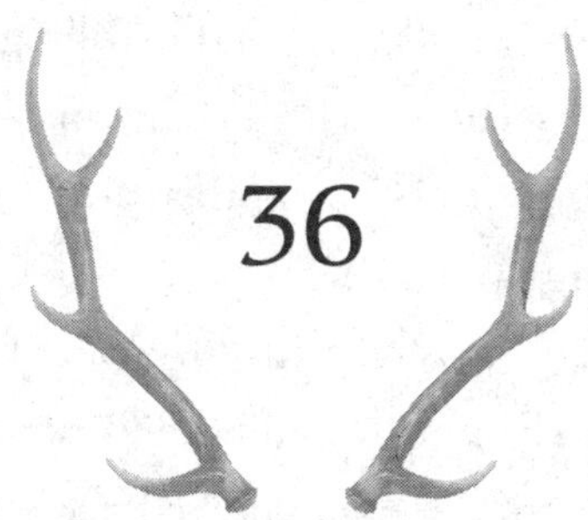

36

É lisabeth stared at her sister slumped against the doorframe. She recognized the scene. In her memory, the doorframe was wider, the woman older. Her clogs had come off, and she could see the dirt ground into the bottom of her feet. Beyond her, a boy running down the lane, coming back with the neighbour's wife, scattering the chickens in the yard. But they were too late. The first baby was stuck, and the other's passage was blocked. The neighbour knelt down and put her hand over the woman's eyes. *Your mother tried her best*, she had said, *she just couldn't birth them both.*

She couldn't birth them both.

Marthe's head lay on her knees. Her eyes were drifting into the distance, looking for the path to Heaven.

Just like Maman.

Barbe Poulin tutted. "Don't be sharp with me, Lili. Marthe's child is coming. Five or six weeks too soon, by my count, and she's far too large for it to be Verger's child. If I say she's a common hedge-whore, it's because she is!"

Élisabeth could not restrain herself. She lunged forward—a demon with wings—and slapped Barbe Poulin's face. The widow stumbled backwards.

"She's carrying *twins*! That is why she is so large."

"Do you think me stupid?" The widow's hand flew to her cheek. "If Marthe were carrying more than one child, the coin I put under her pillow would have turned black." The widow swivelled to find a willing ear. "Verger, cast your wife into the street! You'll be landed with another man's bastard if you do not."

"Verger, do not listen to her. Our mother died birthing twins. Marthe is large because she is carrying two babies. Do not drink that old serpent's poison."

The widow Poulin's face twisted with fury. She drew her hand back as if to hit Élisabeth but then changed her mind and turned to land the blow on Marthe. Before she could strike, Verger grabbed her hand and held it firmly.

"It's past time for you to leave," he said evenly. "Get out of this house."

He released her and she staggered backwards. Verger dropped to his knees. "Marthe? Chérie, do not despair, by God and Saint Anne, I swear you will come through your ordeal."

Marthe did not raise her head from her knees. "Lili is right. This is how Maman died."

Verger turned to Élisabeth. "What can we do?"

"We need a midwife. Marthe cannot do this alone." Élisabeth took a deep breath. "We need Jeanne Roy."

"That witch is halfway to Hell," the widow sneered from the corner of the room.

Élisabeth bared her fangs in Barbe Poulin's direction and the widow shrank. "Verger, lock Poulin in the outhouse so she cannot thwart us. I will run and see if I can get into the fort to speak with Jeanne." Élisabeth crouched down and took Marthe's hand in hers. "Can you hold on?"

Her sister's face was flushed and her jaw clenched. Élisabeth took the grimace as a sign of determination and leapt up. She grabbed a loaf from the counter and checked her cloth satchel. The ragdoll's unravelling eyes stared at her from within. She had all she needed to free Jeanne.

She burst out of the house and ran across the little bridge towards the fort. The bells had stopped ringing; Father de Sancy and the executioner must have finished their grim task. At the gate stood a thin man, not much older than a boy, in a stained doublet. Élisabeth recognized the executioner's teenage son. She waved the bread in his face.

"Let me pass," Élisabeth said. "I've come with the prisoner's food."

The boy stood back. "She's in here," he said, gesturing to a building next to them. Élisabeth stepped past him and opened the door. The room was dark, the air thick with the smell of blood. A few shards of light spilled through the cracks in the log walls to reveal a figure on the dirt floor.

"Jeanne?"

Élisabeth blinked, trying to adjust to the dim light. Jeanne was lying on her side, her hair matted around her face. Her chemise was filthy and torn. Élisabeth recoiled when she saw the back was shredded and covered in dried blood, the lash of the whip having ripped right through the linen.

"I brought you some bread," she said feebly, crouching down and putting the loaf on the ground.

Jeanne Roy's head was twisted at an awkward angle, her legs splayed out as if she had been dumped and did not have the strength to move. Élisabeth could see her ankles were bruised and swollen. She squatted next to Jeanne.

"I am sorry," she whispered. There was no reply. She glanced over her shoulder for a sign of the young jailor. But they were alone, the door shut behind her. "Does it . . . does it hurt?"

She cringed at her own question, but she could not think what to say. She felt sick, both at what had been done to Jeanne, and knowing she was to blame.

"Jeanne, listen. I am going to undo what I did. I will make it right. We can petition the king. We can explain that all the women on this island need you as their midwife. And that I was stupid . . . and a liar . . ."

Still Jeanne Roy's eyes remained closed and Élisabeth felt the hope drain from her. Jeanne was barely alive. They needed magic now more than ever.

"Look," Élisabeth opened her bag. "I brought you your doll. It will be able to help you—"

Jeanne Roy's eyes flew open. "What have you done?" she croaked. She reached a bloodied hand out for the doll. "You risk everything by bringing it here."

"I thought . . ." Élisabeth did not want to admit that she hoped the doll was a magical creature that could somehow save her. She knew Jeanne would mock her for her faith in witchcraft. Instead she swallowed and spoke in a small voice. "I thought it would bring you comfort."

The witch struggled to sit up. "This doll is not for my *comfort*. It is not a *toy*." She grabbed it by its neck and brandished it at Élisabeth. "This is the sum of my life's work."

Élisabeth felt her cheeks burn. Once again, her ignorance had made her a fool. "I am sorry."

The witch closed her eyes and tried to take a deep breath. She winced at the effort. "You were not to know its value."

Silence enveloped them and Élisabeth groped for something to say.

"I'm sorry for all that I have done," she repeated. She could not think how to mend her mistake except by uttering the words, yet like a spell without magic it seemed to have no effect. Jeanne was already in her grave; she would not be able to save Marthe now.

"Do you see my boots?" Jeanne asked.

Élisabeth looked in the direction Jeanne pointed. There were two wooden boxes cast aside by the bench. She shook her head, not understanding her meaning.

"Brodequins," Jeanne explained. "Made especially for me, or so he says. Do you know what I think of when he ties them to my ankles and strikes them with the hammer?"

Élisabeth shook her head again.

"I think of you."

The shame rose from Élisabeth's belly to her chest, then her cheeks, turning her flesh the colour of wine. "You must hate me," she said in a voice she herself could barely hear.

"No. I hate myself."

Élisabeth was startled by the witch's words. She waited as Jeanne Roy gathered the strength to speak.

"Wari believes that if I had listened with more kindness to your concerns, you would not have accused me. All that I am suffering now is God's punishment for my arrogance."

Élisabeth reached out a tentative hand. When Jeanne did not recoil, she laid it on her arm. "I admit that I was hurt when you called me ignorant. But I . . . I did not listen when you offered me a cure."

Jeanne looked down at Élisabeth's hand. Perhaps it caused her pain. Outside she heard the young jailor greet a passerby.

"I should not have called you ignorant," Jeanne whispered. "I am sorry too."

Élisabeth swallowed. The apology was a salve to her soul. She drew her hand back and smiled shyly at Jeanne.

"Wari told me a little about your past. She said your tutor accused you on the pretence of stealing his knowledge." She paused, remembering what Wari had said. *As if knowledge is something that can be owned by one man alone.* "I am sorry you were so wronged."

"But I did steal his knowledge. That is what made him so angry."

Élisabeth sat upright. "You did?"

Jeanne Roy grimaced, then flinched, as if the movement caused her pain. She touched her fingers to her broken lip. "Yes, I stole Chamberlen's Secret. I will tell you the tale. I should have told everyone about it, the moment it was in my hands. The great tragedy is that it is a secret at all."

Élisabeth caught her breath. She felt as if she were back at the Roche d'Oëtre, teetering on the edge of the cliff, the whole world at her feet. She waited for the witch to speak.

"François Mauriceau, my tutor, was not cruel. Not in the least. Indeed, we were . . . fond of each other." Jeanne's voice grew soft and wistful. "A friendship developed. Some days we would step away from our work and walk together from the Hôtel Dieu to Notre-Dame in the middle of the day just to take in its glory." A bug crawled up Élisabeth's leg from the dirt floor, but she did not move lest she interrupt Jeanne's tale. "Paris is the heartbeat that gives life to all of France. It is as intoxicating as you can imagine: the cathedral, the hospital, the bridges, the fishermen along the river, the markets every day of the week. But what Mauriceau and I loved most were books. I read all day and every night until my candles burned to stubs: Galen, Hippocrates, Vesalius's *Fabrica*, Galileo's *Two New Sciences*, Paracelsus—dear Paracelsus, like a watchful parent urging me to put my books aside and turn to nature for wisdom. I read it all and more; anything to do with medicine, chymistry, astronomy, mathematics, I devoured. Then I would discuss all that I had learned with Mauriceau."

Her words wove an enchantment around them. Élisabeth did not know what all of them meant, but she could see in her eyes the glamour the witch used to transport herself from the dimly lit prison back to a city on the other side of the sea.

"Two years ago, during my association with Mauriceau, he had a visitor from England. A man called Chamberlen wanted to share with him a secret—one his family had hidden for many years. Chamberlen feared the knowledge of it would see him executed, and he came to ask for Mauriceau's counsel. We were both intrigued and excited by what the Englishman showed us, but Mauriceau wanted time to consider what should be done with it. I was incensed. What Chamberlen had in his possession was so . . ." Jeanne hesitated and glanced at Élisabeth. "You would call it magical, I believe.

"I knew it could not be kept hidden—it had to be shared with the world. So, against my nature, I took it. I did not think twice. I stole it and fled back to my estate in Normandy with it. That was what drove Mauriceau mad. That I had the Secret, and its exceptional power, and he did not."

Élisabeth could not contain herself. "But Jeanne, what *is* Chamberlen's Secret? If it is magical, can we use it to free you from—"

Sudden light spilled into the shadowy room, startling them both. Élisabeth jumped up as the jailor's thin frame appeared in the doorway. Behind him stood another figure.

Father de Sancy.

"What is this woman doing here? Villagers are only permitted to bring the food, not to stay and dine."

Élisabeth's heart began to pound so loudly she could not hear the jailor's mumbled reply. She drew a deep breath and turned to face the priest.

"Father, I have come to recant my accusation," she said, as firmly as her quaking body would allow. "My neighbour Dufossé died because he was drunk. His wife told me he drank a bottle of brandy the night he froze to death. This woman is not a witch, she is innocent."

The old priest raised his eyebrows and looked her up and down. Behind her she could hear Jeanne Roy struggling to sit up.

"You are the girl with all the questions."

"Yes, Father. I'm Élisabeth Jossard. I was jealous of this woman and sought to do her harm. I am a busybody and a gossip."

The priest gave her a piteous look. "I was never in any doubt that whoever accused this witch possessed a backbiting tongue. It's a wonder women's tongues aren't forked like the Devil's own, so much do they spread scandal."

Élisabeth dug her feet into the ground. She would not back down. "I swear to you, she is innocent."

The priest waved her away. "You may have led me to this lady, but she is not here on your accusation alone. She has already confessed to being Angélique Aubert de Brétigny, whom I know to be the queen of the most powerful coven of witches France has ever known. She slipped away once before, but there will be no reprieve for her this time."

The priest's eyes drifted to the floor. "What is this?" He bent down and reached a liver-spotted hand towards the ragdoll.

"No," Jeanne Roy said, clutching it to her chest.

"Boy, bring me the creature the witch is holding."

The young jailor hesitated until the priest snapped his finger. Then he stomped two paces towards Jeanne and gave her a hard kick in the hip before darting backwards. She writhed in pain but did not drop the doll. The boy bent down and pulled it roughly from her grasp, scampering over to hand it to Father de Sancy. The priest received it as carefully as if it were a golden chalice.

"Heavy," he noted, weighing it up and down. "Is this some kind of familiar? Or a replica of a child you meant to torment?" Father de Sancy turned the doll over in his hands several times, looking from Jeanne Roy to Élisabeth for an answer before tucking it under his arm.

"I wish I had more time to question you, Lady Angélique. For someone of such high rank to have been seduced by the Devil is a rarity. I long to know more about you. It would be wondrous material for my treatise on *maleficia* . . ." The priest seemed lost in his thoughts, then he sighed. "Still. This doll will give me something to study long after you've been burned to ash."

The priest turned and pushed his way out of the makeshift prison. The jailor gripped Élisabeth firmly by the arm and marched her out of the barracks and through the fort's gate, pushing her onto the path outside. Élisabeth stumbled into the mud but did not let herself fall. She righted herself and stared back at the fort.

She had no idea what to do next. There was no time to get a petition to the intendant. Marthe was already in labour. Even if the doll could somehow free Jeanne, she had let it slip into Father de Sancy's possession.

She clasped her hands together and prayed to all of the angels—and all of the demons—to help her.

37

Marthe was in a sea of pain, bent over, hands on her sides, feeling a surge of agony until the wave crested and she was left bobbing along, exhausted, waiting for the current to drag her under again. Verger had moved her into the widow's room, to the bed with the cattail mattress. In between the waves, Marthe wearily rubbed her palms over the ticking and noticed that indeed it was much finer than straw.

"What can I do? I am not usefully employed. Employ me!" Verger fretted, at once by her side and then instantly pacing the room in long strides. Élisabeth had been gone more than an hour. In that time Verger had run his hand through his hair so often that flour had coloured his hair white.

"Thirsty," Marthe said in a small voice.

Her husband leapt to fetch her small beer. He returned and held the pewter mug to her lips as she drank, sickly swallows that would never quench a thirst. He pushed her hair back from her face, tucking a loose tendril behind her ear.

"You will survive this," he said, full of determination. "You will."

Marthe did not respond. She sat in the bed with the cattail mattress, her head on her knees, bobbing in the sea.

"You must survive, my Marthe," Verger said, more plaintive now. He rubbed her back and she felt her shoulders slump with relief. They had not sent for any of their near neighbours, lest they discover the widow in her outhouse prison and release a tornado of trouble. Once Élisabeth returned, Verger would run for one of the *Saint-Jean-Baptiste* girls. For now, Marthe had only her husband.

"You must survive, my Marthe. For we have so much we want to do. You are going to sell jam, remember? Remember all our plans?"

She thought of raspberries and blackberries and the dark currents they called blueberries and could almost taste the summer fruit on her tongue. She would love to have sold jam in her little shop on the corner of Rue Saint-Paul. A white shelf with jars full of deep reds and near-black purples. She would have loved that.

"You will survive, Marthe," Verger pleaded. "From the moment I saw you in the chapel, I knew . . ." He lost his words, then tried again. "You said to me, that first day, that your mother had died when you were a child. I thought it would make you happy, to have an older companion. I thought that Barbe Poulin would be the mother you had lost. I failed you. And I know you are disappointed with me, wanting us to have more—"

"Verger?" Marthe struggled to raise her head off her knees.

"Yes?" He laid his hands on top of hers. "Yes, my Marthe?"

"You've not failed me." She wanted to explain how powerless she felt, watching her father die, slowly, then all at once when the blood ran from his vein. She wanted to explain to him she only ever wanted to be rich so that she would not lose someone she loved again. She wanted to confess that she liked spending time with him alone, that his kisses were as good as any gold. She could not summon the words. "I . . . I hoped for a different fate" was all she said.

This prompted Verger to leap from her side and run out of the room. He returned a moment later, a purse in his hands. "I have put aside a few coins every month. I have a small sum saved. I will call for the barber-surgeon, he will help you. I will go now—"

"No," Marthe gasped weakly. "Not the surgeon, I beg you."

She remembered what Apolline had said. The surgeon was only called when a father wanted his child cut out of the mother's belly. But Marthe could not explain; she hadn't the strength or the time before the next wave was upon her. The whip cracked. She circled her belly with her arms, laid her head on her knees and groaned.

The sea dragged her under again.

38

É lisabeth pushed the door open and was struck by a waft of pipe smoke and the smell of sour wine. Half a dozen heads turned towards her. She cringed to be back in Folleville's tavern so soon; she could not quite remember what had happened when Marcosi confronted the governor but realized that many of the men staring at her certainly did.

She had nowhere else to turn but to the sorry little tavern. She had half a notion that Anne Lamarque, with the taint of witchcraft upon her, would somehow help release Jeanne Roy. Or, Élisabeth thought, if she were indeed a witch, perhaps Anne could fly to Jeanne's aid.

Élisabeth strode up to the bar, looking for the innkeeper. Instead, she saw Anne Lamarque's husband staring at her. He had a soft, grey beard and gentle eyes, quite the opposite of his hard-bitten wife.

"Can I help you, mistress?"

Élisabeth stumbled as her muddy skirts clung to her legs. She tried to kick herself free, like an animal caught in a trap.

"May I speak with your wife, Monsieur de Folleville?" she asked, loosening her legs from the clinging cloth and bobbing politely on the spot.

"She's not here," he said, eyeing her warily. Élisabeth saw that her association with Barbe Poulin, Anne Lamarque's bitter rival, made the innkeeper doubt her intentions.

"It is very important." She lowered her voice. "It is about Jeanne Roy."

"She's most certainly not here," he said more emphatically. Élisabeth's heart sank. Everyone in the village knew it had been her accusation that had brought Jeanne to justice.

"Please, I won't cause any trouble. I am so very desperate. I need help—"

"Élisabeth."

She turned so quickly she felt lightheaded. It was Francoeur. Her Francoeur.

"It's you." Her eyes lit up. "I was praying for a miracle. And the Virgin sent you."

Her husband's beard was shaggier, his chemise dirty around the collar. "I've not been sent. I've been staying here this past fortnight."

"It feels like a miracle to me."

Francoeur clenched his teeth. He held out his arm, indicating that she join him at a table away from the bar.

"What are you doing here?" he asked when they were seated.

"I came to free Jeanne," she said. "Though I am armed only with magic and prayers, and it has all gone wrong. She is so battered, so weak, I doubt she can even walk. Francoeur, you must help her—"

"I have been trying to help her," he said tersely. "The priest will not listen to reason. There is no governor here now to counter his authority, thanks to my petition. There is nothing I can do."

"Knock the jailor down! Carry her out of the fort! Do something!" she pleaded.

Francoeur's lips pressed into a firm line. "If I steal one witch, do you not think they will come for another in her stead? You, perhaps? Or your sister? Or all of the girls-for-marrying who came over on the *Saint-Jean-Baptiste* last summer? Not only would I spend the rest of my days with Jeanne, running from the Sulpicians, but you would all be suspect."

She grabbed his hands. "Marthe will die in childbed if Jeanne is not freed. She is trying to birth twins and I fear she will not survive the night."

Francoeur pulled his hands away. He looked down at the table, rubbing the edge of the maple, as if checking the grain. "So, you are here to save your sister. Do you even regret accusing Jeanne?"

"I do. I came to Ville-Marie to recant. I told Father de Sancy that I lied. But he did not believe me when I said that Jeanne was innocent, or that I was a shrew and a gossip."

"But you agree that I was right, that Jeanne is not a witch?"

Élisabeth hesitated and his face instantly fell.

"No, wait! Francoeur, listen! I know now that Jeanne means us no ill will. She has not made a pact with the Devil. She merely believes in things like black bile and melancholy and strange humours because she read about them in her books. It is only . . ." She searched for the words.

Consider, consider. Witchcraft is real.

If only she could explain how she felt, how a witch's curse had changed her, but somehow not for the worse. How she could feel that Marcosi's blood coursing through her veins made her bold and resilient, how his rage had protected her when she could not protect herself. How she had grown strong with the knowledge that she had chosen her own path.

She took a deep breath.

"I have spent a lifetime in prayer. Yet at times it felt as though the saints had turned their back on me and my prayers. My mother died before she could raise me. I saw my father work in the fields until he was too sick to stand. For all his work, for all my brothers' toil, some years we never had enough to eat." Élisabeth struggled to find the words. "In my life, I have felt so powerless, Francoeur. But in a world where there are witches and demons and magic, there is hope."

Francoeur raised his eyebrows. "The priests would call that heresy, I think."

"No, not at all. The priests believe in demons and witches too. They are, somehow, proof of God." Élisabeth leaned forward. "And I believe that even if witches are frightening and dangerous, they do lend us their power from time to time. And isn't their magic our only hope in a world where God has made everything so hard?"

Francoeur continued his study of the tavern's woodwork until she grabbed his hand and made him look at her. "You see, it's not that I still believe that Jeanne Roy—the Lady Angélique—is a witch. It is that I *hope* for it, I *pray* for it. I *wish* for it with all my heart. I need her to be a witch, to save us. We need her magic."

"She is not a witch," Francoeur said evenly. "She is an ordinary woman who will soon be put to death."

"Then let us break her out of jail." Élisabeth slapped the table. "Break her free so that she might save Marthe, and then I will run with you, and her, for the rest of our lives."

Francoeur stared, as if he were seeing her for the first time. She was suddenly aware how dishevelled she was; her hair was tangled and wild, the ribbon that laced her bodice was coming loose. She returned his steady gaze.

"If we are going to break her out of the fort . . ." Francoeur said slowly. "We will need a distraction. And some help."

Élisabeth's heart skipped and she caught her breath. "Jambon and Lajeunesse will be here soon with Rose and Lou. Jeanne's friend Wari went east to fetch them."

Francoeur rose. "Very well. We will do this. But afterwards, Élisabeth, we will treat your melancholy—"

"My demon," she corrected him.

He hesitated as he opened the tavern door. "When this is over, you must seek help." He stopped when he saw two men rushing towards the tavern, one tall and skinny, one short and wide. Élisabeth stifled the urge to cheer at the sight of Jambon and Lajeunesse hurrying to join them.

"Our wives have gone to the bakehouse to attend to Marthe," Jambon said. "We are at your disposal."

"We will speak more later," Francoeur said to Élisabeth in a low voice before turning to his comrades. "So, lads. How would you like to break the law?" Lajeunesse grinned and Jambon rubbed his hands together. Francoeur nodded. "Good. Do you remember the night at Fort Sainte-Thérèse when we gave Lafred the runaround?"

Lajeunesse chuckled. "Of course."

"Never seen the governor so confused," said Jambon.

Francoeur managed a grin. "Then you know what to do."

Jambon slapped his thigh and hooted. Lajeunesse adjusted his hat on his head and pulled a flask from his pocket. He took a gulp and then passed it to his friend.

"Ready?" Jambon asked, pulling a knife from his belt. Lajeunesse nodded. With a flash of his blade, Jambon cut the sleeve off his friend's shirt as if he were skinning a hare. Then, with a clean stroke he slashed the knife across Lajeunesse's arm. The tall lad flinched. Blood ran towards his fingers.

"Smear it," Francoeur ordered. They painted their arms and faces red. When they looked as if they had mauled each other like dogs, Francoeur took Lajeunesse's ripped sleeve and tied it around the wound. "Now go."

The two men lurched forward, staggering, swinging at each other and shouting, as if they had been born to the stage and not the plough. As they tumbled along Rue Saint-Paul, the residents of Ville-Marie began spilling from their houses, checking to see what the matter was. The first cry from the crowd was fear for their own safety—*Iroquois!*—but when the villagers saw it was only two old soldiers in a drunken tussle, they were glad to gather round and cheer them on. The long winter had left everyone in need of entertainment and the crowd quickly swelled. Jambon and Lajeunesse led them down the street until they reached the Little River. The young jailor stepped out of the guardhouse and eyed them warily.

Jambon threw a punch at his friend, made a show of missing, and spun in a pirouette.

"Follow me," Francoeur said to Élisabeth. Together they approached the boy standing guard outside the fort. "Aren't you going to stop them?" Francoeur asked.

The executioner's son craned his neck to see which fighter would get the better of the other and shrugged.

"You're right," Francoeur said with a shake of his head. "The short one's got a knife. Takes a braver man than you or me to get in the way of that."

The boy threw Francoeur a defiant look, then cast aside the twig he'd been chewing. He strode into the crowd, grabbing first for Jambon, then for Lajeunesse. The fighters evaded his reach, keeping up their drunken charade, dancing and weaving away from his grasp.

"Now," Francoeur urged.

They slipped through the wooden gate while the boy was distracted. Élisabeth then led her husband to where Jeanne was being held. She looked around the compound for signs of anyone else before lifting the latch. Darkness spilled out of the old barracks, but Élisabeth rushed in, finding Jeanne in a heap by the wall.

"Jeanne, wake up. It's me, Élisabeth. I've brought Francoeur," she whispered. "We've come to free you."

The witch raised her head. Élisabeth looked at her swollen ankles, crushed by the brodequins.

"You will need to carry her," she told Francoeur.

He wasted no time. He scooped her up and put her arms around his neck. Jeanne clung limply to him as he made his way across the barracks and out the door.

Outside the fort the crowd was still focused on the spectacle. The jailor had managed to grab Jambon by the back of the shirt, who twisted and tried to hug the boy by his waist, weeping with feigned gratitude. Lajeunesse was rallying the mob with his arms in the air, before spinning back and pulling Jambon's breeches to the ground. The crowd roared and called for more. The boy jailor lunged for Lajeunesse, letting go of Jambon. The ham pulled up his breeches and then did his own tour of the crowd, wiggling his bottom to great cheers. No one noticed as Francoeur and Élisabeth slipped out of the jail with the witch in their arms.

"Walk between me and the crowd so that they cannot see Jeanne," Francoeur told Élisabeth. She nodded and held her head high, as if she could grow several inches just by wishing it. They rounded the corner of the fort and had nearly reached the bridge when they heard a shout.

"Stop!"

Élisabeth whipped around. Lajeunesse and Jambon had kept the crowd in thrall but the boy had marked their exit and followed them. Jeanne lifted her head. Élisabeth crossed herself and waited, frozen, to see who would move first.

"Bring the witch back," the jailor shouted. There was a tremor in his voice.

"No. We need her," Élisabeth called back.

The boy took a tentative step forward, then immediately hopped back when he saw Jeanne groggily lift her head. He danced on the spot, unable to take his eyes off the figure in Francoeur's arms. Élisabeth was struck by a sudden thought. She nudged her husband backwards and slowly he took a step. The jailor moved towards them, thought the better of it, and darted backwards. The boy clearly did not have the spine to cross the witch. They turned and began to run, Francoeur lumbering forward with Jeanne in his arms, Élisabeth close by his side. As they crossed the bridge, she could hear the guard call after them.

"You will rue your actions!"

They weaved across the commons towards Rue Saint-Paul; Élisabeth was careful not to tempt fate by looking behind them, only sneaking a quick glance at Francoeur by her side. He caught her eye and Élisabeth felt a twist of hope as her husband broke into a smile. She blushed and quickened her pace.

They burst through the bakery door a moment later. Francoeur eased Jeanne Roy into a chair in the widow's salon. The witch's head rolled back, and she groaned. Wari rushed in from behind a curtain at the back of the room.

"Angélique," she whispered, placing her hands on Jeanne Roy's cheeks. The witch gave her a weak smile. "You are free."

"Where's Marthe?" Élisabeth demanded, striding towards Verger. The baker was standing dumb by the fire. He jerked his thumb towards the curtain. "Back there. In the widow's bed."

"Then what are you doing out here?" Élisabeth snapped, sick with fear.

"There is no room for me! There must be nearly a dozen women with her. Rose, Lou, Thérèse, Françoise. And more whom I do not know. Apolline bid me to come out here and heat some water. So that is what I'm doing." Verger frowned, staring at the cauldron as if willing it to boil.

"The *Saint-Jean-Baptiste* girls have come." Élisabeth exhaled, feeling the weight lift from her shoulders. She turned to kneel by Jeanne Roy's side. Wari was wiping her face with a cloth, cleaning away the dirt and blood to reveal the damage the hangman had done.

"Jeanne, I am sorry to beg for your help when you are in such pain. But Marthe is trying to birth twins. And I fear they will kill her, like they did my mother."

Jeanne's eyes were bleary. Still, she raised her head. "Where is she?" she croaked.

"I'll carry you." Francoeur stepped forward, lifting the crippled witch once again into his arms. He followed Élisabeth as she pushed back the curtain to reveal a small space crowded with women: some holding Marthe's hand, some mopping her brow, and one crooning a lullaby. When they saw Jeanne Roy they leapt and crowded around the witch, trying to touch her face and kiss her hands, as if she were a saint come to life in their midst.

"Put me down," Jeanne instructed. The girls stood back, and Francoeur eased Jeanne to the ground. She winced as her feet touched the floor, but once she found her knees, she edged towards her patient. "Marthe, let me have a look at you."

Marthe tried to nod but winced instead and made a guttural sound. Jeanne Roy was not dissuaded. She placed her hands on Marthe's belly, feeling the flesh with her fingertips, then she reached one hand beneath Marthe's shift. Marthe grimaced at Jeanne's touch. After several minutes the witch withdrew her hand and spoke calmly.

"Everything is as it should be. You will be a mother before the night is out."

Jeanne Roy nodded to Francoeur and he lifted her back into his arms. He carried her into the front room, Élisabeth following quickly behind.

"All is well? She will deliver soon?" she asked. Francoeur eased Jeanne back into a chair.

"No," Jeanne said softly so that Marthe would not hear. "It is as you suspected. I can feel two babies. But she is clearly weak from her labours. I do not know if she has the strength to continue."

Élisabeth closed her eyes and clasped her hands together. "Oh Blessed Virgin, have mercy on her soul," she began. "Saint Anne, you who gave birth to the mother of Christ our saviour—"

"Élisabeth."

She stopped and opened her eyes. Jeanne was looking at her dead in the eye. "I might be able to save her. But I'll need Chamberlen's Secret."

She stared at Jeanne Roy. Verger spun away from the cauldron of boiling water.

"You need *what?*" he balked.

"It is a tool of unimaginable power," Élisabeth said softly. "A magic wand, I believe. Or possibly a knife."

"Élisabeth," Jeanne Roy interrupted. "Don't try to guess what it is. Just go and find where the priest has taken it."

"The priest has Chamberlen's Secret?"

"Yes, Élisabeth. Go and get my doll."

39

There were hands upon her brow and another pair on her back. No sooner had she cried out for the Virgin to ease her pain, than thumbs kneaded her shoulders and fingers traced a circle on her belly, coaxing the child to be born. Rose tried to massage her feet, but Marthe kicked her hands away.

"Verger?" she moaned. She tried to pull her shift over her head, but another pair of hands soothed her arms back to her sides so that the rough cloth stayed clinging to her chest. She wished Lou would stop singing.

"It's all right," Apolline told her. "It's only us. We sent Verger away."

Marthe collapsed backwards onto the bed, disappointed. Strange that she would want her husband by her side in her confinement. With his shy smile and encouraging words about summer fruit, she wished that it were he who was rubbing her back and mopping her brow.

She wondered if what she was feeling was love.

A wave of pain cascaded over her. She lowed, the sound resonating around the room, causing a flurry of small hands to stroke her face and back and legs. When the wave crested, she turned and tried to bury her face in the mattress.

What a tragedy, she thought.

She had only just realized that she had married for love, and now she was going to die.

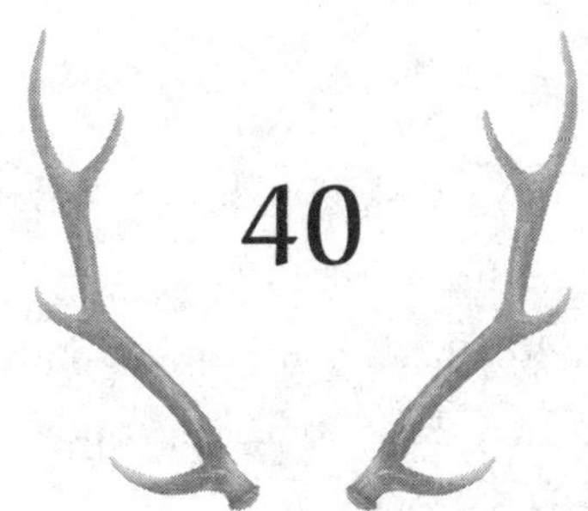

40

The brides had not been pressed together this tightly since they had stood on the wharf in Dieppe the year before, waiting for the *Saint-Jean-Baptiste* to take them away from all they knew.

Élisabeth had called them into the front room, leaving Marthe alone with Jeanne Roy. She looked at the faces all around her. Rose and Lou, of course, ready to do whatever was asked of them. Thérèse and Françoise, one with a worried frown, one with a leer. Several of the other girls who had married and spread across the island, all of them rounded up by Apolline, who stood tall and smug in the centre of the group. Only the youngest, Claire, was still unwed and living with the nuns. Still, she had leapt at the chance to join them when Apolline had arrived with her husband's cart and horse.

"For who, when called to help a witch, would dare refuse?" she had said with a nervous giggle.

Élisabeth wondered how they would succeed. In the back room she could hear her sister's moans and Jeanne Roy's murmurings. Verger had been sent outside to guard the privy to ensure the widow did not escape. Francoeur had run back to the prison to see if Jambon and Lajeunesse had been captured by the boy jailor. Now it was up to her. To find the magic wand that would somehow save Marthe's life. She climbed up onto a chair.

"Girls, please listen to me."

They shuffled to attention. Some eyed her and muttered to those standing next to them. Élisabeth's heart sank, for she knew they did not trust her after what she'd done. But she persisted.

"You all know Jeanne Roy has a cloth toy, a poppet made of rags and yarn. What you do not know is that this doll has great power. And Jeanne needs it to save Marthe's life. Father de Sancy has it—"

"And who's the idiot who gave it to him?" one of them called out.

Élisabeth took a breath and called upon her demon for strength. She would not falter now. "I am. But I am begging you all to help me take it back."

"Why does she need the doll?" It was Claire, her voice wary.

"It's where her magic comes from," said another.

"How do you mean to steal it back?" Françoise asked.

Élisabeth waited for the questions to die down before she spoke again. "The doll is called Chamberlen's Secret. It is a magic wand. It will save Marthe, and when your time comes, it may save you as well."

A chorus of whispers rose up. Most of the girls were already with child. Perhaps they would be moved to help for their own sakes, even if they feared the task ahead.

"Why do you need so many of us to steal a wand?" Françoise called out again. "The Sulpicians will surely spot a dozen women sauntering up to their seminary. They aren't *that* blinded by faith." She sniggered and nudged Thérèse. But Thérèse brushed her elbow away, not taking her eyes off Élisabeth.

"Well, I have a notion . . ." Élisabeth began. She remembered how the young jailor halted in his tracks when he saw Jeanne Roy in Francoeur's arms, stupefied by his fear. Once she too had been frozen by fear. Fear was a powerful enemy, but could it also be their ally? The demon Marcosi was her steadfast ally now. She stood a little straighter on the chair.

"Father de Sancy has been hunting witches these many months. Tonight, it is time to turn the tables. Tonight, it is the witches who will go hunting."

"W-witches?" Claire stammered. "Do you know of witches *other* than Jeanne here in Ville-Marie?"

"*We* will be the witches," Élisabeth told her.

The girls looked from one another to Élisabeth, shaking their heads and crossing themselves.

"This is madness," Apolline protested. "She intends to make heretics of us all!"

Élisabeth held her hands out, trying to quieten them down. Jeanne Roy hobbled out of the back room on Wari's arm, wincing as she walked. Only then did the brides fall silent.

"I cannot wait much longer," Jeanne said.

"I have a plan," Élisabeth assured her. "There are thirteen of us, including Wari. Enough for a full coven."

"A coven!" Lou laughed. "She does want to turn us into witches!"

"Élisabeth, what are you plotting?" Jeanne Roy's voice was sharp.

"The priests will cower when a coven of witches arrives to claim Chamberlen's Secret. They will faint dead from fear."

"Élisabeth, the fire you intend to conjure will burn everything it touches," Jeanne said. "You cannot know the risk you are facing."

"We are already at risk." Élisabeth raised her voice to be heard above the mounting clamour. "If we do not claim the doll, Marthe dies. I will not let that happen. I will steal it myself. And once I do, every woman in the colony will be under suspicion. The old priest will wake tomorrow and discover it missing. He will seek witches at every turn. Which farmer's wife in her garden will Father de Sancy decide is a witch to be burned? Which wife gone to market will be put to the Question? Any woman trying to help another through her labours? A witch."

One by one the girls stopped talking. Élisabeth took a deep breath. "Once I take back Chamberlen's Secret there will be such a witch craze in Ville-Marie none will be safe. None can hide. Thus, I propose that we do not cringe. We do it together. The more powerful we appear, the safer we will be."

"This is not right," Jeanne Roy said. "The solution to a witch craze cannot be to create more witches—"

Élisabeth hopped down from the chair and took her neighbour's hands in hers. "I believe what you've told me about natural philosophy, I do. But science and reason will not get your doll back from a priest. Tonight, you must listen to me. You must believe in magic."

Jeanne Roy opened her mouth, as if to object, then she stopped. "Heaven help me for what I am about to say." She cleared her throat and closed her eyes. "Let the witches' hunt begin."

Élisabeth leapt back onto the chair. "There is no time to waste. Take off your bodices and strip to your shifts. Rat your hair and use the flour in the workroom to powder your faces white. Make yourselves alarming, deranged. From this moment, we are the Normandy coven!"

No one moved. The brides from the *Saint-Jean-Baptiste* eyed her doubtfully. Then Apolline spoke.

"Surely we are not the Normandy coven," she said. There was a pause, and the only noise was Marthe's fretful moan from behind the burlap curtain. Apolline raised one eyebrow. "Surely we are the Montréal coven."

It was the spark that lit the fire. Chaos broke out in the bakehouse. Girls unlaced their bodices and flung them in the air. They tore off each other's caps and pulled ribbons out of their hair. Élisabeth took off her skirt and ran her fingers through her already tangled brown curls. She twisted and teased until her mane was thick and terrible to behold.

"You have the cunning of a wolf," Wari told her. "Do not forget that."

Élisabeth smiled shyly. She felt somehow as if she had been blessed, as surely as if she had put the Eucharist on her tongue. She gazed around the room, her eyes landing on each of the wild girls, and for a moment she saw each of them as they should be. Their true selves. If Élisabeth had the cunning of a wolf, then Lou had the stealth of a wild cat, Rose the heart of a bear. Apolline the wisdom of an eagle. Each of the girls was transformed.

Witches, all of them.

"It's time," Élisabeth declared.

One by one the ghostly brides slipped out into the dusk. The sky was bruised and purple, day hovering on the cusp of night. Apolline took her place at the head of the coven, Élisabeth walked beside them, imparting instructions along the row. When they reached the stone seminary, she put her hand on the wrought-iron gate and pushed it open. The witches floated towards the priests' home.

They spread out and walked slowly as they approached the manor, the white of their chemises shining in the rising moonlight. When they reached the front door, Élisabeth tried the handle. It was locked.

"What do we do now?" Lou whispered.

Élisabeth scanned the rough-hewn edges of the stone building, then drifted towards the windows. The shutters of the study were not fully closed. She pushed one back and pried her fingers underneath the window.

"We climb," she announced, pushing the frame up and open. She put her foot into a space between the stones in the wall and pulled herself up. With her hair loose and her cheeks white with flour, she was a demon climbing her way out of Hell. Using all the strength in her arms she hauled herself up and over the windowsill.

She landed in an empty room. It was the library, where not many months before she had come to ask the famed witch hunter her questions. She blinked rapidly, trying to force her eyes to see what she was looking for. Rose clambered up and onto the sill behind her, followed by the rest. Some were too heavy with child to climb forward and so were dragged in backwards. Lou swung over the sill more forcefully than she expected and swore out loud when she landed hard on her bottom.

"God's wounds!" she cried.

Élisabeth heard a noise overhead. She knew they only had a moment before the priests came down the stairs to discover them. She turned around, trying to get her bearings in the dark. Where would Father de Sancy have put the doll?

"Try the cabinet," she whispered to Lou, as a voice rang out from the hallway.

"Who is there?"

Élisabeth raised her hand above her head, a captain readying her troops. The brides waited, frozen, as they heard the sound of footsteps shuffling across the paving stones. The door swung open, and the glimmer of a candle spilled into the room.

"Christ in Heaven!" a young priest shrieked. He quickly slammed the door shut. Élisabeth put her finger to her mouth. From the other side of the door they could hear Father de Sancy's voice.

"What is it?"

"It is a . . . an abomination," the young priest stammered.

"Be ready," Élisabeth signalled, turning to face the door. The girls spread out, their hands stretched before them. Élisabeth heard sturdy footsteps and knew the witch hunter was coming to see for himself. The door opened slowly.

"Onésime Gaudin de Sancy," Élisabeth intoned, and raised her arms slowly. The other brides repeated her words in heavy, lifeless tones. The priest's name echoed around the room into a crescendo of sound.

Father de Sancy stood in the doorway with a taper in his hand, two younger priests cowering behind him. One held an iron poker.

"Who *are* they?" the younger priest whispered. "*What* are they?"

"You know who I am," Élisabeth said. One by one the girls repeated her words. *You know who I am. You know who I am. You know who I am.* They were back on the ship, singing in rounds. But this time, rather than joy and hope, their song brought darkness and despair.

"I am Angélique Aubert de Brétigny," Élisabeth bellowed as the ghostly chorus picked up the words and turned them into an incantation.

The priests cowered, just as she said they would. The one with the poker brandished it at them. Élisabeth pushed on, hoping the girls could keep up.

"I am la Fille du Roy," she declared. "I am the Warrior Maid. I am the Winter Witch." The spell echoed around the room. *The Winter Witch. The Winter Witch. The Winter Witch.*

"It is just as I said it would be!" Father de Sancy exclaimed with a voice full of wonder as he lifted his candle to peer at them. "Why—the witch queen is controlling the coven. She . . . she is commanding the others to do her bidding. Just as I said!"

"They look like a gaggle of women in their shifts to me," a young curé countered warily.

Élisabeth quivered with fear. If the priests doubted them, the witches would be lost. They would be rounded up, publicly whipped for their deception, and Marthe would die in childbirth. Her knees started to knock as badly as they ever had when Marcosi roamed free inside her.

Marcosi. The she-wolf with wings.

Élisabeth knew what to do. Drawing on the demon's strength, she threw back her head and with all the force in her body let a howl rip from her throat.

The sound was so raw, so painful that one of the priests dropped his candle to cover his ears. After a moment's hesitation, Lou also threw her head back and howled, then Rose and Françoise followed, and the rest. The priest with the poker flung the tool down and bolted back up the stairs.

"I am Angélique Aubert de Brétigny!" Élisabeth cried. "La Fille du Roy! The Warrior Maid! The Winter Witch!"

The Winter Witch. The Winter Witch.

"Begone, demon!" Father de Sancy wheezed, his voice high and panicked. He panted, struggling to catch his breath.

"Give me back my doll," Élisabeth commanded, and the other women echoed her demand.

"No." The priest lunged forward and grabbed her by the arm. His grip was so fierce that Élisabeth thought she might cry out. Instead, she flopped forward at the waist as if she were the ragdoll they had come to find, leaving the priest holding on to an empty husk. He stared at Élisabeth's limp body.

"You cannot stop me," Rose said, picking up the lead, and the other brides repeated her words. *Cannot stop me. Cannot stop me.* "I can fly at will between the innocents. I am the witch queen. I inhabit whomever I please."

Father de Sancy dropped Élisabeth's arm and spun to face Rose. He opened his mouth as if to speak, then closed it again. By the light of the candle she could see the sweat glisten on his reddened face. Élisabeth slowly raised herself back upright, as if she were a marionette being lifted from on high. She watched out of the corner of her deadened eye as the old priest glanced over his shoulder. The other Sulpicians had fled upstairs. He was alone. Still, he took a step towards Rose.

Suddenly Wari spoke from the other side of the room. "Give me back my doll." The witches echoed her words. *Give me back my doll. Give me back my doll.*

De Sancy spun around, and seemed startled to find that there was a native woman among the coven. "I will not . . . will not . . . bend to evil."

"*You* are the Evil One," Élisabeth cried.

The Evil One. The Evil One. The Evil One.

"Give me back my doll!"

"Never." The priest lunged to one side of the room and grabbed Jeanne Roy's ragdoll by the neck. It had been sitting in the shadows, unseen, on top of his books. "Is this what you seek, witch?"

Even by the dim candlelight she could see the strain on his face and the flush spreading up his neck as he brandished the doll at the group of women. The priest was sweating, trembling, an old man with hunched shoulders and shaking turkey jowls. He was weak.

She raised her right hand and pointed her finger at him. Straight and strong, like she had seen the old woman in the tavern do, that night so many months ago. The finger that had put so much terror into her own heart. One by one, faces blank, the other girls did the same. Soon the old priest was surrounded by a coven of witches ready to lay their curse.

"My hand shall drop, and you will writhe in agony!"

In agony. In agony, the brides repeated.

"Unless you give me back my doll."

My doll, my doll, my doll. The ghoulish brides formed a circle around the priest.

"Stay back," he cried, holding it above his head. Élisabeth let out another chilling howl. The sound of twelve more wolves reverberated behind her. She stepped forward.

"No," Father de Sancy gasped, clutching his chest. The doll drooped in his hand. He could no longer hold it up.

"Writhe in agony," Élisabeth chanted, casting her spell. *Writhe in agony*, the brides repeated. The priest fell to his knees, the doll tumbling from his hand. His eyes widened at the coven surrounding him. His face had grown ashen. His mouth opened and closed, a fish on land unable to breathe. He stared at Élisabeth with a face full of horror.

She let her hand drop. A dozen arms fell to their sides, rustling as they collapsed against crisp nightdresses. The priest grabbed his heart with both hands and fell forward, his head smashing against the stone floor.

"It is just as I said it would be," he sighed, as a slow trickle of blood pooled beneath his head.

Élisabeth grabbed the doll from his lifeless hand and sprinted for the window. "Run," she yelled over her shoulder.

The coven dissolved, breaking off in every direction, some following Élisabeth through the window, some slipping through the front door onto the seminary lawn. The witches screamed and whooped at their triumph, throwing their heads back to laugh at the risen moon. Élisabeth saw a face peeking from an upstairs window and let another wolf howl rip from her throat as she clutched the doll and ran as fast as she could.

Élisabeth flung open the bakery door and saw Francoeur at the hearth with Jambon and Lajeunesse. They had escaped the jailor.

Her husband's eyes widened at the sight of her. "Élisabeth, what—"

She ran past him to fling back the curtain to the widow's room. There was Marthe, her eyes closed, her face pale and damp. She was barely alive. Élisabeth thrust the doll at Jeanne Roy.

"Here," she heaved. "Here is Chamberlen's Secret."

The witch took it from her. "Thank you," she said calmly. "Now, get me a knife."

"A knife?" Élisabeth hesitated only for a moment, then plunged back into the widow's salon. "A knife!" she shouted at them all. Jambon's hand flicked to his belt and handed her his hunting blade. Élisabeth grabbed it and turned to duck behind the curtain again. She held it out to Jeanne Roy, flat in her hands like a sacrifice.

In one swift movement the witch grabbed the knife and sliced off the doll's head.

The rag lump rolled onto the floor. Jeanne Roy stuck the blade into the doll's back and gutted it. The cloth and stuffing fell away and its bones were revealed.

"What . . . what is that?" Élisabeth gaped.

The doll's bones were wrought-iron blacksmith's tongs. In the place of pincers were a pair of curved iron hands.

"*This* is Chamberlen's Secret," she said. Even the witch's voice was full of awe.

Élisabeth stared at the device in Jeanne Roy's hands. The black claws looked like an instrument of torture that might be heated in coals and used to pull out a liar's tongue. Jeanne Roy kneeled in front of Marthe.

"Marthe, come to the edge of the bed. I am going to use these forceps"—

Jeanne Roy held up Chamberlen's Secret—"to pull out your baby's head. If I can free the first child, I think the other will follow naturally."

Élisabeth swallowed as she stared at the iron hands. Father de Sancy had been right. Chamberlen's Secret *was* a magic wand that could pull a child from its mother's womb. She hoped that Jeanne Roy was a skilled enough sorceress to know how to wield it.

"Marthe, this is your salvation." Élisabeth crouched by her sister's side, taking hold of her hand. "Say your prayers with me now. Hail Mary, full of grace, the Lord is with you. Say it with me, Marthe. Blessed are you among women and blessed is the fruit of thy womb . . ."

The sisters prayed together. Jeanne Roy crouched between Marthe's legs, murmuring to herself as she cast her spell. Élisabeth watched as the witch pulled Chamberlen's Secret apart, putting her hand inside her sister to insert one of the two tongs. Marthe whimpered and convulsed and called out to Saint Anne. When the second tong was inserted, Marthe hollered in pain.

"I know it hurts," Jeanne Roy said. Élisabeth heard a metallic click as Jeanne joined the forceps back together. "I'm ready. I have a hold of your baby's head. So push with all your strength and I will pull the child out."

Marthe's body sagged. Élisabeth squeezed her hand.

"Come, Marthe. Push."

"I can't." Marthe's face was flushed, her eyes unfocused.

"You *can* do it," Élisabeth insisted. "You would not let me falter on the ship when I could not even rise from the bunk, when fear had me gripped by the throat. And I will not let you die now. So take my hand. We will do it together."

Slowly Marthe raised herself onto her elbows. Élisabeth kept a tight grip on her hand, squeezing all of the demon's strength into Marthe's exhausted frame.

Marthe locked eyes with the witch and furrowed her brow.

She pushed and Jeanne Roy pulled. The witch gave the order for another push, and another and then her arm arced towards the sky as she used

Chamberlen's Secret to guide the child into the world. When the child's head was delivered, she crouched and caught his body with her free hand.

"Rose, a cloth," she commanded. Rose leapt forward so that Jeanne Roy could wrap the tiny baby in clean linen and rub its back until Élisabeth heard the sound of its cry. She thought she would faint with joy. Jeanne passed the baby to Rose and crouched again between Marthe's legs. Élisabeth placed a kiss on her sister's sweaty brow and rubbed her shoulders to distract her from the delivery of the afterbirth.

"You are a mother, Marthe. You have a son."

Marthe looked groggily about the room for the child but before Rose could present him, she started moaning again.

"Jeanne?" Élisabeth's voice rose in fear.

"It is the second child, clamouring to be born. I may not need the forceps this time."

Marthe let out a cry loud enough to shake the entire village. Élisabeth knew that if she had the cunning and strength of a wolf, Marthe could claim the spirit of a lion. After several moments, she delivered the second child, a red-faced cherub with a squall to match her tiny brother's. Jeanne cut the cord with Jambon's knife and handed the baby to her mother as Rose handed over her twin. Marthe held them tightly, staring into their pomegranate faces.

"A boy and a girl, Marthe. Aren't you clever?" Rose whispered.

"We have been blessed," Marthe said, a note of awe in her voice. "Wait, where is Verger? Verger!"

The curtain twitched and Verger stuck his head into the room. Marthe looked up at him, her eyes shining.

"Come, meet our children."

He tumbled over his feet to rush to her side. He laid a kiss on his wife's forehead.

"Thank God," he prayed, his eyes closed. "You're alive."

"Well, I couldn't leave you," she murmured. "We have a lot of jam to make."

Verger started to laugh and cry, first covering Marthe's forehead in kisses, then each of his infant children. Élisabeth took in the sight of her sister, safely delivered, and then gazed at Jeanne Roy. She crouched at Marthe's feet, her raven-dark eyes heavy with fatigue, her skin bruised beneath her torn and bloody chemise. Gone were the velvet witch's fine clothes and curled lip.

She had been broken for her beliefs. A saint in the making.

Shimmering with knowledge.

Jeanne tried to stand, but her ankles wobbled. Élisabeth leapt forward and took her arm. They hobbled out of the back room, leaving Marthe and her family in peace.

"How can you pretend you are not a witch, when you can work such magic?" Élisabeth blurted.

Jeanne Roy looked at Élisabeth "I will admit that the moment a child comes into the world is magical, even to me."

Élisabeth gave her a triumphant smile. "So it is true. Magic is real. Witchcraft does exist."

"I . . ." Jeanne Roy looked weary. They stepped back as Rose rushed past them to the workroom, where the rest of the brides had gathered. They heard a cheer go up next door as the news was delivered. Jeanne drew a breath. "Chamberlen's Secret is just practical philosophy, the result of careful study and experimentation."

"Yes, exactly. Knowledge is magic. And you have so much of it, you must teach us all. So that we too may become witches."

Jeanne Roy laughed then, and the sound of fairies' handbells chiming filled the room. Élisabeth felt her heart lift, then a sudden worry struck her. "Jeanne. The twins are so small. And more than a month early. Can your magic, or practical philosophy, help them live?"

Jeanne nodded. "They have every chance. I will watch over them as long as I can." Then her smile wilted. "Though I may not be here for long. I will have to flee the Church soon."

"No, Father de Sancy is dead," Élisabeth told her. "He can never trouble you again. And with the witch hunter gone, perhaps reason can now prevail."

"I will make sure of that," Francoeur said, stepping into the room. "In the morning, I will go to the Sulpicians and say that there are rumours afoot they were bested by witches. That will quash their talk of a Montréal coven. For who would put their trust in an order that can't cure an outbreak of demonic possession? They will hold their tongues and suppress that news, for fear of losing followers to the Jesuits."

Jeanne Roy swallowed. "What of the accusation of witchcraft against me?"

"You never confessed to anything! And Dufossé's wife will testify that he was drunk and fell asleep while stealing our wood. She will swear to it." Élisabeth crossed her arms. "I will see to it that she does."

"So it is over? Truly over?" Jeanne crumpled into a chair. Wari wrapped her arms around her.

"I'm sure every sermon for several months will preach nothing but the immorality of drunken wives and powdered faces," Francoeur said. "But for you, Jeanne, yes. I believe it is over."

Jeanne Roy put her face in her hands and wept. Élisabeth looked away, straight into her husband's eyes.

"Francoeur?" Élisabeth stepped away from the witch and her friend, towards the bakery door. She motioned for her husband to join her. He followed, and then leaned against the wall opposite, eyeing her carefully. Élisabeth gazed back, not sure where to begin.

"You told me on our wedding night that you were glad to have married me," she started. "Do you still feel the same?"

He locked eyes on hers. "You're not what I expected in a wife."

From his words, Élisabeth could not glean his mood.

"I'm sorry for my deception," she said in a small voice. She meant it truly. Not for hiding the demon from him, but for convincing herself that Rémy loved her, and believing it for so long that she did not let herself fall in love with

Francoeur until it was too late. That was the deception she truly regretted. For she would never meet as good a man as her husband again. "I am glad that I married *you*. Even if . . . Marcosi has kept us apart."

Francoeur frowned and started to speak. "About that. You promised—"

"I will let Jeanne bleed me."

"You will?"

"Yes. I have seen her skill. She has more power than any sorceress in the New World or the Old. If my blood is the price I must pay to end the curse, then I will give it, willingly."

Francoeur gazed at her. "Your curse is melancholy."

Élisabeth let the word hang in the air, wondering at its true meaning. She could not believe there was black bile coursing through her veins, no matter what Jeanne said. But she understood fear, and she knew sadness, a sadness so deep that she could barely lift herself from her bed to carry on. She did not know how God expected her to continue with such a heavy heart, except by giving her children to love to replace the family she had lost.

Another notion started to tingle in Élisabeth's mind.

Had this all been God's plan for her?

If she had not chosen her own path and walked up to the clifftop with Rémy, if she had not run to New France to escape her demon, would she have arrived where God meant for her to be?

She pushed back her sleeves and held out her bare arms to her husband. She felt, somehow, absolved of her sins. She was who God meant her to be: a demoniac, a wolf, a sister, a witch.

Just not a wife.

"I will let Jeanne open my vein to see if it helps my . . . my melancholy." She gave him a wistful smile. "I only wish I had the courage to do it before the Sulpicians annulled our marriage."

Francoeur's hodgepodge hazel eyes flickered with a spark of—what? Mischief?

"I never asked for the annulment," he said.

She blinked. "You did not?"

"No."

"You said . . . we could not be saved."

Francoeur rubbed his chin. "I wonder now if I might have been mistaken."

"I am not what you expected in a wife," she said, repeating his words.

"I wonder, though, if it might be helpful to have a wolf around the house. A passably pretty wolf." Francoeur started to smile. "I've seen what you can do with witch hunters. I wonder if you might also keep the rabbits at bay?"

"Rabbits!"

"Very meddlesome for crops."

She pushed herself off the wall and took a step closer to him. "You could not ask them for an annulment . . . because you want me to be your wife."

The smile on Francoeur's face grew wider until it was impossible not to smile back. Élisabeth took a step closer until her lips hovered near his.

"Because you love me."

She kissed him, and all at once the taste of cloves danced on her tongue. Francoeur put one hand on the back of her neck and crushed her mouth, squeezing her as if he were testing to see if she would break.

She never would. She had the heart of a wolf, the strength of a demon. Her sister had been saved. Her friends stood by her. And her husband, her sandy-haired soldier, was in love with her.

She knew then that the luck of the stars shone down on them.

And she understood that she would not just survive in New France.

She would thrive.

Epilogue

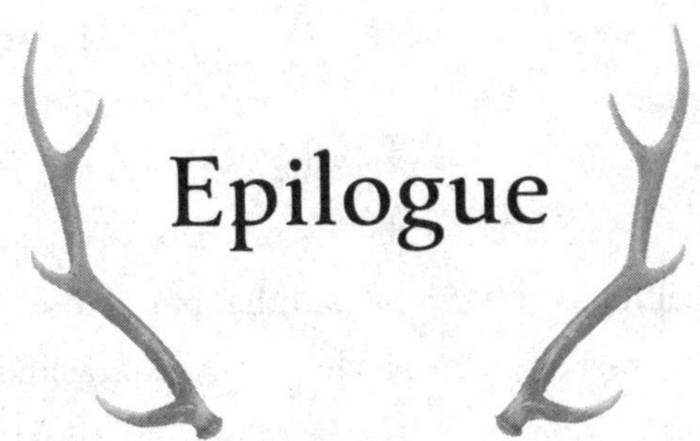

Of all the babes I have brought into this world, none have I held so close as this child.

My goddaughter. My namesake.

Most children that I deliver I do not see much of, unless they take a tumble and need a bone set or a salve to ease an infection. But my Angélique visits me every day, an hour here and an hour there so that her mother might have time to tend her garden and mind her chickens. As I walk along the river path to return her to her parents' home, she is nestled into the cradleboard on my back. Wari has beaded pink and red flowers and curling vines onto the leather carrier. It is now my most prized possession, even more so than the satchel that contains my tools: my lancet, my fleam and cups, and of course, my forceps, Chamberlen's Secret.

I do not think I shall ever have a child of my own. My husband has not returned from upcountry. If he ever does, I suppose that would be another journey for me. In his absence his friends insisted on building me a more comfortable home. It is, of course, nothing like the château where I grew up, or the estate where I lived with my first husband, but it is all mine. And it means I no longer need to sleep on furs on the ground, though some nights when the moon is bright and the wind rustles in the trees, I choose to do so anyway. I do not think I will ever stop spending my winters with Wari in the mission village at La Prairie, whether my husband returns or not. I will never stop learning about the world around me.

"Jeanne, come join us."

It is Élisabeth. She is waving me over. She and her husband are on the bench he built for them to sit and admire the river. I believe the sweet waters of the Saint-Laurent are a balm to her. I am pleased that one course of bloodletting was all that it took for the worst of the melancholy to be put behind her, though Wari doubts it was the reason for her recovery. She thinks Élisabeth is healing all on her own. If that is true, then it must be sitting by the river that calms her nervous edges.

"Take my seat, Jeanne, I must get back." Francoeur stands and picks up his hoe, yet he places his hand on his wife's shoulder, as if even during the hours he works in the fields he cannot bear to be parted from her.

"I cannot. Wari is coming tomorrow for the celebration, and I have many notes to finish before she arrives."

"Jeanne, sit," Élisabeth pleads. "I am worn to the bone cooking and baking for the wedding feast. Tomorrow Marthe and Verger and the twins will arrive. We will be run ragged chasing those two around the house. If you insist on working, then I will feel that I must as well. Sit with me a while."

I cannot argue, for it is I who encourages her to rest. As I loosen the cradleboard's laces, Francoeur steps forward to lift the child from my back.

"This wedding is at a most inconvenient time of year," he grumbles. "Whoever would think to marry in June?"

"When else would a sailor marry than on his patron saint's day?" Élisabeth chides him. "Besides, if Hélène listened to you farmers, she'd never be wed. The warm months are too busy, the cold months are too cold. Let them have their summer wedding. The crops can wait."

"Her sailor is so lovesick for her I don't imagine they will plant a single seed this year," Francoeur says.

Élisabeth laughs. "I imagine he'll get around to planting at least one."

He gives her the child and I notice their hands touch for longer than is necessary. I understand this, the laziness of new lovers, though I am surprised it is still upon them, with a nursling at the breast.

"I will see you later, Liliwolf," he says, leaving her with a look that I can feel burning from where I sit. He puts the hoe on his shoulder and saunters back towards the house.

"So that is true love," I observe when he is gone. Élisabeth places Angélique in the crook of her arm and helps her latch on to her breast. My goddaughter has her father's sandy curls and her mother's blue eyes. She is not interested in feeding, though. She is twisting to see me. I make a face to encourage her laughter.

"You will know love one day, Jeanne," Élisabeth says.

"I am quite content with my work. Wari has brought me the most fascinating flower. It's used for sore throats and mouth sores. I have been thinking about combining the goldthread with a bark I've been studying to see if I might improve its effectiveness."

"Mmm," Élisabeth says, and I know her well enough to know when she is only half listening. Then she looks up.

"Stay for supper. We can talk about your studies while I practice writing my name."

I sit back. That is a welcome invitation. Yes. I will dine with them and then return to my work.

I watch the sparkle of sunshine dance on the river while Angélique nurses. Perhaps Élisabeth is right and one day I will know love again. Maybe even have children of my own.

Or perhaps I am right, and I will take satisfaction in my work and my standing in the community. In the lives I have saved and will continue to save.

I close my eyes. I can feel the sun kissing my cheeks.

Perhaps we are both right.

Author's Note

This book is a work of fiction, although some of the events described in these pages did happen.

In early modern Europe, ordinary people believed in magic. Some practitioners were considered helpful: the sorcerer, the magical healer, the soothsayer. Witches, though, were considered evil because of the pact they made with the devil, and they were feared.

By the late seventeenth century, the royal court and upper classes in France had started to embrace science and reason, while across the countryside witches were still being accused of crimes like curdling milk and causing infertility. It was a time when people did not share a common set of beliefs, and it resulted in real turmoil.

That's what happened in 1670, when a dozen witches were sentenced to death for attending a Witches' Sabbath in Normandy. Louis XIV intervened and commuted their sentence to banishment. The provincial parliament in Rouen was indignant, writing a long appeal to beg the king to reconsider interfering in its jurisdiction. What's especially intriguing about that act of clemency is that in the same year, a short coach ride away, more than one hundred women—filles du roi, the king's wards who were known at the time as "girls-for-marrying"—boarded a ship for New France.

Is it possible, given the proximity of those historical events, that some of those banished Norman witches took the fastest route out of the country and ended up in Quebec?

In fact, New France was quite unique when it came to accusations of witchcraft. Unlike the rest of the Europe and America, the colony never experienced a witch craze. There were a few sporadic accusations involving supernatural elements, but nothing like the mass hunts that led to cascading accusations, torture, and terror elsewhere.

There are a few possible reasons for this. People did not live on top of each other in villages where grievances could fester but were spread out in lonely seigneuries. European witches were typically older women, and in the early days of New France there were few non-Indigenous women. Even widows, who in Europe might have had to beg to survive, becoming vulnerable to suspicion, remarried quickly. It might also be that because people came from different regions of France, bringing with them different customs and dialects, Canadians didn't fear strangers as much as European societies did.

As far as my depiction of 1670 Ville-Marie goes, I nudged some of the dates of the real historical events so that they occur in the same year. Hugh Chamberlen revealed the secret obstetric forceps his family had invented to the French obstetrician François Mauriceau in 1670. The nun and protector of the filles du roi, Marguerite Bourgeoys, left the colony that same year to return to France for a short trip. However, Anne Lamarque de Folleville may not have opened her notorious tavern until the late 1670s. Her trial for "magically" attracting more customers than any other drinking establishment took place in 1682. The acting military governor of Montreal, Hannibal Flotte de Lafredière, was wounded in the campaign against the Iroquois in the winter of 1666, though it was his superior, Daniel de Rémy de Courcelle, who ordered the disastrous march. Lafredière was sent back to France the following year after the citizens complained about his drunkenness, immoral behaviour, and sale of liquor to Indigenous people. While it is not known whether the real Lafredière owned slaves, more than four thousand people were enslaved in Canada from the early 1600s until 1834, the majority of whom were Indigenous. They had a life expectancy of only seventeen years.

I will add finally that most of Maman Poulin's tales about witches and wayward women come straight from the pages of Canadian history.

Acknowledgements

I am deeply indebted to many wonderful people for their magic in making this book happen.

There was probably no moment more like a fairy tale in my life than when Samantha Haywood tapped my manuscript with her wand and said she would be my agent. Thank you to Sam and the Transatlantic team, Eva Oakes, Megan Philipp, and Leah Shangrow, for all your support.

I'm awestruck by my editors, Adrienne Kerr and katherena vermette. I still can't believe I get to work with such talented and creative women. Thank you for your care and dedication to this book. Also many thanks to copy editor Shelly Perron, publicist Natasha Kempnich, and marketing manager Cali Platek. Thank you also to Elita Sidiropoulou for designing the beautiful cover.

It's nerve-racking publishing a novel, so I'm grateful to my first readers for their helpful notes: Sarah MacLachlan, Katie Seaman, John Maker, Margo Ledoux, Marilotte Bloemen, Rosanna Tiranti, Freddie Lofthouse, and Lisa Greaves; and to my writers' group for all their advice: Tamara Miller, Suha Mardelli, and Alexis MacIssac.

I am particularly indebted to Kahente Horn-Miller for being so generous with her time, and her thoughtful feedback on how I portrayed the lives of the Haudenosaunee and other Indigenous peoples in Montreal, and to

Emma Anderson, a kindred spirit, for her help in understanding early modern Catholicism.

Although I read a few dozen history books as part of my research, there were still aspects of life in the seventeenth century that eluded me. I'm grateful to the historians Réal Fortin, Carolyn Podruchny, Jan Noel, and Jack Little for allowing me to interview and email them about cassocks, bandolier bags, marriage contracts, and more. Any mistakes are, of course, my own.

It was a pleasure to meet the Maison Saint-Gabriel's Alexandra Prieur for a private tour of the museum that celebrates the filles du roi. Thank you for that privilege and our conversation. I was also delighted to meet Beverly Delormier at the St. Francis Xavier Mission in Kahnawà:ke. Thank you for explaining the Kanien'kéha alphabet and helping me settle on the name Wari.

Modern-day accoucheur Dr. David Millar kindly talked me through how to do a forceps delivery. My brother Eric Chevalier, a shipwright, examined the text for nautical errors. My godmother Marci Edwards nudged the book along with her help. I will pay your kindness forward.

I'm blessed to have the unwavering support and encouragement of my parents. Thank you also to my children, for not minding when I shut the door to dream.

Finally, writing this book would not have been possible without the help of Andy Lofthouse. I stumbled on the idea for *The Winter Witch* not long after we got married, so he's had to live with my obsession with witches and demons for almost as long as he's known me. Thank you for your cheerleading and constructive criticism, your cooking and (halfhearted) cleaning. Now that it's done, I may vacuum.